THE HELMSMAN

Timberwolf Press

Tune in to the dramatic series
and visit the online world of *Wilf Brim* at
http://www.TimberWolfPress.com

INTRODUCTION

Rewriting *The Helmsman* was one of the most fascinating adventures of my life—it was also *fun*. Imagine meeting a version of yourself twenty years younger: with the same skills, attitudes, and beliefs—all surprisingly familiar, yet undeniably skewed from the present version after twenty years' grating against the millstone we call *life*.

That younger version had just sold his first novel, and a whole unexpected set of possibilities was suddenly open. Wilf Brim was twenty years younger, too, with a whole new set of possibilities of his own to wrestle with—even if was quite unclear at the time if the novel he lived in would survive in the glare of the public eye.

That 20-year-younger author wrote with a much more conservative style than the older one. The very real possibility that this might be his only novel ever affected every word in the manuscript. And the story—the very *story*—seems now to occur in a small, narrowly bounded Universe. Certainly it is the same Universe that exists in the older mind today, but the intervening six novels added a lot more detail—and a wealth of roominess, that continues expanding to this day, as that older mind works on the eighth in the Series, *The Turning Tide*.

So what to expect from the new *Helmsman*? It's certainly the same story that appeared in 1983. This new one, however, is tighter, makes more sense (if modernistic *balonium* like FTL HyperDrives can ever make actual sense), and fits more perfectly into the entire Wilf Brim Universe that evolved throughout 20 years of writing. I've rarely had more fun than making this new *Helmsman* a better, easier novel to read. I can only hope you, my readers, find it just as much fun to read.

- Bill Baldwin

THE HELM

SMAN

BILL BALDWIN

Timberwolf Press
Allen, Texas
http://www.timberwolfpress.com

Timberwolf Press, Inc.
202 N. Allen St., Suite A
Allen, Texas 75013 USA

Visit our Web site at **http://www. TimberWolfPress.com**

Printed in the United States of America
10 9 8 7 6 5 4 3 2 1

Special "Director's Cut" Revised Edition

ISBN: 1-58752-150-4

1 Only three travelers shambled from the coach at Gimmas-Haefdon's badly lighted Eorean station. Two of them disappeared into the ozone-pungent darkness even before the train's warning lights were out of sight along the causeway. Alone on the platform, Sublieutenant Wilf Brim, Imperial Fleet, dialed his blue Fleet Cloak's heating element control another notch toward Warm, then clambered down the wet metal steps from the elevated tracks. The whole Universe seemed dismally cold around him as he reached the landing. He listened to wind moaning through the station shelter while he oriented himself, then picked his way around ice-crusted puddles barely visible beneath infrequent Karlsson lamps and started out toward the dim shape of a distant guard shack. He was shamefully aware of the single traveling case following him. It fairly shouted his humble origins, and he was joining an Imperial Fleet once commanded exclusively by wealth-privileged officers—until First Star Lord Sir Beorn Wyrood's recent Admiralty Reform Act (and six years of war's insatiable attrition) forced inclusion of talent from whatever source it could be obtained.Shivering despite the warm, high-collared cloak, he peered at the predawn sky. Enough light from the star Gimmas now filtered through the clouds to disclose the fundamentals of sprawling Gimmas-Haefdon starbase: Lines of low, gray-painted buildings, a world of dissected starships, and forests of shipyard cranes stationary against a starless sky. Along the waterfront, indistinct shapes of more or less intact vessels hovered quietly on softly glowing gravity

9

pools while the outlines of others projected above covered wharves and warehouses, all a uniform shade of weather-faded gray relieved occasionally by stains of oxidation or charring. In the distance, mountainous forms of capital ships dominated a lightening horizon from still another complex. Brim shook his head bitterly. Fat chance for a Carescrian Helmsman aboard one of those!

He stretched to his nearly three-iral height and yawned in the clammy dampness. The sky was now spitting snow occasionally, with a promise of more substantial amounts soon to come. He sniffed the air, sampling the odor of the sea as it mixed with ozone, heated lubricants, and the stench of overheated logics. At best, the Eorean Starwharves—one of fifteen starship construction-and-maintenance complexes on the watery planet of star bases called Haefdon—could accurately be described as an untidy sprawl. To the twenty-one-year-old Brim, it was far more than that: It was also the realization of a dream that until only recently had seemed impossible. His fellow cadets (and many sullen instructors) quietly did their utmost to make it thus, and prevent his recent graduation from the prestigious Helmsman's Academy near the Imperial capital planet, Avalon. He somehow had prevailed, determined he could raise himself from the grinding poverty of his home in the Empire's Carescrian Mining Sector. A combination of fierce tenacity, hard work, and native talent finally won him his commissioning ceremonies and this lonely outpost in the Galactic Fleet. He counted on those same attributes to take him a great deal farther before he traded in his blue Fleet Cloak—a lot farther indeed.

Picking his way carefully over a series of glowing metal tracks that paralleled a high fence, he stopped at the gatehouse to rap on the window and rouse its single, nodding occupant. Inside, the ancient watchman wore age-tarnished medals from some long-forgotten space campaign. He was tall with thin shoulders and enormous hands, a beak of a nose, sparse white hair, and the sad eyes of a man who had seen too many Wilf Brims enter through his gate and never return. "A bit early," he observed, opening the window no more than a crack to admit the other's proffered orders card, while denying passage to as much of the cold wind as he could manage. "First ship, I'll wager," he said.

Brim smiled. Metacycles ago at the massive Central Terminus of Gimmas-Haefdon starbase, he had indeed conceded the remainder of his sleep to excitement and anticipation. "Yes," he admitted. "In a way, at least."

"Well, you're not the original early riser, young man," the watchman chuckled, "nor I suppose the last, either. Bring yourself in here while I try to find where you belong. And don't open the door more'n you must!"

While Brim parked the traveling case and made his way into the pungent warmth of the shack, the old campaigner placed his orders card in the side of a battered communications cabinet (which also doubled as storage for six cracked and stained teacups, none particularly clean). Presently, a shimmering display globe materialized over the crockery. He studied the contents. "Hmm. All the way from Carescria," he observed without looking around. "Caught in the League's big sneak attack, I suppose?"

Brim only nodded to the man's back. "Lose anybody?"

Brim shut his eyes. Did people have to ask? All he personally wanted was a chance to forget. Even after six years, the war's sudden onset was as real as the night before. Wave after wave of heavy cruisers from Emperor Nergol Triannic's League of Dark Stars attacking Carescria's famous asteroid fields; he'd been on home leave in the ramshackle orbiting "city" where his parents lived. Concussion. Agonizing heat— his tiny sister's last, anguished screams. He shook his head. "Every one," he whispered almost to himself, "everyone except me."

"Sorry," the old man said. "I didn't mean to..."

"It's all right," Brim interrupted dully. "Forget it."

Neither occupant found more words until the old man broke his silence with another pregnant "Hmm." He scratched his head. "T.83, eh?" Apparently, this needed no answer, for he continued moving age-spotted fingers over his small control panel, concentrating on rapidly changing patterns in the globe. Finally, he looked up to consult a large, three-dimensional map tacked above a ragged chair. Tracing a long finger along the causeway, he stopped near the image of a tiny, fenced-in square. "You're here, now, d' you see?" he asked.

Brim peered at the map. "Yessir," he said. "I see."

"All right, then," the watchman continued. "Now let me think, G-31 at, ah..." He peered nearsightedly at the globe again without moving the finger. "Oh, yes, G-31 at B-19." Now he continued across the map until he stopped at a basin carved into a far corner of the island. "B-19," he announced. "Your *Truculent's* moored here, Carescrian. On the gravity pool numbered R-2134. D'you see?"

Brim squinted at the map near the man's black fingernail. A tiny R-2134 was just visible, printed inside one of seven rectangular gravity pools bordering the circular basin. "I see it, all right," he said.

"Bit of a distance on foot," the old man observed, stroking his thin, stubbled chin. "First skimmers from the transport pool won't run for another metacycle or so, and I can't imagine the ship'll send one of their own. You're not even signed aboard as a crew member yet."

Brim snorted. He knew what the watchman really meant—that they wouldn't send a skimmer for a no-account Carescrian. He'd been here before, often. The old man smiled sympathetically. "I can offer you a spot of tea to warm your stomach until then, if you'd care to have a seat."

"Thanks just the same," Brim said, making his way toward the door. "But I think I'll walk off some of this excitement before I try to check in." He nodded. "R-2134. I'll find it."

"Thought you might do something like that," the old man observed. "You'll get there with no trouble. Just keep the set of blue tracks on your left. Snow won't stay on 'em."

Brim nodded his thanks and stepped quickly into the cold, summoning the traveling case to his heel. A thickening carpet of snow lay over the still-sleeping complex, already hiding much of the unsightly dockyard clutter beneath a mantle of white. Carefully keeping the blue-glowing tracks on his left, he made his way along a dark concourse, noting that his pace curiously increased as soon as he cleared the gate. While he hurried along the rough pavement, he asked himself if it was the cold that made him hurry so—or was it the excitement?

On either side of the road, powerful forms of warships loomed through the falling snow, hovering ponderously over shallow gravity pools, dimly lit from beneath by the glow of shipyard gravity generators. Those near the water were often lighted. On a few, he saw occasional crewmembers performing routine poolside duties (cursing both their superiors and the snow, he guessed with a smile). The signs of life made him feel less alone in the sprawling confusion of hulls, KA'PPA masts, and ubiquitous cranes which now crowded the lightening sky.

Other ships—those grotesquely damaged or undergoing dissection for repair—hovered like metallic corpses over inland gravity pools half hidden by stacks of hullmetal plates and heavy shipbuilding equipment. Brim shuddered as he passed one particularly savaged wreck. On the convoy from Avalon, he helplessly watched one of the escorts, an old destroyer named *Obstinate*, take a HyperTorp hit amidships. She had blown up with all hands. That crew would have deemed themselves fortunate indeed to bring her back to base at all, even in this condition! He shook his head; everything in the Universe was relative, as they said.

***

Abruptly, he was there. A rusting sign announced GRAVITY POOL R—2134. Beyond floated 190 lean irals of T—class destroyer: starship T.83, I.F.S. *Truculent*.

He picked his way along stone jetties surrounding the gravity pool, seldom taking his eyes from the hovering, wedge-shaped form. In the amber glow of gravity generators below, shadows from ventral turrets moved gently over her underside as she stirred to urgings of the wind. Above, huddled battle lanterns still cast dim circles of light outside her entry ports, and a sparse web of emerald mooring beams flashed occasionally as the resting starship gently tested her anchorage.

T—class starships weren't big as destroyers went, and at rest they weren't especially pretty, either. But inside their pointed, angular hulls they crowded four powerful Sheldon Drive crystals and two brutish antigravity generators with at least triple the thrust claimed by other ships their size. These latter provided astonishing acceleration below LightSpeed, a regime in which much of their close-in patrol duty was performed. And every iral spoke power. They were rugged, sturdy machines with all the mass of space holes. In the hands of a good captain, any one of them was more than a match for the Cloud League's best. In excellent repair, they could attain speeds in excess of 35 LightSpeed, or 35 Light Years per Standard Metacycle; they had a cruising range in excess of 4,000 light years.

Truculent's sharply angular hull formed a pointed, three-sided trilon resembling the curious lance tips of Furogg warriors from the K'tipsch quadrant. Her flat main deck widened cleanly from a needle-sharp

13

bow nearly a quarter of its length to the rounded shape of an A turret with its long, slim 144—mmi disruptor. Faired in and raised three levels from this was the starship's frowning bridge, covered by a presently transparent "greenhouse" of Hyperscreen panels (required for hyper-LightSpeed vision), which reflected the weak dawn in runnels of melting snow. Projecting from either side of this structure, bridge wings extended like shoulders nearly all the way to the deck's crisply defined edge. A sizable globe atop each of the wings housed fire directors controlling her seven main turrets. From the aft center of the Hyperscreen canopy, her tall, streamlined mast supported a long-whiskered KA'PPA-COMM system beacon that, by a curious loophole in Travis physics, enabled nearly instantaneous communication both below and above the velocity of light and over enormous distances.

Immediately aft of the bridge, the starship's silhouette fell sheer to the single-level 'midships deckhouse, which extended into the aft third of the deck. Wide as the bridge itself, this was flanked by four stubby launches, two in succession to port and two to starboard, protected by the projecting bridge wings. A swiveling, five-tube torpedo launcher was mounted on the flat surface of its roof.

Behind this, a two-level aft deckhouse completed the top deck centerline superstructure. The torpedo launcher abutted its second-level torpedo reload and repair shop. Torpedo magazines and general repair shops occupied most of the first-level space—vital necessities for the long tours of blockade for which she and her sister ships were commonly employed. Slightly aft and outboard of this deckhouse, W and X turrets with 144—mmi disruptors occupied the widest, and most vacant, portions of the upper deck.

Like all other surfaces of *Truculent's* hull, her stem was also a triangular slab of hullmetal. From his studies at the Academy, Brim knew this one measured 97 irals along the "top" edge with its inverted apex only 21 irals below. Pierced by four circular 3.5-iral openings, the surface was otherwise featureless. Each of the openings (outlets for the ship's Drive crystals) was presently sealed from Haefdon's elements by a system of circular shutters.

Both ventral decks were also virtually featureless, except for 144—mmi disruptor turrets mounted fore and aft along each centerline. Those on the port surface were designated "B" (forward) and "Z" (aft); those starboard, "C" and "Y". On each side of her bridge wings, "T.83" appeared in square Avalonian glyphs.

Wistfully, Brim pondered her size. Even with her powerful sort of beauty, she still lacked the sense of hauteur he associated with big capital ships like the ones based just over the horizon. "Pick and shovel" were words that came readily to mind. Smiling wryly, he allowed as to how he was fortunate indeed just to have a berth on her at all. Not many Carescrians ever made it out of the asteroid mines.

As he stared through the hissing snow, a hatch opened in the deckhouse just opposite an arched gangway to the waterside jetty. Presently, a huge Starman lumbered through, watched his breath congeal to steam, and pulled a too-short Fleet Cloak closer to his neck. Reaching inside the hatch, he removed a broom.

"Shut the xaxtdamned hatch, Barbousse!" a voice echoed through the cold air.

"Aye, aye, Ma'am!" The clang of hullmetal rang out as the hatch slammed closed. Shrugging, the oversized seaman triggered his broom and began clearing snow—precisely in time for Brim and his traveling case to meet him at the end of the gangway. The man piled considerable snow over Brim's booted feet before he recognized something was amiss. He looked up with a startled expression.

Brim smiled. On this first contact with his first ship, he was determined nothing would, or could, go wrong. "Morning, Barbousse," he said with all the equanimity he could muster.

In sudden confusion, Barbousse dropped the whirring broom as his hand jerked to spasmodically salute. The device promptly spat clouds of snow over Brim's face and cape, then rolled backward toward the tumbling water of the basin, burbling evil satisfaction. By reflex, each bent at the same time to check its travel—and nearly knocked the other from his feet. At the last possible milliclick, Brim grabbed the throbbing machine from the edge of sure destruction and switched it off, letting it spit snow and particles of rock into the water. He handed it carefully to the seaman while he brushed debris from the front of his cloak and desperately bit his lip to contain his amusement.

"Oh...ah, sorry, Sir," Barbousse stumbled mournfully.

Brim forced himself under control. "Think nothing of it, Barbousse," he said with his last shred of dignity. He spat gritty stone crumbs into the water, then stepped left toward the gangway. At that very moment, Barbousse attempted to remove himself from the path by stepping right. In midstep, Brim deftly switched to his right—as Barbousse dived left. Once more, Brim jogged right, blocked again by the wretched Barbousse, who now wore a frantic look in his eyes.

"FREEZE, Mister!" Brim commanded, stopping himself short in the trampled snow. "And don't drop the broom!" Barbousse froze in apparent rigor mortis, began to topple toward the water, caught himself again, and came to an uneasy rest. Calmly as possible, Brim walked past and onto the gangway, only to stop once more in his tracks. Carefully, he turned to check on Barbousse; the man was still standing before the gangway, broom in hand at parade rest. "Carry on," he ordered smartly, then hurried up the steep incline toward the ship.

Stepping over a high sill, he drew the hatch closed and breathed deeply of starship odors: the too-fresh redolence of ozone and rank stench of electronics mixed with odors of hot metal and scorched sealants. Food. Bodies. And on every starship in the Fleet, an unmistakable scent of polish. He chuckled as he made his way along the short companionway—everything military smelled of polish. Before him, a petty officer glared at her hovering display. Her desk plate read, "Kristoba Maldive, Quartermaster."

"All right, Barbousse," Maldive growled without looking up. "What now?"

"Well," Brim said, "you might start by signing me in..."

Maldive wrinkled a large, thin nose and continued to stare into the display. "Sign you what?" she demanded, fingers flying on a nearby control panel. Hues and patterns in the globe shifted subtly (Brim politely avoided reading any of them). "What in Universe do you mean by th...?" she continued, then stopped in midword when her narrow-set eyes strayed as far as Brim's cloak and the Sublieutenant's insignia on the left shoulder. "Oh, Universe," she grimaced quietly. "Sorry, Sir; I never expected anyone out so early." She stared down at the desk. "We don't often get a chance to sleep so long. And the skimmers..."

"It's all right," Brim interrupted. "I walked."

Maldive looked up again. "Yes, Sir," she said with an embarrassed smile. "I see you certainly did." She inserted Brim's card in a reader, then peered at the display. More soft hues and patterns filled the globe. "Everything seems in order, Sir," she said. From her desk she hefted an old-fashioned book, elegantly bound in polished red fabric with gold trim. *Truculent's* emblem of a charging bull Hilaago (deadly predator from the planet Ju'ggo-3 in the Blim Commonwealth) was engraved in its front cover. "Sign here, Sir," she grunted, opening the heavy book on the desktop facing Brim. "We'll have you aboard in no time at all."

Brim bent to the book and signed full fingerprints of both hands. "Well," he asked with a smile, "how was that?"

"I'd bet you're in, Sir," the Quartermaster said, returning the smile. "Can you find your way to the wardroom? It's on the same deck level. We'll need a few cycles to make up your cabin."

"I'll find it," Brim said with more confidence than he actually felt. He'd been at pains to learn the starship's layout in the Academy library back on Avalon, but now everything looked unfamiliar and confusing.

"We'll come for you there when your cabin's ready," Maldive promised. "And you can leave that traveling case with me, too."

Brim nodded thanks and shook his head. What a difference the tiny device on his left shoulder made! Having someone else look after his luggage was a far cry from life flying ore carriers to and from the Gantaclair wharves on Navron/Linfarne, a planetary system in the vast collection of stars called Carescria. Of course, in poverty-blighted Carescria, he would have been counted fortunate indeed to have any baggage at all—aside from a patched safety suit and the few surface clothes he could carry in a sack.

Along the companionway, he paused at a gleaming metal plate set with old-fashioned rivets. I.F.S. TRUCULENT, it read, JOB 21358 ELEANDOR BESTIENNE YARD 228/51988. The plaque might have been polished every metacycle on the metacycle from its looks— and by persons who cared considerably for the ship. A fine portent, he decided, and gave it a few good strokes of his own with a sleeve. He smiled. Something like that might even bring good luck.

Finding the wardroom proved easier than he expected—he was lost only twice. He opened the door almost bashfully—officers' country had been strictly off limits as recently as six days ago. With sincere relief, he discovered it was unoccupied and stepped over the high sill. A large picture of Emperor Greyffin IV, Grand Galactic Emperor, Prince of the Reggio Star Cluster, and Rightful Protector of the Heavens, adorned the forward bulkhead (identical poses stared beatifically from every available wall in the Empire). Battered recliners lolled here and there along a narrow deck dominated by a massive carved table with ten matching chairs. Eight places were set at the table; two additional chairs faced only polished wood.

Beyond the table, a window opened through the aft bulkhead into a tiny, dark pantry. From within this space, two incredibly rheumy eyes peered at him from atop a thin nose that ended in a bushy white mustache. This time, it was Brim's turn for surprise. He jumped. "Er, good morning," he said.

"It certainly does, Sir," the face stated with conviction.

"Pardon?"

"But then I understand all you young fellers love snow."

Brim was just opening his mouth again when he was interrupted by the appearance of a Great Sodeskayan Bear with engineering blazes on the high collar of his Fleet Cloak. The newcomer—a full lieutenant—peered through the door, appeared to immediately grasp the situation, and wiggled long, unruly whiskers. "Lieutenant Brim?" he asked.

"Yes, Sir," Brim answered. "Ah...?" He inclined his head toward the pantry door.

The Bear smiled. "Oh, that's Chief Steward Grimsby," he explained. "He's all right; he just doesn't listen anymore."

"Doesn't listen, Sir?"

"Well, not in the half year since I signed on he hasn't."

Brim nodded, more in capitulation than anything else.

"Don't let him bother you, friend," the Bear said. "He seems to anticipate most everything we require. Anything else, we get for ourselves."

"I, ah, see, Sir."

The Bear grinned, exposing long, polished fangs, each with the tiny jeweled inlay all fashionable Bears seemed to consider indispensable. "'Sir' is not really my name," he said, extending a large furry hand.

"On the Mother Planets, I am called Nikolas Yanuar Ursis, but you should call me 'Nik', eh?"

Brim gripped his hand. "Nik it is," he replied. "And you seem to know mine's Wilf Brim, Wilf Ansor Brim, that is."

"Kristoba told me you were here," Ursis said, drawing a battered Sodeskayan Zempa pipe from a pocket of his expensive-looking tunic. Six strong fingers delicately charged its bowl from a flat leather case, and he puffed vigorously until the hogge'poa glowed warmly, filling the wardroom with its sweet, heavy fragrance—object of centuries of aggravated complaints by suffering human crewmates all over the Universe. "You don't mind, do you?" Ursis asked, settling into one of the less seedy recliners.

Brim smiled and shook his head. Hogge'poa never especially bothered him. Nobody seriously expected the Bears to stop anyway, but the tolerance had less to do with altruism than with recognition of the extraordinary genius by which Bears engineered HyperSpace Drive systems, and besides, female Bears simply loved the smell of it.

"Fresh from the Academy, eh?" Ursis asked, crossing his legs comfortably. His high boots were perfectly polished, as if he expected an imminent inspection.

"I only graduated last week," Brim admitted.

"Then you came in from Avalon on *Amphitrite*, didn't you?"

Brim pursed his lips and nodded. Indeed, he had arrived in the big converted liner only the night before. "Convoy CXY98," he explained.

"Word has it we lost heavily in that one," the Bear said.

"More than half the cargo vessels," Brim asserted. "Twelve, I think."

"And most of the escorts," the Bear stated.

Brim nodded again. The. Eorean Complex boasted an accurate rumor mill. "I watched old *Obstinate* blow up no more than a c'lenyt off our port bow," Brim said.

"No survivors you could see?"

"I can't imagine anything living through that blast," Brim answered. "All four Drive chambers seemed to blow at the same time; there wasn't even much wreckage."

Ursis got out of the recliner thoughtfully. Standing, he was average for a Sodeskayan native: powerfully barrel-chested and slightly taller than the three irals Brim claimed for himself. Like other Bears, he had short pointed ears and a short muzzle for natural heat retention on the cold planets of his origin. He looked Brim in the eye. "Two cousins," he pronounced slowly. "Voof."

"I'm sorry," Brim said lamely.

"So am I," Ursis said with a faraway look in his close-set predator's eyes. "But then Hagsdoffs always gore the hairiest oxen first, don't they?"

"Pardon?"

"An old saying from the Mother Planets," Ursis explained. "And it is I who ought to be sorry for unloading troubles on you." He put a hand on Brim's arm. "Your people suffered with mine in the first raids."

Brim bit his lip.

"Despots like Nergol Triannic strike Bears and men alike," Ursis said. "Our work is to finish him—and his thrice-damned League—eh?" He puffed thoughtfully on his Zempa pipe. "Some news of your coming preceded you, Carescrian. Many of us have looked forward to your arrival with great interest."

Brim raised an eyebrow.

"Soon, my new friend, we will talk of many things," the Bear said. "But for now, the Drive demands my presence. And I am certain you will be delighted to see your cabin, which at last seems to be ready." He nodded toward the door.

Brim turned. A starman waited outside in the companionway.

"This way, please, Lieutenant," the young woman said.

"Later..." Ursis declared, leading the way through the door.

Within a few cycles, Brim stood proudly in a tiny stateroom, the first in his memory he would not share with someone else. Luxury like this was a far cry indeed from life on Navron/Linfarne and the Carescrian ore trade—and he had paid dearly to win it. For the moment at least, all seemed worth the price.

***

He had only just stowed his traveling case beneath the narrow bunk when he noticed a message frame that had materialized on the inside of his door.

"Yes?"

"Captain's compliments," the frame said. "And interviews will begin in her office at Standard 0975."

Glancing at his timepiece, Brim saw he had more than three metacycles to wait. "Very well," he answered, then settled back on his bunk as the indicator faded. Clearly, he was one of very few early risers aboard *Truculent*, at least when she was in port.

Well before Standard 0975, Brim climbed two levels to the aft end of the bridge tower. Near the ladder, a door was engraved simply CAPTAIN, below which removable adhesive stickers spelled out R.G. Collingswood, Lt. Commander, I.F. While he waited, he was joined by a second Sublieutenant with Helmsman's blazes on his collar. The newcomer was pink and chubby and had an uneasy look about him. His belt divided an expensive-looking tunic into two rolls which flubbered up and down as he hurried. "I thought I'd never find the Captain in this awful warren," he grumped in a high-pitched voice. "What time is it anyhow?"

"If you're scheduled at Standard 0975, you've made it," Brim assured him, checking his own timepiece. "We have nearly a cycle to go."

"No little wonder," the man said, panting, then suddenly looked at Brim with something like recognition. "You're not that Carescrian Sublieutenant, are you?" he asked.

"I am," Brim asserted, immediately on the defensive.

The other grunted. "Well, you certainly don't look odd," he observed.

From bitter experience, Brim knew Imperials often had no idea they were giving offense; and now was not the time to teach this one. "Ready?" he asked evenly.

"As I'll ever be, I suppose."

Brim rapped firmly.

"It's open," a voice called from inside.

Brim pushed the latch plate.

Inside, with her back to the door, Lieutenant Commander I.F. Collingswood stared intently at a display. Soft chords of stately, unfamiliar music beguiled Brim's ears from the background. "Come in," she urged without turning around. "I shall be finished momentarily."

Brim led the way, then stood uncomfortably in the soft, haunting music until she cleared the display and swiveled her chair, looking first at one and then the other. She had a long, patrician nose, hazel eyes, and soft chestnut curls. Graceful fingers interlaced on her lap.

"Well?" she asked.

"Sublieutenant Wilf Ansor Brim reporting for duty aboard I.F.S. *Truculent*, Ma'am," Brim said with as steady a voice as he could muster. In the following silence, he realized he was very nearly terrified. He also noticed he was not the only one—his overweight counterpart hadn't even opened his mouth. Still in silence, he offered his orders card, carefully turning it for insertion in a reader.

Collingswood read the printed name, then—accepting the other's without a glance—placed both behind her on the desk. She frowned. "So you're Brim?" she asked in a quiet mezzo.

"Yes, Ma'am."

"That makes you Theada," she said to the other.

"J-Jubal Windroff Theada the Third," he said, "from Avalon."

"Yes," Collingswood said with a frown. "At one time, I knew your father." Silent for a moment, she smiled distantly, then went on. "I suppose both of you are fresh from Helmsman's training."

Brim nodded. "Yes, Ma'am," he said again. The other continued his silence.

A tiny smile escaped Collingswood's thin mouth. "Ready to take old *Truculent* into space from the command seat, then?" she joked.

"I'd gladly settle for any seat up there, Ma'am," Brim said with a grin. For the first time, it occurred to him the woman was dressed in a threadbare sweater and short skirt that revealed slim legs and soft, well-worn boots. Somehow, even at her leisure, she looked every inch a captain.

"You are the one who piloted those horrible ore carriers on Navron/Linfarne, aren't you?" she asked.

"Yes, Ma'am," Brim answered, again braced for the inevitable insult.

"Hmm," she mused, "I understand they require some rather extraordinary flying."

Brim felt his face flush and kept an embarrassed silence.

Collingswood smiled again. "You'll show us your talent soon enough, Lieutenant." she said. "And you, Lieutenant Theada. Shall I put you in the command seat straight off?"

"W-Well, Captain," Theada stammered, "I only h-have about three hundred metacycles at the controls...and some simulator time. I don't know if I'm actually ready f-for the left seat right away."

"You'll build your metacycles quickly in *Truculent*," Collingswood interrupted with just the shadow of a frown. Then her neutral smile returned. "Lieutenant Amherst will expect you to check in with him; he's our Number One. And of course you must see Lieutenant Gallsworthy when he returns to the ship. He's chief Helmsman—you report to him." Abruptly, she smiled, then swiveled back to the display. "Welcome aboard, both of you," she said in dismissal.

Brim led the way out the door. Just as he stepped over the sill, Collingswood turned his way again. "By the by, Lieutenant Brim," she said, looking past Theada. "When you address me, it's 'Captain,' not 'Ma'am.'" She smiled with a warmth Brim could actually feel. "Nothing to worry about," she added. "I thought you'd want to know."

When Theada disappeared along the companionway without uttering another word, Brim decided his next move should be to report to *Truculent's* first lieutenant. He tracked the man down in the chart house portion of the bridge at work before a small disorderly table that projected one of the ship's ubiquitous display globes. "Lieutenant Amherst?" Brim inquired politely, eyeing a richly lined Fleet Cape carelessly heaped on a nearby recliner.

"Never forget it," Amherst growled coldly as he turned from his display. His were the same aristocratic features as Collingswood's, only strongly masculine. He had a thin, straight nose with flaring nostrils, two narrow mustaches, a lipless slit for a mouth, and wavy auburn hair. It was the eyes, however, that set him apart from Collingswood. While hers greeted the world with easygoing intellect, Amherst's revealed the quick, watchful manner of a true martinet. "You certainly took your time reporting, didn't you?" he sniffed, ignoring Brim's original question.

"I was with Captain Collingswood, Sir," Brim explained.

"Plead your rationalizations only when I ask," he sneered. "Lieutenant Theada came to see me straight off—as befits a proper Imperial officer." He swiveled his chair and smoothed his blue-braided breeches where they became close fitting just below the knees. Elegant knee-high boots exuded the soft luxury of expensive ophet leather (which Brim had seen before only in pictures). "Colonials always have so much to learn about proper deportment," he sighed, then peered along his nose at Brim. "You Carescrians will probably prove the worst of all."

Brim held his temper—and his tongue. After the Helmsman's Academy, Amherst's manner was all too familiar.

"Well?" the other demanded suddenly. "What have you to say for yourself?"

"I was with the Captain," Brim repeated, "at her request."

"You'll soon learn to be smart with me, Carescrian," Amherst snapped, eyes flashing with quick anger.

"I meant no insult, Sir," Brim stated evenly, still under relatively firm control.

Amherst glared coldly. "I shall be the judge of your pitiful insults, Sublieutenant." He joined long fingers at the tips, contemplated the roofed structure they formed while Brim stewed in uncomfortable silence. "I believe I shall do the whole crew a favor," he said presently, looking Brim in the eye for the first time. "The sooner your kind display your true abilities, the sooner we can replace you with your betters." Abruptly, he turned to his display. "Imagine, " he muttered to no one in particular, "a Carescrian with a cabin of his own!" He shook his head and moved long, pink fingers over the control panel. "We are scheduled out of here the morning after next," he chortled. "And you are now posted as co-Helmsman for the takeoff. Old Gallsworthy ought to be in a spectacular mood after another two nights' gaming. He'll make short work of your no-account talent."

Trembling with frustration, Brim remained in the doorway, waiting for whatever might come next.

"You may go," Amherst said, turning his back. "You have the remainder of today and tomorrow to enjoy the ship. After that, good riddance, Carescrian. You have no place with a gentleman's organization—in spite of what Lord Beorn's perverted Reform Act might allege."

Brim turned on his heel, and with the last vestiges of his patience eroding like sand on a beach, he stormed off to his cabin.

***

Long metacycles later—he lost track of time—Brim sat, head in hands, on his bunk, halfway between murderous anger and deep, deep despair. It was cadet school all over again. The few Carescrians who even made it to the Academy had to be better than anyone else just to be accepted as living beings. And the very weapon Imperials always used was a person's own temper. He shook his head, painfully rehearsing his meeting with Amherst for the thousandth time when a mighty pounding rattled the door to his cabin. "Wilf Ansor, my new friend, come! Now is the time for libations in the wardroom, eh?" In all his twenty years, Brim could not remember a more welcome sound.

Now, late in the last watch of the day, the wardroom was dim with hogge'poa smoke and crowded by people who had clearly collected from all over the base. Brim picked out uniforms of spaceframe structure masters, logic boffins, and a whole cadrè of Imperial officers—many with impressive ranks. Most of the latter wore insignia from other ships. And beautiful women! They were all over the room. Some young, some not so young. His eyes had just fallen willing prisoner to an artfully tousled head of golden curls and soft expressive eyes when Ursis returned with two largish goblets of meem—and another Bear in tow.

"Come, Anastas Alexi," Ursis called to the smaller edition of himself. "Let me present new Helmsman just reported in. Wilf Ansor, you must meet glorious engineering officer, and my personal boss, Lieutenant A.A. Borodov!"

Borodov grasped Brim's hand in a firm hirsute paw. "Brim?" he exclaimed. "But I have heard of you—greatest Helmsmen of all in latest Academy class, is it not so?"

Brim felt his face flush. "I am pleased to meet you, Sir," he stammered.

"Ah-ha!" the Bear exclaimed, turning to Ursis triumphantly. "Blush gives him away, would you believe?"

Ursis chortled heartily. "All's dark when snow flies blue, eh?" They both laughed.

"Well, Wilf Ansor," Borodov rumbled on. "Many of us have looked forward to flying with you at helm. Tonight we shall drink toasts to Navron/Linfarne and Carescrian ore barges." He placed a paw on the chest of Brim's uniform. "I myself started Drive work on same star beasts, eh? Many years before you were little cub." He chuckled.

"Destroyers should prove easy work in comparison, believe me."

He turned suddenly and caught the arm of a dainty lieutenant. "Ah, Anastasia," he said. "You must meet our new Helmsman, Wilf Brim!"

"Beautiful woman here is Anastasia Fourier—weapons officer, Wilf," Ursis added with a wink. "So small for such large job..."

"Big enough to bruise your shins, you chauvinist Bear," Anastasia said as she bussed his furry cheek. Her face was almost perfectly moon-shaped with wide-set eyes and heavy, pouting lips. She had a high-pitched voice and talked at such a rate that Brim marveled she could make herself understood at all. Her Fleet Cape revealed just enough in the way of curves to assure Brim that great intrinsic worth lay beneath. Her wink made him believe that much of it might, under proper circumstances, be readily available. "If this is the kind of company you keep, Lieutenant," she squeaked, "I shall have to keep a close eye on you, and the sooner the better." Then, suddenly as she appeared, she was swept away giggling on the arm of a smiling commander. He wore the insignia—if Brim's eyes didn't lie—of a battlecruiser.

Ursis touched his ann. "When you stop drooling, friend Brim," he said, "I want you to meet our Dr. Flynn—keeps us alive and moderately healthy despite all efforts to contrary." The Medical Officer was short, fair, and balding, with a reddish face and quick smile. His uniform was also—noticeably—standard issue.

"Xerxes O. Flynn at your service," he said with a wide-eyed leer. "You look terrible."

Brim flinched. "Pardon?"

Flynn shrugged. "I need the practice, Brim," he said with mock seriousness. "These Bears keep the crew so filled with Sodeskayan wood alcohol nothing has a chance to get started." He cocked one eye and stared in the direction of Brim's ear. "You certain you haven't brought some sort of epidemic with you? I mean, Number One is spreading the word you're unsanitary or something!"

When all three howled at this bit of rare humor, Brim's temper threatened to erupt anew. Then suddenly he perceived an important difference. These people were laughing with him. Before he knew it, he was laughing, too, for the first time in years, it seemed—perhaps longer than that.

"And you'd better meet this lovely lass," Flynn panted, grabbing the arm of a plain young woman with her back to Brim. "Sophia, my dear," he said. "I want you to meet Wilf Brim, your new partner in crime. Lieutenant Sophia Pym, Sublieutenant Wilf Brim."

Ursis grinned. "Lady Helmsman, would you believe?"

Relaxed for the first time since boarding *Truculent*, Brim turned and extended his hand. "I didn't catch your last name," he said, smiling. Then his heart literally skipped a beat. Sophia was talking to the girl with the tousled hair. He said something inane, took Sophia's proffered hand, and tried not to stare at her friend. When a voice from somewhere pronounced, "Margot Effer'wyck," the rest of the wardroom ceased to exist.

If this tall, ample young woman was not the most beautiful in the Universe, she nonetheless appealed to Brim in a most profoundly fundamental manner. Her eyes flashed nimble intelligence. Her oval face was framed by the loose golden curls that had drawn his gaze originally, and her skin was almost painfully fair, brushed lightly with pink high in her cheeks. When she smiled, her brow formed the most engaging frown he could imagine. Whatever it was she had, it was sufficient for him. "Margot," he stammered. "That's a beautiful name."

Her cool blue eyes remained neutral, but the large hand and tapering fingers in his grip were warm and friendly to his touch. "I like the name, too," she said, "even if everyone does use it these days."

Brim watched her full, moist lips, and suddenly he was a bashful schoolboy allover again—he couldn't even look her in the eye! On the left shoulder of her cape, she wore insignia of a full lieutenant, and her nametag read, CHIEF, THREAT ASSESSMENT SECTION, TECHNOLOGY DIVISION. An impressive-sounding job for one so young. Even her uniform looked perfect (and reminded him, for the millionth time, of his own shabby, regulation-issue blues).

While Flynn and Sophia (what was her last name?) exchanged words, with considerable friendly laughter, he met her glance again. This time, some of the coolness was replaced with interest. "You're new aboard *Truculent*, aren't you?" she asked.

"Yes," Brim answered, wretchedly wishing he could think of

something more clever to say. "I reported this morning."

The smiling frown reappeared. "You drew a good ship," she said, looking about the room. "And a lucky one, too. People like to share the wardroom when she's in port." She laughed. "I think they secretly hope some of the luck may rub off."

"Not you, though?" Brim asked with a grin.

Margot's eyes sparkled. "Perhaps me most of all," she said, laughing again. "I accept all the good luck I can get." Suddenly she gazed at the blazes on his collar. "What made you become a Helmsman?" she asked.

"Oh, I'd done a bit of flying before I was called up," Brim explained modestly. "But I think the Admiralty was getting desperate, if you want the absolute truth."

Her eyes drew his. "I'd certainly say so," she agreed with a twinkle. "It's known that only madmen fly those ore carriers on Navron/Linfarne."

Brim took a deep breath. Everyone seemed to know about him. "Being a Carescrian," he answered coldly, "I was fortunate indeed to achieve the exalted status of 'madman'. It put me at a Helmsman's console. Most of my contemporaries were privileged to suffer radiation sickness in the cargo holds…"

"I'm terribly sorry," she said, wincing. "I suppose I know better than that." She put a hand on his arm. "Your name came up at a party the other evening. They say you are a superb Helmsman."

Brim grimaced. "They should have informed you I am also an unreasonably touchy Carescrian," he said, suddenly ashamed of his outburst. "Will you forgive me?"

"I shall call it even," she said, color rising in her cheeks. 'I have not loved my words, nor my words me/nor coin'd my voice to smiles…'"

Brim frowned, concentrated for a moment, then snapped his fingers and grinned. "'Nor cried aloud'," he continued, "'In worship of an echo in the crowd.'"

Her sudden smile seemed to light the room. "You know that?" she asked.

"Star Pilgrim," Brim said. "I suppose I've read a lot of Alastor's poems." He smiled, a little embarrassed. "I've had a lot of time on those old carriers—and secondhand poetry books are pretty cheap."

"But nobody reads poetry anymore."

"Evidently you do," Brim said with a smile. "And I do. I'd like to think neither of us is a nobody."

A new look was now on her face, one that hadn't been there before Alastor. "Who else do you read?" she asked.

"'Father of this unfathomable Universe/Hear my solemn song, for I have loved your stars...'"

"That...that's 'Solitude' by Nondum Lamia," she said with delighted eyes.

"Yes. That's right," Brim said. "Verse two."

"And how about, 'Roll on, thou deep and star-swept cosmos—roll/ Ten thousand starfleets sweep thy wastes in vain...'"

"Yes!" Brim said, frowning again. He raised a finger. "Lacerta. 'Rime of the Ancients', I think. 'Men mark their worlds with ruin—their power/Stops with their puny ships; upon the starry plain...'"

Clearly speechless, she shook her head. "That's beautiful," she finally whispered. Then she raised her hands, abruptly serious. "It's nice to know I'm not totally alone sometimes..." Her voice trailed off.

Taken aback, Brim raised his eyebrows. "I don't understand," he began, but was interrupted by an elegantly uniformed commander.

"Sorry, Lieutenant," the man said without bothering to introduce himself. "It's about time I escort this young thing back to headquarters."

"My date seems to be here," Margot said, instantly recovering her previous mood of reserved amiability. "I'm very glad I met you, Wilf." Their eyes met once more, lingered for a heartbeat. "Until the next time," she whispered in a husky voice. Then, before he could answer, she was on her way through the crowd.

Entranced, Brim shamelessly stared as she walked away: long, well-built legs revealed below her cape through skintight trousers, feet in tiny, ankle-length boots. "You are spilling your meem, friend Wilf Ansor," Ursis said, once again breaking into his reverie.

"Yes, thanks," he mumbled, shaking his head.

"Quite a lady, Miss Effer'wyck," Flynn sighed. "But then you've already noticed, haven't you?"

Brim felt his face flush. He was sure he had already made a fool of himself.

29

"I think you may have to admire that one from a distance," Sophia observed tactfully. "Turns out she's already spoken for: The Honorable Commander LaKarn, Baron of the Torond, no less."

"Story of my life," Brim grumped good-naturedly. "Too late for everything."

"Well, perhaps not quite everything," Sophia observed. "You've still got more than a day before you face old Gallsworthy on the bridge."

"It's true, Wilf Ansor," Borodov interjected. "Lots of time to spend learning those deep-space whiz-clanks you Helmsmen play with on the bridge." He winked meaningfully.

"Not that we'd want you to disappoint Number One or anything so subtle as that," Flynn said under his breath.

Brim grinned. "I think I'm beginning to understand a lot of things," he said.

Borodov put a hairy finger on Ursis' cuff. "After chill and darkness of storm, wise Bears run without snow, eh?"

Ursis raised an index finger. "Is much truth in that, Anastas Alexi," he said sagely. "Without snow, indeed."

By the time Brim returned to his cabin, the face of Margot Effer'wyck was already vague in his mind's eye. If nothing else, he had learned long ago to take life one step at a time.

***

Weary metacycles before Haefdon's dawn lightened Gimmas' cloudy sky, Wilf Brim was already busy on *Truculent's* empty bridge. "Good morning, Mr. Chairman," he said, settling carefully in the right-hand Helmsman's seat.

"Good morning, Lieutenant Brim," replied the Chairman's disembodied voice. "What service can we render?"

Brim peered into the darkness through the Hyperscreens where yesterday's snowfall had again relapsed to driving sheets of rain. Below, wet hullmetal decks gleamed under hovering battle lanterns; beyond, the Eorean Complex was revealed by half-lighted shapes of sleeping starships, grotesque forms on other gravity pools, and the ever-present shipyard cranes. Compulsively, he pulled the cloak tighter about his neck, though the air was warm and dry. "Simulation, Mr. Chairman," he said at length. "All systems."

"All-systems simulation, Lieutenant," the Chairman repeated. "Starboard Helmsman's console in simulation mode." Soft-hued patterns filled the displays before him, moved and changed. "Will you require special circumstances?"

"Later, Mr. Chairman," Brim answered, concentrating on the start-up data flashing past his eyes. "Right now, you can do something a bit easier—like the last takeoff here on Haefdon. Do you still have that stored?"

"A moment, Sir," the Chairman answered. Presently the Hyperscreens became opaque, flickered, then abruptly came to life in the illusion of gloomy daylight, this time a mile or so out to sea from the complex. "Found it," the Chairman intoned.

Brim looked around the simulated seascape, checked systems parameters once more on his displays, then gently lowered his hands to the consoles. "Mr. Chairman," he said, "we'll take this one from the very beginning..."

All that morning and far into the afternoon, Brim exercised *Truculent's* controls, simulating takeoffs in good conditions and bad. Like most contemporary starships, she employed antigravity generators for HypoLight-speed travel, switching to her four matched Sheldon Drive crystals (for both propulsion and negation of relativistic mass/time effects) only when it was desired to surpass the critical velocity of LightSpeed.

Specially designed for blockade and close-support work, all T— class starships flew with two oversized CR-special 258x gravity generators astride the keel at the deepest (and aftmost) point of the hull. These powerful units provided extraordinary acceleration and maneuverability when working close-in to planetary systems where HyperLight travel was impractical (and potential targets were themselves either accelerating from or decelerating to zero velocity). A third unit of normal output and configuration was housed in a long chamber over the keel directly beneath the bridge. This generator supplied direct thrust along the ship's vertical axis for intricate maneuvering or warping into an anchorage.

As the session wore on, *Truculent's* Chairman provided antigravity failures of every kind and significance, then added steering-engine problems and systems troubles as the session progressed. By mid-afternoon, the bone-tired Carescrian felt rancid with dried sweat from metacycles of mental and physical effort. But he was also reasonably certain he could fly the starship through anything the Universe might throw at him. In the back of his mind, he knew well enough that simulators never really duplicated real-life flying experience, but the combination of a day's practice on these well-maintained controls and nearly three years' bullying deteriorated Q—97 ore carriers in and out of Navron/Linfarne's asteroid-cluttered HyperSpace provided him with considerable confidence in himself as well as the ship. Compared to even the best Carescrian C-97s, *Truculent* came off like a scalpel to an ax—not altogether shabby, he allowed (smiling at himself), for a "pick and shovel" tub like a destroyer.

Tired as he was, he lingered at the console, working the controls even after technical ratings began to appear here and there on the bridge to bring their respective systems on line for the morning's takeoff. But when two yeomen noisily commenced work on the principal Helmsman's console to his left, he knew it was time to wrap things up. "Mr. Chairman," he announced, "I'm finished with the controls."

"A moment, Sir," the Chairman said, then, "Simulation terminated. Starboard Helmsman's console returned to direct connect." The Hyperscreens faded momentarily, then restored themselves to the dreary landscape of Haefdon. It was again snowing outside as spume tore from wind-lashed whitecaps in the basin and the last yellowish tinges dissolved from the low-hanging clouds. Brim laughed grimly to himself. Weather on Haefdon was so bad—so horrible—even poor Carescria seemed appealing in comparison.

He slid wearily from the recliner, then dallied for a moment, staring through the Hyperscreens at the driving snow. While he watched, haloed headlights from a distant surface vehicle caught his eye as it picked its way through the shipyard in the direction of the basin. Abruptly, the vehicle turned onto *Truculent's* jetty and pulled to a hovering stop under the battle lanterns at the gangway. Brim frowned, thankful it was not he who was out on a night like this.

He had just started back to his cabin when it occurred to him that nothing more seemed to be happening on the jetty. The skimmer continued to hover in the driving snow, but no one got out, or in. The whole affair piqued his tired curiosity—now what?

As if in answer, two men appeared on *Truculent's* gangway, trudging through the driving snow toward the jetty and its waiting skimmer. Heads down and capes plastered to their bodies, they gave mute testimony to the wind that he knew was howling through the nearby lifelines. One of them, by his very size and gait, was surely the inane Barbousse.

Curious, Brim considered. Where was a man like Barbousse going in a skimmer, especially with *Truculent's* lift-off little more than a few Standard Metacycles away? He watched with renewed interest. Shortly, the two reached the skimmer, now hovering in a cloud of stirred-up snowflakes. They hammered on the forward compartment until they were joined by an agitated driver waving his arms and stamping his boots emotionally. Presently, Barbousse stepped to the man's side and plucked him from his feet by the scruff of his collar. This had an immediate quieting effect, and the three of them opened the passenger compartment of the skimmer and peered into its darkened interior.

Shortly thereafter, Barbousse disappeared through the door—only to emerge almost immediately, this time with the limp figure of a man in his arms. His companion from *Truculent* reached inside the skimmer and withdrew a Fleet Cape, which he used to cover the motionless individual, then completed some sort of transaction with the driver of the skimmer. This finished, he turned on his heel to follow Barbousse back up the gangway to the ship.

As the skimmer pivoted and started its journey back along the jetty, Brim scratched his head. Who? he asked himself, but deep inside, he feared he already knew.

The bridge was again deserted some four Standard Metacycles before *Truculent's* scheduled takeoff time, though things were well astir below as ratings prepared the ship for flight.

"Morning, Mr. Chairman," Brim said, again settling into the right-hand Helmsman's station. "Today, we'll do those checkouts for real."

He worked without interruption until the Bears arrived at their power consoles, by which time most of the other stations were occupied and the bridge was humming with activity. "Don't they let you sleep in new cabin of yours?" the Bear asked with mock solicitousness as he strode along the main aisle of the bridge. "Power-systems log says you've already checked everything couple thousand times." He chuckled. "You have no trust in Chairman, maybe?"

Brim felt his face flush. "I thought I'd better get everything right this morning if I hope ever to do it again," he said with a chuckle.

Ursis smiled. "Is worth doing," he pronounced seriously. "No fool, Bear who first said, 'First impressions are lasting'. You must have been listening, eh?"

"Just scared," Brim said honestly.

"Probably good time for being little scared," a displayed image of Borodov interjected darkly from the power exchange deep in *Truculent's* hull. "Word is they carried him aboard!"

Brim looked the old Bear's image in its eye. "Gallsworthy?" he asked.

"Is same," Borodov answered. "Bad, they say."

"I think I watched it from here on the bridge, then," Brim said. "I wasn't certain at the time."

The old Bear looked thoughtful as Sophia Pym arrived, towing a flabby Theada to his jump seat at the side of the bridge. The latter's eyes widened considerably when he caught sight of Brim at the right-hand console. "You may well find yourself on what you call 'hot seat', Wilf Ansor," Borodov pronounced soberly.

"We've seen him like this before," Ursis interjected.

Brim smiled and looked at the two Engineering Officers. "What are you trying to tell me?" he asked.

"Simply this," Borodov explained with a serious mien, "Nikolai Yanuarievich and I, we can make seem like *Truculent's* power systems won't run. None of you humans will be able to tell difference—begging your pardon."

"Many of us in crew do not think is fair you must go through with this, Wilf," Ursis added.

Brim glanced at his boots, wrestling with his emotions. He wasn't used to Imperials who even cared if he lived or died. Finally, he shook his head, looking first at one and then the other. "Thank you," he said quietly. "Thank you both. But sooner or later, I'm going to have to face up to this, and I suppose now is as good as any other time."

"Is brave decision you make, Wilf," Borodov said.

"Is also too late to change mind," Ursis interrupted, inclining his head slightly toward the back of the bridge. "Now comes Gallsworthy." Without another word, the Sodeskayan dissolved into a suddenly quiet bridge.

2 As he strode among the consoles, Bosporus P. Gallsworthy, Lieutenant, I.F., wore the look of a man so secure in what he did that mere outward appearance was of no importance. His face was almost wooden in calm, though bushy eyebrows failed to mask a glint of cold intelligence in his red-rimmed eyes. He had short-cropped hair and loosely-jowled, pockmarked cheeks, a dark complexion, and thin, dry lips. His height was average or a little less, and his uniform, though most obviously clean, revealed the ghost of a stain halfway down the left breast of his tunic. Reaching the principal's console, he casually flipped his cape to one side and slid into the recliner. Brim watched him from the corner of his eye, motionless.

"Mr. Chairman," Gallsworthy said curtly.

"Good morning, Lieutenant Galls..."

"I'll have the systems checkout right away," Gallsworthy interrupted. "Altimeters?"

"Preverified," said the Chairman. "Set...and cross checked."

"Engineers' preflight?"

"Preverified: complete."

"G-wave service?"

"Preverified: forty-four, five hundred Go and GH."

"What in xaxt is this xaxtdamned 'preverified' business?" Gallsworthy demanded.

"The systems checkouts are already complete, Lieutenant," the Chairman said. "We are ready for immediate generator startup."

"Who ran those checkouts?"

"Lieutenant Brim, Sir."

"Brim? Who's Brim?"

"Sublieutenant Wilf Brim," the Chairman replied, "at the console next..."

"Takeoff bugs ninety-two, one thirty-eight, one fifty-one," Gallsworthy interrupted, continuing the checkout. "And drop that 'preverified' muck."

"One sixty-nine five," the Chairman answered.

"Four eight oh four?"

"One hundred and seventy thousand, Lieutenant," the Chairman said. "Within tolerances."

Gallsworthy paused, frowned. "I know," he growled. "All right. You can skip the rest of that one, then. We'll do the 'start' checklist next."

"The 'start' checklist is also complete, Lieu..."

"I said 'start' checklist, Mr. Chairman. Now."

"Start pressure ninety-one forty. Sub-generator on," the Chairman said.

"Gravity brake?"

"Set."

"KA'PPA beacon?"

"Energized."

Again Gallsworthy stopped. "Skip down to...No. Stow that." Without turning his head, he spoke from the side of his mouth. "All right, Brim, or whatever it is they call you. If you think you're so xaxtdamned expert at checkout all by yourself, maybe you'll want to fly this beast yourself, too?"

"That will be fine, Sir," Brim answered, without turning his own head. But his heart was in his mouth. He endured Gallsworthy's stony silence for a personal eternity, staring through the Hyperscreens into the dirty gray sky and driving rain and forcing himself to relax. Every eye on the bridge would be watching.

At some length, Gallsworthy turned in his recliner. "Smart-aleck kid," he snarled under his breath, biting each word off short. "Right out of the xaxtdamned Academy and you puppies think you know how to fly a starship. I've got half a notion to let you try it, then kick your ass off the ship when you can't."

38

"I'm ready, Lieutenant," Brim asserted quietly, still staring out the Hyperscreens, "anytime you are." In the corner of his eye, he watched a startled expression form on the senior Helmsman's face, then turn to cold anger.

"You just thraggling asked for it, Brim," Gallsworthy hissed through clenched teeth. All of it. The controls are yours." He sat back in his recliner and folded his arms.

For the first time, Brim turned and faced the waspish individual who was to be his first commandant. "As you wish, Lieutenant," he said evenly.

Gallsworthy snorted, smiled, and began to return to the controls when he stopped short and turned in his seat again. "What was that?" he demanded.

"I said, 'As you wish, Lieutenant'," Brim repeated.

Gallsworthy's face clouded; his bushy eyebrows descended to almost hide his eyes. "You mean you're actually going to try to...?" he stumbled, clearly unprepared for Brim's answer. "Why, you can't fly this ship any more than a..." He stopped, clearly groping for a suitable term of disapprobation.

"I can't believe you plan to finish that sentence, Lieutenant Gallsworthy," Collingswood interrupted. "Certainly you would never turn over the controls to someone whose competence you question. Would you?"

The senior Helmsman jerked around in his recliner. "When did you...?" he growled, then bit his lip. "My apologies, Captain," he said lamely. "I, ah..."

"Oh, please continue, Lieutenant Gallsworthy," Collingswood commanded sharply.

"Nothing, Captain," Gallsworthy grumbled. "Really."

"Good, Mr. Gallsworthy," Collingswood answered. "And I am highly gratified to see you and Number One working so closely together today."

At this, Amherst looked up in alarm. "Together?"

"Why, yes," Collingswood answered, the very picture of innocence. "It was you who suggested Lieutenant Brim have a chance to show us how he graduated first in his class at the Helmsman's Academy. Wasn't it?"

"First in his...?" Amherst stammered. "Ah. Why, ah...of course, Captain." He turned to Gallsworthy. "Didn't we, Lieutenant Gallsw..."

"We shall discuss this cooperation at a more appropriate time, gentlemen," Collingswood interrupted pointedly. "Lieutenant Brim is about to transfer control to his console, aren't you, Lieutenant?"

Brim nodded. "Aye, Captain," he agreed quickly. Then, before anything further might transpire, he acted. "Mr. Chairman," he ordered, "swap command to this console immediately."

Gallsworthy stiffened, opened his eyes and his mouth at the same time, and turned toward Collingswood, but he was already metacycles too late. Before retiring the previous night, Brim had carefully preset all necessary turn-over transactions, and the complex ritual was accomplished almost instantaneously.

"Start checkout is complete, Lieutenant Ursis," the Carescrian said to an image of the Sodeskayan that suddenly shimmered in a hovering display globe near his right hand. "Fire off the generators, please."

"Starboard antigrav," Ursis rumbled quickly. "Turning one; wave guide closed." From far aft and deep within the hull, a low whine dropped slowly to a wavering drone. This steadied. "Turning two." A thump passed through the spaceframe. "Guide open."

Brim watched colored patterns race across his power readouts as antigravity pressure built. A gentle rumble, more felt than heard, replaced the drone, building rapidly in volume and strength. "Call 'em out, Mr. Chairman," he ordered.

"Normal pressure," the Chairman confirmed. "Plus nine. Plus twelve. Plus fifteen—we have a start, Lieutenant."

Ursis' beady eye winked at Brim from the display. "Port generator, Mr. Chairman," he continued without interruption. "Turning one; wave guide closed." A second whine mingled with the sound of the running generator and dropped in pitch. "Turning two. Guide open." The combined rumble was a substantial presence on the bridge as the second antigravity generator reached operating parameters.

"Normal pressure on starboard," the Chairman reported. "Plus fifteen. You have a second start, Lieutenant Ursis."

"Number three," Ursis said quietly. "Standard start. You do it, Mr.

Chairman." A third and higher pitched thrumming soon joined the first two.

"All generators running and steady," reported the Chairman.

"Your ship, Wilf," the Bear pronounced. "Drive systems are checked and waiting."

"Thank you, Nik," Brim said, trying desperately to avoid matching eyes with the clearly thunderstruck Gallsworthy. He mentally ran through a dozen personal checklists, scanned the readouts once more—all normal. Satisfied for the moment, he relaxed in the recliner. "Mr. Amherst," he announced to the clearly disapproving Number One, "the Helmsman's station is ready for immediate departure."

"Let's be at it, then, Number One," Collingswood's voice prompted as Brim watched the freezing rain spatter against the heated Hyperscreens. A large tracked vehicle had just pulled onto the jetty, lining up in front of *Truculent's* sharp nose. Presently, three great amber lenses deployed from its back and positioned themselves so that only one could be seen from Brim's console. They glowed once, twice. Brim's hands eased over his control panel. "Ground link complete," he reported tersely.

"All hands to stations for lift-off, Mr. Chairman," Amherst commanded. Brim listened to alarms going off below. "Special-duty spacemen close up!" On the forward deck, lights appeared in the mooring-control cupola. A nearby display showed the two mooring cupolas aft were now manned and ready. All over the bridge, a familiar litany of departure was in full activity. Below, at least ten maintenance analogs were racing along the decks making last-minute checks for loose gear. From the rear of the bridge, Maldive spoke into a dozen interCOMM systems. "Testing alarm systems! Testing alarm systems! Testing..."

Outside, an indistinct movement on the basin caught Brim's attention. Imagination? No—there it was again! Nearly lost in the grayness, a light of some sort was battling through the driving rain.

"Ship approaching from green, yellow-green, Lieutenant Brim," a rating warned from his center console.

"Very well," Brim acknowledged. "I'll keep an eye on it." Within clicks, he could make out a darker mass within the gray, which steadily defined itself into an angular shape. First, a KA'PPA beacon broke clear among the sheets of driving rain, then a bridge, and finally a hull, riding fast about twenty irals off a flattened, frothing area of water amid the thrashing waves of the storm-swept basin. Brim made out A.45 on the side of a bridge wing; she was one of a relatively new class of large, fast, and heavily protected destroyers that had been constantly in the public eye of late because of their prominent employment in the Empire's critical convoy lifelines. From her bridge, she also displayed the flashing triangular device that signaled she carried a flotilla leader aboard. A ship of some consequence, this one, and she approached *Truculent's* gravity pool with an important mien, drawing to a stop in a sweeping cloud of ice particles as her reversing generators bled off the tremendous momentum she carried.

"I.F.S. *Audacious*," Amherst observed with ill-concealed awe as he looked up from a data display. "With Sir Davenport himself aboard. Do you suppose she's the next one for our gravity pool? We could run the next checklists out on the water."

"Why should we do that?" Collingswood asked with a frown.

"Well," Amherst said with raised eyebrows, "Sir Hugh is an influential person in the Fleet, after all."

"And he is at least a quarter metacycle early," Collingswood answered. "We shall clear the mooring in our own good time. You will proceed with our departure in a normal manner, Mr. Amherst."

"As you wish, Captain," the senior Lieutenant said, a half-troubled timbre in his voice.

Brim mentally shrugged, storing that tidbit in a safe corner of his mind. If Collingswood wasn't worried about a flotilla leader, then neither was he. He grinned to himself while all around the gravity pool, mooring beams flashed as ratings in the mooring cupolas drew the ship solidly into place. Suddenly, treble-pitched steering engines overlaid the rumbling gravity generators. *Truculent's* bridge quivered as side thrusts jolted through her spaceframe. "Steering engine thrusts in all quadrants, Lieutenant," the Chairman reported.

"Very well," Brim said calmly. "Pretaxi check, Mr. Chairman, bridge report..."

"Bridge is secure, Lieutenant."

"Electrical?"

"On generators."

"Environmentals?"

"Packs are set for 'flight'."

"Auxiliary power?"

"Running."

"Launches stowed and secured for deep space," a voice reported at Amherst's console behind him.

"All working parties on station, Lieutenant," said another voice. "Analogs report decks clear and secure."

"Pretaxi check complete," Brim announced, forcing himself to relax. He felt the gentle throb of the gravity generators, watched Ursis' face as the Bear made last-minute adjustments to their controls. *Truculent* was nearly ready for lift-off.

Suddenly, KA'PPA rings flashed from the waiting ship's high beacon like concentric waves from a pebble in a pool.

"Message from I.F.S. *Audacious*," a balding signals yeoman with fat cheeks reported to Collingswood.

"Very well, Mr. Applewood," Collingswood replied. "I'll have it."

"'Flotilla leader, the Honorable Commodore Sir Hugh Davenport, I.F, informs I.F.S. *Truculent* that he is now assigned this gravity pool,'" Applewood read in a high-pitched voice.

Brim heard Collingswood chuckle. "Is that so?" she asked. "Well, Mr. Applewood, you can make this back to the Honorable, etc., aboard I.F.S. *Audacious*: 'Pity. Where does the Commodore propose to moor his starship?'"

"All stations ready to proceed, Captain," Amherst reported, this time almost in a gasp.

"Lieutenant Brim," Collingswood's voice boomed confidently in the pregnant silence of the bridge, "you may proceed to the takeoff zone when you receive taxi clearance."

Brim smiled to himself. It was one of those moments he imagined he would recall for the remainder of his life—as long as that might be, considering the going mortality rate for destroyers. "Aye, aye, Captain," he said. "Proceeding to the takeoff zone. Mr. Chairman, have the cupolas single up all moorings," he ordered. Immediately, beams winked out all around the ship until only a single shaft of green remained attached at any of the optical bollards in the jetty walls.

"All mooring points singled up, Lieutenant," the Chairman reported.

"Very well, Mr. Chairman," Brim announced quietly, "you may now switch to internal gravity—Quartermaster Maldive on the interCOMM, please."

"Aye, aye, Lieutenant," Maldive answered from a display.

"All hands stand by for internal gravity," Maldive's voice echoed from the ship's interCOMM as alarms clattered in the background.

Brim braced himself as the first sudden rush of nausea swept his stomach. He swallowed hard, forcing his gorge back where it ought to be. Loose articles all over the ship rattled and clanged. He felt sweat break momentarily from his forehead. Then, quickly as it struck, the sensation passed. A muffled thump announced detachment of the ground umbilicals; the ship sagged precariously to port, then righted as her stable platforms adjusted to independent operation. From a corner of his eye, he watched the brow swing away from the hull and retract into the top of the jetty. He glanced at the tracked vehicle; its lenses were still perfectly lined up with his console but now glowing cool green. A white cursor was centered on the foremost surface. He flexed his shoulders and shook his head, smiling to himself—another gravity switch without losing his breakfast. "I'll speak with Ground Control now, Mr. Chairman," he said, glancing quickly at the waiting vehicle on the jetty wall.

"Ground Control," a narrow face with huge, bushy eyebrows announced from a display.

"T.83 to Ground," Brim replied. "We're ready to taxi out when you are."

"Ground to DD T.83," the Controller said. "You're cleared to taxi. And you've got a destroyer standing off your stem."

"T.83 to Ground: I see that one," Brim replied.

"DD A.45: hold your position," the Controller warned *Audacious* through another display in the tracked vehicle. Brim overheard Davenport's curt "Holding" through the same roundabout means. It provided scant comfort; the waiting destroyer could hardly have drawn up any closer to *Truculent's* gravity pool—nor been placed in a more inconvenient position with regard to the wind. Starships were forbidden to fly low over any land areas because overpressure from their gravity generators simply caused too much damage and noise. That ruled out exiting the gravity pool in a normal, forward-running attitude. The same overpressure (and resulting noise levels) also prohibited altitudes higher than thirty irals anywhere within a c'lenyt of land. And because *Audacious* blocked any chance for a snubbed swing with mooring beams rigged as old-fashioned spring lines, it was now Brim's difficult task to back the starship around the other destroyer—in a high-wind situation. Moreover, he was painfully aware that if he so much as grazed Davenport's spotless new escort, the resulting board of inquiry would destroy his career before it had much of a chance to begin. Wrestling his jangled nerves to a tenuous draw, he shrugged and smiled to himself. Best to be on with it. In the next few cycles, he'd either win all the maneuvering room he wanted, or he would be on his way back to Navron/Linfarne's ore carriers. And in no way did he intend a return to Carescria!

"Ground to DD T.83: wind zero four zero at ninety-one," the Controller reported.

"T.83 copies," Brim acknowledged, shaking his head. "I'll have a balance on the forward gravity generator, Nik," he said. "Then give me a point ninety-one gradient at zero four." That would at least give him a chance with the wind.

"Ninety-one gradient at zero four," Ursis repeated.

The low rumbling of *Truculent's* forward generator increased as it shouldered the weight of the ship. "Balanced," Ursis reported.

"Helm's at dead center, Lieutenant," the Chairman announced. "We are ready to move."

"Stand by," Brim warned. He checked the control settings once more, feeling a balm of resignation soothe his nerves. *Truculent* could never—in his wildest nightmares—be as difficult to control as a loaded ore carrier. And he'd mastered them. "Let go all mooring beams," he ordered quietly, eyes glued to the cursor in the center of Ground Control's lenses. Instantly, the beams vanished. "Dead slow astern all," he ordered, feeling sweat break out on his forehead.

"Dead slow astern," Ursis echoed tensely; the ship began to move.

With one eye on *Audacious*, Brim struggled to keep the cursor centered, but in spite of every effort, it started across the glowing lens—sure indication *Truculent* was drifting upwind. Brim's heart leaped into his mouth. "Too much gradient, Nik!" he warned. "We're sliding into *Audacious*."

"I've got fix on it," Ursis answered tensely. "Sorry."

"'S all right," Brim croaked with relief as the drifting slowed and finally ceased, but he didn't breathe again until *Truculent* was backed all the way off the gravity pool. "Stop together," he ordered. She was now directly beside *Audacious*, separated at the stem from Davenport's spotless decks by no more than a score of irals.

"Stop together," Ursis echoed.

Now came the tricky part.

Screwing up his courage again, he ordered, "Dead slow astern, port."

"Dead slow astern, port." *Truculent's* bow began to swing sharply toward disaster waiting only irals away.

"Brim! What in the Universe are you...?" Gallsworthy growled beside him.

"It is Lieutenant Brim's helm, Lieutenant Gallsworthy," Collingswood interrupted. "By your orders."

Brim put them both from his mind. The next clicks were critical. He tensed, waited..."Quarter astern starboard, dead slow astern port," he uttered with a dry mouth.

"Quarter astern starboard, dead slow astern port," Ursis echoed. *Truculent's* bow stopped its swing only an iral or so from *Audacious*, then slowly began to draw away to safety. This time, the gravity gradient held and—as Brim planned—she continued in a wide turn to port. But an eternity passed before the starship's needle bow finally pointed out on to the rolling waters of the basin.

Brim never so much as looked back. "Ahead one-quarter, both," he ordered weakly.

"Ahead one-quarter, both," Ursis echoed, this time with an ear-to-ear grin. He knew.

At that moment, a display winked into life with the image of Sophia Pym touching thumb to forefinger. "Too bad you can't see Amherst's face," she whispered gleefully. Beside her, Theada's look of astonishment had grown to one of total disbelief.

While *Truculent* moved into the relative freedom of the basin, the Controller called once more from the jetty: "Ground to DD T.83: you're cleared for taxi out to sea marker 981G. See you all next time you're in port. Good hunting!"

"DD T.83 to Ground," Brim replied. "Proceeding to marker 981G. And thanks." He peered into the driving rain ahead. "I am taking the helm, Mr. Chairman," he announced.

"You have the helm, Lieutenant Brim," the Chairman acknowledged. For the first time that morning, Brim's hands touched the directional controls. He was now in direct command of the ship itself. Inadvertently, he glanced at Gallsworthy—who was now staring back with unconcealed curiosity.

"Yes, Sir?" Brim asked.

"Mind your own business, Carescrian," Gallsworthy replied expressionlessly. But somehow the coldness had gone.

Brim nodded and turned away silently. Now was not the time to work out his basic relationship with this taciturn individual. "Taxi checks, Mr. Chairman," he said. "Lift modifiers?"

"Fifteen, fifteen, green," the Chairman replied.

"Yaw dampers and instruments?"

"Checked."

"Weight and balance finals?"

"One sixty-nine five hundred; no significant changes, Lieutenant."

"Twenty-one point two on the stabilizer. Engineer's taxi check, Nik?"

"Complete," Ursis growled.

"Taxi checklist complete," the Chairman pronounced.

With a feeling of relief, Brim watched the opening to the basin slide past. *Truculent* was now over open water. "Half ahead, both," he said, setting a course for marker 981G across the ranks of marching waves.

"Half ahead, both," Ursis echoed.

During the nearly ten cycles required to taxi into place, Brim made his own final checks of the starship's systems, finishing only moments before the flashing buoy hove into view ahead in the Hyperscreens. "DD T.83 to Harbor Control," he announced. "Starship is in sight of marker 981 G. Heading two ninety-one." He grinned in spite of himself. "Lift-off checklist, Mr. Chairman," he ordered.

"Transponders and Home indicator on. Fullstop cell powered. All warning lights off," the Chairman reported.

"Engineer's check?"

"Complete," Ursis said.

"Configuration check...Antiskid?"

"Skid is on," replied the Chairman.

"Speed brake?"

"Forward."

"Stabilizer trim—delete the gravity gradient, Mr. Chairman."

"Gravity gradient eliminated. Ship carries normal twenty-three one on lift-off."

"Very well, Mr. Chairman. Course indicators, Mr. Gallsworthy?" Brim prompted politely.

Mind clearly elsewhere for the moment, Gallsworthy jumped in his recliner. "A moment, Lieutenant," he mumbled with a reddening face and busied himself frenetically at the course controls. "Set and checked," he croaked at length.

"Lift-off check complete, Captain Collingswood," Brim announced. "At your command."

"Your helm, Lieutenant Brim," Collingswood replied from a display, thumb raised to the Hyperscreens—just as a nearby COMM globe flashed its priority pattern and displayed the Harbor Master's face.

"Harbor Master to DD T.83," he announced. "Hold your position at marker buoy 981G for cross traffic." Collingswood chuckled from her display and smiled understandingly.

"Holding," Brim grumped. "Full speed reverse, both," he said to Ursis' image.

"Full speed reverse, both," the Bear echoed. *Truculent* glided to a hovering stop just short of the tossing buoy.

"All stop."

"All stop."

"Steering engine's amidships," the Chairman announced.

In the driving rain outside the ship, Brim could see neither sky nor horizon; but twenty-five irals below, the sea's great swells were thick and black looking, peppered with ice rubble. Abruptly, a chance break in the downpour revealed the specter of another mass looming from the grayness, this one infinitely larger than *Audacious*. It quickly defined itself as the profile of a monster starship moving rapidly in *Truculent's* direction near the surface of the water. Scant moments later, she fairly burst from the storm, majestic and powerful, sea creaming away ahead of the roiling, foaming footprint she punched deep in the flattened surface, a haze of spray lifting hundreds of irals in her wake to rival the clouds themselves. Brim gasped in spite of himself. Perhaps no one in the galaxy could mistake that grand panorama of stacked bridges, great casemated turrets, and wide-shouldered, tapering hull: *Iaith Galad*, one of the three greatest battlecruisers ever constructed, and sister ship to *Nimue*, in which the famous Star Admiral Merlin Emrys was lost (nearly two years ago now, if Brim's memory served him). Waves of chill marched his back in icy regiments. To serve as Helmsman on something like her! He shook his head in resignation. Carescrians didn't get assignments like that. But what a dream.

"We shall require a salute, Lieutenant Amherst," Collingswood's voice prompted.

"Aye, Captain," Amherst replied. Immediately, glowing KA'PPA rings shimmered out from *Truculent's* beacon in the age-old Imperial salute, MAY STARS LIGHT ALL THY PATHS.

Brim had to crane his head back to see *Iaith Galad's* beacon when she made her traditional reply: AND THY PATHS, STAR TRAVELERS. He glimpsed tiny figures peering down from the vast panoply of Hyperscreens atop her towering bridge as she passed. One of them waved. Then, quickly as she appeared, she was gone, swallowed again in the gloom. *Truculent* bounced heavily in her gravity wake while a deluge of spray from the warship's backwash cascaded in sheets over the Hyperscreens and decks below. Then the destroyer steadied and the sea rolled again beneath the hull as if the great starship had never passed.

"DD T. 83: you now are cleared for immediate takeoff," the Harbor Master announced. "Wind is zero four at one oh three. Heavy battlecruiser just landed reports considerable turbulence on final: your path."

"Thank you very much," Brim acknowledged, then looked Ursis' image in the eye and winked. "Finally," he whispered, then louder, "Full speed ahead."

The Bear nodded. "Good luck," he mouthed silently. "Full speed ahead." Immediately, *Truculent's* two oversized gravity generators began to thunder deep in the starship's hull, shaking the whole spaceframe.

While thrust built, Brim held the bucking, vibrating starship in place with gravity brakes. He got a definite feeling the devices were only just adequate for the job, and was distinctly glad to hear Gallsworthy's voice when it came.

"Lights are on; you've got takeoff thrust!"

Brim released the brakes. "Full military ahead, both, Nik!" he bellowed over the roar of the generators.

"Full military ahead, both," Ursis answered. The noise intensified and *Truculent* began to creep forward.

Brim managed a last glance aft through the rain. The huge rolling waves were now flattened in a wide, flowing trough that extended out from their stem to a great cloud building skyward at the very limits of his vision. Then the ship was suddenly racing over the water, and no time remained for thoughts, only reflexes and habits. Stabilizers and lift modifiers, helm and thrust controllers. And even his long afternoon simulating on the bridge was poor preparation for the destroyer's astonishing acceleration. "Great—thraggling—Universe!" he gasped.

"Moves right out, doesn't she?" Ursis commented through a grinning mouthful of teeth.

Awed, Brim watched the surface rush by for only clicks before Gallsworthy's voice beside him announced, "ALPHA velocity." Then he carefully rotated the destroyer's nose upward a specified increment for lift-off. *Truculent* was smooth and responsive on the controls, almost skittish. She was his first real thoroughbred, a hundred light-years beyond even the best of the training ships he had flown.

"BETA velocity," Gallsworthy announced a few moments later, then, "Positive climb." Within clicks, *Truculent* was thundering through Haefdon's heavy cloud cover, bumping heavily in the everlasting turbulence.

"Haul 'em both back to full speed ahead, Nik," Brim ordered.

"Full speed ahead, both," the Bear verified. Generator noise in the bridge subsided considerably.

"DD T.83: contact departure one two zero point six," the Harbor Master called. "Good hunting, *Truculents!*" The transmission faded quickly as they broke out in smooth air above the overcast: Dirty gray billows that extended forever and forever in Gimmas' weak sunlight.

"Departure Control to DD T.83," said a woman's face in the display. "You are cleared Hypo-light to the Lox'Sands-98 buoy, zone orange— with immediate transition to Hyper-Drive on arrival. Good-bye from Gimmas-Haefdon starbase. And good luck, *Truculent.*"

"T.83 to Departure Control," Brim seconded, "proceeding Lox'Sands-98 buoy, zone orange with immediate HyperLight transition on arrival. Thanks, Gimmas-Haefdon. See you next time." Before he finished speaking, *Truculent* swept through the planet's atmosphere and was streaking along in darkness on the edge of outer space. He busied himself with additional checkout routines and monitored the ship's systems for the next few cycles, keeping a wary eye on his LightSpeed indicator as the ship accelerated. "Let's cut in the Drive, Nik," he said presently. "Lieutenant Gallsworthy, will you call out the readings?"

Ursis winked and kissed his fingertips. "Drive shutters open. Activating Drive crystals," he echoed. "Firing number one." A single shaft of green light extended far out into the blackness aft. Instantly, Hyperscreens dimmed to protect the bridge occupants while a deep, businesslike grumble joined the roar of the gravity generators.

"Point seven five LightSpeed. Point eight," Gallsworthy called out.

"Readouts normal," the Chairman reported.

Ursis nodded, cross-checking his own instruments. Apparently satisfied, he went on to the next: "Firing two. Firing three."

"Point eight five LightSpeed," Gallsworthy continued. "Point nine."

"Firing four."

Truculent's light-limited gravity generators were now just about played out. In the forward Hyperscreens, the first glowing sheets of Gandom's V_e effect were already crackling along the starship's deck when Brim turned his attention outside.

"Point nine seven LightSpeed."

Presently, the visible Universe became laced by a fine network of pulsing brilliance spreading jaggedly from the last visible stars as if the whole firmament were about to shatter into the very pebbles of creation. Now all he had to do was pass the Lox'Sands-98 buoy. The ship would have to tell him when; until the Drive could be deployed, *Truculent's* bridge crew was virtually blind to the outside Universe.

Suddenly: "Lox'Sands-98 buoy in the wake, Lieutenant Brim," the Chairman confirmed. Brim smiled with anticipation. "That's it, Nik," he said. "Half ahead, all crystals."

"Half ahead, all crystals," Ursis echoed. Quiet thunder from *Truculent's* four Drive crystals joined the roar of her straining gravity generators, the starscape wobbled and shimmered, then blended to an angry red kaleidoscope ahead until space itself came to an end in a wilderness of shifting, multicolored sparks. When this phenomenon (the Daya-Peraf transition) at last subsided, the LightSpeed indicator had moved through 1.0 and began to climb rapidly again as *Truculent's* Drive crystals took over the job of hurtling her through HyperSpace.

"Finished with gravity generators," Brim announced.

"Gravity generators spooling down," Ursis confirmed.

Immediately, the Hyperscreen panels darkened while their crystalline lattices were synchronized with the Drive, then they cleared once more, blazing with the full majesty of the Universe. On this side of the LightSpeed barrier, however, flowing green Drive plumes trailed the ship for at least two c'lenyts, surrounded by a whirling green wake as *Truculent's* HyperSpace shock wave bled off mass and negative time ("T_{neg}" of historic Travis equations) in accordance with the complex system of Travis Physics. In a few moments, the noise of the generators faded completely. Brim glanced at Collingswood. "Twenty-eight LightSpeed, Commander?" he asked.

"Twenty-eight LightSpeed will suffice," Collingswood replied with a slight grin.

"Mister Chairman, set and hold the ship on twenty-eight LightSpeed," Brim ordered.

"Twenty Eight LightSpeed cruise set," the Chairman confirmed.

Without warning, Gallsworthy caught Brim's eye.

"Yes, Sir?" the surprised Carescrian asked, braced for still another rebuff.

A shadow of humor passed the senior Helmsman's reddened eyes, before they clouded again. "You may have proved a point or two this morning, Brim," he allowed emotionlessly. "I shall take over now and let you watch the scenery."

Jolted, Brim suddenly understood he had just received rare praise from this taciturn officer and groped for something appropriate to say. Then he brought himself up short with the sure realization that words were tools Gallsworthy simply didn't understand. "Thank you, Lieutenant," he said matter-of-factly. "I should be glad for a moment to relax."

When control was subsequently restored to the left-hand console, Brim settled back in his recliner and closed his eyes for a moment, smiling inwardly. It was a morning of two victories so far as he was concerned, though few of the Imperials on *Truculent's* bridge could have logically explained why. As thralls to Avalon's Galactic Empire, Carescrians were rarely praised for anything they accomplished. Most became highly adept at ferreting out life's little triumphs wherever and whenever they could be found. And even Gallsworthy's acceptance of his flying skills could in no way match Brim's satisfaction in the sour look still manifested on Amherst's long, homely face.

Truculent was well on her way to war—so was Wilf Brim.

* * *

Blockades in intergalactic space were mounted for pretty much the same reasons they were mounted anywhere else: starve a critical component of a civilization into collapse and other, dependent components suffer with it. Starve sufficient critical components, and the whole civilization suffers. To this end, I.F.S. *Truculent* was assigned patrol duty off the periphery of the League's great Altnag'gin hullmetal fabricating complex orbiting the star Trax. Without imported metallic zar'clinium, a rare trace element, its mills could forge no hull metal plate, and without hullmetal plate, dependent shipyards could turn out no more warships.

The actual implementation was as simple as it was effective: transport starships cruising HyperSpace at roughly ten to thirty light years each metacycle were simply not "maneuverable" in any normal sense of the word. It was first necessary to exit HyperSpace before approaching anywhere near a space anchorage, and this meant HypoLight runs of at least two or three metacycles at the end of each journey. During this interval, "runners" (enemy ships headed in either direction) were quite visible in the normal spectrum—and vulnerable to attack from predators like the Empire's specially equipped T-class destroyers. *Truculent* was one of six patrol craft assigned to sealing Altnag'gin; she relieved a smaller N-class destroyer, which had been constantly on station for three Standard Months.

It came as no particular surprise to Brim when the duty quickly broke down to mostly hard work and boredom; a lot of work in deep space was like that. However, the routine was often enough punctuated by periods of deadly action, and *Truculent* found herself immersed in one of these no more than a few Standard Days after the ship she replaced gleefully turned her bow homeward and surged off into deep space at full thrust.

A chance break in one of the region's interminable gravity storms some thousand or so c'lenyts off the Nebulous Triad (a key departure point from one of the Cloud League's most important manufacturing centers) had just revealed two fast transports racing in from deep space.

Besides metallic zar'clinium, blockade runners in this part of the League nearly always carried other basic commodities to fuel the maw of Nergol Triannic's war machine: food ripped from starving farmers of Korvost, freshly mined crystal seedlings, and always quantities of the potent narcotic TimeWeed from the Spevil virus beds—frequent drafts of the latter were necessary for addicted members of the dreaded Controller class and their rulers, expatriates from Triannic's royal court in far-off Tarrott city.

Only cycles out of HyperSpace, the enemy ships had run out of luck.

Gallsworthy and Pym worked briskly at *Truculent's* Helmsmen's consoles, Collingswood on her feet behind them, one hand on each recliner, staring through the Hyperscreens. An off-duty Brim sat as observer in a jump seat, concentrating on the proceedings as if his life depended on learning each movement at either console—someday, he knew it would.

No escort craft accompanied these two high-speed beauties; Leaguer Admiral Kabul Anak had recently siphoned nearly all protection from the area to support a large combined attack on nearby targets in the Empire. And the gravity storm that only cycles in the past covered their dash for safety also served to conceal *Truculent*. But the latter's military scanning devices picked up the two traders long before her own image activated their civilian proximity alarms. Now the deadly warship was positioned so as to deny any possibility of escape to HyperSpace and was surging along in their wakes like the legendary wraith of Zoltnark, Dark Lord of the Universe.

"We shall have a warning salvo, if you please, Anastasia," Collingswood ordered quietly. "They are surely aware of our presence by now."

"And probably yelling for help on every channel they scan," Amherst grumbled nervously. Brim's glance strayed to the Communications consoles where two ratings quietly nodded to each other. No time to waste today. The broadcast alarms would soon attract every enemy warship remaining in the area.

Outside, he watched *Truculent's* three upper-deck turrets index slightly to port, then return to starboard, finally coming to a stop with their long, slim 144s pointing dead ahead: toward the distant targets. His mind's eye visualized four identical turrets that had just danced the same little gigue out of sight on the starship's dorsal planes.

"Stand by for a close pattern about half a c'lenyt off their bows," Fourier ordered.

Brim watched fascinated while firing crews hunched over their Director consoles, faces lit from beneath by the ever-changing colors of information pouring into their globes.

"Range six thousand and closing. Fifty-nine hundred...fifty-eight hundred..."

"Connect the mains, all disruptors."

"Connected."

"Deflection seventy-six left. Rate eighty-one plus."

"Range fifty-five hundred and closing. Sharply now..."

"Steady."

"Fire!" At Fourier's word, all seven disruptors went off in a salvo of blinding light and raw energy—*Truculent's* deck bucked violently; clouds of angry radiation cascaded into the wake. In spite of himself, Brim thrilled to the rolling, earsplitting thunder rumbling through the spaceframe. Instantly, a whole volume of space ahead of the League ships convulsed with brilliant flashes of yellow fire.

"Eyes of Vothoor!" Theada quipped in an undertone, "That ought to slow them down some."

"Don't count on it," Collingswood warned, eyes riveted on her fleeing quarry. "They'll not give up so easily as that. Triannic's forces everywhere are clamoring for supplies—he makes it well worthwhile for the ones who do get through." Indeed, nearly a full cycle later, the two ships were still speeding toward their destinations.

She frowned, nodded her head. "Reason with them again, Anastasia," she ordered. "Closer, this time."

"Aye, aye, Captain," Fourier answered. "A bit closer, if you please, at the Directors."

"Aye, Lieutenant. Down five hundred. Deflection fifteen minus. Rate sixty-four plus."

Brim's untrained eye could detect little movement of the disruptors as they were relaid, but he knew the next shots would be a great deal closer, if recent target exercises were any indication at all.

"Fire!"

This time, the darkness ahead was shattered by one huge upheaval, which appeared as if it must have taken place only irals from the targets themselves. And though it did produce immediate results, they were not quite the ones expected on *Truculent's* bridge. "Voot's gray ghost," Collingswood grumped under her breath. "Wouldn't you know!" Only one of the ships had slowed down to surrender—the other was still speeding toward Altnag'gin, leaving its partner as sacrifice. A rare show of teamwork for the independent Cloud League's blockade runners.

"Must be something xaxtdamned important in that second one," Gallsworthy observed angrily. "Those zukeeds rarely help one another."

"That's the truth," Anastasia agreed. "We'd better catch it, all right."

"I want them both," Collingswood said, tossing her head. "Those ships are valuable prizes, and I do not intend either will escape." She turned abruptly, peering into the darkened bridge. "Lieutenant Amherst!" she called.

"Captain?"

"Lieutenant, round up those hands we designated Boarding Party Alpha," she said in an excited voice. "Ten with side arms and blast pikes. Have them ready no later than ten cycles from now: Before we catch up to the first ship," she ordered. "Because you are going to take it home as a prize while we continue 'discussions' with its friend."

"Me? Home?"

"Yes, Puvis—home," she said, gaze sweeping across the bridge— where it came to rest on the off-duty Brim in his jump seat. "And by Slua's third eye!" she continued, "you are going to do it with our Carescrian prodigy as your pilot. How do you feel about boarding that transport, too, Lieutenant Brim?"

Grinning like an addled tree h'oggoth, Brim clambered out of his recliner and hurried along the aisle to Amherst's console. "I'm on my way to the transfer tube, Captain."

"Pity," Collingswood laughed. "You may well miss all the action there, for I do not plan to board her by conventional means—that would absolutely insure the second ship's escape."

Brim watched Amherst match his own frown. "Captain?" the latter asked.

"I shall only slow when I pass that first ship," she said, eyes narrowed in excitement. "Something neither of those rather clever blockade runners expects." She pointed a finger at Brim's chest, "Instead, Lieutenant Brim, you will fly the boarding party—in one of our launches—alongside the enemy bridge. Where you, Lieutenant Amherst," she continued, "will have the job of boarding her through any kind of a hatch you find there; they've all got something. Then take immediate possession of the controls. Ten men should be more than sufficient. If you work quickly, it will all be done while she's still in the range of our 144s—they should guarantee active cooperation from your hosts. After that, Lieutenant Brim, it will be your job again to take her into any Imperial port you can reach. Don't worry about the launch. We'll pick it up if we get the chance, otherwise she's a small price to pay for either of those beauties. I shall expect you back aboard *Truculent* soon as you can hitch a ride. Now get moving— both of you!"

Moments later, Brim and Amherst were bustling down a ladder

toward the ship's small armory as Maldive's voice broke into the interCOMM, "Boarding Party Alpha: Form in battle suits immediately at Launch Hatch Three. Boarding Party Alpha to Launch Hatch Three—immediately!"

Well within the ten cycles allotted by Collingswood, Brim sat perspiring at the command console of *Truculent's* number-three launch, a stubby, powerful affair Sophia Pym swore was designed first for ugliness, and only then for performance. Behind him, similarly peering from the armored blue globes of Imperial battle-suit helmets, Amherst and nine men—led by the hulking Barbousse—clambered through the hatch to perch on jump seats in the crowded utility compartment, jostling to position their long blast pikes under the low canopy. Last aboard was Ursis, waving a huge side-action blaster of Sodeskayan manufacture.

"Hatch is closed and dogged, Wilf," the Bear reported, thumping into place beside Amherst. "Terribly sorry, Lieutenant," he grunted, as he wedged the First Lieutenant against a rack of stringers. "Collingswood sent me to keep an eye on Brim here," he continued as Amherst dissolved in a fit of coughing.

Brim stifled a delighted grin, nodded assent, and confirmed the hatch seal on an instrument panel before him. Then he started the powerful little antigravity generator aft and immediately spooled it up to maximum output; he hated that kind of heavy-handed Helmsmanship, but had little choice under the present circumstances. When the registered output steadied, he nodded to the image of Theada in an overhead display. "Swing us out, Jubal," he barked through the suit's interCOMM. Moments later, two heavy davits sparkled with emerald light as mooring beams flashed to the launch's optical capstans. Less than a cycle later, the beams thickened, then the davits began to move: first upward, then sideways, hauling the launch from behind the protection of *Truculent's* bridge wings. It provided Brim's first unobstructed view forward since he left the bridge: the first enemy ship—a typical Cloud League transport made up of globes and cylinders co-located along a single tube—was now pothering along less than a quarter c'lenyt ahead and being overhauled rapidly.

"Stand by to cast off the launch," he yelled over the roar of the generator.

"Standing by," Theada asserted shakily.

Brim carefully judged his distance and rate of closure; launches were not capable of sustained high-speed travel, even at military overload. Aft, the straining antigravity generator already threatened to rip itself from its mountings. He tensed. "Now, Jubal!" he yelled.

Theada made no clean job of it. The forward beam winked out a fraction of a second before the aft, and very nearly dragged their launch end around end before Brim fought her back on course, heart pounding against his chest. Then, miraculously, he was bucketing along beside the enemy transport's globular forward module with an already distant *Truculent* pulling away all too rapidly for comfort—her big 144s provided a distinct feeling of security in the thin-skinned launch.

"There's the emergency hatch, Lieutenant," Barbousse exclaimed, pointing a fingered glove toward a faint outline just aft the port arm of the ship's cross-shaped Hyperscreens.

"He's got it," Ursis seconded. "Bring us alongside, Wilf. We'll blast it in if they won't open on their own. They xaxtdamned well know why we're here."

Brim maneuvered the launch until his main hatch was opposite the enemy's bridge, then watched Barbousse yank it open and aim his blast pike, finger twitching on the valve. He could see the enemy flight crew peering back at him—helplessly, he hoped.

"Give them a moment, Barbousse!" he yelled.

"Aye, Lieutenant," Barbousse assured him. "I'll wait." But in point of fact, the blockade runners did not need even a moment; their escape hatch flew off into the wake before Barbousse's voice faded from the bubble of Brim's helmet. The opening was immediately filled by one of the Cloud League's jet-black battle suits, arms crossed against the chest in the Universal gesture of surrender.

"Snag 'em, Barbousse," he yelled as he jerked the launch sideways, smashing the two hatches together in a cloud of sparks. Deftly for his awesome size, Barbousse lofted two explosive grappling hooks accurately through either side of the opening, then dragged them taut when they fired, securing each to baggage tie-downs on the launch's floor.

After that, nothing happened. Puzzled, Brim shut down the straining generators, his attention glued to Number One, waiting for further commands.

"Well, come on, Amherst," Ursis growled in the resulting silence. "You are waiting perhaps for personal invitation from Admiral Anak?"

"Oh. Er…yes. I mean no, of course not! Ah…this way, men," Amherst stuttered, pushing Barbousse through the opening first. Ursis clambered through on his heels, followed by Brim and the nine ratings of the boarding party.

Inside, a small group of civilian spacers huddled glumly on one side of the bridge, nervous eyes darting in every direction. One, a woman, was tall with a figure even a space suit couldn't hide; she also had a nose only a mother could love. Beside her a fat old man stood with his paunch straining the power belt around his waist. Another had no hair on his head. And still another wore a crumpled little peaked cap inside his bubble helmet and sported a huge black mustache drooping from his upper lip. Brim stopped in his tracks. So these were the enemy he so often read about. The Cloud League's storied blockade runners. He snorted in irony. These? They looked like nothing more—or less— than any workaday spacer he'd known from the ore carriers; ordinary, everyday faces. In an Avalonian byway, he would not have noticed any one of them. And to a man, they were frightened, no doubt about that!

In the center of the bridge, however, three very different human forms stood before the controls, these dressed in the black battle suits of Controllers. For no apparent reason, they instantly returned Brim to the dark mood of war. Black-uniformed Controllers were a separate, elite branch of the normally gray-uniformed League armed forces. In the eyes of most Imperials, they were the true Cloud League villains: Killers of little Carescrian girls and destroyers of undefended villages. He could almost see bloodstains on their spotless gloves as they waited with looks of insolence on their faces.

"Ah," Amherst started lamely, "wh-what ship is this?"

"And who asks?" one of the black-suited Leaguers demanded haughtily.

"It is not your time for questions, Black Suit," Ursis growled as he ever so slightly moved the big side-action blaster in his hand. There was nothing subtle at all about the gesture—either meant by the Bear or interpreted by the Controllers.

"S-Starship S.M.S. *Ruggetos*," one said quickly.

"Good," Ursis rumbled, taking control of the situation. "You now understand our relationship. For your own good, I urge all to remember well." He licked his chops with a long red tongue. "Has been almost a year since I visited Mother Planets for chasing live red meat."

Sweat broke out on the brows of all three Controllers. Rumors had long circulated about Sodeskayan Bears and their annual home leave for "The Hunt." It seemed only natural; certain places in the galaxy permitted non-sentient bear hunts, too.

"Take these men and lock them somewhere, Barbousse," Amherst ordered imperiously, recovering some of his confidence. "And see those Controllers are kept off to themselves," he added. "I don't want them mixing with the rest."

"Aye, Sir," Barbousse, said, nudging the three black-suited Controllers into the companionway with the tip of his oversized space boot. "They won't stir no one up when I'm done with them." Cycles later, he reappeared to herd the civilians from the bridge in a different direction. Brim filed all this away for future reference. Today, the huge Starman was not at all the bumbling dunce who appeared on *Truculent's* gangway the morning of his arrival.

Then there was no more time for random thoughts as he took his place at the master control console in the center of the ship's peculiar cross-shaped Hyperscreen arrays. He heard Ursis thump down behind him in what appeared to be a propulsion console. The simplified layout on *Ruggetos'* tiny bridge was surprisingly easy to comprehend, yet as distant from Imperial design philosophy as the Cloud League's spoken Vertrucht was from Avalonian. "We'd better get some speed on this bucket of bolts, Nik," he called back as he studied the readouts before him. "Our COMM people picked up the messages these birds broadcast. We'll likely have visitors around these parts before we know it, and the first of them probably won't be *Truculent*."

Always different in minor respects, flight controls on one starship usually turned out to be fairly similar to those on any other-anywhere in the Universe. These were no exception. Brim soon mastered all three panels and prudently set a course for deep space, waiting for the sound of the crystals when Ursis fired them up. But—at least by the chronometer on his console—five cycles later, nothing more happened. In the corner of his eye, he detected a concerned look on Amherst's face and continued to study his own readouts, hoping to avoid drawing further attention to the clearly troubled engineer at the console behind him. The ploy was totally without success.

"What seems to be the trouble, Ursis?" Brim heard the First Lieutenant ask nervously.

"Cannot change the Drive's power settings," Ursis growled absently. "Something has been altered here." His voice trailed away as he continued to concentrate.

Amherst fairly ran across the bridge to the console. "Something has been altered?" he asked, his voice suddenly tinged with fear.

Brim turned in his seat as Ursis looked up at the First Lieutenant, blinked his eyes, then shook his head as if what he had to say pained him. "Yes, Number One," he said, frowning, "something has been tampered with that I do not yet understand. But if you do not interfere for a few cycles, I shall master it. Now..."

"Don't touch that console, you damned Sodeskayan fool!" Amherst squeaked in a high-pitched voice. "They may have rigged it to blow us up!" Sweat suddenly stood out on his forehead.

"With them still aboard?" Ursis demanded indignantly as he continued to manipulate the controls. "Ridiculous."

"Get your hands away from those, Ursis!" Amherst hissed nervously. "That is an order. Understand?"

"Would you rather wait until one of their patrols intercepts us, Lieutenant?" Ursis asked, frowning.

"I don't want to die, Ursis," Amherst spat. "Stay away from those controls before you blow us all over the Universe!"

"Wha-a-a-t?"

"You have no idea what they might have patched in there, Sodeskayan. By Slua's third eye, you toy with our lives. There's high power at the end of those controls."

"I know from power for xaxt sake," Ursis rumbled, head cocked to one side in anger.

"You know about power systems that have not been turned into death traps, Bear," Amherst argued hotly.

"True, but I do not think such is the case here. Can you seriously believe they'd blow themselves up with us?"

"I shall believe anything I wish. And get your paws off those controls—that is a direct order! Do you understand?"

Ursis thumped angrily back in the recliner, a grim look on his face.

Unable to contain himself further, Brim jumped into the fray. "If we don't start moving a whole lot faster than this, we are very liable to end up looking down the barrel of a disruptor, and it won't be ours, Lieutenant Amherst," he protested. "Both these ships broadcast calls for help."

"Would you rather risk being blown to subatomics, Carescrian?" Amherst snapped angrily.

"I don't see what Nik's doing as any sort of risk," Brim argued, temper only barely under control. "What I do see as a risk is sitting around here at less than LightSpeed. Anybody can catch us the way we are now, and unless I badly miss my guess, we shall soon be joined by a lot of 'anybodys'."

"Well!" Amherst fumed. "I suppose I have no reason to be surprised. You Carescrians would be expected to side with the Bears, now that I think of it. Subhumans..."

Brim shook his head, ashamed to meet Ursis' eyes. "Perhaps you'd rather deal with our black-suited friends from the Cloud League," he said hotly. "Shall I send Barbousse to fetch them? Maybe you can persuade them to explain what they've done."

Amherst tensed. "We...we all know how much good that would do," he said, a shadow of fear passing into his eyes. "And besides, I prefer to keep them where they are."

Brim set his jaw and glowered at the starship's useless controls. He was still fighting his temper when the ship's proximity alarm started clanging overhead. He swiveled in his recliner, activating the aft Hyperscreens before he stopped.

"What is that?" Amherst asked, face ashen. "Are we going to blow up after all?"

"No," Brim assured him grimly. "And you are now quite safe from foreign hands tampering with the ship's Drive mechanism."

"Well, that's better," Amherst said, taking a long breath of relief. "But what was that ringing?"

"The proximity alarm, Lieutenant," Brim said, adjusting the focus of the aft Hyperscreens and shaking his head. "Help has just arrived."

"Oh," the First Lieutenant said, "then *Truculent's* back?"

"No," Brim said, "but there is another starship outside. I can't make out the name. She's a Cloud League corvette—Number HS-91. And both her long 99s are pointed right here at the bridge."

3

Arms embracing his knees, Brim sat with his back against a chilly metal bulkhead, gritting his teeth in frustrated anger. Twelve more would-be raiders from *Truculent* idled about in the gloomy compartment, faces set in like attitudes of disgust, helmets confiscated from their battle suits. Outside, in the merchantman's central K tube, he could hear disjointed bursts of guttural Vertrucht—and a lot of laughter. He understood most of what he heard: before the war, all ore-carrier Helmsmen had to learn Emperor Triannic's official language. League buyers were some of the Empire's best customers in those days. He snorted; the lot aboard this ship didn't know that about him. And he wasn't about to volunteer the information, either, though so far his little secret had netted him no particular advantage. Except the knowledge that all thirteen Imperials were up for immediate transfer to the waiting corvette.

He listened to the uneven thrumming of the merchantman's unsynchronized gravity generators. Every so often, they rattled a bolt somewhere on the bulkhead at his back, but he couldn't locate it in the dim light. Turning his head, he glared at Amherst's rigid figure still nearly frozen by fear as he stood bolt upright, staring at the door. Nearby, Ursis and Barbousse each occupied a corner, asleep and snoring profoundly. Brim chuckled in spite of his wrath—nobody in a right mind would disturb those two.

He shook his head in resignation: if nothing else, he'd learned a good lesson (though a fat lot of good it would do him grinding his strength away in some Cloud League slave brigade). But if he did taste freedom again someday, Wilf Brim swore he would never again acquiesce to anyone's reasoning flawed by fear. He shook his head in disgust. Had he taken steps to silence the frightened First Lieutenant (or had Ursis disregarded the man's orders and continued to work on the sabotaged Drive controls), they might now be boring their way through HyperSpace toward home and safety. Instead, *Ruggetos* and her vital cargo would soon resume their interrupted journey into a safe Leaguer harbor.

The Carescrian shrugged angrily. It was far too late now for thoughts of that sort. He purged them from his mind—self-recrimination was patently useless anyway, especially once basic mistakes were aired and thoroughly understood. He forced himself to random thoughts, conjured loose golden curls and frowning smiles; red, moist lips; Lacerta's "Rime of the Ancients..." He heard the husky voice in his mind's ear as if it were yesterday: "Roll on, thou deep and star-swept cosmos." Margot Effer'wyck, her large hand warm and soft in his for a too-short instant of total enchantment. Sturdy legs and tiny feet. Suddenly, another line of poetry crossed his mind; written especially for her, it seemed, though Lacerta penned the words more than a thousand years before those blue eyes first saw the light of day. "She walks in beauty, like the stars/Of cloudless climes and worlds afar." He shook his head. Strange how meeting her affected him. Just that once, and her face was never again far below the surface of his mind. "She walks in beauty..."

He chuckled to himself. Always an eye for the best! But this time those tastes had surely betrayed him. Incredible now he hadn't tumbled to the name when he first met her. Pym had to explain the whole thing days after they'd met: Effer'wyck! The beautiful blond Lieutenant was not only grandchild to Sabar Effer'wyck (ascetic mogul of the powerful star nation), she was also a full-blooded princess and kin to the late Emperor Erioed III himself.

He snorted in embarrassment. A Carescrian talking face to face with an Effer'wyck. Even taking her hand. He pictured her and the elegant Baron LaKarn together in some ornate setting, sharing a laugh about his pitiful love of poetry. His cheeks burned with shame. Given his background of poverty, he'd need to become another Admiral Merlin Emrys—save a whole star system, perhaps—before she'd notice any interest he might have in her.

He shrugged. It was all over now anyway. Not much chance to accomplish anything heroic where he was going, or contribute anything to anybody, except perhaps to League Admiral Kabul Anak's war effort. Well, he considered, if nothing else, he had his anonymity. She couldn't laugh at someone she didn't remember. And Wilf Brim was about to disappear completely, another small statistic in a very large war.

The hatch abruptly clanged open, nearly blinding him with light. Shouted commands propelled him to his feet, and a sharp blow to his head brought sudden pinpoints of light to his eyes as he started through the hatch and down the companionway. In a black mood, he stumbled off toward incarceration aboard the enemy corvette.

Shambling helmetless through the transparent transfer tube, he glanced toward *Truculent's* ugly little launch hanging forlornly at the merchantman's bridge, silhouetted against the blazing stars of outer space. How differently things had begun only a few short metacycles ago! Ahead, the glasslike tube ended at a circular hatch opened in the corvette's second module, a fat cylinder mounted astride the ship's central K tube: Crew quarters, he guessed. Next aft, the spherical battery module carried both 99-mmi turrets mounted at opposite poles. After this...He craned his neck, but he was already too close alongside now to see. If he remembered correctly, though, most Cloud-League ships started with a spherical bridge module forward, then alternated cylinders and globes along the central K tube. This ship, then, would continue with a second cylinder, then a globe, and presumably end with a final cylinder containing the Drive and antigravity machinery. He wished he'd paid more attention when he had seen the whole ship in the merchantman's bridge display.

Then he was inside the hatch, where a sharp kick by a hulking, lantern-jawed Controller rating sent him reeling along a companionway into the K tube itself. There, a second black-suited rating with scowling mien and great bushy eyebrows waved him aft with an ugly-looking blast pistol. A few steps farther on, a Controller officer stopped him in his tracks—an Overmann (the League equivalent of an Imperial lieutenant). Her face was horribly disfigured by a purple scar that ran diagonally across her mouth from her nose to her chin.

"You will halt!" she commanded, large almond-shaped eyes blazing with hate. Somehow Brim couldn't bring himself to blame her; no question she'd received her wound at the hands of someone dressed in the same kind of battle suit as his. He stopped and prudently froze, listening behind him to other voices, thumping, stomping, and occasional grunts of pain, as his comrades from *Truculent* were herded into the corridor. The black-suited lantern jaw at the hatch evidently enjoyed kicking. His own shin throbbed, but he dared not move to rub it.

At some length, the woman banged on a hatch beside her. "All right, Overmann," she said gruffly, "here's the lot. They're yours."

The hatch opened and a serious-looking, bespectacled officer in the stiff-necked gray tank suit of the Cloud League's "normal" military starfleet stepped through. Thin and ascetic-looking, his face had more the intense seriousness of a lifelong student than the careful awareness Brim associated with military professionals. A person more likely to be addressed by "Professor" than "Overmann." The antique timepiece on his wrist sparkled in the overhead lights. He was followed by two elderly gray-suited ratings, one fat with squinting eyes and flushed face, the other with the looks of a farmer, spare and muscular, whose callused hands had not yet lost the hardness required of those who tend the soil. Each carried a wicked-looking blast pike of League manufacture. "Ah, yes, ma'am," the gray Overmann said in a cheerful voice to his disfigured Controller counterpart. "Just leave the whole thing to us. We'll take good care of them for you." He smiled hopefully.

The black-uniformed Overmann only raised her eyebrows. "How good of you," she sneered, then turned on her heel and walked away as if the studious-looking starfleet officer simply didn't exist. It was graphic proof to Brim that even though rank names might be the same in both Starfleet and Controller organizations, actual power was lopsidedly vested with the latter.

The man shrugged, embarrassed, then watched his counterpart disappear along the K tube in the opposite direction Brim had come. "Controllers," he said, shaking his head. After a moment, he turned to the slim rating beside him. "Locar," he ordered, "you and Koch'kiss follow while I lead 'em to the interrogation chamber." Then he stopped and frowned. "Ah...how many of 'em are there anyway?" he asked.

"I don't know, Overmann," Locar said. "She didn't say."

The officer raised an eyebrow. "I suppose we'd better know that," he said, standing on tiptoe. "Let's see..."

Brim suddenly jumped as he heard his name growled in a whisper from directly behind his back. "Make a break for it, Wilf Ansor," Ursis' voice urged in a fierce whisper. "Now, before they can make that count!" Immediately, he roared at the top of his voice in feigned, deafening, agony. Brim whirled just in time to see the Bear sink to the deck, writhing in the grip of what could only be a seizure of the deadliest kind. Stunned by the sudden outcry, the two gray-suited ratings jerked around in dumb surprise, only to be knocked into a welter of flying arms and legs by a suddenly howling and wide-eyed Barbousse. In the burgeoning confusion, Brim dropped to his knees and scuttled toward a nearby hatch, praying to every power in the Universe it was not secured. With a paroxysm of tension, he grabbed the latch. It moved! In one motion, he smashed the hatch open with his shoulder, blindly threw himself through, and slammed it closed behind him, gagging on the sudden sick-sweet foulness of TimeWeed, the mysterious, poisonous narcotic many Controllers were known to smoke (indeed, some were rumored to eat it!). Before him, dressed only in ceremonial loincloth, the room's occupant bounded up from his bunk, slowed by the drug but surprisingly agile for all that—and clearly alerted by the commotion outside his room. Roaring in anger, the Leaguer grabbed a blast pike from a nearby rack and swung the heavy weapon toward Brim's stomach. Desperately, the Carescrian grabbed its barrel and fiercely wrenched it off to one side, jerking awkwardly. The dazed Controller howled in surprise, overbalanced, and began to tumble forward, a look of bestial rage on his face. He recovered and ripped the weapon from Brim's hands, swinging its clumsy barrel like a club. Spontaneously, Brim stepped in close, the man's breath stale in his face, grabbed his slippery armpits, and drove a knee into the loincloth with all the strength he could muster.

Eyes wide as saucers, the Controller bellowed in hoarse agony.

Retching on Brim's battle suit, he dropped the pike and grabbed convulsively for his smashed testicles. Instinctively, Brim reverted to Academy training: He cocked his fist at a right angle, then smashed the heel of his hand upward into the base of the other's nose. With a brackling crunch, snapped bone and cartilage punctured the frontal lobes of the man's brain like tiny stilettos.

The Controller's eyes—still open in mortal agony—glazed and rolled upward as he sank to his knees, blood guttering from his nostrils, then he toppled face first to the deck.

Panting desperately, Brim sank to his own wobbly knees, hands trembling convulsively. Air! Light-headed, he shook his head wildly— the TimeWeed! It was still burning somewhere, filling the room with deadly narcotic fumes. The whole Universe seemed to have slowed around him. He felt light-headed and introspective. His mind was expanding, growing more and more perspicacious, more conceptualizing...He was losing control!

Using his last vestiges of strength, he willed himself to the bunk. There! The man's pipe of TimeWeed lay in a bulkhead alcove, thick smoke writhing heavily from its bowl. He lifted it in weak hands, then somehow found himself at the metal washstand. He mashed open the water valve, shoved the pipe into the trickling stream. The fragile bowl hissed, shattered with a snap, but the smoke stopped. Senses reeling, Brim next pulled himself up to the basin, reached above the top of the wash fixture itself, and dialed the atmosphere controls to ALL FILTERED. A sudden hissing filled the room as he slithered again to his knees, gasping desperately. Why? How could anyone do such things to himself? He felt himself falling, hit his chin on the basin, almost blacked out from the pain. Then a rush of cool air hit his lungs like a runaway starship, and his head began to clear. Some cycles later—he never remembered how many—he was on the deck, grinning stupidly, huffing like some sort of animal. He'd made it!

Suddenly, a persistent buzzing overhead brought him jumping again to his feet. What now? His watering eyes searched the room. An alarm? Finally, there, over the door, an old-fashioned summons hooter, like the ones on ore carriers. Heart beating with fresh apprehension, he stepped over the sprawling corpse, reached above the door, and flipped the device from MONITOR to RECEIVE. Then he waited in sudden and terrifying silence. Whatever new fate awaited his twelve comrades outside in the K tube, it was evidently now decided.

In due time, the hooter answered his summons with the tinny imitation of a woman's voice: "*Officient* Zotreb?"

Brim eyed the body at his feet. So that was the name of the man he killed. He shuddered. "Yes?" he responded in Vertrucht, muffling his voice through a fist.

"*Officient?*"

"Yes."

"You do not sound yourself, *Officient* Zotreb."

Heart in his mouth for the hundredth time since he left *Truculent*, Brim searched the bare walls for an answer—deciding attack was his best defense. "And just what is it you expect?" he snapped angrily, still muffling his voice.

"N-Nothing, *Officient*," the voice responded placatingly.

"You will concentrate on your own concerns in the future," Brim growled. "Now, what message disturbs my contemplation of the Weed?" he demanded.

"S-Sorry, *Officient*," the voice said. "The call was placed at your personal request."

"Well, get on with it, damn your worthless hide!"

"Y-Yes Sir. You are due on the bridge in twenty cycles, *Officient*."

"And that is all?"

"Yes, *Officient*."

"Acknowledged," Brim spat, then turned the device back to MONITOR. He frowned, concentrating. Twenty cycles of relative safety before they started looking for Zotreb. After that, it was just a matter of time until...He snorted. He couldn't very well just sit in the cabin. Ursis hadn't set up his escape so he could run away to hide. And now that he found himself with a few options again, it was necessary he make the most of his time and do something about the disaster their mission had become. Soon! Every cycle brought the little crew closer to an enemy spaceport and slavery or death—eventually the latter, in any case.

Brim suddenly grimaced. Of course. That was the answer. Whatever else he might accomplish, it was necessary first to stop the corvette. That meant getting himself to the engineer's flat in the aftmost module and somehow disabling the starship's single gravity generator. Its uneven rumble irritated him almost as much as the Controllers. But how could he get all the way back there? His answer came from the corpse.

The late *Officient* Zotreb had no further use for his uniforms now, but Wilf Brim did. In less than five cycles, the Carescrian was dressed in one of the dead man's hated black uniforms, too big overall, but a lot less noticeable than his own bright blue Imperial battle suit. He consulted his timepiece. About fifteen cycles remained, perhaps forty until they started looking and found the body. After that, Universe knew. But one step at a time.

Wiping clotted blood from Zotreb's big blast pike, he carefully opened the door, peered both ways along the empty K tube, then started aft toward the propulsion module at what he hoped was a casual rate of speed.

Footsteps echoing in the smooth-walled tube, Brim didn't get far at all before his disguise was put to the test. A gray-clad rating, arm around a bundle of logic assemblies, appeared suddenly from a companionway, turned on his heel, and passed at a fast walk. He saluted but never lifted his eyes. Brim breathed a deep sigh of relief as he entered the ship's central module, carefully memorizing everything he saw. One never knew...

Unlike similar modules built around a K tube, this corvette's central globe was part of the tube itself: A place where the long, cannular structure swelled to a spherical chamber before shrinking again at the point opposite his present position. The walkway cantilevered across twenty irals of open space to meet its counterpart on the other side.

Centered in the chamber, a glowing vertical tube divided the catwalk and extended through wide, circular openings at the top and bottom of the room, beyond which would be control rooms located just inboard of the ship's 99—mmi disruptor turrets. Brim easily picked out the firing consoles (triggering gear all looked pretty much the same everywhere) in the harsh light that streamed from the rooms and provided most of the illumination around him. Elsewhere in the chamber, great power conduits sprang from the aft opening to the K tube and disappeared within the brilliance of the rooms. Numerous ledges jutting from the curved inner walls contained consoles—some manned, most not—many of which Brim could not identify. These oddly placed displays cast random, moving patterns of colored lights throughout the strange spherical chamber and everything it contained. Clearly, a great deal of the activity that took place on the bridge of an Imperial warship was decentralized throughout this ship. A nice point of design, he allowed, for a warship. It would make her much harder to knock out with one well-placed hit. But it also denied the close team atmosphere that resulted from concentrating decision-making power. He filed it away in his mind as he strode (more confident looking, he hoped, then he felt) across the catwalk, gripping Zotreb's blast pike and trying to act as if he belonged where he was. If he ever got back to his own side of the war, the information he memorized could prove handy in many ways. He snorted to himself. If he ever got back.

As he moved into the aft continuation of the K tube, more and more gray-clad crew members passed, all avoiding his eyes—most, in fact, cringed while they hurried by as if they were relieved to be out of his way. He smiled to himself: No more relieved than he!

Then, passing an open door in the next-to-last module, he heard voices, glanced inside, and was rewarded with a view of five Controllers seated at a circular table, clearly pursuing serious matters among themselves. Putting his haste aside for the moment, he stepped to a position outside the door where he could hear what was going on but still remain unseen by the conferees. He rested the butt of his blast pike on the deck beside his right boot, then assumed the Universal position of a bored guard. So far as he could remember, he himself seldom questioned armed guards—especially commissioned armed guards—and guessed it was a pretty typical reaction. This was verified only moments later when he was passed by three gray-suited ratings (who saluted) and two Controllers (who did not). Not one of them so much as met his eyes.

"The Bear incident is now under control?" a smooth, perfectly modulated voice demanded in Vertrucht from inside.

"It is, Praefect Valentin," a younger voice declared, fear just below its surface.

Brim felt his eyebrows raise. Praefects were the equivalent of Imperial lieutenant commanders. The corvette was too small for more than one of these, so it was a good bet this Valentin was the ship's commanding officer.

"And the count of prisoners, Placeman Naddock—how many prisoners were there?" Valentin's mellifluous voice demanded.

"Ah," Naddock's younger voice began. "Ah, I..." A chair scraped the deck.

"Well, Placeman?"

"We have all twelve of them locked up, Praefect," a self-assured female voice interrupted impatiently. Brim recognized it as belonging to the scarred Overmann Controller from the K tube. "Gray Overmann Mocht counted the prisoners just after the Bear experienced his fit."

Brim smiled: Twelve, eh? Ursis' distraction had come just in time. They didn't know he was loose—yet.

"You had better hope the Gray fool's count is accurate, my scarred beauty," Valentin said with an audible sneer. "Or I shall make certain you both spend the remainder of the war on the ground—armed only with blast pike and sword. I am certain you will enjoy brawling with the Wild Ones on the Sodeskayan front!"

This was followed by a sharp intake of breath and then silence.

In the hall, Brim returned the melancholic salute of a fat, gray-suited rating with a painful-looking, very swollen, black eye, who limped slowly along the corridor. Souvenir of Ursis' free-for-all in the K tube, he guessed, hard put to stifle a smile.

"Well, what then have you planned for our visitors from the Empire, Placeman Zodekk?" the Praefect's voice demanded from inside. "I haven't all day. We dock in only a few metacycles."

"Oh, we are keeping the prisoners busy, Sir," another female voice answered, this one with just the hint of a lisp. "They are being questioned one-by-one, even as we speak."

"Well, go on, pretty fool. What follows that?"

"Wh-When we finish, we shall s-simply shoot them, I suppose...push them out into space."

"You'll what," the scarred woman's voice interrupted. "Use your head, fool. Sentient laborers are scarce on Altnag'gin. Our captives might well serve there as slaves. All appear to be well fed and could survive a long time on next to nothing; am I not correct, Praefect?"

"Hmm," Valentin's modulated voice intoned. "Indeed a point. Of course, I have heard of your—shall we say—predilection for the slower forms of death, my dear. So I cannot grant full credit for your suggestion." Then he laughed. "But what of the Bear? What should we do with this most troublesome Bear?"

"Ah, the Bear receives special treatment, my Provost," the lisping voice interrupted gleefully. "Bearskin coats and carpets are in much demand among Emperor Triannic's royal court in Tarrott this season. It has been quite cold, as you might have heard."

"The Bear's skin is mine, Placeman," the Praefect's voice said with an ill-concealed irritation.

"Without question, my Praefect," a number of voices chimed in. "Without question."

"That's better," Valentin said. "Now, as to the recent trouble in the vestibule module: The next time we take prisoners, you will be extra vigilant at all times; otherwise..."

Heart pounding, Brim left the doorway and started aft again along the K tube. It was imperative that he prolong the corvette's trip in space—once it reached its destination, they all were good as dead. Especially Ursis.

Free passage along the tube ended abruptly in a solid-looking bulkhead and dogged-down hatch at the entrance to the ship's aftmost module. Illuminated warnings mounted on either side of the hatch read AUTHORIZED PERSONNEL ONLY and SIGN IN/ OUT REQUIRED BY THE PRAEFECT. Below these, a tabulator board hung from a hook, complete with logic scriber, the same kind of portable writing device carried by everyone in the Universe who ever took an inventory or made a survey. It was all Brim needed.

Checking behind himself for activity, he suddenly ripped the tabulator free from its hook—only one person had signed inside. He scrolled the sign-in form from its display, then touched a glowing panel on the hatch before him and waited.

"Yes?" a voice asked from a speaker.

"Radiation-level survey," Brim answered briskly, pointing to the blank tabulator board as if it were his own.

"Name and rank," the voice demanded.

Brim grimaced, heart pounding. "I have already signed that information in the tabulator board you have hanging from your hatch, fool!" he blustered, pointing to the empty hook as if it were visible from the other side of the hatch. "Now you open up before I have you fire-flogged. Do you hear?"

"Aye, Sir. Aye, Sir! I h-hear," the voice stammered as a series of clanks and chatterings announced the opening of the hatch. Brim was almost knocked to the deck as it swung open toward him.

"Th- This way, please, Overmann, Sir," a frightened rating stammered, face white with fear. He was short, wiry, and middle-aged with narrow-set eyes and a sharp-looking chin covered by uneven gray stubble. His hands bore the blue stains of a sometime kupp'gh cleaner.

Brim pushed his way past and into an antechamber, which ended in a second hatch. This one looked even more secure than its outside counterpart. Keeping his nerves under control, he slammed the first hatch shut and whirled on the rating with the best imitation of haughty anger he could summon. "You will also open this immediately," he demanded through tight lips.

"Oh, ah, aye, Overmann," the cowed guard said, taking a key from around his neck and unlocking the inner hatch. "And will you need assistance, Sir?" he asked.

"You dare question my ability?" Brim hissed through his teeth.

The rating shrank back away from the hatch. "S-Sorry, Sir," he whispered. "Don't have me whipped, Overmann. I mean no harm askin' ye."

Brim looked down his nose at the wretched rating, hating himself and what he had to do. He knew what it was like to be on the receiving end. "Perhaps I may overlook the lapse this time," he said. "But I shall brook no interruption of my work. Do you understand? No interruption."

"I understand, Sir," the wan-faced rating said, taking his seat . "No interruptions. I'll make sure."

"See that you do," Brim growled, then stepped into the bright, humming module and closed the door. He had just dogged it down tight from the inside when he heard alarms go off everywhere. He glanced at his watch—time was up by almost ten cycles.

"Warning!" the speakers brayed. "Warning. An Imperial murderer is loose within the ship. He is armed and dangerous. Shoot on sight and shoot to kill. Repeat: shoot on sight and shoot to kill."

Brim shrugged as he threw the tabulator in a corner. It probably wouldn't fool anyone else now.

One eye out for his lone companion in the module, Brim jog-trotted from cabin to compartment, desperately seeking entrance to the generator chamber. No time to waste now. He soon found himself deep within the module, but unable to exit from the deck on which he entered—and from the intensity of sound and vibration corning from below, he knew the mechanism he sought was located somewhere deeper in the hull. Frowning, he had just returned to the K tube from another fruitless search of a parts storeroom when a dazzling explosion seared the wall beside his head and nearly knocked him from his feet. He whirled around, firing the pike by instinct as a second explosion ruptured the space he had occupied only clicks before. The shadow of a black-suited Controller disappeared inside a nearby hatchway only clicks before Brim's bucking weapon blasted the hatch panel from its hinges in a wild tattoo of destruction. He rushed for the blackened, dented opening and flattened himself outside.

Panting, he readied the pike again, then blew out a whole section of overhead lights. This resulted in almost total darkness—except the bright glow streaming from the hatchway into which this new adversary had disappeared. He dropped to a crouch, the pike ready at his hip. Gathering himself, he flexed his shoulders, took a last deep breath, and leaped through the doorway, spraying the room with deadly bursts of energy and radiation. As his feet hit the floor, a figure armed with what must have been a RocketDart pistol ran screaming toward him, launching a flurry of deadly sparkling missiles. Two hit with a searing— unbelievable—agony in his left shoulder. He heard himself scream, sank to his knees, and fired the heavy weapon point-blank into the man's stomach.

With a horrible scream of anguish, the Controller doubled over, sprayed a stinking froth of blood and vomit over Brim's blouse, then collapsed nearby in a heap on the floor, his still-smoking torso blown nearly in half.

Gritting his teeth from the burning pain in his shoulder, Brim felt blood running inside his tunic and realized he had no more than a few cycles to disarm the ship's generator before he lost consciousness. He struggled awkwardly to his feet, stuffed the dart pistol in his belt, and dragged the blast pike by its scorched barrel to a large open hatch set in the deck. Light and noise streaming through from below assured him he had finally reached the generator chamber. And not a moment too soon. Far down the K tube, he could already hear thumps and clangs as the ship's crew—almost certainly alerted by the sight of their dead comrade in the crew section—attempted to force the inner hatch.

Balancing himself precariously on the narrow rungs, he found the howling bass of the machinery nearly as painful to his unprotected ears as the throbbing darts in his charred shoulder. Somehow, he managed to descend with his good hand while he doggedly clutched the heavy pike in his left, but at the bottom he couldn't remember navigating the last two rungs at all.

Mounted overhead directly to the underside of the K tube, the generator itself looked much like the rest of the antigravity generators he had seen. It was big, taking up the major volume of the round-bottomed chamber; the deck on which he presently stood was no more than a small platform mounted over the stout longerons and curved hullmetal plates that formed the underside of the module itself. Brim estimated the machinery stretched nearly twenty irals in length from its forward cooling vanes to the gleaming, pressure-regulating sphere, where it connected to the ship's primary power supply by means of two finned wave guides arching down from the flat ceiling, then up and around to a radiation-blackened collar.

Thrusting aside the torment in his shoulder, Brim considered his options. There were only two. He could blast the regulator globe; either of the weapons he carried could do that easily. Or he could shoot out the machine's all-important phase latch—if he could find it. The second choice was much more attractive from a personal standpoint: rupturing the regulator globe would release all the generator's output directly into the chamber. The burst of raw energy would last only a gigaclick at most before logic fuses sensed the runaway flow and choked it off at the source. But that was ample time to fry him (and any other organic compounds in the generator chamber) to fused carbon atoms. Grimly, he studied the big machine. Familiar as it looked overall, individual parts made little sense by themselves. He shook his head with frustration as he eyed the pulsing regulator. He grimaced. Death held no particular terror for him, especially after what he'd already been through. But he hated to give in. He concentrated again, trying desperately to discover some thread of functionality amid the complex network of conduits, insulators, logics, and odd-shaped housings. Then, almost by accident, his eye was caught by a big synchronous compensator, calibrated in the League's crazy ROGEN scale. No wonder he hadn't found it the first time! Directly below was its logic shunt; to the right of that, a beam multiplier, no doubt about it! And a Fort'lier tube—they'd call it a "multigrid-A" here. He was getting close now. A good thing, too: The pain in his shoulder was almost stopped, but he had become very drowsy now—and dizzy. He steadied himself with the hot barrel of the blast pike, forcing his eyes to focus. A distant clanging and hammering commenced on the hatch above him. Not much time left now. He compelled his tired mind to function...The Fort'lier tube. It controlled a radiation modulator somewhere. Therefore...

Things had become terribly foggy. He traced a thick wave guide from the oblong device through...Yes. That was the modulator, and beside it the phase latch he was looking for. He could tell by the big rectifier mounted on its side. All so easy once he knew where to look!

He sniffed the air anxiously, looked up. The hatch was glowing cherry red. Bastards were burning through. Desperately, he raised his pike toward the generator—Universe, how he was shaking. The hammering commenced again. He blurred, squeezed his eyes clear. The latch was in his sights. He fired...and missed.

With a sharp ripping noise, a bolt of energy cut through the hatch and sent sparks all over a nearby bulkhead. Gritting his teeth, Brim wrestled the weapon to his shoulder again, aimed. This was his last chance. If he missed, he'd go for the regulator and a quick, painless death. He willed himself to steady the sights, counted backward. Three...two...one. Then he fired. This time, he was rewarded with a satisfying flash of light as the phase latch shattered in a wobbling ball of violet radiance. Immediately, the noise of the generator began to fade with a great, almost-human sigh.

Presently, his eyes began to fog over again. By now, Brim had no strength to counter it. He felt himself falling. The last thing he heard was the hatch grating open on its ruined hinges...guttural shouts he no longer understood. Then he heard nothing.

***

He noticed the glare forcing itself through his closed eyelids at about the same time his cheek told him he was lying face-down on something cold and very hard. Groggily, he caught himself before he opened his eyes, voices on every side, all speaking Vertrucht. Where was he? So hard to remember...But with all the Vertrucht being spoken, it couldn't be very healthy for him, wherever it was.

"Try it again," a gruff voice commanded, clearly under some sort of strain.

"I already did," a nasal voice answered. "And I'm telling you, the whole damned thing's dead. What's the big rush anyway? They've already sent a ship out to help."

"You know the Praefect as well as I do," the gruff voice said. "And he's not going to be happy taking anybody's help. So try it."

"Yes, Sir. Shunt's in place. Inverters on. Grav housing closed."

Other voices stopped, listening.

"Hit it!" the gruff voice commanded. "Now."

Silence. Brim's shoulder throbbed painfully. He was cold, shivered in spite of himself.

"That's all?"

"That's all," the nasal voice confirmed. "Bastard really cocked up the phase latch, didn't he?"

The gruff voice swore an unintelligible oath. "Whole damned generator's dead as an xchort, then," it said.

The generator! It all came back to Brim in a rush. But where had they taken him? Was he still in the chamber? Somehow he didn't think so. This sounded more like the bridge.

"How long before you can get us going again?" a new, deeper voice demanded.

"None will say as yet, Placeman," the gruff voice answered. "When that one on the deck over there murdered Overmann Zotreb, he did more damage then he knew."

"Well?"

"Zotreb's assistants are a good deal slower, it seems."

"Curse all of them—especially him," the deep voice growled. Brim's side exploded with a blow that knocked the wind from his lungs and opened both eyes wide with pain. It took only a moment to determine he was indeed on the corvette's bridge.

"Look out! He's awake," someone yelled. This was followed by a second vicious kick. Brim shut his eyes and clenched his teeth, waiting for the next one.

"Placeman Zimmermann!" another voice squealed. "Would you kill him before we search his mind?"

"Putrid spawn of Greyffin's scum!" the deep voice growled. "You can be sure I shall kill him—but not before we extract certain information, fool."

"Oh, ah...no, Sir, Placeman Zimmermann!" another voice stumbled. "Certainly not before."

"One must be subtle," Zimmermann's gruff voice interrupted, as though the other had never spoken. "Like this..."

Brim opened his eyes wide in renewed agony as a scuffed jackboot ground the fingers of his left hand into the metal decking. He gasped in pain, trying to pull his hand away, but the arm didn't seem to work anymore. Blinking angry tears from his eyes, he looked up into the flushed, angry face of another Controller. Greasy haired, stubble-jawed, and hard-featured, the man was outfitted in wrinkled black breeches, an open tunic with yellow Placeman's patches on its collars, a dirty-gray sweater, and a shapeless peaked hat with the tarnished decoration of a Controller.

"Keep your eyes open and attend my questions, slime of slime," Zimmermann commanded in broken Avalonian. He sneered as he removed his heel from Brim's bleeding fingers. "You clearly understand you will die soon," he said matter-of-factly, "therefore it should be of little concern to you what we do with your body." His face wrinkled in cruel laughter. "How quickly and painlessly you die depends upon your answers. I reward truthfulness even for your kind."

"Hab'thall," Brim spat defiantly, picking the most insulting malediction he could dredge from his store of gutter Vertrucht, then grunted in pain as the jackboot smashed into his mouth, snapping teeth and throwing his head back against his shoulder.

"That should teach you better use of Vertrucht."

Brim willed the pain away and glared up in silence.

"Good," Zimmermann said at length, studying his fingernails. "Now, what is your ship? Name and home port, if you please."

Brim continued his silence as blood seeped from the corner of his ruined lips and ran warm along his lower cheek to puddle silently along the deck.

"My, my," the officer said with an innocent mien, "others in your crew have shared that secret with me. And much more, too. Now..." He stepped on Brim's helpless fingers again. "Won't you?"

Brim threw up on Zimmermann's boot.

The Controller roared in anger, jumped back, and kicked Brim full in the stomach.

By this time, Brim hardly noticed.

"I'll show you, cretin son of a capcloth," the enraged Controller shouted, pulling a blaster from a black, shiny holster on his hip. He pointed it in the direction of Brim's stomach. "You will die slowly, Avalonian scum. As I promised."

Morbidly fascinated, Brim watched Zimmermann's finger curl over the trigger. Then, suddenly, the man lowered his blaster as an angry voice shouted, "Idiot, what in the name of Korzol do you think you are doing?"

Glancing to the left, Brim saw for the first time what could only be the calm face of the corvette's commanding officer. Blond, square-jawed, young, and strikingly handsome, even from a deck-level view, the man called Valentin was the very opposite of his underling. Outfitted in immaculate black breeches, a tight, form-fitting tunic with crimson

Praefect's patches on his collars, and a peaked hat with a highly-polished Controller's insignia, he was the perfect embodiment of Triannic's officer corps—clearly a man on his way up someone's ladder of success. The look of anger on his reddened face gave clear signal he was also a man who brooked no mistakes from his subordinates.

"A, n-nothing", Praefect Valentin, Zimmermann stumbled, "...ah, I w-was merely questioning the..."

"And pray how do you plan to question the prisoner after he is dead, Placeman?" Valentin interrupted, his lips drawn back in a snarl.

"Th-the prisoner is n-not dead, Praefect. He is..."

"Go to your cabin, Zimmermann," Valentin ordered. "I will deal with you later—painfully, you may be certain. Now go!"

As Zimmermann slunk from the bridge, a rating suddenly shouted in panic. "Praefect Valentin, Sir!"

Valentin growled and turned. "Well?" he demanded furiously. "What now?"

"Another sh-ship, Praefect," the voice stammered.

"Drat!" Valentin swore. "They got here much sooner than I expected." He glared at the generator console. "Now I suppose I shall have to accept their help."

"It...it's the w-wrong kind of ship, Praefect Valentin," the rating declared.

"Well, what kind of ship, fool? How does it answer the challenge?"

"It does not answer, Praefect."

"What?"

"See for yourself, Praefect."

"Silence, fool! Where is it coming from?"

Brim couldn't see where the man pointed, but watched Valentin's boots spin round.

"Train the guns," the officer bellowed. "And..." He stopped in mid-sentence. "Sweet Hok'kling Poknor," he swore through his teeth. "Belay that last order. It's one of their T—class destroyers. Our 99s don't stand a chance."

Brim laughed through his cut and bleeding lips, though it came out as more of a bubbling noise. He mouthed the next words slowly and carefully. "What number, Hab'thall?" This time, he spoke entirely in

Vertrucht, then waited for the foot. It didn't come.

"You sneaking slime," Valentin snarled. "Vertrucht, eh?"

"What number, Hab'thall?" Brim bubbled, this time with a smile worth twice the pain it caused his lips.

Valentin narrowed his eyes, peered through the Hyperscreens. "T.83," he snapped furiously, then biting his lip in concentration, he stepped to one of the empty Helmsman's consoles. "Get this ordure into the seat here. Perhaps he can be of further value after all."

Rough hands hauled Brim from the deck into the recliner. He almost passed out from the pain; new blood was trickling along his chest again. His eyes fogged over and he felt himself slump toward the console. "I think you're too late, Praefect, old cock," he mumbled as a tiny popping noise exploded on his right arm.

"There, that'll bring him around for a while," another voice said.

Warmth spread rapidly from Brim's right arm, and his eyes abruptly cleared. A rope under his arms secured him to the back of the recliner; he could see the Hyperscreens now. He focused his eyes, grinned as well as he could. I.F.S. *Truculent*, all right. Never had a "pick and shovel" starship looked so beautiful. Bow on, she was standing about a thousand irals off the corvette's port quarter, all seven of her powerful 144—mmi disruptors pointed, it seemed, directly at his head. Even while he watched, they flashed in unison, accompanied by great coruscating eruptions of flame and glittering clouds of radiation. Outside, the Universe went mad in a paroxysm of erupting, runaway energy. The corvette bucketed violently, seams creaking and groaning as her spaceframe twisted in the backwash of space falling back in on itself. Screams of terror filled the bridge. The lights flickered out, then re-lighted, much dimmer this time.

Too near the onset of death to care, Brim turned to the young Praefect. The hypodermic that cleared his eyes also seemed to have stemmed the pain—at least most of it. He smiled crookedly. "She's about to blow all of us to subatomics, Valentin," he bubbled happily. "I'm sure the others won't mind."

"She?"

"Captain Collingswood," Brim said, reverting to Avalonian.

"By Poknor's beard," Valentin whispered. "Perhaps there's a chance yet," he whispered to himself. "Universe…"

"Not 'Universe', 'Collingswood'," Brim corrected gleefully.

"Silence, fool!"

"As you wish, Praefect."

Valentin shivered, peered through the Hyperscreens at *Truculent's* seven 144—mmi's. "I shall talk to her," he said almost to himself, then turned to a rating at a nearby console. "Make me a connection to that ship," he ordered, smoothing his wavy blond hair. "Immediately!"

"Aye, Praefect," a rating with a bald head and large ears answered, bending over his console. Within scant clicks, a blank globe appeared on the console nearest the black-suited officer.

"Not yet to me!" he bellowed. "Him!" He pointed to Brim. "Quickly."

A second blast from *Truculent*, this time much closer, sent every loose article on the bridge crashing wildly to the deck. The ship's gravity pulsed and the Hyperscreens flashed wildly.

"Hurry, fool!" Valentin wailed, nervously shooting his cuffs "Hurry!"

"Aye, Praefect," the rating answered. "They're listening now, I think." A new globe appeared on Brim's console, flashing once...twice. Then it filled with a Blue Cape rating, bald with fat cheeks. It was Applewood.

"Connection's made, Praefect," the League rating reported. Applewood's image peered out from the globe, talking with someone off the display. "We've got a connection to them, Captain," he said hesitantly. "I seem to be looking into the bridge." His eyes came to rest on Brim's ruined face. He stopped, a look of horror on his face. "Oh, sweet thraggling Universe," he groaned. "It looks like Lieutenant Brim."

Brim nodded, raised his good hand. He felt hot and weak. The hypodermic was rapidly wearing off and his vision was starting to fog again. Blood still trickled onto his chest.

"There's blood all over him," Applewood exclaimed. He was suddenly thrust aside, replaced by Collingswood in the globe.

"Lieutenant Brim," she said, clearly struggling to keep herself under control. "What has happened to...?" She paused. She seemed to know the answer to that. "To the rest of the crew?" she asked.

Smiling toothsomely and fairly dripping masculinity, Valentin moved beside Brim and spoke into the globe. "They are safe, Captain

Collingswood," he said with the earnest look of a schoolboy. "I am Praefect Kirsh Valentin, Captain of League warship HS-91, and you have my word as an officer of the League."

"Oh?" Collingswood answered. "Lieutenant Brim certainly doesn't look particularly safe to me."

"As you can see from his dress, Captain," Valentin said smoothly, "Lieutenant Brim is a special case. Disguised, mind you, in the uniform of my beloved homeland—against all established conventions. Further, he ruthlessly murdered two of my officers in cold blood." He shrugged. "We were forced to question him."

"I see," Collingswood said slowly, a look of disgust in her eyes. "And you have, ah, 'questioned' my other crewmen in the same manner?"

"You can believe me when I say the remainder of your crewmen are, shall we say, safe for the moment." Valentin's eyes hardened theatrically the length of a well-measured instant, then the boyish smile returned.

"'For the moment'," Collingswood repeated evenly. "Perhaps you had better tell me what that means." The corvette's bridge was deathly still by now, every officer and rating watching breathlessly as if life itself depended on the next few words.

"Simply this, Captain Collingswood," Valentin said, his voice growing oilier by the moment. "Should something untoward happen to my ship, your men would surely be affected also. And I am sure a lovely woman of your stature would never want something like that."

"Silence!" Collingswood snapped, her eyes blazing with anger. "I have no more patience with your game—and it is now clear to me you cannot move under your own power. Therefore, listen to me well," she continued, "for I am about to destroy your ship."

Valentin's eyes opened wide in surprise. "With twelve—thirteen of your men aboard?" he demanded. "Would you kill them, too?"

"Absolutely," Collingswood assured him.

"She means it, Valentin," Brim laughed weakly. "I'm ready; look at me. And I imagine the others are, too." Blackness was sweeping over him and he had no strength left to fight. He closed his eyes, felt his head lolling as he collapsed against the rope that held him in place. He heard Collingswood gasp, then abruptly her voice hardened.

"Despite my own wishes to the contrary, Praefect," she said through clenched teeth, "it is not necessary that anyone die with your ship—if my orders are followed accurately. Do you understand? No deviations. Your fate is entirely up to you."

"Wh-What can I do?" Valentin asked in a shaky voice. His part in the game was clearly over before it began.

"You have only ten cycles to carry out my orders," Collingswood said, the sound of her voice fast fading in Brim's ears. He strained to hear the next words, too, but they were drowned by a sudden thundering roar having nothing to do with starships or disruptors either: he was dying and he knew it. Strange it didn't matter now the time had come. He even managed to relax as the last light faded from his eyes and the Universe ceased to exist. He'd done the best he could...

***

This time, light filtering through his closed eyes was gentle—and wherever he was now come to, things were blessedly quiet, even warm. Comfortable. A definite improvement, he thought. Even the pain was gone, replaced by a wild tingling in his shoulder.

Alive?

He opened his eyes cautiously. A curved, transparent canopy arched overhead no more than half an iral from his face. For lack of anything better, he concentrated on that, and blinked his eyes. In one corner, it carried the stylized comet insignia of the Imperial Fleet.

Safe, too! Somehow—miraculously—he was in somebody's sick bay. He didn't even particularly care whose it was, or how he got there.

He turned his head in the cramped enclosure, sighted along his left shoulder. It had come free. The healing machine's amoebae-like apparatus was evidently finished with him and had retracted, or whatever it was pseudopods did when they went away. The shoulder itself was wrapped in a softly glowing cloth that extended all the way to his elbow. The remainder of him appeared to be dressed in a standard-issue, one-piece Imperial hospital suit—minus the left sleeve and shoulder. He moved his left hand, clenched a fist. Very little tenderness.

Not bad.

In a state of almost total exhaustion, he closed his eyes again and drifted off into contented sleep.

Later, when he woke again, the canopy was open and the deep rumble of Drive crystals soothed his ears. A familiar face peered down from a balding head with considerable professional interest. "You xaxtdamned Carescrians will do anything for a little attention, won't you?" admonished Xerxes O. Flynn.

Brim grinned. "Well," he conceded, "almost anything. I didn't let 'em kill me, after all."

"Could have fooled me," Flynn said with a serious look. "Those League bastards sure thought you were dead. Frightened to death of what might happen to 'em because of it."

Brim frowned. "Yeah," he conceded, "Well, they weren't alone by a long shot. I was pretty sure it was all over, too. Just how in the bloody Universe did I get here?" he demanded. "When I passed out, that Praefect bastard, Valentin, was still trying to play sex roles with Collingswood."

"Collingswood wasn't playing," Flynn chuckled, "but I did hear her telling Pym she thought he was xaxtdamned cute."

Brim raised an eyebrow. "Collingswood? Valentin?"

"Valentin, indeed," Flynn answered. "He's rather famous over there, in case you hadn't heard. Quite a hero, among other things." He laughed. "And there's nothing wrong with our little Regula Collingswood, either. She's a perfectly healthy specimen in every respect. Just wasn't in the mood at the time. Probably the sight of all your blood, or something. Anyway, she worked everything out. It's a long story; you can get the details later. But she nearly melted that thraggling corvette before she left, not long after Ursis carried you over himself. In a LifeGlobe."

"Melted the corvette?" Brim asked in amazement. "Universe, you can't expect me to wait for that story. Come on now, Doctor. I'll never get back to sleep."

Flynn opened his mouth for a moment, pointed a finger at Brim, then shook his head and smiled resignedly. "All right," he said, leaning his elbows on the side of the healing machine. "I suppose it makes sense. I wouldn't be able to sleep, either." With that, he related how Collingswood offered Valentin a very simple plan. He and his crew could safely embark in their LifeGlobes—so long as the captured

Imperials were also provided their own LifeGlobe in which they could separately return to *Truculent*. Once they were safely aboard and the Leaguers were a safe distance away, Collingswood would signal Pym to destroy the corvette—and one Leaguer LifeGlobe for each Imperial who was dead or had failed to return. "They were xaxtdamned careful with you after that," Flynn concluded.

"What about Ursis and Barbousse and the rest of the crew?" Brim asked.

"Oh, they're all healing, more's the pity," Flynn said. "Pym got no further target practice, and you're the only one I was able to really practice on."

"Universe," Brim said, "I'll bet everybody else all felt terrible about that."

"They didn't," Flynn grumped. "Unsympathetic bastards. But you made up for it, Brim, old friend," he said with a smile of satisfaction. "Isn't much under that bandage you brought from Carescria. I practiced on you for a long time; practically had to grow you a whole new shoulder, plus a few teeth."

"Thraggling wonderful," Brim exclaimed in mock dismay. "Does any of it work?"

"Smart bastard," Flynn fumed. "I couldn't very well cock up the teeth, now could I? They come in a box." Then he frowned. "I am sort of worried about the arm and shoulder assembly, now that I think about it. Might be only good for piloting starships and lifting glasses of meem." A quiet chime interrupted his banter, and he looked over his shoulder, grinning. "Couple of strange-looking individuals asked to see you when you awakened, Wilf," he said. "Feel up to talking some more?"

"If they can stand me, I can probably stand them," Brim assured him.

Flynn nodded, again over his shoulder. "All right," he said, "come on in."

Brim heard a door slide open on quiet rollers. Directly, Ursis and Barbousse appeared on either side of the Doctor, grinning from ear to ear. Both wore heavy bandages. "Remember now," Flynn warned sternly, "only a couple of cycles. Then out you go."

The Bear looked down at Brim with one eye (his other was hidden by a patch), fang gems flashing a soft light. He cocked his head toward the Doctor. "Flynn here can be great nuisance when he wants," he said. "Is not so, Starman Barbousse?"

The big rating's face reddened. "Well, Sir," he said, "he does appear to do passing good work. Ah..." He peered down at Brim. "Glad to be seein' you, ah..."

"How about alive?" Brim suggested. "And speaking of that, what happened to you two?"

"Oh," Barbousse said lightly, "them Cloud League scalawags didn't take kindly to Lieutenant Ursis' fake fit there in the K tube, what with all his rollin' around on the deck an' all."

"And you piling in for good measure," Ursis chuckled with a toothy grin. "As they say on Mother Planets, 'When Hagsdoff scratches rock, Bears move snow houses out of sunlight', eh?" He nudged the big rating in the ribs with an elbow.

"Oh. Ah...aye, Sir," Barbousse answered with a confused look. "Hagsdoffs."

Flynn's eyes met Brim's, then rolled toward the ceiling. "Hagsdoffs," he repeated.

"You were both great, "Brim piped up to stifle an oncoming chuckle. "Even if you did almost get me killed."

"Sure glad you made it, Lieutenant," Barbousse repeated. "If you hadn't done what you did, we'd likely be startin' an all-day night shift at some Altnag'gin hullmetal mill."

"Not all of us," Ursis interjected with a dark growl.

"I heard," Brim said. "The bastards..."

"At any rate," Flynn interrupted quickly. "You two did show up here for a particular purpose, didn't you?"

"Yes, that we did," Ursis answered, turning to Brim with a serious look on his face. He narrowed his eyes. "Someday, Wilf Brim," he said, "I shall properly thank you for all you did for us. Not now. But I want you to know your bravery would be legend, even in my homeland." He shook his head, momentarily a long way off. "Meantime," he said, turning to Barbousse, "you give it to him. You found it."

Barbousse's cheeks went red again, but he looked Brim in the eye.

"Ah, I, ah, c-copped this on the way out of the corvette," he stammered as he lifted a big side-action blaster into the startled Carescrian's right hand. "Tried to return it to Lieutenant Ursis, but he wouldn't take it back."

"We agreed you should have it," Ursis thrust in. "It belonged to my grandfather: A man of great gallantry. You will honor it, Wilf—and him, rest his spirit."

Brim opened his mouth in surprise. "I...Oh, Universe, Nik," he exclaimed emotionally, "I can't take that."

"Sorry," Flynn interrupted, "but if you people are going to argue, these two will have to leave, which they are going to have to do soon anyway."

Brim shook his head in defeat, tears of emotion burning his eyes. "Thank you," he choked when he was able. Not eloquent, but all he could manage.

"You are most welcome, Friend Brim," Ursis said with a huge grin. "And before this very inhospitable medicine man rescinds his tenuous welcome, I have something else here for you—from no less a personage than Bosporus P. Gallsworthy."

Brim raised an eyebrow. "Gallsworthy?" he asked incredulously.

"None other," Ursis said. "As your boss, he has collected all messages sent to your person since you last accessed your queue."

"And?" Brim asked. "Nobody sends me anything but debit notices."

"Don't remember Gallsworthy handing me anything like that," Ursis said, a look of ill-concealed merriment in his eyes.

"What else could it be?" Brim asked, genuinely mystified.

The Bear laughed. "This," he said, handing Brim a small plastic card. "Hard copy of personal message from Gimmas-Haefdon. Thought you might want to see straightaway."

"For me? I don't know anybody on Haefdon. I didn't even get there until two nights before we..."

"Hmm," the Bear replied. "Perhaps is a mistake. But I think not. Read...."

Frowning, Brim took the card, turned it to catch the light—his heart skipped a beat. Four short lines of poetry from the ancient pen of Sante' Eremite blazed from the tiny page. The power of the simple words transcended centuries; he'd read them often: "My fire burns among the stars/My long lance thrusteth sure,/My strength is as the strength of ten,/Because my heart endures." One more line completed the short message: "Congratulations, Wilf Brim." It was signed simply, "Margot Effer'wyck."

4 More than two Standard Weeks
passed before Brim's weakened body accustomed itself to its brand-
new parts, but the day at last arrived when Flynn dismissed him
permanently from *Truculent's* sick bay—with strict orders to go
cautiously until more of his strength returned. Now, only cycles after
pressing the doctor's hand in heartfelt thanks, he was back inside his
tiny cabin, seated on the edge of his bunk and accessing the ship's
message system. He cycled his pitifully small mail file three times: Eight
messages in all, only one sourced from Effer'wyck@Haefdon.

He immediately brought this one to his display, which filled with
loose golden curls and a frowning smile. Margot! He thrilled while the
image recited Lacerta's timeless lines in a soft, modulated voice. She'd
be proud of that voice, he reflected, and wondered how he'd managed
to miss it before.

Far too soon, the little message ran its course. He played it again—
and then again. He rotated the display and watched her from every
angle. She might be far beyond his reach, but that didn't stop him from
dreaming!

With a sigh, he finally sent her message to his permanent storage,
then selected a note from Captain Collingswood. Voice only, this
requested he "drop by" her office to file a verbal report whenever he
felt "up to it." He took care of that immediately, appending his name to
her appointment schedule for just after the next change of watch.

The remainder of his messages, save one, were all debit notices.

His single exception was a short communication from Borodov containing a cross-reference to the prestigious *Journal of the Imperial Fleet*. "A most valuable article, Wilf Ansor," the shifting patterns read. "You must file this with your most important documents. Good as credits in the pocket, perhaps better. (signed) A.A. Borodov."

The Journal? With a frown, Brim fetched Borodov's reference to his display. Characteristic patterns in the style of the highly venerated publication replaced Borodov's covering message, then indexed to a small article almost lost toward the back of the issue. It was clearly little more than filler placed during a time of little important activity elsewhere, but it was there nonetheless:

> Gimmas-Haefdon (Eorean Blockading Forces) 118/51995: Carescrian Sublieutenant Wilf Brim, recently graduated Helmsman assigned to Lieutenant-commander Regula Collingswood's I.F.S. *Truculent* (DD T.83, see other reports, this issue), distinguished himself recently off the Altnag'gin periphery during a boarding action that resulted in destruction of League corvette HS-91 commanded by Kirsch Valentin, infamous young Praefect with five Imperial kills.

As Borodov suggested, he carefully filed the reference on his permanent storage, grinning in spite of himself. Strange, he reflected, how much that little bit of recognition meant to him. He'd been such an outsider since he joined the Fleet under Lord Wyrood's Admiralty Reform Act. It took only this insignificant crumb of acknowledgment to make him feel a lot less like one.

Then he busily applied himself to composing Margot's answer—no easy task, he discovered to his surprise. When he scanned his books of verse for a fitting line or two, nothing seemed to fit, though a number of the same poems seemed perfect when he first thought about them in the solitude of the sick bay. He made a second pass, then a third, before settling down for a detailed search. Shortly before his appointment with Collingswood, he had completed only two books with three-quarters of a third remaining to be studied. So far, nothing even resembled his requirements. In the end, he decided he might easily spend years without finding the proper words. Shaking his head ruefully at the time he had already wasted on the project, he quickly chose a few lines that approximated his thoughts, composed a short covering message of thanks, then sent everything on its way before he could change his mind again.

That out of the way, he smoothed his tunic, brushed his boots on his bunk cover, and made his way forward to the captain's cabin, one level above his own.

***

"Sit down, Wilf," Collingswood said as she relaxed in her chair. Subtle harmonies insinuated themselves from the cabin background: soft instruments blending, separating, then blending once more to form emotional tapestries of surprising beauty. He seemed to recall the same sounds from his first visit to her cabin, but they hardly registered then. "The last time I saw you," Collingswood was saying with a twinkle in her eye, "you appeared to be rather soundly asleep."

Brim grinned. "I seem to have been doing a lot of that lately, Captain," he answered.

"Almost a permanent condition, from what Dr. Flynn tells me," Collingswood declared, her face becoming serious. "I watched Ursis and Barbousse carry you in from the corvette. You'd been rather thoroughly worked over by that frightful Valentin character and his crew—you evidently caused a bit of trouble during your short visit."

"I tried to, Captain," Brim said.

Collingswood laughed quietly. "I'm quite certain you did, Lieutenant. But I shall need to know a bit more than that," she asserted. "I am required to file an official report, you know."

Brim felt his face flush. "Sorry, Captain," he said. "I didn't understand." He stared at his boots, reflecting for a moment, then rubbed his chin. "So far as I can remember," he began, "this is what happened after we spotted that corvette..." For the next metacycle, he described what he had seen aboard the enemy warship, including his own activities when he felt they had any relevance.

Collingswood sat relaxed in her recliner while he spoke, taking notes, interjecting occasional questions, or clarifying certain points. When he finished, she re-crossed her legs, frowned thoughtfully, and looked him straight in the eye. "Strange," she mused, "how much like your shipmates you have become. None has mentioned Lieutenant Amherst so far, nor his part in this little adventure of yours. I wonder why."

Brim frowned. In the seclusion of the healing coffin, he considered himself ready for questions about that part. Now all his confidence seemed to dissipate like smoke. He fumbled with a loose fastener on his tunic. "Well," he uttered, groping for something to say, "I can't speak for the others, of course. I was alone most of the time we spent aboard the corvette, Captain."

"I see," Collingswood said, brushing aside a stray lock of hair. She studied the fingernails of her right hand. "Would you," she began, "make any further comments were I to ask you for information concerning alleged incompetence on the part of Lieutenant Ursis?"

"In what context, Captain?" Brim asked warily, not yet willing to meet her eyes.

"Why, in the context of his attempts—or should I say, non-attempts—to alter the control settings of the Cloud League merchantman *Ruggetos*, of course," she answered, her expression suddenly cold as space itself.

Brim took a deep breath and met her gaze squarely. "In that case, Captain," he said evenly, "I should probably have a great deal more to say."

"Would you testify, Lieutenant?" she continued, sitting well forward in her recliner, elbows firmly on the armrests.

"If it came to that, Captain, you can bet I would testify," Brim answered. He waited for an explosion—both she and Amherst were clearly Imperials of no mean station, and in his experience, Carescrians didn't usually get away with taking stands, no matter who was in the right.

As if considering her next words, Collingswood remained for a moment staring into his eyes. Then, suddenly she relaxed and sat back in her recliner, smiling broadly. "You have joined my old *Truculent*, haven't you, Brim?" she pronounced. "I rather thought you'd have little trouble doing that once you got started."

Brim blinked. "Pardon?" he stammered.

"Protecting Amherst the way you are," Collingswood explained. "You're already part of my crew." She laughed quietly. "In rather record time, too."

Brim kept his silence, unsure of where she was leading him.

"You probably wonder what I plan to do about him, don't you, Lieutenant?" she went on, holding up a graceful hand. "His part in the loss of that merchantman was easy enough for me to piece together—and caused you considerable difficulty and pain. You deserve an answer."

Brim nodded his head noncommittally. "Thank you, Captain," he said simply.

"I shall not rid the ship of him," she said with no further preamble. "Because Amherst is a powerful name throughout the Fleet—and other reasons which have nothing to do with either of you—he shall have one more chance, at least." She smiled and shook her head. "No one ever said life would be fair, Lieutenant. In spite of what Amherst might really deserve, I shall not commit political suicide to secure his punishment—though I shall attempt to insure he is never again in a position to cause so much harm, should he fail a second time."

Brim nodded again. At least she was honest.

"And no record of Amherst's report will ever find its way into your friend Ursis' records." She glanced at her empty display, then grimaced in an unmistakable sign of dismissal. Brim got up to leave.

"Your report was first rate, as were your actions, Lieutenant," she added. "You weren't thinking of returning to bridge duty immediately, were you?"

"Not for two more days, Captain," Brim answered.

"Dr. Flynn knows best," Collingswood said as her display began to fill with data.

Brim left feeling better about his future than he had ever dreamed possible. So long as the Fleet had a few Collingswoods, Carescrians still had a chance.

***

The endless succession of days that followed was notable only by its sameness until danger and boredom became two great stones that ground *Truculent* and her crew alike. And all around, the larger war waxed and waned. Victories and defeats: There were still more of the latter, but one could sense an occasional ray of hope among the grim news KA'PPAed in from powerful transmitters halfway across the galaxy.

To Brim's utter astonishment, his abbreviated answer to Margot's note established a lively—if disappointingly chaste—correspondence. During the long stretches of boredom, he often argued with himself concerning that. After all, any kind of treatment was more than he should ever expect. She was, aside from being promised to someone else, a person of noble blood. Very noble blood. And a full military rank above his own into the bargain. What more could he expect?

Sometimes this sort of logical approach worked. Sometimes it didn't. But most of the time, it didn't.

And for some exasperating reason, he never did quite condition himself to the point where he could comfortably think of her in the company of Rogan LaKarn. That became painfully apparent when a chance news program pictured the two together during a leave in Avalon:

> Princess Margot Effer'wyck and Commander the Honorable Baron Rogan LaKarn share a well-deserved leave in Avalon's Courtland Plaza near the Imperial castle. Engaged nearly two years now, the popular couple have postponed their nuptials while they work to defend the Empire from its enemies.

Somehow, the sight of them holding hands in that manicured garden tied his heart in a knot. He gritted his teeth and felt his cheeks burn, hoping against hope nobody in the wardroom noticed his helpless discomfort—he a Carescrian worked up over an Effer'wyck. What a joke that was!

In private, he railed at himself. He could claim no part of her life. How she chose to spend her leave was certainly none of his business. He meant nothing special to her, and she ought to mean nothing to him.

But he really didn't believe the second part.

That night, as he fitfully dozed, his mind was torn by weird, wildly erotic dreams. He pictured her beckoning to him through a soft, warm fog. But when he reached to touch her, Rogan LaKarn interposed.

And each time, Brim awoke to find himself alone in his tiny cabin, sweating and frustrated, the rumble of the generators no longer comforting to his ears.

In a foul mood, he dressed and made his way up to the bridge, where he spent the remainder of his free watch tutoring Jubal Theada for a battery of upcoming tests. Even that kind of frustration was better than fighting his own imagination!

***

For the next three Standard Months, Collingswood's aggressive blockading techniques eroded both *Truculent* and her crew. Space off the Altnag'gin Complex at Trax was a busy crossroads of the League's commerce. Always there was another "runner" to be pursued—or a pursuing Cloud League warship determined to rid the space lanes of Imperial blockaders. Borodov and Ursis constantly rushed through *Truculent's* battered hull, patching battle damage or repairing components worn to uselessness from constant duty at maximum settings.

Flynn was similarly busy patching burned and blasted bodies: Carelessness caused by advanced fatigue was at least as deadly an enemy as the League itself. Yet no relief was forthcoming, and everyone knew why. The Imperial Fleet was stretched so thin that every ship and every crew member served past all reasonable limit. No alternative existed; everyone was well aware of Triannic's vow to punish the Imperial Fleet to its last man.

Only continuing success made any of it bearable. Collingswood was an extraordinary tactician, and *Truculent* sent a steady stream of prizes off toward Avalon—often seriously shorting her own crew complement for weeks at a time. Everyone was now accruing Imperial credits in individual accounts, and even Brim found himself debt-free one day, for the first time he could remember.

Following still another stormy month of desperate fighting and wearing fatigue, *Truculent* was even more patched and dented than before. Many of her less critical mechanisms were by now completely inoperative—the crew worked around these when possible, but mostly did without. Some of the important systems were little better than these, and operated only marginally, when they worked at all. Often, Brim looked over the battered decks from his position high on the bridge and wondered if anyone back in the Imperial Client States had any idea at all what it really took to keep Triannic from their gates. A small part of him wanted desperately to believe they did. The remainder doubted many of them had any idea what was going on at all.

Only when Borodov managed to convince his Sodeskayan superiors at the Admiralty that *Truculent* could no longer be patched enough to fight and win did Flight Operations deign to send their replacement, and by then it was nearly too late. The Drive itself failed three times on the way home and fully half the Atmospheric Controller Modules consumed themselves in a cloud of sour-smelling vapor and sparks before the ship was two days en route. The nearly desperate crew completed their return with most of the ship's environment simulating the worst elements of a steamy Crennelean Narr jungle.

One way or another, they made it. Both Gimmas and Haefdon were sizable disks in the Hyperscreens ahead when Brim heard the Drive finally eased all the way back to idle. He and Theada occupied observers' seats while Gallsworthy and Fourier flew the approach. "You may prepare us for landfall, Lieutenant Gallsworthy," Collingswood said, her voice loud in the unaccustomed silence.

"Aye, aye, Captain," Gallsworthy growled. Immediately, Brim heard distant alarms go off below in the ship, and docking crews began to fill the bridge.

Fourier signaled to Ursis; a few moments later the generators shivered to life.

"Finished with the xaxtdamned Drive," Gallsworthy rumbled.

"I think it's finished with us anyway," Collingswood said grumpily.

"Drive deactivated," Borodov chuckled. Astern, the flowing green of the Drive plume flickered and disappeared.

"Drive shutters closed," Ursis said.

"LightSpeed point zero," Fourier called out as Gandom's 'V_e effect went into full flare and the Hyperscreens stopped translating. Gradually, the view cleared as the speed dropped below the critical mark. Applewood contacted Haefdon Approach soon afterward, and within a few metacycles they were in a holding pattern for clearance at the Lox'Sands control ring, this time in zone green. Traffic was light during that watch, and presently *Truculent* was on final, thundering down through Haefdon's cloudy turbulence.

With a sense of weary excitement, Brim waited impatiently for *Truculent* to break out of the overcast. So far, all he could see were regular flashes of the beacon reflected back from the streaming haze outside and the occasional glow of KA'PPA rings expanding outward as Applewood talked to Approach Control. The sound of the generators moderated to a burbling grumble, and the muted drones and thumps of imminent landfall were well under way. Gallsworthy banked to port, revealing glimpses of gray, fog-strewn seascape wrinkled by the thickly sluggish patterns of frigid-looking swells and jagged ice fragments everyone associated with the base.

As they returned to level flight, Brim spied two or three lamp-studded causeways below like the thin spokes of some great wheel converging at an unseen hub somewhere far off to port, but the haze swallowed them completely in damp-looking muzziness before he could distinguish any details. As usual, there was no real difference between land and sky aloft on Haefdon—no horizon, only fog and clouds and occasionally the wrinkled blackness of the inhospitable sea below.

Another turn to port, generators roaring momentarily, then *Truculent* settled gently onto her forward gradient and churned over the icy rollers that shone dully in the landing lights twenty-five irals below her stained and dented hull. Through a chance break in the fog, Brim saw they were now running parallel to another causeway. He watched giant waves batter themselves to wind-blown spume against its rocky bulwarks. A beacon flashed indistinctly in their direction. Ahead, fog-shrouded blue and red lights marked the opening to the Eorean section. He smiled to himself. The last time through here, he'd been considerably more occupied than he was now, sitting at his leisure in an observer's seat. Beyond, a forest of KA'PPA masts jutted from the starwharves themselves.

With Fourier at the controls, *Truculent* changed course smoothly, slid through the entrance, and in a few moments glided to a halt above a gently glowing gravity pool. Thick mooring beams leaped from lenses in the seawalls and Brim's nausea made itself known when the umbilical arm connected, switching *Truculent* back to local gravity. Gallsworthy raised his hand silently and their gravity generators spun down and stopped—the unaccustomed silence after nearly six months of one kind of propulsion system or another was almost physical. A tentative "Hurrah!" sounded from the back of the bridge. Then another, and another—in a moment, the whole ship was gone wild in a paroxysm of cheering. Even the normally reserved Collingswood could be seen pounding Gallsworthy on the back.

Theada grasped Brim's hand. "We made it!" he gasped joyfully. "We actually made it!"

"Yeah," Brim said, himself overcome with a strange sort of relief. He could plan on living at least a few weeks more. It was a strange feeling. He hadn't encountered that kind of confidence since their departure.

Truculent was home.

***

With little to occupy him at the moment, Brim forsook the noisy throng exiting from the bridge. A traditional homecoming celebration was scheduled shortly for the wardroom, but according to wartime rules, crew members joined only after completing a session with someone from a debriefing team, and with his lack of seniority, Brim appeared next to last on the schedule of officers. He looked out through the Hyperscreens at the gray landscape: Another of Haefdon's long, drab evenings was beginning in a driving snowstorm as the Harbor Master's peculiar vehicle scuttled off down the snow-hazed road. A large group of utility skimmers in various sizes was already parked near the breakwater, and below the bridge he watched a line of figures leaning into the wind-driven blizzard as they trudged across the brow toward the ship. One particularly heavy gust momentarily freed a shock of golden hair from beneath a parka before its owner hurried out of his sight. It made him laugh at himself. Nearly anything was sufficient to remind him of Margot Effer'wyck these days! He shook his head. Beyond all reason, and he knew it.

Nearly three metacycles passed before he was finally summoned for his debriefing—in Amherst's cabin, of all places. Somewhere in the Universe there was irony in that, he chuckled as he knocked on the door.

"Come in," a familiar voice called out from the other side. Brim frowned as he pushed the door open. Where had he heard that? His heart skipped a beat.

"Wilf Brim," Margot exclaimed, brushing a soft blond curl aside. "I have surely saved the best for last."

He stopped short in the doorway when he felt his face flush. His breath had suddenly gone short, his ears burned, and he felt like a foolish schoolboy with his first serious crush. She was even more beautiful than he remembered. The image she had sent in her message didn't begin to do her justice at all! "M-Margot," he stammered, then his eyes went to the full lieutenant's insignia on the left shoulder of her cape. "I mean, 'Lieutenant'."

She smiled warmly. "'Margot' is fine, Wilf," she said. "And we shall never get to the wardroom if you don't come in and let me start your debriefing."

Somehow, those words brought him around. "Sorry," he said, regaining at least some of his composure and breaking into his own smile of honest pleasure. He shook his head. "I guess I never expected to see you here," he said.

"Some ships get special treatment, Wilf," she said. "Ones that carry special people."

Brim looked at her hands, smooth and shapely and perfectly manicured, as she set up the keyboard of Amherst's Communicator. He listened to the sounds of the cooling hull, the raucous celebration in the wardroom. "Thank you" was all he could think to say. She was disconcertingly beautiful. Then he lost all track of time while she probed his mind with a professionalism and skill that nearly took his breath away. He was first surprised and then fascinated by her deep understanding of the technology of warfare, and especially starflight mechanics. She posed questions that led to others and to others still— forced him to recall details that he had forgotten as unimportant but which were decidedly the opposite, from her viewpoint.

"The triggering gear you saw in the corvette's central globe, Wilf, was it in the upper firing room only, or was it in both?"

"Both, I think," he answered.

"Then, were they the same?" she asked, blue eyes searching his very soul. "Could both disruptors be operated from the same firing room if one room was shot out?"

He thought for a moment. "Yes," he answered finally, "because the power cables went to both firing rooms."

Every word he uttered seemed to have some value. He had never met anyone like this before, never a woman both so beautiful and so talented all at once. When she finished, he found himself dazed with mental fatigue. They had worked without interruption for nearly three metacycles.

"You have quite a memory, Wilf Brim," she said, fatigue slowing her own voice, "which has provided me a great deal of material for study." She smiled comfortably. "Now I shall claim the further pleasure of sharing some meem from your wardroom. How does that sound?"

"Wonderful," Brim said, looking at her softness. "Just wonderful." Then other words suddenly crept into his mind. He grinned. "'Oh weary lady Geraldine,/I pray you drink this crystal wine'," he recited, gesturing dramatically.

Margot closed her eyes for a moment and frowned. Then she laughed, a look of pleasure spreading from her lips. She pointed a finger at him. "'It is a wine of virtuous powers;/My mother made it of wild flowers'. There! Something out of Leoline's "Silver Lamp," isn't it? You've yet to stump me, Wilf Brim. Even when you choose some of the very worst poetry in the whole Universe!"

They both laughed at that, then she deactivated Amherst's Communicator and they made their way to the wardroom.

***

They were late to the party, much of which was by now moved off to other ships and wardrooms across the sprawling base. *Truculent's* badly depleted meem supplies would be better stocked for the next round of celebrations. The wardroom was still well-populated, but the early frenetic energy was now worn into a comfortable hum of conversation and the musical clink of goblets. Most of the lights were dimmed, and here and there couples shared the privacy of shadowed tables. A gathering of Bears talked quietly at one end of the room; Ursis signaled "hello" from a seat close to a slim female whose eyes never strayed from his face. The air was heavy with the scent of perfume and hogge'poa. Two other female Bears talked animatedly with Borodov while a number of other furry couples toasted in the Sodeskayan manner: Goblets raised empty and upside down while they chanted the age-old Bearish drinking litany, "To ice, to snow, to Sodeskaya we go!"

Margot nodded toward Borodov. "He's everybody's darling," she said with her husky laugh. "The sly old Bear."

Brim smiled and nodded. "I didn't realize so many of their females had joined the Fleet," he commented.

"More of them arrive from Sodeskaya all the time," Margot continued as he helped her into a chair at a table away from the lights. "Bears can't get along without them any more than men can," she laughed softly. "Professionally, that is."

"The Logish Meem you ordered, Lieutenant," Steward Grimsby said, materializing cadaverously from the smoky darkness.

Startled, Brim looked up as the ancient steward placed two goblets before them. "I didn't order..." His eyes met Margot's; they were laughing and sleepy all at the same time.

"It's a fine choice, Wilf," she said as Grimsby half filled her goblet.

"Thank you, Lieutenant, ma'am," Grimsby said to Margot. He poured Brim's with total aplomb. "My compliments, Lieutenant Brim," he said. "I can only agree with Princess Effer'wyck. It is a fine choice. Saved for a special occasion." Then, quickly as he appeared, he was gone again.

Margot shrugged and raised her goblet. "To you, Wilf," she said, "and to old *Truculent* here—and to Nergol Triannic's slipping on a ca'omba peel."

He lifted his goblet and touched hers with a tiny musical note. "I'd duel a dozen Nergol Triannic's—ripe ca'ombas at ten paces—if you would promise to debrief me each time I got home." The Logish Meem was like silver fire in his throat. He had never experienced such fine vintage.

"One Nergol Triannic is quite sufficient for this war," Margot said with a wink, "in spite of what I am sure are your very formidable talents throwing ripe ca'ombas."

As the cycles slipped by, they talked of poetry, Haefdon, and the endless duty watches. She clearly had the broader picture of their war, and by the time Grimsby materialized with a second bottle of the same rare Logish Meem, Brim had a confused impression that her mysterious Technology Division was actually beginning to grasp some of the enemy's *metiér*, that Baron Rogan LaKarn didn't find his way to Gimmas-Haefdon as often as she thought he should, and that even when he did, her own work schedule took its toll of an already abbreviated love life. Somehow Brim found nothing unusual about her last comment. She was that sort of person. Besides, he reminded himself, this was simply a social occasion shared between two professionals. But, oh, how he wished he could satisfy that particular area of her needs!

He savored her oval face, her loose curls, her sulky eyes—now even sulkier as fatigue and the meem took effect. And he drew her out, learned what he could of her life, her family, her loves from her days as a little girl. She spoke freely, clearly relishing the memories of carefree dalliances before the war. Brim smiled with her, but somehow the words were bittersweet in his ears.

Then, suddenly she looked about the wardroom. His eyes followed. Except for Grimsby's spectral presence in the pantry, they were alone. Margot glanced down at her timepiece and shut her eyes. "Oh, Universe, Wilf," she whispered. "I'm on duty in less than five metacycles. I've got to go—now!" She touched his hand and drew his eyes to hers. "Thank you for a beautiful break in a long tour of duty," she whispered. "'Rarely, rarely, comest thou,/Spirit of Delight!/ Wherefore hast thou left me now/Many a day and night?'"

As he helped her into her Fleet Cloak, Brim found his mind a poetic blank. "All I can think of right now are my own words," he stammered. "But I need to tell you that...that this evening has made some of the tough parts of my life suddenly well worth living through." For a few moments of absolute unreality, he stood so close he nearly touched her. And found his carefully nurtured professional attitude was rapidly evaporating with each passing cycle.

Then, from nowhere, Grimsby appeared again, this time with Brim's own Fleet Cloak. It broke the spell.

"M-Many thanks, Grimsby," the Carescrian stammered, looking perplexedly at the strange little man.

"Yes," Grimsby agreed with a warm smile. "She is lovely, isn't she, Sir?" Then he saluted and scuttled off toward the pantry.

Margot looked at him and smiled sleepily. "I shouldn't begin to question him, were I you, Wilf," she giggled. "This old Universe has always contained its share of magic; Grimsby's clearly a part of that."

"So are you, Margot," Brim whispered as he followed her into the companionway.

"What was that?" she asked.

"Nothing," Brim replied. "Just saying good night to Grimsby."

Outside, the wind had abated somewhat, but the cold nearly deprived Brim of his breath while they picked their way over the icy brow. In the snow-strewn mist at the breakwater, they stopped outside her little skimmer.

"I'm glad I scheduled you last, Wilf," she said—almost disconcertedly.

"You did that on purpose?" he asked.

Margot smiled. "My professional secret," she said. "But aside from missing all the important data I took from you, I might also have missed the pleasure of these last few metacycles with you, mightn't I?"

Brim looked down at his boots. "Yes," he admitted. "I would never have dared to even ask you to drink with me." He shook his head and shrugged. "So many other officers must want..."

She put a gloved finger to his lips. "The Universe doesn't have many Wilf Brims to offer," she said. "Let me choose my friends. All right?"

"All right," Brim agreed with a smile. He opened the door to her skimmer in a shower of tiny snowflakes that tingled against his face and flashed in the dim light of *Truculent's* battle lanterns.

She slid into the seat, then looked him in the eye once more. "Few people here recite poetry, either, so don't be a stranger, Wilf." She tilted her head slightly. "Soon," she added, then shut the door.

"I promise," he said.

Moments later, the little machine trembled into life and shook itself of snow. Then it rose and skimmed off over the drifts, lights beaming through the tendrils of fog. Brim stared silently at the point where it disappeared a long time before he trudged thoughtfully back to the starship. A bloody real princess—but the title didn't matter any more.

A fitful night ensued as Brim tossed endlessly in his narrow bunk while his timepiece metered away the early morning watch. When occasionally he could trick himself into something resembling sleep, he was beset by further dream sequences with Margot—whose beauty remained frustratingly untouchable (for one reason or another), but who was at least now unencumbered by Baron Rogan LaKarn. When more commonly he couldn't sleep at all, he lay staring at the dark ceiling attempting to convince himself his impossible relationship with this beautiful young noblewoman was nothing more than a friendship growing naturally out of some shared professionalism.

"Shared professionalism." The term pleased him: Ample foundation for a friendship, even with a royal princess so far above his station she ought rightly to be completely out of sight. It explained everything. Made it all right.

Eventually, he did succumb to a deeper sleep, but it lasted only into the first portion of the morning watch: two metacycles at most, then chimes woke him, directing his attention to his message frame, which announced a wardroom meeting for officers in twenty cycles. Sleepily, he pulled on his uniform. Shared professionalism, he thought while he polished his boots. Well, if that's what it was, then it was clearly his turn to get them together. Muzzily, he combed the knots from his thick black hair. What did one do with royalty? He shook his head and chuckled. This time, he'd have to improvise as he went because the average Carescrian simply wasn't outfitted with that kind of knowledge, at least as standard equipment. Then he smiled.

Yet...

"I shall detain you only a few moments," a smiling Collingswood called out from the head of the table. "I know everyone is as anxious to be about their business..." the merest blush of color rose high in her cheeks, "as am I."

A joshing kind of rustle swept the table, punctuated by, "Hear, Hear!" and, "Good on you, Captain!" Brim looked down the table while the small stir settled. Nik sat to his right, outfitted in his usual finery, the heel of one expensive-looking boot hooked to the front of his chair, hands folded across a sturdy Bear ankle. At the opposite end of the table from Collingswood, Amherst sat imperiously looking neither right nor left, and to his left Gallsworthy already swayed drunkenly in his seat. Next to him, and closest to the door, a tired-looking Sophia Pym slouched in loose-jointed comfort, her red-rimmed eyes dreamily focused somewhere a long way from *Truculent*.

"We have a whole lot of repairs to put to rights this trip," Collingswood was saying, "as all of you know so well." More laughs and comments punctuated that. "Well, they're going to make it worthwhile for us, too. This time, people, I have been notified we shall be in port for one full Standard Month, starting today. And we shall be processing applications for leave directly following this meeting."

At this, the wardroom fairly erupted in cheers and applause. Nik pounded his fists on the table, great diamonds flashing in his fangs. Fourier and Pym slapped each other on the back, and Borodov nudged Flynn in the side with a wicked look on his furry face. Only Gallsworthy seemed not to notice—a momentary cloud of sadness passed over his face. Then it was gone, replaced by the impenetrable mask of drunken indifference.

Collingswood completed her presentation quickly after that, finishing with the usual port announcements, duty-roster requirements (to be satisfied before any leave applications would be processed), and official Fleet notices. One of these had to do with a call for volunteers—a special mission of one sort or another—but Brim missed most of it in the chorus of hoots and general disparagement that followed the word "volunteer." Something about a converted starliner registered in the back of his mind. I.F.S. *Prosperous* was it? If memory served him, a ship by that name was among the fastest in the peacetime fleet. Then the meeting was over and everyone was suddenly fighting over the duty roster.

Brim walked quickly past the happy throng signing up for leave. He had none coming, nor anyplace to spend it if he did. Alone in his cabin, he sat before the Communicator and reported in to the Base's general-availability roster for the duration of *Truculent's* stay in port. Dutifully removing one of the Fleet's ubiquitous personal transponders from his cabinet, he sent in its serial number, activated power for one Standard Month, then swallowed the tiny device and waited.

"Recorded and verified, Lieutenant Brim," the Communicator said. "We shall be in touch if necessary."

So much for that...

Within the metacycle, Brim was on *Truculent's* bridge once again, watching a husky, broad-shouldered tug materialize out of a thick fog to tow the destroyer to one of the inland repair pools. Collingswood had long since signed her over to the base repair organizations and would not return for at least two weeks. For that matter, nearly all the rest of the officers were gone, too. Only Ursis remained with the ship to run the center gravity generator while the ship was towed—and even he was scheduled to depart with Borodov when that was done. The Bear watched approvingly while the tug's crew grappled on to *Truculent's* hull with the huge mooring beams the little ships seemed to use whether they needed them or not.

"One would think we displaced as much as *Benwell*," the Bear chuckled as *Truculent* was eased backward off her gravity pool.

"So long as they're the ones driving us to the repair pool," Brim laughed, "they can use real rope for all I care—just so I don't have to keep track of the silly rules they've got for overland running."

In no time at all, their original mooring was swallowed in the fog. Brim watched in silence from the bridge as occasional buoys passed below in the swirling wake of the generator's footprint on the water. Then they slowed and passed between two great, age-blackened stone pylons, and the ice-filled water of the basin was abruptly replaced by grimy, dirt-tracked shipyard snow.

The tug was soon towing them over a pair of glowing rails, the kind Brim had followed on his arrival at the base. And Gimmas-Haefdon had meanwhile transformed itself into a disjointed parade of weathered buildings, suddenly looming gantries, and dismantled starships, which appeared and faded in the grayness as the destroyer glided backward in the swirling mists. Here and there, they saw trackside parties of grinning, heavily bundled workmen who alternately held their ears and waved as the ships rumbled past, cheering soundlessly outside the destroyer's bridge.

Finally, *Truculent* jolted to a stop on a pool surrounded by a forest of towering cranes and dozens of new umbilicals to sustain the ship's logic systems while her main power supply was shunted elsewhere for diagnostics.

Ursis no sooner shut down the center generator than a monstrous brow gently latched aboard, and presently the bridge filled with a rowdy gaggle of rough-hewn shipyard engineers and technicians.

"I shall offer my farewell here, Wilf Ansor," Ursis said gravely. "I would remain, but I am sure you understand one takes leave when he can." He solemnly raised a long finger. "'Dark snow and thrice-frozen lamps beckon old Bears and cubs alike to caves in the Great Vastness', as the saying goes," he observed.

Brim smiled and put his hand on the Bear's shoulder. "I think I understand, Nik," he said. "And thanks for the thought."

Ursis bowed formally. "Besides," he said, "Borodov and I have a..." he frowned, "feeling, shall we say, that you will not lack for companionship—if last night is indication."

"Last night?"

The Bear merely laughed as he peered through the Hyperscreens, then nodded toward the breakwater where an elegant chauffeur-driven skimmer had drawn up opposite the gate. "Last night," he pronounced, grinning now. "We shall talk again, eh?" He clapped Brim on his arm. "Enjoy Princess Effer'wyck, my good friend. She is known among Bears as a fine young woman, in spite of her royal blood." Then he was gone. Brim watched him stride across the brow toward the waiting skimmer, six great traveling cases bobbing along in his wake.

Soon after Borodov's massive skimmer disappeared into a new snowstorm, *Truculent's* bridge became a confused mass of incomprehensible voices and engineering babble until Brim could stand it no more and escaped to the relative tranquillity of his cabin. While these crews were on the job, *Truculent*, or at least the *Truculent* he knew, would cease to exist.

With little to occupy his normally busy mind, his thoughts returned quickly to Margot—and the promise he had made her. He frowned. Well, why not? He reached for the Communicator, then shook his head, suddenly unsure of himself. Wardroom parties were one thing, but right now, he didn't even have the prospect of a wardroom, much less another party. What would he say to her? One didn't just invite someone to visit a gravity pool! And he knew nothing about the rest of Haefdon—or how to entertain a full-blooded princess.

He laughed. He didn't have to know anything about either, for

Margot Effer'wyck did. She'd been around the bloody base for years now! Screwing up his courage once more, he activated the COMM and talked his way into the Threat Assessment Division (Universe, but they were secure!). At some length, her face appeared in the display.

"Wilf," she said, brushing aside a stray curl. "How nice. I hoped I'd hear from you."

The warmth of her smile managed to calm him before her physical beauty made a gawking schoolboy of him again. He laughed. "I hoped you'd hope," he quipped. "Now, all I have to do is find something to say next."

Margot grinned. "Hmm," she said. "Perhaps I can help. What was it you had in mind?"

"Actually," Brim answered, "I had you in mind."

"Well," Margot said with a look of mock thoughtfulness, "you have come to the right person, then."

"I thought so," Brim said. "Perhaps, then, you can tell me how I might suggest another evening together."

Margot smiled again, her heavy-lidded eyes alive with warmth and humor. "That's not difficult," she said. "You could ask me to supper; I'm quite available for something like that." She winked. "Including tonight."

Brim felt his heart skip a beat.

"Universe," he stammered, "I'd love that, b-but I have no idea where."

"I see," Margot said in mock seriousness. "Well, were such an invitation tendered, I should be glad to take care of the other details— including transportation."

Brim laughed. "I was going to cross the transportation bridge when I got to it," he admitted.

"Gets cold around here for a lot of walking," Margot asserted. "But, then, I haven't been invited anywhere, either."

"You did say tonight, didn't you?" Brim asked, hardly willing to believe his ears.

"Well, I am free."

"Would you..."

"Wilf, I swear I thought you'd never ask."

"Universe."

"Pick you up right after the third watch. Does that sound all right?" she asked.

"Rebuild pool 581," Brim answered, regaining some control of himself.

"I know," she said. "Bring an appetite." Then she was gone.

Grinning to himself, Brim shook his head happily. Whatever else she might turn out to be, Margot Effer'wyck was also a whole new set of rules. He looked forward to learning as many as he could.

***

By precisely the end of the third watch, Brim had carefully picked his way over the icy surface of the repair pool's monster brow and now stood impatiently on a platform before the main gate. Light snow was falling, and for the first time he could recall, the wind was still. Even Gimmas-Haefdon had its peaceful moments—but not many.

Margot arrived only slightly late; Brim was checking his timepiece for the ten-thousandth time when headlights glowed softly down the road. Moments later, her well-used little skimmer was hovering at the platform.

"Hungry?" she asked when he settled into the seat beside her.

He nodded. With the hood of her cape back over her shoulders, she looked tired, relaxed, and ravishing. Brim felt his breath quicken. "Where are you taking me?" he asked in mock-frightened innocence.

She looked his way for a moment. "A favorite place of mine," she answered. "I think you'll like it, too—and it's not very far, either." They were soon off the main highway and climbing a gentle grade over what Brim guessed was once a country road, now buried irals deep in Gimmas-Haefdon's everlasting snow. On either side, tall, tangled forms of ancient trees wound themselves into a sinuous wall of bare branches draped by garlands of snow: Mute reminders of summers now lost forever as the dimming star Gimmas continued its long march toward ultimate death. Ahead, at the summit, soft lights shone in glittering circles through the gentle snowfall.

"It must have been beautiful once," Brim pronounced, looking out at the dark landscape.

"It still has its beauty, Wilf," she said quietly. "You've got to look for

113

it, though." She smiled. "'Spirit who sweepest the wild Harp of time!/ It is most hard, with an untroubled ear/Thy dark inwoven harmonies to hear!'" They glided through an ornate metal gate set in a high stone arch; a huge lantern at its center illuminated the swept cobblestones of a spacious courtyard. She brought the skimmer to a halt before an age-blackened stone building with a great vaulted entrance whose dark wooden doors were covered by intricate carvings. Over these, a ponderous sign hung from stout chains below an age-bleached yardarm set into the stone. MERMAID TAVERN, it read, ESTABLISHED 51690, nearly three hundred of Haefdon's long years in the past.

"Universe," Brim whispered in a hushed voice as he peered up at the snow-covered jumble of steep peaked roofs and tall stone chimneys. Huge wooden beams appeared everywhere, in every architectural capacity imaginable, each carved in bas-relief with shapes of strange animals and birds. Translucent first-floor windows glowed warmly in the darkness; here and there, a softer light emanated from the upper floors.

"Like it?" Margot asked, her voice soft in the stillness of the tiny passenger compartment.

Brim could only nod emotionally.

"Wait till you see the inside," she said, smiling.

Still shaking his head, Brim opened the door and stepped into cold air scented with the sharp spice of wood smoke. Snow tingling on his nose and cheeks, he held the opposite door while she stepped out, a long, shapely leg escaping from her slit skirt with a giddy flash of white. Brim felt himself blush as his breath caught in his throat. Then all too soon she was on her feet, Fleet cape wrapped demurely around her.

She smiled impishly. "Did that pass inspection?" she asked, eyes sparkling with good humor.

Brim felt his face flush anew, thanking Providence for the darkness. "I suppose I'm sorry I stared," he stammered in embarrassment. "I'd forgotten the uniform included anything like a dress gown." Then he chuckled. "And, yes," he admitted, "you certainly pass any inspection I'll ever give."

"In that case, I shall take it as a compliment," she said, wrinkling her nose and smiling. "I always did have great legs." Then she started for the entrance, Brim trailing in utter disarray.

He opened one of the huge wooden doors—it moved silently on massive hinges so perfectly balanced he thought for a moment it might be servo-activated. Then he smiled to himself as he helped her over the high stone stoop. No automatics here. In a place like the Mermaid Tavern, servomechanisms would be an intrusion.

Inside, with the doors closed, the spicy odor of burning wood was much stronger, an impossible luxury here on Haefdon, where the last tree must have died hundreds of years in the past. They were standing in a dark room with a low, beamed ceiling and rough-textured walls decorated with ancient landscapes mounted in massive frames. Flickering candelabra softly illuminated stout wooden furniture, richly patterned carpets, and a gleaming stone floor. Liveried domestics in long, ornate coats with oversized golden cuffs and collars materialized from nowhere and quietly helped them from their Fleet capes, then disappeared into one of many doorways leading from the room in all directions.

"Good evening, Princess Effer'wyck, Lieutenant Brim," a voice said softly from beside a high wooden desk half hidden in the darkness. "We are most gratified you have chosen the Mermaid Tavern." Brim frowned as he turned to face the speaker.

Like the domestics of his employ, the steward of the Mermaid Tavern wore a long red coat with oversized cuffs and collar. There, however, resemblance ended. If by no other means, he was utterly distinguished by an explosion of curly white hair that reached all the way to his shoulders. A veritable landslide of ruffled lace separated lavishly embroidered lapels, and his silken breeches were white as his hair. Huge golden buckles decorated his gleaming shoes. He spoke with the guarded, inexpressive mien of those used to dealing with wealth and power—no trace of subservience, only a practiced grace and an unerring precognition of what people expected.

Brim nodded silently when the man offered his arm to Margot. The place made him remotely uncomfortable, though he couldn't pinpoint the reason why. He had the feeling it had more to do with his Carescrian background than anything else.

He followed them through another of the many doors into a second candle-lighted room with a low ceiling and exquisitely carved beams.

Bill Baldwin

The tables were placed on islands of rich-looking carpet where shadowed couples sat close by each other in the soft warmth; here and there, he glimpsed badges of unimaginable rank. Eight formal musicians in black ruffles played quietly from a raised dais in the center of the room. They made a sound of such exquisite elegance Brim was reminded of his visits to Collingswood's cabin. Perhaps the same music or composer? He listened, enraptured. Another kind of poetry, he guessed. It would bear study someday—if he survived the war.

The shadow of Valentin's face suddenly intruded in his mind, and his skin prickled with remembered agony. He ground his teeth. Before he might involve himself in anything so beautiful as music, he would first have to deal with that evil zukeed and a lot more like him. Then he grimaced to himself and forced the anger from his mind. Tonight...Tonight, there was Margot. And he didn't intend to share her with anyone in any way—especially thraggling Leaguers!

The quiet music blended with the murmur of intimate conversation and the gentle, ringing assonance of goblets. At the far end of the room, huge glowing logs blazed in a high stone fireplace. Delicate odors of spice and rich perfume blended with the smooth effervescence of meem, hogge'poa, and burning wood, the whole muzzy atmosphere creating an aura of absolute luxury Brim found difficult to believe.

The steward assisted Margot into a high-backed chair at a table close to the warmth of the fireplace—the other was placed so the table's occupants were compelled to sit together facing the fire. Somehow, the whole arrangement gave an illusion of privacy. Once they were seated, it was almost as if they occupied a warm, spice-laden room all their own. In the softly flickering firelight, Margot's lovely oval face seemed even more beautiful than ever, her moist red lips and sleepy eyes more desirable than any he could remember, or imagine.

"You're quiet, Wilf," she said with her smiling frown. "Is there something wrong?"

"No," Brim answered bemusedly. "Nothing's wrong at all. It's more like nothing has ever been quite so right."

"That's good," she said, closing her eyes and leaning back in her chair. "It's awfully nice for me, too." She smiled. "'All precious things discover'd late,/To those who seek them issue forth'."

116

Brim nodded. "'For life in sequel works with fate,/And flings the veil from hidden worth:' Latmos the Elder always did write your kind of verse, you know," he added.

Margot kissed her fingertips in admiration. "My kind?" she asked.

"Well," Brim said, "so much of you as I know."

She blushed. "I'm terribly honored," she said.

"You should be," he commented, watching a domestic serve from a dust-covered bottle of Logish meem. "He wrote for no one else but you—and did so more than five hundred years before you were born. Makes you quite special, you know."

She laughed. "You're pretty special yourself, Lieutenant Brim. And you don't even need Latmos."

"Me?"

"You," Margot affirmed. She frowned. "You know, Wilf, I haven't heard a word from you about what you really went through out there, only the technical detail." She raised her eyebrows and moved her face close to his. "Anybody else would still be crowing about how brave he was."

Brim snorted. "Nothing much to brag about," he said. "They beat me up some, and we lost the merchantman we went after in the first place."

"You did have something to do with stopping the corvette, though."

"Well," Brim admitted with an embarrassed chuckle. "Yes, I suppose I did. But anyone could probably have done the same. The brave ones were Ursis and Barbousse; they started the commotion that let me get away."

She laughed—a wonderful, honest laugh Brim wished he could somehow keep going for the rest of his life. "Wilf Brim," she declared, "you are impossible. Nothing to it, eh?"

Now it was Brim's turn to laugh. "Well," he said, "I had to let one of them shoot me, if I remember correctly."

Her face was suddenly serious, and she brought her face close to his again. "That's what I mean," she said. "You are special. Do you have any idea how many people wear the Fleet uniform—call themselves Blue Capes—and never even hear a shot fired. People like me, Wilf."

"Wait a cycle," Brim protested suddenly. "Getting shot at or not getting shot at has little to do with much of anything. It just turns out that I fly starships pretty well. And people naturally shoot at starships—big targets." He shrugged, looking her in her sleepy eyes. "If I could do something else better, they'd probably have me doing that."

Margot sighed. "I stand by my words, Mr. Brim," she said. "You are impossible." She smiled sleepily, her face soft in the firelight. "Given sufficient impossible people, we might even win this awful war."

Later, they dined sumptuously on food Brim recently thought he would never live to savor again. And they talked—about starships, the war, poetry, and love. But as the evening passed, they settled more on matters of love. For a while, Margot drew him out, listening to his words with a faraway look in her eyes. Later, she spoke of her own first lover. "I was terribly fortunate," she told him, her eyes focused across unbridgeable gulfs of space and time. "He had so much love to give. So gentle..."

Brim felt a thickness in his throat. He knew he would carry her words to the end of his days—and an irrational jealousy he would never manage to overcome. Without thinking, he took her hand, then panicked when he realized what he had done. To his surprise, she responded with her own hand, then looked silently into his eyes.

It was suddenly difficult to breathe in the tropical wash of her perfume. She was speaking as she squeezed his hand. She had a confused look in her sleepy eyes. "I hardly know you, Wilf," she was saying hesitantly. "What's the matter with me?" Then she closed her eyes and shook her head—but kept her tight grip on his hand. In a moment, she seemed to regain herself and took a deep breath. "Hello, Lieutenant Brim," she said huskily as she opened her eyes.

"Hello," Brim answered. He took her other hand, oblivious to anyone else in the room, then abruptly threw caution to the winds. "I noticed they have rooms upstairs," he said. "Should people find themselves, ah..."

"O-Overcome...." she stammered.

"Yes. By, ah, whatever," Brim finished.

She laughed suddenly. "'Whatever'," she repeated. "I hate that terrible word, Wilf. My mother used it when she wanted to avoid me." She drained her goblet. "And, yes," she said, bringing her face close to his. "They do have rooms upstairs." Then she looked at her hands as if she were afraid to say the rest.

Brim never wanted anyone the way he wanted Margot Effer'wyck now, ever in his life. He squeezed her hand, took a firm grip on his fast-eroding emotions. "Th-Then..." he stammered shakily, "then, would you...?" Before he could finish, he was stopped in midsentence by a hand on his shoulder, and taken completely by surprise, he turned in the seat, heart pounding, to confront the tavern's white-haired steward.

"A thousand pardons, Lieutenant Brim," the man whispered. "Your transponder."

"Sweet thraggling Universe," Brim swore fiercely under his breath. The thrice-xaxtdamned personal transponder he'd swallowed! He closed his eyes in total and absolute defeat. "Very well," he said with resignation. "Let's have the bad news."

The steward handed him a tiny message packet, which he authenticated with a fingerprint and placed in his ear.

"You are summoned immediately to I.F.S. *Prosperous*," it said, "at emergency priority. Your kit is already packed and delivered from *Truculent*."

"I deeply regret the intrusion, Princess Effer'wyck," the steward said as he turned to leave. "We had no choice."

"I understand," Margot answered with a wry look. Then she turned to Brim. "What?" she asked.

"I.F.S. *Prosperous*," Brim whispered. "I've been summoned."

With an incredulous look in her eyes, Margot suddenly dissolved into giggles. "A transponder?" she asked incredulously. "You really swallowed one of those things, didn't you?"

"Yeah," Brim admitted, cheeks burning from sudden embarrassment.

"Oh, Wilf," she exclaimed. "Didn't anybody tell you?"

"No," he admitted. "I haven't been around long enough to learn much of anything that's not in a textbook."

She shook her head. "Well," she said, "you've just had lesson one." She smiled sadly. "There's no getting out of emergency priority. At least none I know." She squeezed his hand for a moment more, then gently withdrew. "I can probably save you a few steps in my skimmer. We Assessment types get cleared for all sorts of strange places."

They were on their way back down the tree-lined road in a matter of cycles.

No sooner had Margot swung onto the causeway than the Mermaid Tavern, the fire, everything but the woman herself quickly faded to an aura of unreality. Even with shared expenses, he'd never before spent so much for a single meal, nor been in a position where he could. He had no illusions about why everything had gone so well. The name Effer'wyck was well known—often feared, he understood—all over the galaxy and beyond. But she'd never mentioned it. He smiled to himself. This beautiful young woman had no need to try to impress anyone; she simply did.

The wind had picked up considerably since the third watch, and she drove skillfully in the gusts, picking her way among rapidly forming snowdrifts. Now, it was she who was strangely silent when they quit the main thoroughfare, this time for a side road crowded with heavily-loaded vehicles of all kinds. She drew to a stop before one of a dozen heavily-guarded sentry booths and offered her ID card. It flashed an unusual color passing through their reader (which it did, Brim noticed, with singular ease). "I'm delivering Lieutenant Brim," she said simply as she handed his card through the window after her own. Both were returned with a half-heard, "Thank you, Princess," then they were waved through into the milling confusion of the loading complex.

"It's been a wonderful evening, Margot," Brim said lamely as she drove carefully through the crowded system of ramps leading to the 'midships brow. Beyond, a mammoth liner floated on a gravity pool of truly heroic proportions—easily five or six times the size of those in the Eorean starwharves. The Fleet's ebony hullmetal could by no means hide her thoroughbred lines. She was *Prosperous*, all right. More than 950 graceful irals of blue riband starliner, with speed and power in her gigantic hull to outrun all but the fastest warships.

Margot stopped the skimmer short of the orderly mob passing through the gate, then turned his way, face softly lighted by the instruments. Her heavy-lidded eyes were moist, and she had a serious appearance that Brim had never seen before.

"It was a wonderful evening, Wilf," she said. She blew her nose

120

softly on a lace handkerchief. "And I think I owe you an apology. I'm afraid I let things get way out of hand back there."

"We both did," Brim agreed. "But then, nothing really came of it, either."

"No," she said quietly. "But you don't understand."

"I don't want to understand anything," Brim asserted suddenly, surprised at the force of his own voice. "I want your lips, Margot-after that, we can reset and start over again. But I want a kiss from you more than anything else in the Universe."

Without a word, she was in his arms, her lips pushing eagerly against his, wet and open—and hungry. Her breath was sweet in his nostrils as she clung to him, big in his arms; an ample woman. Their teeth touched for an instant, and he opened his eyes; hers opened too, blurred out of focus before they gently closed again. He felt her tremble, then her grip suddenly loosened. She took a great gulp of air, and he released her.

They sat in panting silence for a moment, Brim's heart pounding all out of control.

"I th-think I'd better go right now, Wilf," Margot said in a shaken voice. "My 'reset' is going to be difficult enough as it is."

Opening the door of the skimmer to the noisy bustle and confusion outside, he nodded wordlessly and jumped to the snow, touching his fingers to his lips. She returned the salute as he gently pressed the door closed, then moved off in a cloud of snow and was quickly lost to sight in the throng of vehicles.

With an unaccountably heavy heart, Brim pushed his way through the crowd toward the guard shack where someone who looked very much like Utrillo Barbousse waited with a familiar battered traveling case.

"Barbousse?"

The huge Starman saluted as Brim stepped into the lighted area at the entrance to the brow. "Lieutenant Gallsworthy thought you might need some assistance, Lieutenant, Sir," he shouted above the noise of the big ship's generators. "An' I hadn't made plans for the layover, so I took the liberty of signing on the cruise with you." He handed Brim the side-action blaster. "It's the kind of mission you might be needin' this."

Brim shook his head and grinned with honest appreciation. He clapped the big Starman on the shoulder (which felt like Octillian shore granite). "Let's be on our way, then, Barbousse, my friend," he said. "It's becoming very clear I have an awful lot to learn about the Fleet—and everything else as well."

5 Swept along in the lines of soldiers
and military vehicles coursing up the wide lanes of the brow, Brim and
Barbousse caught only glimpses of the great starliner as she hovered
on her monster gravity pool. She seemed to stretch for c'lenyts on either
side, and lighted only by the weak glow from beneath, she still looked
splendid. Her forward deck tapered gently upward from a conoid bow
to a high, rakish superstructure surmounted by two enormous KA'PPA
beacons and a dwarfed control bridge, the latter providing the ship
with a nearsighted and, to some extent, surprised expression overall.
The remainder of the wide, shallow hull—at least three-quarters of her
overall length—appeared to be covered by cascading Hyperscreen
terraces, which gleamed brightly from within as the big ship loaded.

Below, streams of tarpaulin-covered cargo lumbered along under
the lights of at least a dozen cargo-level brows; Brim glimpsed giant
cargo tractors levitating a line of self-propelled disruptor cannon into
an access hatch deep in the hull. Enormous machines. A great turret
squatted on each flattened hull, ridiculously small for the apparent
weight it bore, and angular glassed-in driving cabins projected
awkwardly like afterthoughts from the forward port and aft starboard
corners. Inboard of these, massive cooling systems were ample proof of
the prodigious energy required to fire the thick, stubby disruptors that
protruded from the turrets.

"What do you make of those?" he asked Barbousse, nodding toward
the big vehicles crawling along below.

"Captured Leaguer field pieces, by the looks of 'em, Sir," the big rating answered. "I think 'e call 'em 'Nine-ks.'"

"No wonder they looked strange," Brim remarked. "Won't they be a surprise to a couple of Leaguers somewhere?"

Barbousse laughed as they crested the uphill portion of the brow. "Serve Triannic right to have those turned against him, Lieutenant. Nine-Ks are mean weapons, I've heard. Big, but exact for all their size. Use 'em for knockin' armored vehicles around, as I hear it. Like battle crawlers and things."

Suddenly the whole ship was spread before them. Brim shook his head in wonder, imagining how she might have appeared before the war, hullmetal in brilliant white and the legendary IGL logo shining ostentatiously on her bridge. "She must have been beautiful," he whispered, literally stunned by the immensity of the gigantic machine floating before him.

"Aye, Sir," Barbousse agreed beside him. "Another world all by herself, so they say."

"Not a Carescrian's world, you can bet," Brim said as they continued their journey down the other side of the brow toward the main aperture 'midships.

"Nor mine, Lieutenant," Barbousse said, then he chuckled. "But in the Fleet she belongs to all of us, in a manner of speakin'. War has a funny way of redistributing the wealth."

Even stripped of peacetime luxury, *Prosperous'* Grand Receiving Lobby was everything Brim expected—and more: A spacious pillared concourse with wide, arched corridors leading off in all directions to other parts of the ship. Tracks glowed everywhere in the deck, and they guided dozens of hooting trams piled high with military luggage pushing slowly through the noisy crowds. The air was alive with the smell of excitement, and everyone seemed to have somewhere important to go, although it was not at all clear any of them knew precisely where that somewhere might be located.

In the center of the lobby, a crew of harried-looking clericals toiled desperately within the perimeter of a huge circular desk, fielding questions, peering into half a hundred terminals, and generally assisting the mob of newcomers struggling into the ship. It was here Brim and

Barbousse found themselves separated, the latter assigned to a damage-control unit, Brim to Flight Operations.

"I'll keep an eye on you, Sir, just the same," Barbousse said, voice raised to be heard in the crowd. "When you want me, just ask any of the ratings." Then he was gone, pushing his way confidently toward one of the large companionways as if he had been assigned to the mammoth starship all his life.

Brim smiled as the big man disappeared in the crowd. *Prosperous* was a large ship, with a lot of strangers on board—a likely place for feeling lonely. He laughed to himself, before *Truculent*, he hadn't really thought that much about loneliness; he'd been simply used to it. Now...It was nice to have Barbousse around. Someone from home, so to speak.

"You'll want to check in with the Flight Ops," a bucktoothed rating with narrow eyes and a long nose said as she handed him back his identification. Her perfume suggested crushed ca'omba cookies, somehow. "Concourse 3, Fifth level, zone 75—catch the 16-E tram, Lieutenant..." She pointed vaguely across the room. "One comes by every few cycles during loading operations."

Brim nodded and started through the crowd, chuckling to himself. So far as he could remember, this would be one of his very first rides in a shipboard tram. All the really big ships had them, of course—even giant Carescrian ore carriers. The big difference was that presumably the ones on *Prosperous* worked!

***

"Oh, you're welcome on the bridge anytime, old boy," said a youngish-looking Operations lieutenant commander wearing prominent Ka'LoomKA signet rings (one of which displayed his name as C. A. Sandur). With a bulbous nose, pursed lips, and enormous gray eyes, his round face wore a perpetual look of pleased astonishment. "But probably you'll never touch a control," he added uncomfortably. "Pity they dragged you along at all. You're clearly dressed as if you had better plans for the evening."

"I did indeed, Commander," Brim answered, looking bleakly around the spacious cabin assigned to Flight Operations—everything was big on this ship. "I'm replacing someone suddenly ill, is that it?"

"That seems to be the drill," Sandur said.

"Just my luck," Brim grumped, thinking of a warm room in a warm tavern with a warm Margot. "All that trouble and now I've got nothing to do."

"The woman you are replacing had nothing to do, either, if it makes you feel any better," Sandur answered patiently. "She was just a temporary Helmsman like yourself. We always have full crews of IGL people to man this particular liner—same ones who fly her in peacetime. Like myself." He snorted humorlessly. "Yet the movers and shakers in your Admiralty think we need Fleet types to help us run our own equipment now they've got a war." He shook his head in good-natured frustration. "It's not as if we hadn't been piloting this elegant rustbucket for close to seven years now." Then he laughed amiably. "But that isn't your fault, is it, Brim? Any more than it is my fault you find yourself here. Is there anything I can do to make your stay more, ah...?"

"I'll say there is," Brim piped up. "Sir," he added hastily. "They called me out so quickly, nobody told me anything about the mission."

Sandur shook his head. "Oh, my," he said sympathetically. "They really did the job on you, didn't they, Brim?" He laughed. "Well, that seems about the very least I can do." He swept his Fleet Cloak from a nearby recliner and fastened it around his neck with an expensive-looking—and very nonstandard—collar clasp. "Why don't you follow me up to the bridge? We can observe the takeoff from there, and then I shall tell you what I know."

Less than a metacycle later, Brim watched Gimmas recede in the aft Hyperscreens from a large, but discouragingly normal-looking control bridge. He chuckled to himself, wondering why he'd expected anything special about *Prosperous*. Bridges were, after all, bridges—some larger than others, but in most aspects alike as so many shells on a beach. Another study in relativity, he decided while he settled down to his first details of the mission code-named Raid Prosperous.

As Sandur put things, the operation had been sorely needed for a long time now. A'zurn, a mild, lushly vegetated world on the edge of Galactic Sector 944-E, had been violently seized by Triannic at the outset of the war. The solitary planet of Brandon, the star that gave it sustenance, lay directly astride one of the principal trade routes leading to the League's most important starports. Location itself made the invasion one of military as well as economic necessity, at least the way the Leaguers saw things. To provide a modicum of propriety in which to wrap this outright rape of a blameless republic (and longtime ally of the Empire), Triannic immediately constructed a colossal research center within the capital city of Magalla'ana. Then he broadcast far and wide that the new facilities would be dedicated to beneficial purposes, i.e., ridding primitive worlds populated by avian beings of viral diseases that threatened their most promising life forms.

Of course, nobody believed a word—special weapons research is difficult to conceal anywhere. And the center was successful at its real work from the outset: so much so that its destruction soon became an obsession throughout the Home Galaxy, especially in the Empire. But the Leaguers stayed one step ahead in defenses. They cleverly used A'zurnian natives (a race of flighted humanoids) for on-site laborers and hostages—with the latter function much more vital than the first. While big, starship-mounted disruptors could easily wipe out the whole complex without even coming into orbit around A'zurn, they could not do so without slaughtering thousands of innocents imprisoned in a circle surrounding the target area. Only if the hostages could first be evacuated to safety could units of the Imperial Battle Fleet accomplish their mission. Essentially, the operation called for a swift ground foray to save the natives closely followed by heavy bombardment. Coordinating the diverse units necessary to field such an operation eventually led to Raid Prosperous, hosted by Imperial Fleet Operations and implemented as a joint effort by the tradition-steeped Imperial Avalonian Expeditionary Forces, units of the Nineteenth and Twenty-fifty Destroyer Flotillas, and His Majesty's Royal Transport Command, whose temporarily Blue-Caped IGL employees operated *Prosperous* in war as they did in peace.

During the last day out, Brim audited a series of briefings conducted by native A'zurnian officers. These onetime diplomats and military attaches had been stationed in Avalon at the outbreak of war and found themselves unable to return home before their dazed government capitulated to Triannic's massed invasion forces.

Even Carescrian children studied pictures of A'zurnians—everyone in the Universe did, it seemed. But Brim had not yet encountered one in real life. Close up, they were stunning. Men and women alike were tall, barrel-chested individuals who dressed in wonderfully old-fashioned regimentals: tight gray tunics with high crimson collars (elaborately embroidered), gold epaulets, dark knee breeches with crimson side stripes, and high, light-weight boots. The uniforms cast an odd but beguiling grandeur wherever they were worn.

From the front, A'zurnians were normal enough humanoids, resembling most all of the space-traveling sentients Brim had encountered so far. From the back, however, their wings—really a second, very specialized set of arms—set them apart from all the rest. Midway between the shoulders, their tunics opened to accommodate a down-covered, pillow-sized lump common to all adult A'zurnians known as a tensil. This protrusion (manifesting itself at puberty) covered an outgrowth of the reflexive nervous system that automatically coordinated the complex motions of feather and flesh necessary for flight. From each side of the tensil, great folded wings arched upward like golden cowls, trailing long flight feathers in alabaster cascades that reached all the way to the floor. Brim found himself awestruck.

The briefings themselves were well prepared and easy to understand. Careful lectures from a whole staff of experts gave Brim details of the landscape and climate, planetary transportation system, the Magalla'ana city layout (including the research center itself), and known effects of the League occupation.

This last subject was covered by a tall female with the huge eyes and large retinas of a born hunter—she instantly captured Brim's imagination. Her presentation, however, drove all thought of pleasantries from his mind, for she described an A'zurn that suffered mightily under Triannic's iron fist.

As she explained it, League soldiers intended no special malice toward their A'zurnian thralls, but the net effect was much the same as if they did. Triannic's military structures were specially designed to stifle independent thought of any kind. Pragmatic rules covered everything—including how conquered peoples were to be governed. So, when the fragile A'zurnians were subjected to the same general treatment that subdued a planet of sturdy warriors like the seven-iral giants of Coggl'KANs, their hollow bones and fragile wings literally tended to

128

crumple and shatter upon contact. Broken extremities were so common that fully a quarter of the A'zurnian population was known to have succumbed in the first two years of occupation alone. And if this were not enough, the feared black-suited Controllers (who were occasionally permitted independent thought) soon discovered it was much more convenient to imprison A'zurnians once their wings were snapped in half just below the elbow. Captives altered in such a fashion could then be impounded without the Leaguers' first having to construct sky barriers as well as walls. It wasn't so much cruelty that led the Controllers to devise such gross tortures—it was simple pragmatism coupled with a total absence of empathy.

When the briefing ended, a much-subdued Brim made straight for his stateroom and pondered the utter callousness of war. At that point, he would almost have joined the ground forces himself.

***

Less than a day later, the big liner arrived in high orbit over A'zurn. Below, on the surface, a small but well organized A'zurn underground was already well into a noisy, highly successful, uprising in the distant city of Klaa'Shee to draw League occupation troops away from Magalla'ana while Imperial land forces disembarked for operations on the surface. In the air, the Imperial Fleet held complete, if temporary, command of the skies. After six years of League occupation, the A'zurnians were so totally devastated that the Controllers had seen fit to reassign all but a few surveillance warships to other occupied planets where more active opposition to League ministrations made such equipment more in demand.

"I say, Brim," Sandur exclaimed, bursting onto the bridge where Brim idly watched a stream of shuttles ferry men and equipment toward the surface. "Someone claims they've actually got work for you down there. How does that sound?"

Brim laughed. Used to constant—grueling—activity on blockade duty, he was more than halfway desperate for something to at least occupy his mind. "Where do I sign up, Commander?" he asked immediately.

"Well," Sandur said, smiling and cocking his head, "you won't need to sign anything. Seems they've already saved that trouble and volunteered you."

Brim smiled. "How thoughtful, Sir," he chuckled. "What sort of work do they have in mind?"

Sandur frowned, managing somehow to look even more surprised than normal. "I don't know, Brim," he answered. "You're to receive your orders from an Army type once you've arrived: A Colonel Hagbut, I believe." He cleared his throat. "I suppose it could be dangerous."

Brim nodded with equanimity. "Boredom can be dangerous, too, Commander," he chuckled again. "I'll be packed in five cycles."

Sandur grinned. "That's the spirit," he said. "And you won't go alone, either. There's this absolute giant of a rating who insists he travel with you." He scratched his head. "Don't rightly know how he even found out about the whole thing—nor how he managed to get orders cut and signed by the ship's Captain himself. But he did. Said he'd wait for you in the shuttle, Brim. You *Truculents* stick together, don't you?"

Brim smiled. "Have to, Commander," he agreed. "It's a rough war out there."

"Isn't it," Sandur said soberly. "And getting more so all the time, as I am about to inform you." He squared his shoulders. "Seems Triannic's occupation forces got off every broadcast for help we predicted they would. Maybe even a few more. We were pretty accurate guessing those." He gazed thoughtfully out the Hyperscreens, drumming his fingers on a nearby console. "Unfortunately, we also predicted Triannic wouldn't be able to free up much equipment for a counterattack," he continued, "at least not before we finished most of our work." This time he ended with a grimace.

"You weren't so accurate there, Commander?" Brim asked.

"Not quite," Sandur answered.

"What went wrong, Sir?"

Sandur laughed. "Nothing actually went wrong, my young friend. We simply did not count on Admiral Kabul Anak and his battlecruiser squadron to be in quite such close proximity." He shook his head in disgust. "You've heard of him, of course."

"Once or twice," Brim growled, his little sister's face flashing painfully in his mind's eye. "And us with only destroyers..." He stared out into the starry blackness. "How long do we have, Commander?"

"Perhaps three Standard Days," Sandur said, frowning darkly. "Instead of the five Planning Ops allotted." He grimaced. "I thought I'd better let you know beforehand, because whatever you're going to accomplish down there, you'd better do it quickly. When we receive orders to move *Prosperous*, we'll move her, let me guarantee you that. This starship is more than just a fast transport; she's one of the biggest and fastest liners in the Universe, but she can't fight and she can't outrun a battle cruiser. So when those orders arrive, we'll pick up whomever and whatever we can on the way out—and we'll leave everything else here." He placed a hand on Brim's shoulder. "There's ample time to accomplish the destruction of the research network; that's important to the Admiralty, too. But once those objectives are accomplished, well, remember, Brim, after the raid, everything and everyone is expendable except *Prosperous* herself."

Later, the Carescrian hurried toward his cabin, chuckling in spite of storm clouds gathering in the back of his mind. He could distinctly remember the Commander's original warning that he might likely have nothing to do on this trip.

***

Barbousse arrived on A'zurn's surface armed to the teeth. He carried two heavy-looking meson pistols on his belt and a wickedly curved knife strapped to the top of his right boot, this latter in a splendid jeweled scabbard that glittered in the bright afternoon sunlight as he jumped to the ground from the shuttle. He surveyed the noisy, crowded landing field for only a moment, then pointed to a big L-181-type armored personnel carrier hovering nearby, its driver beckoning with a burly arm. "Transportation into town, Lieutenant," he announced while Brim adjusted the small knapsack attached to his battle suit.

The crowded roadway was not in the best of repair, but Magalla'ana itself was beautiful, though mysteriously bereft of all but a few winged inhabitants—at least from what little Brim could see through the side port of the L-181 as it lumbered along at high speed through equipment-crowded suburban streets. He fancied exploring every tree-shaded square and shaggy, moss-covered carved stone spire (all looked as if they had been in place since the Universe cooled). Here and there they passed side lanes lined by deserted-looking homes with upper-story doors and overgrown gardens of multicolored flowers in place of roofs. Then they rattled between two heroic obelisks and out across an ornate stone bridge spanning what appeared to be a major canal. Through intricate balustrades, Brim could see a great waterway fronted by palaces or at least important houses of state, each terraced with the remains of once-tended gardens, most gone wild with neglect. The burned-out wreck of a graceful watercraft rose gruesome from the center of the channel like a charred finger of warning. Brim grimaced as they drove through more deserted streets and lanes. Heroic efforts would truly be needed to restore this tiny paradise to its former tranquillity— beginning with the ouster of Nergol Triannic's jack-booted invaders.

In due time, the personnel carrier rumbled to a hovering stop before a stately portico of ten ornate pillars that fronted a circular stone building topped with a high, age-discolored dome. Carved two-story wooden doors provided street-level entrance through the weather-stained walls.

"You'll find the Colonel in there," Brim heard the driver shout to Barbousse over the noise of the traffic, "and may the Universe spare you both." He laughed, then Barbousse slammed the hatch shut and the L-181 lurched into the thundering flow of traffic amid an angry blare of warning clicks from the other vehicles. Deciding to ignore the overheard warning for a time, Brim silently led the way up a broad stone staircase toward the massive doors. Under the weather-stained portico, they proffered their orders to four white-gloved guards, then stepped inside under the dome where Barbousse audibly gasped with awe.

The whole structure enclosed one grand circular room lined in polished, flawlessly white stone. Elegant inlays divided the curving walls into four quadrants, and on each of these, great carved murals depicted heroic struggles between winged men dressed in ancient-looking body armor and tall, eight-legged creatures with lance-like fangs. Above these, the dome glowed from hundreds of circular doors set into its very plates, and a huge sword dangled perilously, point down, from a curious ornamentation at the very apex. The floor—a confusion of people swarming in all directions— was constructed from the same white stone as the walls and was arranged in three concentric circles, the inner two raised and surrounded by a strange carved-metal balustrade. Aisles ran straight from the mural-covered walls to a circular altar centered on the inner circle. This was presently occupied by a figure in the tan and red battle dress of the Imperial Army.

"D' you suppose that's Hagbut?" Brim asked with a shrug.

Barbousse grinned. "I'd bet on it, Lieutenant."

"I'll be back in a cycle or so, then," Brim said, and started up one of the aisles.

He was no more than a few irals past the first balustrade when he was intercepted by a pink-looking civilian administrator who looked very much out of place in his ill-fitting battle suit. "Your orders, Lieutenant," he demanded officiously.

Brim silently handed over his card for inspection; it was accepted as if it bore some shameful disease.

"You may approach the Colonel," the man said after a long pause, indicating the figure at the center of the room with a pained nod of his head.

Brim's eyes met Barbousse's for a moment; then he was on his way. As he climbed the second alabaster staircase, an ornate nameplate became visible on the surface of the desk. Self-powered and multicolored, the clearly expensive device flashed:

Colonel (the Hon.) Gastudgon Z' Hagbut
X^{ce}, N.B.E., Q.O.C., Imperial Expeditionary Forces
(Combat)

The mustachioed figure behind the nameplate was a small, intense-looking individual of middling years who spoke as though he disliked showing his teeth. His left collar wore distinctive crossed blast pikes, which identified him as a graduate of the prestigious Darkhurst Academy on Fortis-Darkhurst, a close neighbor of Avalon itself. Likewise, his clearly custom-tailored battle suit and mirror-like boots spoke of considerable wealth—wielded by a man to whom the act of commanding probably came as a natural inheritance. His red-veined face further revealed him as an officer of quick temper or little patience or (more probably) both. As Brim approached, the man's coarse gestures to a cowed-looking subordinate gave substance to Barbousse's earlier warning that the undersized field officer was known as a "cod'dlinger" (a uniquely Narkossian-91 reference to excretory organs of a local slops-yard scavenger). "I'll be sure to keep that in mind," he had assured his companion, "but I'm not sure I'll be able to do anything about it."

"YOU THERE!" the Colonel roared in a voice that sounded as if his mouth were open a great deal wider than it appeared. He motioned imperiously to Brim. "OVER HERE! ON THE DOUBLE!"

Brim ran the last few steps, then saluted (smartly, he hoped). "Lieutenant Wilf Brim, I.F, reporting as ordered, Colonel," he said, gazing up in awe of the huge sword dangling from the center of the dome.

"Certainly not a moment too soon," the Colonel rumbled irately. "Where have you been?" He sat back with a sour look on his pinched red face. "You Fleet types are so worthless," he observed at length, spitting noisily over the balustrade. "Well?"

Brim remained at attention. "What can I do for the Colonel?" he asked in a respectful voice, still staring at the sword.

"You mean you don't know?"

Brim swallowed his embarrassment, sure everyone in the room was laughing at him. "No, Sir," he said, looking the Colonel in the eye for the first time. "I don't."

"Universe," the Colonel sniffed, spitting over the balustrade again. "Well, I suppose I shall have to tell you, then—mind you, it won't be the first time I have covered for your organization's incompetence!"

Brim spied a wiry little sergeant standing on the second ring about ten irals behind the red-faced officer. The man winked and rolled his eyes toward the sky; it helped somehow.

"Here," the Colonel shouted, gesturing Brim's attention to a display globe that suddenly materialized over a portable COMM pack. It pictured the eight captured disruptors Brim had watched being loaded aboard *Prosperous*. They were now resting lifelessly on the ground. "You are to take command of those League field pieces," he snorted. "Lost all eight of my regular crews in a shuttle accident last night. Can't trust you Fleet types to get anything right, can I? At any rate, I know you've all been trained to fire a disruptor. It's probably all you can do."

Brim felt his jaw drop open. "Colonel," he stammered, "I'm a Helmsman; I have a lot to learn about operating League disruptors."

"Well, you'd better get busy and learn!" the Colonel bellowed, "because those eight vehicles were starlifted all the way from Gimmas-Haefdon especially to protect this mission from league armor. They were my idea—League vehicles will be nearly invisible to counterattacking forces looking for Imperial equipment. And all eight of those field pieces will move out precisely two metacycles from now. Understand?" He shot a pair of elegant battle cuffs, then raised his eyebrows as if he were reassuring a hopelessly dense child. "This is a brilliant innovation, and you will be proud to have been instrumental in its trial run."

Brim could only stare wide-eyed and silent in disbelief.

Hagbut frowned for a moment, stared closely into Brim's eyes, then grimaced. "You really don't know anything about the job we summoned you down here for, do you?"

"Yes, Sir," Brim assured him. "I do not."

Hagbut laughed aloud. "I'll bet those drafted IGL people never let you in on a xaxtdamned thing, did they?"

"They said I'd receive my orders from you, Colonel," Brim replied flatly.

Hagbut regarded him bleakly. "Wonderful," he muttered. "Just thraggling wonderful."

Brim held his tongue. There was nothing more he could say.

After a few moments in thought, Hagbut shrugged to himself and looked Brim directly in the eye. "Your xaxtdamned fleet stinks, Brim," he said with his upper lip raised. "You can't help it, and neither can I. But it does. Luckily, your uselessness probably won't mean a thing to me this time anyway. Since the A'zurnian underground staged their big show in Klaa'Shee a couple of days ago, those rotten Leaguers hardly have anybody left in the area at all—much less battle crawlers to fight the cannon you're here to drive. All you've got to do is follow along and keep your head down when there's fighting to be done." He drummed his fingers on the altar. "For you, the mission ought to be easy as falling off a cliff. You follow us to the research center in your cannon, wait out of the way while we free the hostages they've got penned up beside the main laboratory, then you call in your destroyers to blow the whole thing up once we're on our way back." He shook his head in disgust. "Do you think you can handle that much?"

"I shall certainly try," Brim answered.

"Well," Hagbut said bleakly, "at least you seem willing. It's better than nothing, I suppose. But not much." He gazed balefully across the altar, apparently lost for a time in some inner thought. "Probably," he continued presently, "the worst part of the trip will come when we get to the hostages themselves."

"I understand they've been pretty roughly treated."

"An understatement," Hagbut said with a grimace. "Those Controllers they use as guards aren't very nice people at all—I even dislike coming up against them in combat," he said. "Hard to go about the job professionally, without emotion, you know."

Brim felt his eyebrow raise. "Sir?"

"We Army officers usually go out planning to fight our opposite numbers in the League Army," Hagbut answered, "—like the guards they'll have at the outer gates to the compound. No emotion there. It's simply professional against professional; somebody wins and somebody loses. But what kind of person do you think they'll have guarding the inner gates to the hostage compound? Army types? Not on your life. They'll have Controllers. Bloody, black-suited Controllers. And when I come up against them, then the fighting gets bitter. Because those scum of the Universe deserve anything we do to them." Suddenly he stopped, looked at his shaking hand, and thrust his jaw in the air. "I don't know why I feel constrained to tell all this to you, Brim," he said. "This interview is at an end." He raised a pontifical finger. "As for your cannon, I shall direct you personally as to where and when I want them fired. It will save you from overtaxing what little of your gray matter remains operable in your head after a tour in the Fleet Academy." He looked down his nose. "Do you have any questions, Lieutenant?"

Brim stifled an urge to laugh in the man's face and nodded instead. "I do have one question, Colonel," he said.

"Well? Be quick about it."

"Who else do you have scheduled to crew those eight field pieces, Colonel?" he asked. "They sent only two of us down from *Prosperous*."

Hagbut laughed triumphantly. "I have already seen to that, Lieutenant," he boomed. "More than a metacycle ago, I deposited eight of your ordnance ratings with the disruptors to help do that." He spat again. "And since I knew they'd be worthless as any other Fleet type on land, I gave you fourteen equally worthless extras to assist." He frowned.

136

"Those last are a BATTLE COMM group, all worthless females, but they're at least warm bodies—I think." He guffawed without humor. "Now get moving. You've less than five metacycles to jump-start that blasted machinery into useful equipment, then get it operating." He turned back to the desk in a clear gesture of dismissal.

Brim saluted uselessly, then trudged back down the staircase to where Barbousse sat waiting, a black look on his brow.

"Cod'dlinger," the big rating glowered in a low voice. "If you please, Sir."

"I xaxtdamn well please," Brim grumped. "Come on. Let's see if we can find someone who knows where those mobile disruptors are. Maybe we can use one to run the bastard over once he's in the field— accidentally, of course."

"Of course, Sir," Barbousse chuckled darkly. "Accidentally, by all means."

Barbousse worked his magic rapidly in the old temple, and within a few cycles, he both discovered the location of the mobile disruptors and lined up another ride. Presently, the two *Truculents* found themselves deposited in a large urban park bordering dense groves of tall, gnarled trees. Nearby, the mobile disruptors sat disconsolately on their warty rounded bottoms, leaning drunkenly at odd angles like toys discarded by some titanic child. A row of twenty-two Blue Capes dangled their legs from one of the hulls, kicking their heels against the giant cooling fins beneath and talking excitedly.

Brim glanced at a flight of starships traveling so high he couldn't even make out what kind they were—but he could hear them. He suddenly felt homesick for *Truculent*. Truth to tell, he felt more than a little out of place here on the land; inadequate was more to the point. Then he laughed to himself. Fat lot he could do to change things anyway! He braced his shoulders and strode across the field. Might as well look confident, he thought, even though he didn't feel that way.

As he approached the field pieces, two of the ratings jumped from their perches and ran to meet him, saluting smartly.

"Leading Starman Fragonard here, Lieutenant," one announced importantly. "I've got seven ordnance men with me." He was short and rawboned, his hair was gray, and he seemed to be in motion standing still. His constantly darting green eyes were those of a master thief — or a master gunner. Right from the beginning, Brim suspected he was both. On his uniform, a number of gold and crimson ribbons presaged excellence in his specialty of Ordnance. Too bad nobody gave awards for mischief, Brim thought with a stifled smile. At least none were approved for wearing on a Fleet Cape!

Brim returned their salutes, then nodded toward the second StarSailor with a raised eyebrow.

"Yeoman of Signals Fronze reporting, Lieutenant," she said—a squat, heavyset woman with broad shoulders and neutral hair. Her flat, amorphous countenance served merely to highlight a coarse, open-pored complexion. Only flashing eyes and a winning smile saved her from total, unmitigated plainness. She was neither young nor old, but her large hands suggested long periods of manual toil long ago in another life. Both she and Fragonard would have been nearly invisible on a crowded metropolitan street in Avalon, but where Fragonard might well have made a diligent effort to achieve such an effect, for Fronze it would have been automatic. She indicated thirteen women of various sizes who jumped to the ground and saluted raggedly. "Two mobile KA'PPA beacons and the best BATTLE COMM in the Fleet," she added with a toothy grin.

Brim smiled back as his heart sank. BATTLE COMM people to drive League battle-crawler destroyers. Wonderful! He supposed somewhere nearby a squad of qualified drivers were probably attempting to fathom the arcane operation of a KA'PPA beacon. "Ordnance and Communications," he said lamely. "Well, I'm, ah, certainly glad to have you...aboard. I don't suppose anyone knows anything about starting one of these mechanical marvels, does he—or she?"

"Us?" Fragonard asked incredulously, holding a slender (and reasonably clean) hand to his chest. "Lieutenant," he said, "we ordinance types only fire the disruptors, we don't do nothin' like drivin'." He stopped suddenly as the rumble of heavy artillery intruded from a distance.

Barbousse stepped quietly to the side of the rawboned little man and plucked him from his feet by the scruff of the collar, smiling pleasantly all the while. "You," he said gently over the far-off booming, "are, of course, volunteering yourself and all seven of your men for whatever duties the Lieutenant suggests. Is that correct, Starman Fragonard?"

Fragonard's eyes bulged, became large as saucers. He tried to swallow something much larger than his throat, but the latter was constricted by the peculiar way his collar was twisted within Barbousse's huge fist. "Of course," he choked.

"M-My s-signal ratings, too," Fronze piped up hurriedly. "Always glad to help out anywhere we can."

Barbousse nodded silently, returning Fragonard none too gently to his feet. "My apologies for the interruption, Lieutenant," he said, regaining his position behind Brim.

"Er, yes," Brim mumbled, struggling to stifle a smile. He looked over the heads of the assembled Blue Capes to the huge machines lying cold and silent in a forlorn pile of—unless he could start them—space junk. He counted heads for a moment, frowned, and scratched his head, listening to renewed artillery fire in the distance. "All right," he said to the two ratings, "we've got eight of these monsters to operate. That means teams of three each. Count off your people, Fronze: Two in a control cab. One of yours in each turret, Fragonard. Understand?"

"Aye, Sir," Fragonard answered, his face a picture of concentration, "but twenty-two people only crews seven of those big thumpers."

Brim nodded his head. "That's right," he said. "Barbousse and I crew the eighth. And you run the turret for us. Does that fit with your previous views on the proper division of labor?"

Fragonard peered at Barbousse for only a moment, then he nodded. "Absolutely, Lieutenant," he said, grinning. "Besides, I'm a very good gunner—and a very bad wrestler."

***

Brim sat uncomfortably upright in the cold, stiff-backed control seat, a dark instrument panel staring balefully at him in the afternoon glare. The distant artillery duels had recessed for a moment, birds sang in the background, and heavy vehicles rumbled somewhere on a crowded highway. His mind drifted to Ursis and Borodov—most likely off at a hunting dacha on one of the Sodeskayan planets, happily drinking Logish meem and hunting the great, two-headed mountain wolves which shared, and ravaged, many areas of the Bears' home worlds. Bears would know how to start this hulking bucket of bolts!

He shook his head enviously as another flight of distant starships thundered across the sky at the edge of space. Little more than a metacycle remained before his own part of the operation was expected to move out. And the thrice-xaxtdamned field piece that fell to his lot to drive was canted at a perfectly sickening angle to the horizon. It made him dizzy every time he looked outside. Drumming his fingers on the console, he gazed in helpless disgust at the bewildering array of controls.

For the hundredth time, he considered the large red button that occupied a prominent place on his lower starboard instrument quadrant. Its center ring displayed the Vertrucht symbol for BEGIN, but Brim was not about to blow himself to atoms by that sort of simpleminded error. In the League's crazy vocabulary, the word DETONATE started with the same symbol. He grumpily looked outside at the other seven inert forms, also canted at uncomfortable angles. In the last, precious forty-five cycles, he had managed to accomplish nothing, and now spare time was virtually gone, along with his options. He shrugged to himself, squeezed his eyes closed, gritted his teeth, and mashed the button, waiting anxiously for the explosion that would snuff out his life.

Instead, he was greeted by bird-punctuated silence, broken now and then by heavy breathing—his and that of his two compatriots.

Cautiously opening his eyes, he found himself confronted by nothing more threatening than all the lights on the vehicle blazing out as if it were the blackest darkness outside. That and a newly-operational instrument panel. Moreover, one of its readouts, C_{L-2} intensity (all C_{L-2} readouts looked more or less the same), was already starting to rise. He watched it for a few cycles, then smiled. Normal. Even at its present rate, he estimated it would take about fifteen cycles to reach operating parameters.

He showed the button to Barbousse and Fragonard, then sent them out to help power up the other machines. "By the time you get back," he called down the ladder after them, "maybe I'll have the next step figured out."

As he expected, the remaining controls and readouts were all more or less incomprehensible, except for a big pulse limiter; anybody could recognize one of those. And to its left, a primitive linear slide control was mounted in the panel. It looked a lot like an adjustable thrust sink—

a common, cost-conscious substitute for antigravity brakes on many large military vehicles built for the League. The slide itself was pushed all the way to the top of its slot, where the highest index numbers were. An ON position, probably, but he couldn't be sure, so he kept hands off while he studied further.

He frowned. Most heavy ground equipment operated by ducting energy from a pulse limiter into a gravity-defraction transmitter. The latter acted as a simplified antigravity generator, providing lift and directional thrust through a simple logic-lens arrangement. It couldn't fly, of course, any more than a traveling case could fly. Antigravity technology guaranteed no more than vectored thrust. To actually fly, one needed a lot more major systems than one could economically cram into a ground vehicle.

Grimacing, Brim pondered the correct amount of energy to gate from the pulse limiter: How much C_{L-2} was good? Or bad? It was still building steadily, according to the readout in front of him—but to what? He considered the possibility he had just sent Barbousse and Fragonard on a mission to blow up the other seven vehicles in his tenuous command, then shook his head. If that was the way things were going to turn out, then so be it! He had to start somewhere. He returned his concentration to the controls.

Ah! There, low in the left-hand quadrant of the center console, his eye caught a primitive sort of phase converter: Regulating mechanism for just about every pulse limiter he'd ever seen. Of course, the ones in his experience were also installed on heavy mining equipment, and never set at more than half conductance. This one indicated at least a full three-quarters, even a little more. He grimaced. He knew he could fine-tune the device by thumbing a notched wheel under its mounting, but if he set the converter too high, it could severely spike the defraction transmitter when that device came on line, and then he'd never get it started. He could also get a runaway power plant, he remembered with a shudder, and decided to leave everything set as it was for the time being.

He narrowed his eyes. To the left of the converter, he recognized a strange-looking resonance-choke readout, which indicated a pulse average of zero. Probably all right, as he recalled; these units ran with really low pulse pressure. But if the reading slid into negative values, he knew he would have to consider dumping the C_{L-2} pressure to start all over again—and he didn't have time for anything like that. Then he noticed the choke was switched to OFF. That explained zero pressure at the readout, but didn't do much to relieve his growing sense of apprehension.

"Lieutenant," a voice called out, breaking into his concentration, "we've got 'em all running now."

Brim looked up to see Fragonard's face peek over the door coming from the boarding ladder. He checked the other seven machines; each was blazing with unnecessary lights. Happily, nothing untoward seemed to have resulted from punching the big red power buttons. "No problems?" he asked.

"None, Sir," Fragonard declared.

"Good," Brim said offhandedly, "because the next thing you'll have to do is teach those same people how to run them."

"How to run 'em, Sir?"

"Not to worry, Fragonard," Brim chuckled darkly. "It isn't clear I shall ever discover anything to tell you about the subject."

"Sir?"

"Nothing," Brim said as he got up to stretch. "But you'd better get our friend Barbousse up here with us. We'll all three of us see if we can't learn how this fool thing operates—together."

"Aye, Sir," Fragonard said, scrambling back down the ladder. He presently returned with Barbousse in tow, and the two were soon breathing over Brim's shoulder, watching every move.

As he scanned the readouts, Brim brought himself up short, peering at the resonance chokes in utter disbelief. The thrice-xaxtdamned zero reading! He snapped his fingers in angry comprehension. Somewhere in the system, a heavy-duty demodulator kept the whole radiation mechanism safe. And chances were that if the resonance choke was off, so was that demodulator! He felt sweat beading on his forehead. The whole subsystem might already be far beyond the limits of safety. He frantically scanned his readouts searching for...There! He breathed a sigh of relief. He found it, and it was ON.

He glanced nervously at the C_{L-2} intensity. Universe! Now that was all the way up to fourteen hundred. He ground his teeth, doing a desperate conversion from milli-ROGEN to something he could work with. Then he shook his head and relaxed. Certainly. Fourteen hundred milli-ROGEN was all right in this sort of system (it had no local storage capacity). In fact, the reading was just a hair under normal.

Getting a firmer grip on himself, he watched the C_{L-2} climb into the operational range, then switched the choke to ON and squinted tensely at the readout. It was just beginning to register. Presently, a great plume of vapor sighed from the cooling mechanism behind the cabin and the gravity-defraction transmitter came on line. The big vehicle automatically righted, lifting smoothly to about eight irals above the ground, where it hovered quietly, at last on an even keel.

"That's the way, Lieutenant!" Barbousse cheered in an awestruck voice.

Brim could hear more cheering from the ground. He leaned his head against the chair's high back for a moment and took a deep breath. He really *had* started the xaxtdamned thing. "All right, Barbousse, Fragonard," he said. "You were both watching. Think you can show the others how to do that?"

"Yes, Sir, Lieutenant," Barbousse declared immediately.

"I think I could, too," Fragonard said after frowning once more at the control panel.

"You only think you could?" Brim asked pointedly.

"No, Sir," Fragonard declared with a grin. "I could."

"That's better," Brim said, grinning at the two ratings. "Get hopping, then, both of you. You've seven more to fire up while I try to get this oversized ore hauler moving next." Walking to the hatch, he listened to the deep, steady growl coming through the logic lenses from the gravity-refraction transmitter, then peered down at the small crowd of ratings gathered below. "Stand clear, down there," he yelled, then made his way back to the front of the cab and took his seat at the controls.

Buckling himself firmly to the seat, he looked at the pulse limiter and shook his head. Its setting of three-quarters conductance was simply too high. The thumb wheel, however, was mounted in an incredibly awkward place, and he found himself hard pressed to move it. Eventually, he prevailed (with a few skinned knuckles) and changed the reading to fifty percent. Next he gingerly reached out and opened the phase converter itself, gating raw energy into the pulse limiter. The machine sounds behind him changed subtly, becoming deeper and more damped as he listened. He bit his lip nervously, considering everything he had done. So far, it all checked: C_{L-2} intensity normal (a little on the high side, but not enough to worry about), phase converter at OPEN and set to approximately fifty percent, cooling on, gyros lighted, hull trimmed level. He checked the ground in front of him. It was clear. His previous audience of spectators had mostly disappeared, but here and there he caught a face peering out from behind the protection of a tree or a large rock.

He laughed. He certainly couldn't blame anybody for that! Shrugging, he acknowledged the vehicle was as ready as he could make it, and retarded the pulse limiter. The sounds in the power compartment increased precipitately, and the big machine began to vibrate. But nothing else happened.

Brim frowned, opening the pulse limiter still farther. Now a great, discordant roar came from the shuddering traction machinery, but he was moving, albeit in palsied jerks and hops. Trouble was, the movement was nowhere near what it ought to be, considering the tremendous power he was gating to the deflection transmitter. He opened the pulse limiter a little farther still, and his forward progress did improve, but the increased speed was accompanied by intolerable levels of roaring from the traction machinery plus an alarming cycle of repetitive shuddering now coming from beneath his feet. Outside, the few stragglers who persisted in watching the big vehicle move were running panic-stricken for the nearest shelter. Behind him, a huge cloud of steam was blasting from the cooling unit as brightly glowing fins stripped vapor from A'zurn's moist air. The cabin air was blue with the acrid smell of red-hot metal.

Suddenly, he pounded his fist on the instrument panel. The thrust sink! That's what was doing it. On its highest setting, it was recycling all the energy back to the coolers. No wonder the traction machinery was tearing itself to pieces. He grabbed at the slide, then bit his lip. "Easy, Brim!" he yelled as he moved it gently to the center of its slot.

The rasping noise faded immediately, although the cooling system continued to race. Brim suspected it would continue to do that for quite awhile to come.

The big field piece was picking up speed smartly now. Tentatively, he pushed the left rudder pedal. The vehicle lumbered off clumsily in that direction but steered well enough to provide at least a modicum of control. It wasn't built for much manual steering anyway—only enough to maneuver to and from the ubiquitous cableways installed wherever the League held sway. Near anyone of these, automatic devices in the hull of the field piece could take over and "follow the wire," as the expression went. Typical, he considered, of a civilization that discouraged any sort of freethinking outside a small ruling class. He could see the thick cable he would soon follow himself disappear around the trees at the far end of the field.

Those trees! For some reason, he was still picking up speed—a lot of it. Already he was running a great deal faster than he should if he were to negotiate a turnaround. He had to stop the big machine. And soon!

Frantically, he smashed the thrust-sink slide back to the top of its slot; the rasping noise resumed immediately, along with the shuddering, which quickly turned into a bone-jarring series of grinding jolts. Everything loose in the control cabin cascaded to the deck, where it added its own distinctive clatter to the rattling of every plate in the hull.

And that hadn't stopped it! If anything, he was moving even faster toward the trees, which now looked like a green wall of solid stone. What had gone wrong?

In something closely related to panic, Brim suddenly realized his latest mistake: The thumb wheel on the phase converter. It was supposed to retard energy flow instead of increase it, so when he'd changed the setting from three-quarters (retardation!) to one-half, he'd actually doubled the device's output. No wonder the thrust sink wouldn't do its job! In horror, he visualized the big machine smashing itself farther and farther into the thick forest ahead until one of the trees was simply too big. He shuddered. In sudden desperation, he awkwardly jammed his fingers onto the little wheel and painfully moved it back close to its original position.

Immediately, his speed began to drop, along with the shuddering rasp from aft—but far too late to do much about the trees. With a shattering crash, the big machine plowed through the edge of the forest, snapping tree trunks like twigs and throwing splintered logs a hundred irals in the air. The cab ricocheted back and forth like a starship caught in the great-grandfather of all space holes as he stood on the port rudder pedal. Ahead, through the armored glass, he watched a monster tree that seemed to have deliberately moved in his way. This was it! He braced himself for the crash just as the runaway vehicle smashed over a half-buried boulder, swerved crazily, then wobbled level again—miraculously turned around the other way—and stopped at last against a sapling no thicker than his forearm.

He sat for a number of cycles in the smell of crushed vegetation, listening to more distant artillery, the angry cries of disturbed birds, and the rattling polyphony of cooling metal behind him. Then he returned to the controls and carefully retraced his well-marked route back to the sunlight.

By the time he reached the forest's edge, his steaming, branch-strewn vehicle was traveling at a normal rate of speed under positive control for the first time since he entered the cab. Brim could feel himself blush as he brought the big vehicle to a stop beside a cheering crowd of ratings. Some days, it simply didn't pay to get out of one's bunk.

Ten cycles before Brim's scheduled departure, all the mobile field pieces were finally operational, their fledgling crews making the most of a few moments' practice. The field was alive with rumbling, steam-breathing machines that staggered drunkenly over the smashed grass in a scene filled with resounding collisions and general confusion. Red-faced and very much out of breath, Barbousse and Fragonard both returned on foot, grumbling they were hard pressed merely to stay alive amid the roaring mayhem outside.

Now, with Fragonard safely ensconced in the turret, Barbousse reactivated the COMM, and within a short time a display globe materialized the wobbly image of Colonel Hagbut.

"Well?" the flush-faced officer demanded. "Are you ready to move out?"

Brim glanced at the clattering disorder outside, gulped, and nodded his head. "Absolutely, Colonel," he declared, thankful the Army officer was not privy to the same view of the field. In truth, he rationalized, the Blue Capes were probably as ready as they ever would be.

"That's better, Brim," Hagbut barked. "We may make a proper soldier of you yet."

146

Brim uttered a silent oath about that.

"In precisely eight cycles," the Colonel continued, "you will lead your field pieces onto the wire at the end of your field and proceed at speed point zero three. That will put you in position to switch onto my cable—behind the personnel carriers—five cycles later. Do you understand?"

"Aye, Colonel," Brim said.

"That's 'Yes, Colonel'," Hagbut corrected. "On land, we do not 'aye' anything."

"I understand, Colonel," Brim said through gritted teeth.

"That's better, young man." Abruptly, Hagbut frowned and peered directly in Brim's face. "Of course," he exclaimed in sudden recognition. "You're that Carescrian they let into the Fleet, aren't you?"

"I am a Carescrian, yes," Brim said stiffly.

"Universe," Hagbut said. "That explains a lot. Well, do the best you can, then. I'm sure you can't help what you are."

Brim felt his face flush—at the same time he also felt a massive grip on his forearm, well beyond the console's video pickup.

"Stand easy, Lieutenant," Barbousse's voice whispered. "Don't let the cod'dlinger make you throw it all away!"

Brim clenched his fists. "Very good, Sir," he spit through his teeth, but the COMM globe had, as usual, already gone out.

Five cycles later, all eight machines hovered idling at the end of the wire in reasonable approximation of line-ahead formation, Brim's foliage-littered field piece at the van. Directly behind him, the cab from the next vehicle in line hung over his savaged rear deck, where it had come to rest as the result of a badly planned stop. A red-faced BATTLE COMM rating smiled in discomfiture from the controls as Brim and Barbousse picked themselves up from the deck, strapped more securely into their seats, and prepared to follow the cable into the leafy tunnel.

Running at precisely 0.3 speed, according to his velocity readout, Brim's group of lurching vehicles cleared the boundaries of the park (and the end of his temporary cable) precisely at the same time as Hagbut's speeding troop-carrier convoy. So accurate was their arrival that they switched in line behind the last Army coach without even slowing, now following the stronger signal of a permanent cable buried in the road.

"Not bad for a worthless gaggle of Fleet types," Brim growled under his breath as the COMM module spawned another display globe.

"Congratulations, Brim," Hagbut barked. "You do tolerable work."

"Thank you, Colonel," Brim grumped, keeping his voice just the safe side of propriety. At least the zukeed didn't sound as if he wanted to press the Carescrian issue.

"Our convoy travels no faster than those field pieces of yours, Lieutenant, so keep a careful watch to the rear," the Colonel admonished. "We have all indications that League forces are nowhere within a day's march—but with operations like this, one trusts one's own eyesight, as they say. Understand?"

"I understand," Brim lied, wondering how much the recent artillery exchanges affected the Colonel's "indications." Turning the controls over to Barbousse, he positioned himself at the COMM module and set up a neat row of seven display globes, one to each of his companion mobile disruptors.

"Now hear this," he said into the COMM console. "Our friends from the Expeditionary Forces tell us all League forces have been drawn from the area," he began. "But just to be on the safe side..." He scanned the seven faces peering at him from the globular displays. Each was serious, but showed no fear whatsoever. "Just to be on the safe side," he repeated, "you will each keep your eyes peeled for anything suspicious, and report it to me immediately."

Seven versions of "Aye, Lieutenant" joined Barbousse in the rumbling control cabin as Brim settled back in the awkward seat for a few moments of relaxation—he had been working at peak output for a considerable time, and was only feeling the first pangs of fatigue. The gentle swaying of the heavy vehicle and the steady thunder of its traction system relaxed him. He leaned back as far as he could in the straight-backed seat and crossed his legs. Forward, the giant shape of Barbousse hunched attentively over a console, poised for instant action should the machine require assistance at the controls.

Brim turned his head and peered through the thick armored glass as they roared past blackened shells of suburban homes, windows and top-story doors gaping hideously like open mouths caught forever in the great gasp of death. No sense of surprise clouded his mind's eye, only disgust. Triannic's invaders laid their cableway with the typical arrogance of all conquerors: Burning their right-of-way straight as a die through the city with no regard whatsoever for the hapless victims in its path.

The neatly spaced ruins with their pitifully blackened gardens and skeleton trees continued for a considerable distance, eventually giving way to shrub-lined fields dotted with tall, dome-capped structures—some connected by fantastic lace-like webs shimmering in the afternoon sun. Nowhere did he see the planet's winged inhabitants aloft. He pondered momentarily on this, then quickly dismissed it. He had plenty of other concerns to solve before he tackled that!

Swiveling in his seat, he looked out the opposite side of his control cabin and across the broad expanse of stained, tree-rumpled metal that formed the front of the vehicle. Fragonard's huge disruptor loomed overhead, pointing their course like a stubby veined finger with three sets of grooved anti-flash shields circling its tip. To starboard, tall, closely spaced buildings replaced the domes, then mixed with residences—these of clearly diminished promise, but whole nonetheless, having glazed windows to flash back the brilliant sunlight as Brim's heavy vehicles rushed past.

Presently, they came upon the banks of a broad canal and took up a new heading atop a moss-covered seawall whose age-blackened stones looked easily twice the size of the mobile field piece in which they rode. They whizzed past a string of rotting pilings out on the water covered with green braids of hairlike moss. The pilings curved abruptly from the seawall and terminated at a tumbledown pier before a crumbling brick structure of uncertain purpose. On the far shore, Brim could see rows of ramshackle warehouses fronted by networks of wooden piers extending far out into the stream—but few water craft anywhere: mute testimony to the ruined commerce of the conquered world.

They soon flashed across a connecting waterway, the exposed cable suspended in an arch by rusty wire bundles attached to the tips of tall pylons paired at opposite sides of the stream. With the speeding field pieces balancing themselves above the cable and wire bundles flashing by on either side at regular intervals, Brim got the definite perception that he was sitting at the controls of a flying brick.

Then abruptly they were thundering wildly along a narrow, shadowed thoroughfare between two close-set rows of giant buildings faced with panels of dreary color decorating vast expanses of featureless wall.

Emerging again into the sunlight, they sped steadily along the stone seawall until the canal itself ended in a great lagoon. Their cable—and travel—diverged, however, in a sharp curve to the right, continuing uninterrupted through marshes and tidelands near the shore until they passed a second dark canyon of buildings in a streaming blur, this much longer than the first. Then suddenly, far off to port, Brim caught sight of a stupendous arch bridge rising gracefully at least a thousand irals into the afternoon sky before it descended again in the hazy distance on the other side of the lagoon.

"Lieutenant Brim! Lieutenant Brim!" an excited voice broke into his thoughts, "I think we've picked up a few extra vehicles to the rear! I can't see how many, but a couple at least."

Instantly alert, Brim frowned at an image of Yeoman Fronze in the last vehicle.

"What do they look like?" he asked.

"Don't exactly know how to describe 'em, Lieutenant," the woman said, looking off to one side. She squinted, frowned. "Big, for sure. An' squatty, like a roach or somethin'," she reported. "They're kind of keepin' their distance right now."

"Ask her if they're square shaped like this one, or long, Sir," Barbousse urged from the driver's seat.

Brim relayed the question.

"Long," Fronze stated emphatically. "With three turrets. A big one to starboard and two on the port side facin' fore and aft."

"Sound like RT-9Is to me," Barbousse pronounced. "About the best the League manufactures," he added.

"Comforting to know those League people are more than 'a day's march away'," Brim snorted, then established connection with the Colonel's personnel carrier.

"Well?" Hagbut demanded.

"Someone seems to be following us along the cable, Colonel," Brim reported. "Were we scheduled to rendezvous with other captured vehicles from *Prosperous*—RT-91 types, perhaps?"

Hagbut's brow wrinkled. "Negative," he said. "You've seen these RT-91s with your own eyes?"

"They've only been reported to me, Colonel," Brim answered. "But I have no reason to question..." He was interrupted by a glowing blue-green geyser that shot skyward about five hundred irals out in the lagoon. The huge waterspout immediately burst about five hundred irals to his left with terrific flame and concussion.

"Don't bother, Brim," Hagbut blustered. "I could see that!" He immediately bawled a string of orders over his shoulder and the troop carriers began to accelerate, soon outdistancing the lumbering field pieces by a considerable margin.

Brim winced as a second explosion leveled a large row of warehouses to his right in a cloud of dirty flame and flying debris. So much for doing the mission in "invisible" captured equipment, he thought. The xaxtdamned ruse hadn't worked as long as a single watch! He shrugged phlegmatically. At least the Leaguers weren't having much luck with their ranging shots.

"I have ordered the troop carriers forward, Brim," Hagbut boomed from the display globe. "To insure the integrity of my mission."

Brim nodded. "Aye, Sir," he said.

"Not to mention the integrity of your bloody skin," Barbousse muttered under his breath. "Beggin' the Lieutenant's pardon."

"What was that?" Hagbut demanded.

"The local grass, Sir," Brim said, desperately stifling a laugh. "Starman Barbousse suffers a violent sneezing reaction."

"Poor fellow," Hagbut pronounced as another explosion destroyed an island of trees a few hundred irals to port. "Damn Leaguers never could seal a driving compartment."

"No, Sir."

"It is now your duty, Brim, to stop the bastards," Hagbut continued in what must have been his best pontifical voice. "Use those cannons soon as you can." He turned in the display for a moment to bark more orders at someone, then swung back to Brim. "Catch up to us when you've stopped whoever it is back there—but not before. Understand? We cannot compromise the mission!"

"I understand, Colonel," Brim said, but again he spoke to a darkened display. He shook a mock fist of anger, then opened a connection to Fragonard in the turret. "You're the disruptor expert, Fragonard," he said. "What do you say? Can these field pieces really tear up a couple of the League's RT-9I battle crawlers?"

"Easily," Fragonard replied with a frown, "if we can just aim 'em well enough. I've told the men to have a go at it soon as they've got their equipment ready. Trouble is, we haven't had time to adjust 'em well enough yet to fire accurately while they're moving. Maybe we can get close, but if we kill more Leaguers than locals, it'll be a case of good luck, if you catch my drift, Sir."

"Tell everyone to do the best he or she can," Brim yelled over the noise of another near miss. This one sent a deluge of green water drizzling into the control cabin between the panes of glass to puddle on the deck and COMM cabinet. He ruefully wished he'd thought to have the BATTLE COMMs rig a permanent KA'PPA to his field piece. Perhaps he might now be calling in some close support from space—one couldn't do that with ordinary COMM gear, of course. He shrugged and dropped the subject from his mind. "Are they gaining on us?" he queried Fronze in the last disruptor.

"Aye, Sir," she answered, face serious. "We're gettin' ready to try an' put the disruptor on 'em, Lieutenant, but Starman Cogsworthy up in the turret don't think we've much chance of hittin' them, what with no stabilizers an' all." Her image bounced in the display as the same enemy fire sounded first from the COMM console, then a click later from the windows.

"Thanks, Fronze," Brim said. "Let me know when you get the stabilizer going." They were passing along a relatively clear stretch of shore marsh now. His mind raced. If he couldn't get at the pursuing battle crawlers, what could he do? Stop and fight? He laughed at that possibility. They'd all be sitting ducks while the ordnance men recalibrated their disruptors. He shook his head. Perhaps he ought to sacrifice the last few cannon in line: Order Fronze to stop and fight a lonely battle of delay. He discarded that idea, too—not enough delay.

Presently, a deeper, more substantial thunder sounded from the rear, with a flash visible at mid-afternoon. A dirty column of smoke and debris shot skyward far to the rear. "Lieutenant!" Fronze yelled excitedly from a display globe. "Cogsworthy got the stabilizer goin', Sir! That ought to give 'em somethin' t' think about!" Her image jumped violently as sounds of heavy return fire filled Brim's control cab.

More of the huge, drumming thunder followed the first. This was succeeded in rapid succession by whole series of smaller bursts. "By Corfrew's goatee," someone said excitedly from a display globe, "I don't think they liked that!"

"Can't understand why not," another voice said after more explosions tore up the marsh. "Look! It wasn't anywhere half near them. Bastards have no sense of humor."

"How's it going back there, Fronze?" Brim demanded.

"Not so bad, Lieutenant," the rating said through clenched teeth. She blanched while a whole volley of discharges thundered from the disruptor above her, then turned to peer out the rear of her vehicle, shaking her head. "'Cept," she added, "I think they're shootin' closer t' us, an' Cogsworthy's gettin' farther away from them." She grinned. "This single-file-on-the-wire stuff cuts our shootin' down to my one projector." Her image danced violently in the globe as Cogsworthy let go with another shot, then continued to shake from a peppering of near misses landed in return. "Course," she added cheerfully, "it also saves our skins from more'n one of theirs, too."

Suddenly, the display globe seethed with a churning glow and disappeared. A violent flash from aft lit the afternoon sky, followed by a grating, trembling roar. Brim swung in his seat in time to see a burning turret arch lazily through the sky, trailing thick clouds of amber smoke until it disappeared with a monstrous splash and cloud of steam far out into the lagoon. "Universe," someone bawled, "that was Cogsworthy!"

"Poor Fronze!" wailed another voice.

"Shut up, the both of you," a third voice rasped. "None of those three felt a bloody thing! So just maybe they're the lucky ones."

"Yeah," said a fourth. "You'll wish that was you if we're ever captured, you will!"

Brim squeezed his eyes closed for a moment, thinking about a praefect named Valentin, then nodded in silent agreement.

"Someone told me you were worried about bein' bored this trip, Lieutenant," Barbousse called out over the roar of the machinery, his face an impish parody of surprise.

"Must have been someone else," Brim said, eyes rolled heavenward. "It surely wasn't this Wilf Brim!" He glanced out the windshield and nearly jumped in surprise. His running battle was rapidly approaching the titanic suspension structure he had viewed from a distance.

He snapped his fingers. That was it! An artificial hill—and a big one.

He activated BROADCAST on the COMM console and began to speak, taking special pains to keep a calm inflection in his voice. "Now hear this, all hands!" he yelled over the rising thunder of the disruptors. "We are about to run the high arch ahead. While we're on this side, you'll each have fine visibility and a clear field of fire below. Make the most of both! And remember that any battle crawlers you don't polish off will have the same visibility and field of fire when you are on the bottom!"

6 So absorbed was Brim with the
unfolding battle that the ascent onto the bridge, when it came, nearly
took him by surprise. Fragonard had the big disruptor in action before
they climbed fifty irals. The noise was deafening, as was the concussion.
Higher and higher they rose, traction system roaring and dense white
vapor streaming from the cooling fins. Brim watched the ground behind
them erupt in gigantic explosions as the wiry little gunner switched to
rapid fire and fairly peppered the right-of-way around the speeding
enemy battle crawlers. He counted ten of the lopsided enemy machines
and thanked whatever powers had dissuaded him from stopping to
fight the battle crawlers in place. His second field piece soon added its
fire to the holocaust below, then the third. The cable pitched and swayed
from dozens of frenzied discharges, sending the field piece careening
wildly from one side to the other as they climbed farther and farther
toward the high arch of the bridge. Without warning, a particularly
bright blast on the ground was followed first by a cloud of peculiar-
looking debris and then by frenzied cheering from the COMM cabinet.

"A hit!" someone yelled.

"I nailed the bastard, I did!"

"Good on you, Ferdie! Give 'em wot for!"

Soon all seven of the captured field pieces were firing rapidly and
wildly, as often as their disruptors could recover. Below, the Leaguers
maintained a furious barrage in return—although two more of their
number were now carbonized junk mounds smoldering at the base of

155

towering smoke columns along the right-of-way. Beneath Brim's straining vehicle, the rampaging cable was bucking violently in two axes, making Barbousse lean desperately on the rudder pedals in a frantic attempt to keep from plunging off into the considerable abyss that now separated them from the surface.

"Sweet bloody Universe!" someone screamed in panic from the COMM console. "I'm losin' it!"

Horrified, Brim looked back along the wire to see one of his field pieces skid up and off the writhing cable, its projector still firing spasmodically. Momentum carried the awkward vehicle perhaps twenty irals higher before it peaked, rolled lazily to port, and plunged like a stone through the suspension wires, disappearing in a great splash that spread rapidly in all directions from the point of impact. Heartbeats later, a single explosion rent the lagoon in a giant glowing bubble that burst with a massive eruption of smoke and greasy flame, quenched almost instantly in a plume of steam and slowly tumbling debris.

Ahead, the apex of the great arch was now visible through the windshield, no more than a few hundred irals distant. Aft and below, the remaining enemy gun layers were finally warming to their jobs—space around Brim's convoy was suddenly alive with explosions and concussion. Three of the armored windows above his head shattered, filling the control cabin with a swarm of whirring glass splinters that buzzed harmlessly along the armored fabric of his battle suit and helmet, but shredded the tough upholstery of his seat. He shook his head. Another near miss tore a huge access hatch from something near the cooling mechanism—which was itself beginning to glow again from the strain of the long, steep climb and the insatiable demands of the disruptor, now firing almost constantly. Renewed clouds of steam billowed in their wake from the cooling fins, and as he looked down along the weaving, swinging cable, he could see his other field pieces were in no better shape at all. It was now or never. He bullied the COMM cabinet back to BROADCAST and yelled over the noise, "Now hear this, all hands! Switch targeting immediately to the buried cableway five hundred irals in front of the bridge. I repeat, in front of the bridge." The disruptors went silent momentarily as he talked. "Dig up the cable so the battle crawlers can't follow right away," he enjoined the ordnance men. "But don't touch the bridge. We need that for our own trip home!"

"Right ya are, Lieutenant!" someone called back over the noise.

"We'll be careful, Sir," someone else echoed.

In short order, the six disruptors directed a new frenzy of flame and concussion onto the buried cableway—no more accurate than before, but at least more-or-less concentrated. The bridge began to sway again, but Barbousse was now mastering the big machine, and he tracked the cable flawlessly as it pitched and yawed like a pendant flying in the breeze.

Suddenly Fragonard's thundering disruptor went silent. Brim looked up from his COMM cabinet. They were over the top! The big field piece could no longer bear on the approach ramp to the bridge. Soon the next cannon topped the bridge, then the next. When the sixth left off firing, Brim leaned out of the cabin in the roaring slipstream. Two thousand irals below, wide areas fronting the bridge approaches looked as if they had been plowed by a large asteroid. Gaping holes here and there told of many near misses, but the area through which the cable had to pass was now a gigantic crater that glowed from within and vomited forth a dense smoke pillar as the underlying rock formations themselves burned from the hellfire of Brim's disruptors. While he watched, the first enemy battle crawler pulled to a halt well short of the zone of destruction, firing off a desultory round now and then toward its escaping quarry.

Brim frowned as he drew his head back inside the cab. "They're stopped," he told Barbousse.

The big rating expressed no surprise at Brim's announcement. "Makes sense, Lieutenant," he said. "I figure in their eyes we've made ourselves out to be a lot more trouble than we're worth." He grinned as the field piece roared between a pair of towering and the cable disappeared once more into the ground.

"I suppose that's right," Brim said, watching the other machines regain the surface.

"It is, Sir," Barbousse assured him. "If you can't beat somebody you're fightin', it never hurts to convince him he can't beat you, either." He grinned. "Besides," he added, "anybody who's spent his life followin' a cable isn't going to be too happy about pickin' his way through that mess of craters—probably fall in and never find his way out."

"Let's hope," Brim agreed, settling wearily back in his uncomfortable seat at the COMM console. "Now all we've got to do is catch up with Colonel Hagbut."

"Beggin' the Lieutenant's pardon, but that bird's liable to be all the way to Avalon by now," Barbousse said.

Brim smothered a laugh—just as the landscape ahead erupted in flashes of light. Clicks later, the cascading, rolling thunder of high-energy artillery reached them. He looked at Barbousse and frowned. "Another battle?" he whispered.

"Sounds like one to me, Sir..." Barbousse started, then he was cut off by the screech of an emergency channel running overload on the COMM console.

"Brim! Stay clear! We're prisoners! Target is map locus 765_{jj}. Everything up to you now..." The display globe went out in a manner similar to Fronze's demise.

Galvanized, Brim displayed the coordinates of the message on the COMM console. "Nine thirteen point five by $E9_G$. Can you help me remember that, Barbousse?"

"Nine thirteen point five by $E9_G$. I'll remember it, Sir."

"Good," Brim said, his mind working furiously as he peered off along the cable right-of-way. "Now get ready to stop us in that patch of trees coming up to starboard. We've got some serious thinking to do before we go any farther."

Scant cycles later, the convoy was hidden under the dense foliage of a large forest glen. Brim clambered onto the cool, fern-carpeted ground and motioned for the rest of the crews to stand down for the remainder of the day, then he leaned on a stump and breathed the clean fragrance of the trees, pondering what he ought to do next.

Suddenly, he was in command.

***

Late into the long summer evening, Brim sat alone on the cool forest floor, back to a stump, hands around his knees while he desperately tried to assemble a coherent mental picture of his predicament. Reduced to absolute basics, the situation appeared to consist of no more than three primary elements, which he absently counted on his fingers for the hundredth time: (1) his chances for calling anyone to assist him, (2) his mission (and what to do about it), and (3) the meager resources at his disposal.

The first element—assistance—was simply unattainable. He immediately dismissed it as such. The Fleet certainly couldn't help him. Even if he asked his BATTLE COMMs to call, any starships they might find were powerless against his target, at least until he could contrive to achieve Hagbut's original mission and remove the A'zurnian hostages imprisoned there.

The second element, his mission, was a different proposition altogether—one in which the word "impossible" had no meaning whatsoever. It represented a commitment to duty he absolutely intended to fulfill. Of course, that involved no less than capture of a major military facility (which he had never so much as seen), freeing a sizable group of hostages who unwillingly—but effectively—protected that same facility from attack, delivery of the hostages to safety (wherever that was), and, finally, getting himself and his charges back to Magalla'ana in time to be evacuated when the mission terminated. All this, of course, had to be accomplished notwithstanding his secondary obligation to search for the captured Colonel Hagbut—if he found himself with spare time on his hands.

The third element, unfortunately, threatened ill for everything else. His resources were nowhere near to being suitable to the requirements of his mission, and that included himself. His fewer than twenty BATTLE COMMs, for example, had superb equipment for calling in destroyers—but before they could use any of it, they first had to double for one-hundred-and-eighty of Hagbut's highly trained foot soldiers!

The combined lack of help, impossible task load, and inadequate resources might have daunted many a normal Imperial. Carescrian Imperials, however, shared a unique background of adversity, one in which even the best of circumstances normally required making do with whatever expedients came to hand. He shrugged. He knew a way existed for getting the job done; no doubt about it. All he had to do was discover what that was.

***

He began early in the first watch of the night with Barbousse, poring over a three-dimensional map, scouring dusty corners of his mind to remember everything he ought to know about field operations from exercises at the Academy. As photomapped in real time by an orbiting reconnaissance craft, his target, the purported research center, sat astride the cableway in a wooded location at the extreme limits of Magalla'ana. A wide, narrow structure, it cascaded down a hillside in three levels of attached terraces, courtyards, and glass-enclosed laboratory structures. Significantly, its doors were on the ground story. Surrounding this structure was a huge campus area protected by a stout fence with gates at two opposing cable crossings. Clearly, the big facility also doubled as a key checkpoint controlling the cableway: Both gates appeared to be protected by large guardhouses. Inside the campus and considerably removed from the gates (as well as the research center itself), a rectangular compound with separate guardhouse was set off by its own double fence. The compound contained ten rectangular buildings in two rows of five each.

"That's where they keep the hostages," Brim declared grimly, pointing at the buildings with the magnifier.

"Looks like, Sir," Barbousse said. "And only one entrance to the compound." He pursed his lips. "Makes things a lot easier for us with all the guards concentrated in one place."

"Maybe." Brim warned with a grin, "But first we've got to get there."

Barbousse nodded gravely. "I've been thinkin' about that, Lieutenant," he said with a frown.

"What's on your mind?" Brim asked.

"Well, Sir," the big man said, "hasn't been much traffic on the cableway since we hid in these woods this afternoon—and during that firefight we had comin' up to the bridge, you just know somebody got a warning off to the lab." He frowned and shrugged. "So by now it pretty well stands to reason they've fixed a special welcome for anyone arriving at this side of the research center. I mean, we know they've got battle crawlers around, so there's no tellin' what else they have in store."

"You're right," Brim agreed gravely. "I guess I've given that some serious thought myself. And I think I've found something that might help." He pointed on the map to an overgrown path that formed a rough semicircle around the campus and connected to the cableway at both ends approximately five thousand irals from the gates.

"I see, Sir," Barbousse said dubiously, studying the map. "What do you suppose it is?"

"Looks like a construction road to this ex-miner," Brim pronounced. "Couple of years old at least. Might well have supplied gravel from these pits it runs beside. The research center probably used plenty, the way it's built." He laughed. "Whatever they used to use the road for, that old right-of-way just might make our job a whole lot easier and less risky tonight."

"How's that, Sir?" Barbousse asked, scratching his head.

"This way." Brim explained with a smile, "We leave the main cable at the road, turn right, then use it to go around to the other side of the research center. When the road meets the cable again we simply get back on the cable again and turn left. This time, we'll be coming from the opposite direction—and arrive from the opposite direction. Like a convoy of Leaguer reinforcements. After all, that's why Hagbut says he brought these captured cannon in the first place."

Barbousse nodded his head and smiled. "Sounds good to me, Lieutenant," he said. "But what if that road doesn't have a cable in it any more?"

"I thought about that," Brim said. "But the way the Leaguers litter the landscape with spare cable spools, I'm betting it's cheaper to leave laid cable where it is than remove it." Then he shrugged. "And if that isn't the case, then we'll have some really great practice with the rudder pedals."

"It's sure worth a try, Lieutenant," Barbousse said, "anything is that makes the odds a little better than they are right now—we aren't exactly the best substitute for the Colonel's hundred and eighty foot soldiers."

Brim chuckled. "You've noticed?"

"I've noticed," Barbousse agreed, "but it's yet to worry me, Sir." He laughed quietly. "We'll make a go of it, Lieutenant. Catch a little sleep now. We've got a lot to do in the morning."

Brim nodded sleepily and leaned back in the uncomfortable chair as the big rating switched out the light on the map table. He remembered nothing more until the first crimson rays of dawn filtered through the trees.

***

Following an early morning assembly, Brim set the various crews to searching their field pieces for anything of possible value to the task at hand. Not surprisingly, they found each vehicle had been well equipped at Gimmas-Haefdon. Emperor Greyffin IV was a steadfast Army man, and consequently the Imperial Expeditionary Forces were known everywhere for the wealth of equipment they carried in the field.

With the sound of distant artillery grumbling through the morning air, Barbousse and Fragonard lowered a number of heavy packing cases to the ground with two cables, then broke the seals with a power draw bar. From these, they lifted packages of blast pikes, oversized power cartridges, cartons of proton grenades, and a brace of battle lanterns—wiping each clean of preservative gel.

"Gantheissers, no less," Fragonard said admiringly, turning one of the big blast pikes in his hands. "Not bad for emergency-pack stuff." He slotted a power cartridge in place and grinned with pleasure as the self-test finished. "All ready to fire, too," he said. "Got to give those weird Ganthers credit. If they do nothing else well, they surely can build weapons." He departed shortly to make sure the other crews had their weapons under control.

When all the stores were prepared and distributed, some of the orphaned BATTLE COMMs set to unpacking one of the portable KA'PPA sets. "Sooner or later we'll need it to call in the destroyers, Sir," Barbousse explained to Brim. "I suggested they get their testing over with now."

"Good idea," Brim agreed, watching two ratings reverse a large plate in the packing crate—which soon became a control panel. Others attached an auxiliary power unit via heavy cables with complex connectors, while nearby a third team unfolded the antenna lattice from a slender silver container. These tasks complete, everyone pitched in to lever the longish structure into the air and guy it in place with a triad of insulated wires. Immediately, operators busied themselves with integration tests using equipment contained in a third pack the size of the power unit. Operation of the complete assembly was verified in half a metacycle, then the whole bulky unit was restowed in five more. Brandon, A'zurn's star, was high in a hazy, cloud-dappled sky by the time the BATTLE COMMs replaced the unit aboard Brim's field piece, then marched off toward still another task with Barbousse in the lead.

***

By mid-afternoon, the clouds had changed to a lowering overcast and a brisk wind rustled the treetops. Brim stood at the edge of the cable right-of-way, inspecting a larger portion of sky than he could view from the forest floor. It was the fourth time he'd come; each time he did, he became more confident than the last. This time, it even smelled like rain. He smiled. Had he ordered the weather himself, he could scarcely have done a better job.

Later, rejoining the mobile field pieces, he visited the ordnance men adjusting their disruptors. "Probably get a mite better performance out of 'em this time," Fragonard assured him from one of the boarding ladders. "None of 'em was ever fine-tuned before—thank the bloody Universe they were ready to fire at all, even if we couldn't hit anything, in a manner of speakin'." He chuckled mirthlessly. "We'd all be dead by now."

"Or worse," Barbousse added under his breath.

Inside the quietly humming turret, Brim watched two ratings concentrating their efforts on the big disruptor, aiming the heavy weapon indirectly by means of a rigged index point: A hatch cover tied in a distant sapling just visible through the trees. Leveling devices and compensators whirred and hummed, dizzily (to Brim) changing the attitude of the huge turret as the ordnance men fine-tuned elevation and transverse targeting controls in both automatic and manual modes. "This time," Fragonard said confidently, "if we need' em, we'll know better how to use 'em."

By late afternoon, everything appeared to be ready, including the rain. A few drops filtered through the trees while Barbousse patched broken glass in the control cab and Brim completed his equipment checkout with Fragonard.

"Got the map," the rating declared.

"Check."

"Blast pikes?"

"Nine. One of 'em couldn't run diagnostics, so I pitched it."

"Good. Positron grenades?"

"Forty-six energized, Lieutenant. Four duds with no power."

Brim nodded. "That's it," he said as the gathering storm began to drum loudly against the field piece's metal flanks. "The KA'PPA's tested, everybody's armed in one way or another, and you've got the disruptors tuned. I think we're about as ready as we're ever going to be." A smell of rain filled the control cabin, fresh and damp to his nose. He peered around at the other field pieces. Probably it was his imagination, but somehow each one looked much more deadly now that he knew the disruptors were tuned. Then he closed his eyes and forced his racing mind to relax. Tonight would be a long night indeed.

Later, when storm-gray daylight faded to the near darkness of A'zurnian evening, the rain—which was previously only falling lightly—now began to come down in torrents. "Even with a cable in place, we're not going to make much speed with visibility like this," Barbousse observed, peering through the water streaming along the windshield.

Brim nodded agreement. It was raining with a vengeance. "At least we don't have far to go," he observed. "And anyway, it'll make it harder for them to spot us."

"Through optical sights, Sir," Barbousse grumped with a smile.

"Those jammers in the hull ought to confuse their other sensors some," Brim offered.

Barbousse smiled. "They won't believe it if they do pick us up, Lieutenant," he said. "Nobody would go out on a night like this."

"Sure hope so," Brim said as he stretched forward and opened the phase converter. "You make sure the traction gear works and I'll test the COMM. After that, we'll get started and find out if you're right."

Five display globes again hovered above the shifting light patterns of the COMM cabinet as Barbousse gunned the traction engine from the driver's seat. "Everybody ready?" Brim asked—this time with the transmitters in short-range, SECURE mode.

Five versions of "Aye, Sir" provided his answer from the other field pieces.

"Fragonard?"

164

"Ready, Sir," came his answer on the interCOMM from the turret.

Brim peered around the hunched form of Barbousse in the driver's seat. The big rating had his windshield cleaners in action, and the trees appeared like specters in the dim illumination of the battle headlights. "All set?" he asked.

"All set, Sir."

"Let's move out."

"Aye, Sir." Barbousse nodded and carefully lowered the thrust sink. The big machine lumbered into motion, its traction system throttled back just above idle. Brim swung in his seat, watching five pairs of battle headlights follow in a serpentine track among the trees. "There," the rating muttered, manhandling the heavy vehicle into a sharp left turn.

"Cableway?" Brim asked.

"Aye, Sir," Barbousse answered. "But I'm not lockin' on the cable-just as you ordered, Lieutenant." He cocked his head momentarily. "Do you suppose they can track who's followin' the cable?"

"Don't know for sure," Brim admitted. "But it's always possible, and besides, the construction road isn't that far away."

"Aye, Sir," agreed Barbousse, peering out into the rain ahead.

To Brim, the raging torrent looked like a meteor shower in the battle headlights' dull glow.

They drove in silence, Barbousse picking his way carefully with the trees a bare ten irals to his left. "Break in the woods coming up, Sir," he said tensely.

Brim peered past the man's shoulder. "About the right time," he confirmed. "Try it." Then he turned to the five COMM displays. "Hard right coming up," he warned the others. "Watch for a break in the woods to starboard." The landscape abruptly skidded to the left and the field piece tipped precipitously, then righted, Barbousse swearing under his breath. Then they were once more under control, picking their way slowly along the overgrown construction road.

***

Considerable time elapsed before the six vehicles completed their circuitous route around the research center—successfully avoiding nine open quarry pits along the way. By the time they drew to a halt at the cableway again, this time on the far side of the campus, nearly half the night had passed.

"Everybody still with me?" he asked the COMM cabinet.

"Aye, Sir," five voices replied from the globes.

"Barbousse?"

"Doing fine, Sir," the big rating assured him.

"Very well," Brim said. "Let's be at it, just as if we'd been coming this direction all day."

"Aye, Sir," Barbousse called over the roar of the traction engine. He swung the heavy vehicle left onto the cableway. "Picking up the cable now," he reported as a trio of green lights began to pulse on the panel before him. "Lock on."

"Good," Brim replied. "Let's put the lights on, we might as well get it over with and be done for once and all."

Barbousse switched energy to the three big forward illuminators and all the running lights. The other five field pieces followed suit. Brim mentally shuddered as trees bordering the cable right-of-way stood out in sudden detail. He imagined the lighted machines looked a lot like six oversized refugees from a Gambbolian Feast of Lights.

In due time, they coasted to the foot of a lengthy downgrade, then began what the map promised was a short climb to their first view of the research center at the bottom of the hill.

***

Just before they crested the rise, Barbousse drew to a halt, hovering in place over the cable. Outside, the right-of-way was now lined with a row of tall night illuminators like Karlsson lamps. They made hazy orange circles in the driving rain. "All right, Fragonard, it's time," Brim called into the interCOMM.

A moment later, the turret hatch opened and the ordnance man scrambled down a ladder, raced across the deck, and fairly burst into the control cab in a spray of rain. "Universe!" he sputtered as he struggled out of his battle helmet. "Make sure you've got your suit dogged down tight; otherwise it could fill up and drown you."

"I'll do that," Barbousse laughed. "We've got a long way to walk in that downpour."

"You two all set?" Brim asked.

166

"Aye, Sir," Barbousse and Fragonard answered together.

"Remember to flash the signal three times—soon as you can see my lights," Brim reminded them.

"Three times it is, Sir," Barbousse assured him. "If the map's right, we shouldn't need more'n twenty cycles to get there." He pulled his helmet over his head, then followed Fragonard over the hatch coaming and out into the storm.

Brim slammed the hatch shut in a shower of flying rain, watching the two men scramble down the ladder. At the bottom, Barbousse waved, touching his thumb and forefinger together, then the two figures set off through ankle-deep puddles toward the top of the hill and soon disappeared into the gloomy downpour.

Brim hovered, idling a full thirty cycles just to be sure, then settled in the driver's seat, lowered the thrust sink, and drove the lumbering cannon up over the crest of the hill, locked on to the cable. Behind, five more brightly lighted vehicles followed.

Interminable cycles later, a ruby glow clawed its way through the deluge three times in succession. Brim stepped up his speed along the downgrade until a number of high illuminators began to show through the rain ahead: Hagbut's target—now his own—was less than a cycle away. He forced himself to relax. Now was the time for calm, not mind-numbing tension.

He pulled up sharply just outside the guard shack, adjusting the big vehicle's traction system to its highest, and noisiest, power level. Then, taking his cue from the officers aboard Valentin's ill-fated corvette, he boldly activated the external amplifiers. "Well?" he broadcast imperiously in Vertrucht. "Hurry, fools. We have little time to dawdle here at your gate. Enemy vehicles are in the area."

"P-Please identify yourself, S-Sir," a voice responded unsurely from the guard shack.

Brim smiled to himself. Just as he guessed. "Identify myself, indeed!" he growled. "You will present yourself immediately to open the gate in person, fool."

"But w-we have orders..."

"How long," Brim interrupted, "has it been since your last fire-flogging, fool?"

"But, Sir..."

"You will immediately present me with your name for the Center's flogging roster or you will, alternatively, open the gate."

"A moment, Sir."

"Immediately."

The door to the guard shack opened and a fat, slack-jawed guard waddled onto the stoop as if his feet hurt. His hand was palm up in a very unnecessary verification of the teeming rain. Behind him, Brim saw a second guard struggling into some sort of foul-weather suit. As the first stepped all the way out into the storm, a great arm materialized suddenly from the shadows and wrapped itself around his face. In the next instant, a jeweled knife flashed in the glare of the headlights. Then the guard's tunic was covered with a rain-thinned curtain of red before everything disappeared again in the shadows. Brim gunned the traction system to muffle any further noise as the second guard met a similar fate. Abruptly, Barbousse and Fragonard scrambled around the corner—battle suits surprisingly free of stains—and disappeared inside the guardhouse. Each carried a big Gantheisser ready at his hip. Light flashed explosively for a few heartbeats from the half-open door, then the two reappeared at a dead run for the main gate.

Barbousse and Fragonard struggled considerably before the huge, one-section gate grudgingly slid aside. Extinguishing his running lights, Brim began to move through the opening. He slowed to a crawl while the two ratings boarded on the fly, then shoved the big traction system to its highest speed and roared into the campus toward their second objective: the hostage compound.

Moments later, Barbousse and Fragonard yanked the hatch open and clambered over the coaming, dripping rain.

"I think it's lettin' up," Fragonard declared, popping off his helmet.

"Has to," Barbousse agreed. "Can't be much left up there anymore." He peered through the windshield. "They've got a map in the guard shack back there, Lieutenant," he said. "We guessed right—that square fenced area is marked with the Vertrucht symbol for prisoners you showed me."

"Good," Brim said, nodding out ahead and to his left. "That's it, just off the port bow." He switched off two of the three cable followers.

"How'd it go back there?" he asked.

"Like it was programmed, Lieutenant," Barbousse declared. "They never got the first warning out."

Brim smiled to himself. So far, so good, he thought—but the nasty business was far from finished. At about three thousand irals, he eyed the entrance to the hostage compound. He could just make out the rooflines beyond against the sky, and in that instant, the last details of his plan fell into place. "Second and third field pieces follow me!" he yelled at the COMM cabinet. "Last three shear off and take out anybody you find at the city-side gate. Got that?"

Five voices returned a confusion of assent just before the last three field pieces pulled out of line. The Carescrian grinned and flexed his shoulders. Then he disengaged the third cable follower and leaned hard on the left rudder pedal. His big machine banked wildly and skidded around until it was racing at high speed for the gate. The roar of the traction system was deafening in the cab. A glance over his shoulder assured him the other two field pieces were in close formation behind him, bobbing and swaying ponderously as they galloped over the uneven ground, battle headlights like the eyes of great steam-breathing nocturnal monsters.

"Halt and identity yourself!" someone yelled over a loud hailer from the guard shack ahead.

Brim opened the phase gate farther and the speed increased again. The big machine was barely under control now, swaying and skidding from side to side, clouds of steam belching from the cooling system and the rain streaming from its sodden flanks. "Buckle in!" he warned.

Ahead, a cluster of figures burst from the guard shack with blast pikes, kneeled, and began to fire, their charges pattering harmlessly against the armored plate of the rampaging field piece.

"Hang on!" Brim yelled over the howl of the straining traction system. Simultaneously, the guards seemed to realize what was about to happen. As one, they dropped their pikes and scattered in all directions—but much too late. They all disappeared beneath the front of the vehicle into the thrashing torrent of gravity from the raging logic lens. An open-mouthed head suddenly bounced forward into the glow of the battle headlights, rebounded from a rock, and trailed a smeared string of dark red offal across the armored windshield as it joined a ragged upper torso that spun lazily in their wake like a thrown rag doll. Then, with a tearing, shrieking crash, the field piece burst wildly over the guard shack, throwing a torrent of debris flying in all directions.

Brim jammed the thrust sink into full detent amid screeching protest from the traction system; they shuddered to a stop not more than fifty irals from the first four hostage barracks. He glanced over his shoulder again as the other two field pieces drew to a skidding halt nearby; the last spun dizzily out of control for a moment before coming to rest precariously against a solid-looking utility building. At the same moment, the sky to his right lit, blazing forth with terrific flashes of disruptor fire, followed by waves of concussion as the last three cannon went to work on whatever League forces they found marshaled at the city-side gate.

Leaving the controls set at a fast idle, Brim joined the two ratings at the hatch. "You know what to do," he yelled over the hiss of the cooling system. "Each of you take a building; get the hostages out quick as you can. Any of 'em can't fly, get 'em on one of the field pieces—anywhere. Understand?"

"Understand, Lieutenant," Barbousse answered, then he disappeared over the coaming, followed by Fragonard. Brim clamped his helmet firmly in place and clambered down the ladder after them. Outside, the storm appeared to have run its course. Only a few drops spattered against his faceplate before they were instantly cleared. Ahead, Barbousse was already inside the first building of the first row. Fragonard was heading for the second. To his right in the darkness, Brim made out six other figures heading in a low crouch for the second row of barracks. All the buildings appeared to be dark, both outside and inside.

Unexpectedly, a group of figures dashed from the third building, firing wildly in all directions. One discharge flashed blindingly beside Brim, knocking him from his feet and rolling him across the muddy turf. He lay low for a moment while deadly beams of energy crisscrossed only fractions of an iral above his helmet. Proton grenades flashed coldly in the darkness and guttural shouts filled the air. Then his vision cleared and he clambered stiffly to one knee, took Ursis's great side-action blaster from its holster, and, in an Academy-perfect, two-hand crouch,

170

blew the nearest Leaguer completely in half. Sodeskayan Bears, he observed, built powerful hand weapons. Moments later, a number of thundering Gantheissers suddenly joined his blaster, and the defenders rapidly disappeared in a welter of flame and concussion.

An instant later, he was back on his feet and at the entrance to one of the barracks. He blew the latch from the door and burst into the poorly lighted room—where he stopped short, shuddering in absolute horror. The stench of rotting flesh alone was almost enough to drive him gagging into the fresh night air before his battle suit switched to internal air. The far end of the room was filled by a pitiful knot of cadaverous things he guessed once were like the flighted people he had seen aboard Prosperous. Now they were unbelievably emaciated—with shriveled stumps where once there had been wings. No wonder he'd seen no one aloft! He'd been warned: Characteristic Triannic pragmatism. He stood for a moment, transfixed, then forced his mind once again into action. "Can any of you walk?" he choked.

"Y-You... an Imperial!" one of them stammered from behind starved, deep-set eyes. "Our hopes are answered."

"Have you come to set us free?" a spectral woman asked in a thin voice.

"Yes," Brim said, his eyes filling with tears. "Can any of you...walk?"

"We can walk if our steps lead to freedom," a gaunt old man with a white beard and spindly, ill-matched wing stumps pronounced somberly. "Freedom of any kind."

Brim fought his emotions back under control. "Three League field pieces wait outside," he said. "Climb aboard—anywhere. They're not very suitable, but..."

"They will serve, young man," another haggard prisoner said. "We shall carry our comrades who can no longer walk. Come, my friends. We make our way to more useful employment."

Brim nodded as the fleshless mass of humanity untangled itself from the end of the room and began to shamble for the door. Outside, he could see other halting lines of people already struggling to reach the waiting vehicles. Barbousse and Fragonard were both in the adjacent barracks as he ran along the walkway. The next building—opened by someone else by now—was a repeat of the last, emptying a pitiful remnant of emaciated bodies with blackened, deep-set eyes and torn, snapped-off wings. Some were already dead, as were many others in the remainder of the barracks he visited.

Then, once all the buildings had been opened, he found himself running headlong through the pitiful lines of shambling hostages. The wind had picked up now and the rain came in spurts. Nearby, Fragonard and Barbousse were boosting hostages gently up the ladder and onto the vehicle's broad back. All three machines were filling rapidly with pitiful knots of what once were graceful flighted men and women. "Get 'em up there quick as you can," he yelled to the ordnance man. "I want us out of here before the Leaguers bring up some real reinforcements!"

As the six machines lumbered back through the gate and up the hill, running lights darkened this time, stars were showing through the clouds. Brim glanced at his timepiece and nodded. They were almost precisely on the schedule he had set. Less than a metacycle remained before dawn.

***

The first recall signal was broadcast from *Prosperous* not long after Brim and his party rejoined the other three field pieces just over the crest of the hill. "League Battlecruisers on the way, Lieutenant," Fragonard reported with a look of concern. "Operations gives us less than four watches before *Prosperous* leaves—ten metacycles at most."

Brim pursed his lips, thinking of Sandur's warning, then he shrugged and smiled. "Ten metacycles gives us plenty of time," he answered in what he hoped was a voice of confidence.

"If you say so, Lieutenant," Fragonard muttered, but his face gave the lie to his words.

"Count 'em yourself," Brim reasoned. "It took us only three metacycles to drive to the high bridge—so four will certainly get us back from here. And with another metacycle for shuttling up to *Prosperous*, we still have most of five metacycles to use looking for Colonel Hagbut."

Fragonard's eyes looked as if someone had just slapped him on the side of the head.

Brim smiled sympathetically at the ordnance man's discomfort. "I understand how you feel," he said honestly. "And I am also well aware of how close that could be cutting things. But we can't just desert those men without at least giving our best shot to bringing them home. Remember, once we're gone, they have no hope at all."

"You're right, Sir," Fragonard agreed. "I understand. I'd surely want it that way if I were in their shoes."

Brim nodded. "Besides," he said with a grin, "we'll have some potent help locating' em soon as we call in the Fleet."

Fragonard knuckled his forehead. "Sorry. I..."

"Sorry nothing," Brim interrupted with a smile. "You gave me a chance to review my plans. Everybody needs a sanity check once in a while." Then he winked and made his way to where the BATTLE COMMs were busily rigging a portable KA'PPA.

"Ready in a moment, Lieutenant," a signal rating said. "By my timepiece, it's just about time to make your call."

Brim nodded, remembering his last view of the research center as he had crested the hill just before dawn. All the lights had been blazing—too late, he'd noted with satisfaction. Now, in the early cycles of the morning, the clouds of the spent storm were disappearing rapidly and a cool breeze rustled the grass outside the field pieces. Everything smelled of A'zurn's rich, wet soil. The sirens were again quiet; he could hear chirps of morning birds and a low babble of conversation from the A'zurnians over the idling rumble of nearby traction systems.

"All ready to call the Fleet in from orbit, Lieutenant," the rating declared. "Your time window begins...now."

Brim nodded. "Call 'em," he ordered.

Instantly, patterns of light changed position and hue on the console while overhead KA'PPA rings spread lazily from the beacon on its portable tower. "Sent," the rating reported. Then, only clicks later, he added, "And acknowledged, Lieutenant. They're ready."

Brim nodded. "Pack it up then, ladies," he said to the BATTLE COMMs. "We'll be moving out momentarily." Then he trotted across the field and hoisted himself up the ladder. Climbing over the coaming, he turned to stare out the open hatch—listening.

He waited only cycles before he heard the distant rolling thunder. Nothing else in the Universe made a sound like that. Big, deep-space antigravity generators, a number of them, if his ears heard correctly. As far as his eyes could see, the overcast was shredded now into distinct layers of gray and white cloud tinged here and there by the gold of a still-hidden dawn. Below these, visibility was perfect. The rumble quickly grew to a crackling, pulsing thunder he could feel as well as hear. Soon the very air was steeped in it, a palpable, physical sensation that seemed to shake the very warp and woof of the planet itself. Direction was obvious now. Brim peered into the fleecy clouds—any moment now. From the research center, he caught the overwhelmed wail of sirens. He grinned to himself. Too late for those, too!

Presently, the ships came arcing down among the distant clouds, growing rapidly as they steered directly for his hill. At the same time, the entire Universe dissolved in an unbelievable storm of raw, physical sound that physically throbbed against the massive field pieces and blasted the forest on either side of the cable right-of-way in a cloud of dead leaves. For a moment, the sky itself darkened, then the three big K—type Fleet destroyers glided overhead not more than two thousand irals high, their slipstreams whistling shrilly past bridges, deckhouses, and casemates as they came. Each hatch and housing on their undersides was visible as twelve long-barreled 200—mmi disruptors indexed smoothly downward, targeted on the research center.

An instant later, all discharged in crackling waves of blinding green plasma and incredible concussion. Brim felt his hair stand on end. Trees glowed and sparked with globs of ball lightning, and the buried cable itself writhed burning from the ground in a traveling burst of soil and debris. Then a monstrous black cloud erupted over the hill with a vivid core of crimson and yellow flame as the three destroyers banked away to port into a gentle climbing turn, their disruptors returning to fore-and-aft parked position. When the noise level dropped again, Brim could hear wild cheering from the A'zurnians. No one remained alive down there, and they knew it as well as he.

"Ships're calling for you, Lieutenant," Barbousse yelled, pointing to the COMM cabinet.

Brim ripped himself from his near trance and stepped into the control cabin. "Sublieutenant Wilf Brim here," he shouted.

"Commander Englyde Zantir here, Wilf," a voice boomed from among the flashing lights. "We're at your service as long as you need us. What else can we do to brighten your morning, Lieutenant?"

Brim stiffened. Englyde Zantir—everybody knew that name: dashing hero of a thousand hard-won battles. At his service. He was stunned. "Th-Thank you, Sir," he stammered, then quickly recovered. Hero worship could wait. "We need to find Colonel Hagbut's men, Commander," he continued. "They've been captured. If they're still in the area at all, they ought to be near their personnel carriers—six of them, I think. Last transmission came from nine thirteen point five by $E9_G$."

"Personnel carriers," Zantir repeated thoughtfully. "Well, we'll have a look for them." In the distance, the rumble from the destroyers began to intensify again.

Brim looked toward the top of the hill, beyond which huge chunks of molten rock and debris were still falling through the towering column of smoke. "You people up to traveling some more this morning?" he called to the A'zurnians. "We need to move up the hill."

"Oh, we're all right, Lieutenant," a voice called out from the pitiful collection of rags and starved flesh. "You Imperials worry about driving this thing, and we'll worry about hanging on."

"Yeah," another called out. "We've got a few scores to settle."

Brim nodded to Barbousse; the traction system roared and the field piece lumbered ahead. At the crest of the hill, Brim gasped first in astonishment, then in dumbfounded horror. Even the A'zurnians hushed with awe. Below, in the place where the research center once stood, all that now remained at the base of the towering smoke column was a glowing, bubbling crater perhaps two thousand irals wide and a hundred irals deep. Around this, a charred circle of smoldering, melted destruction extended outward another thousand irals. The blackened cable trench ran from the top of the hill and disappeared into the lurid incandescence below. He shook his head—a single salvo! So much for map locus 765_{jj}.

It was the renewed A'zurnian cheering that brought him back to reality. The broken-winged wrecks of once-flighted beings were now on their feet, clapping each other on the back and pointing toward the destruction as if they were possessed (which, in retrospect, he supposed they were).

He smiled grimly. Thus grew the seeds of Nergol Triannic's eventual downfall!

"Commander Zantir for you again, Lieutenant," Barbousse interrupted.

Brim nodded. The rumble of the destroyers was getting louder again.

"Believe we've found old Hagbut for you, Wilf," Zantir's voice chuckled from the COMM cabinet. "Six armored personnel carriers, Imperial built. Is that right?"

"Yes, Sir," Brim replied. "Six of them."

"Not far from you, then," Zantir said. "Two hills distant, near a quarry of some sort. Do you have a chart?"

"I've got one, Commander," Brim answered. "An A971FF."

"Good," replied Zantir. "Like mine, with the late research center at the top. Your hill is the next one down. Right?"

"Aye, Sir."

"Two hills to the left of you is what looks like a stone quarry. See that?"

"I see it, Commander," Brim acknowledged.

"That's where they are, Wilf," Zantir said. "The six troop carriers are parked on the paved apron you see surrounding the pit. The whole thing's guarded by eight big Leaguer battle crawlers of some kind: Shouldn't be much of a problem for those field pieces you're in. They're pulled up close around the pit so they can aim at the prisoners."

"Thank you, Sir," Brim replied as he studied the chart. No cableway connected him to the enemy position, but his BATTLE COMMs by now were adept at handling the big machines with rudder pedals alone, and the path to the quarry looked as if it were clear of obstructions for most of the way. "We still need your help, Commander," he added.

"Name it, Wilf," Zantir replied. "We've got more than nine metacycles to get you back to *Prosperous*."

"Aye, Sir," Brim answered. "And what I need more than anything else right now is your noise."

"Our what?"

"Your noise, Commander," Brim repeated. "While you're orbiting the area, we can sneak up on anything, even riding these roaring monsters."

"Aha," Zantir exclaimed, laughing. "Good thinking, Wilf! Regula Collingswood said you were a bright lad, and she's seldom wrong. We'll be back in half a moment—at which time nobody will so much as hear himself think!"

176

Brim looked out at the A'zurnians, no battle suits for them. No protection from anything—and in a very few cycles, a pitched battle was a distinct possibility. He slid the window open beside him, leaned out, and explained the situation in as few words as possible.

"What that means," he concluded, "is that we can leave you here in the safety of the forest or you can go with us. The choice is yours."

Not a moment of hesitation elapsed. They roared back as one voice, "We go. We go against the League!" In moments, A'zurnians on the other field pieces had also taken up the shout and turned it into a litany. "We go. We go against the League! We go!" Then the stillness of the skies shattered once again as Zantir's destroyers returned.

The next cycles were the noisiest Brim could remember in his lifetime. Once he gave orders to move out, the three destroyers took up station around the quarry, circling at a constantly diminishing radius that brought one of them blasting low over Brim's galloping field pieces every fifteen cycles. Even in the protection of his battle helmet, the noise was absolutely deafening. He marveled that the A'zurnians could stand it out on the unsheltered flanks of the vehicle, but all were flapping their pitiful wing stumps excitedly and pointing ahead like children on a holiday outing.

The six bellowing, steam-spewing vehicles covered the distance to the quarry in what seemed to be no time at all. They were soon charging up the last hill toward a wide opening in the surrounding ring of dense forest. On either side of the opening, two huge—incredibly old-looking—carved columns rose into the morning sky, each topped by the figure of a huge flighted warrior, wings outspread as if in gliding flight. "Double up!" Brim yelled at the COMM cabinet, wondering if anyone on the receiving end could hear anything he said.

His answer came in moments, when the second field piece in line pulled abreast on his starboard side and thundered along in tandem with him, hostages grinning and laughing in the slipstream as they clung to the vehicle's bucketing deck. The convoy exploded between the two stone columns, scattering Leaguers left and right as they came. "Stand by," Brim yelled into the COMM cabinet. "Starboard column takes the starboard side of the pit, port takes port—and have your disruptors aimed at one of those battle crawlers!" As they burst onto the apron, he saw a score of Leaguers sprinting for their battle crawlers, but already they were too late. The big field piece careened wildly to port as Barbousse skidded out onto the apron, then again to starboard as they raced along the periphery of the pit. He watched the disruptor indexing smoothly this way and that as Fragonard compensated for Barbousse's wild maneuvering, but it was always aimed for one of the enemy battle crawlers. The ordnance work done in the forest had not been wasted. Then the traction engine bellowed in reverse while the big vehicle shuddered to a stop in a boiling cloud of steam.

As the other five field pieces skidded into place, Zantir's voice boomed from the COMM console. "Looks as if that went well, Wilf."

"Aye, Sir," Brim answered. "So far..."

"I shall put up into orbit above the atmosphere, then," Zantir said, his voice amplified above the roar of his generators. "You'll be able to negotiate with them a bit more easily if they can hear what you have to say, and we'll stick around to back you." The roaring boomed momentarily, then Brim watched the triangular shapes disappear into the clouds and suddenly the landscape was saturated with a delirious silence.

In the first tentative chirps from surrounding trees, Brim watched the stunned Leaguers begin to revive. Beyond, at the quarry pit, the Imperial prisoners started to wave and cheer. Beside him the ex-hostages only stared in deadly silence at their torturers. They sensed their time was near.

Abruptly, the Carescrian was galvanized into action. "Fire up the outside amplifiers," he whispered, thinking furiously. "I have a game to play with these bastards, and I learned the rules from a man named Valentin."

***

The amplifiers clicked on and hummed. Brim watched the dazed Leaguers freeze in place and warily turn toward his field piece, waiting. Then, from the corner of his eye, he caught the turret of one of the enemy battle crawlers as it surreptitiously began to creep around from its bearing on the prisoners. Squelching the amplifier input, he hit the turret interCOMM. "Take out that battle crawler between those two piles of rocks, Fragonard," he ordered calmly. "Right now."

178

"No problem, Lieutenant," the ordnance man said, "now that I've got these honkers calibrated." The stubby disruptor overhead moved smoothly to the left, dropped rapidly, then thundered, rocking the massive chassis back on its gravity cushion. Opposite, the League battle crawler disappeared in a neat cloud of blackish flame, ragged chunks of debris wobbling over the trees and out of sight. The too-clean stench of ozone filled the air, but not a stone was disturbed on either side of the void where the battle crawler had been.

"Nice," Brim commented.

"All in the setup, Lieutenant," Fragonard said modestly.

Nearby, a Leaguer in a black suit had begun to emerge from one of the battle crawlers. The figure stopped to peer at the empty space, turned for one quick glance at the glowing disruptor on Brim's field piece, then disappeared again into the hatch.

Brim lifted the squelch from the amplifiers. "Surrender, or we blast you all to atoms," he broadcast in Vertrucht. "As you can see, we've learned a thing or two about your cannon."

Silence.

"Four archestrals remain for your answer, fools," he said. "Then we destroy you." That gave them two full cycles to make up their minds.

An amplifier clicked on at the black-suited Leaguer's battle crawler. "Another shot from those field pieces, and we kill our prisoners, Imperial fool," a metallic voice warned.

"So?" Brim inquired imperiously.

Surprised silence ensued. "Well... ah...you know," the metallic voice said lamely. "We kill all these Imperial prisoners we have captured. Including your Colonel Hagbut. Make no mistake, Imperial. We mean what we say!"

"Of course you do," Brim said laconically. "But that really doesn't have much effect on me—or my mission, does it?"

"What do you mean?"

"Listen, Hab'thall," Brim chuckled into the amplifier, "my orders say to bring back the six personnel carriers you've got parked on the apron; they're expensive. We can get soldiers anywhere, and of course we'll have to shoot old Hagbut anyway for getting himself captured." He looked at his timepiece. "You have two archestrals left."

More silence. Finally, the voice came again from the battle crawler. "You say you can replace the soldiers anywhere?"

"Well, of course, fool, just like you," Brim answered. He knew he had them now. "You kill those prisoners; we bring the personnel carriers back empty—with you dead, of course. Otherwise..."

"O-Otherwise?"

"Well, you certainly must know that," Brim answered. "Otherwise, we blow up your battle crawlers without you in them. Either way, we get what we came for, understand?"

"Yes...I ah, understand."

"I was pretty sure you would," Brim said. "All right. Time's up. What'll it be? We have a busy day ahead of us." Above his head, he watched the big disruptor index toward the next enemy battle crawler. "Ready..." he broadcast. "Aim...!" The other disruptors indexed slightly.

"We capitulate! Don't shoot!" the metallic voice screeched, this time in broken Imperial Avalonian. "We capitulate!"

Suddenly, the A'zurnians and the Imperial prisoners in the pit erupted into wild cheering. Brim took a deep breath, hoped his voice wasn't shaking too noticeably, then spoke again into the amplifier. "Very well," he broadcast. "Then I want those battle crawlers of yours emptied immediately. Everybody out. Weapons on the ground in front of you. I'm sending the A'zurnians to make sure none of you retain any surprises." He watched the cheering ex-hostages pile off the field pieces and hobble toward the battle crawlers, all of which were soon open, crews standing forlornly before them, their side arms and blast pikes in the hands of their former A'zurnian captives. Brim silently wondered how many of the Leaguers would be alive by the time the sun set. The lucky ones, he concluded, would not be among them.

**

"...And I've given the personnel carriers to the A'zurnian underground as well, Colonel Hagbut," Brim explained. "They'll take them over immediately with the Leaguer battle crawlers, then send crews with us on the run to Magalla'ana so they can drive these field pieces back when we ship out." Two ragged A'zurnians stood quietly at the rear of the control cabin.

Hagbut's eyes narrowed for a moment—Brim could almost swear

he heard clockwork clattering, then the man's face broke into a wide grin. He put a fatherly arm around Brim's shoulders and thumped him on the back. "You make me proud of you, boy," he roared. "I knew you had it in you when I put you in charge. I shall write a favorable memorandum on your behalf."

Brim felt his eyebrows raise, along with his hackles. A half-stifled snort issued from Barbousse at the COMM cabinet.

"I shall tell my high command that the success of the mission is actually a tribute to the fine training I received at old Darkhurst Academy," Hagbut continued, striking a heroic pose. He turned to address the A'zurnians. "This accomplishment, gentlemen, is merely the latest in the unbroken series of military victories which mark my career." He indicated Brim with his free hand, as if the Carescrian were his personal prodigy. "I provided this talented young man with the proper equipment for his task, instructed him as to mission parameters, then commanded him until I could no longer physically command. Once properly instructed and equipped, he merely followed my lead to insure the success of the mission." He turned again to Brim. "Yes, young man," he said, "I shall write a highly favorable memorandum concerning your part in this successful operation. You follow orders well!"

"Four-metacycle departure warning from *Prosperous*, Lieutenant Brim," Barbousse interrupted in a choked voice.

Brim winked at the big rating, then turned to Hagbut. "Perhaps we should consider starting out for Magalla'ana, Colonel," he suggested. "Took us a bit more than three metacycles to drive here in the first place, and we left a real mess to negotiate at the end of that high suspension bridge."

They both stopped to watch the BATTLE COMMs hoisting an Imperial Fleet battle pennant to the top of the KA'PPA tower where it fluttered lazily just below the transmitter—more magic courtesy of Barbousse.

Hagbut nodded his head and glared out of the corner of his eye. Then he took a deep breath. "All right," he conceded. "Lieutenant Brim, you may broadcast orders for my men to mount the field pieces immediately."

***

They only just made it. When Brim's steam-breathing field pieces charged into the pickup zone with battle flags flying, they became the last vehicles to return at all. The whole area was littered with abandoned equipment. Only one large shuttle remained idling in the center of the lift-off area, crewmen at both hatches beckoning frantically with their arms.

"I think they want us to hurry," Barbousse said as he braked the big machine to a halt.

"So do I," Brim agreed. "If that League fleet is still on schedule, Anak and his battlecruisers can't be too far away any more." He switched on the amplifiers. "End of the line, gentlemen," he announced to Hagbut's soldiers. "Everyone into the shuttle over there—on the double!" Instantly, the men began clambering to the ground. Hagbut was out of the control cab before Brim had even stopped speaking and led the sprint across the field. "Don't stop for anything," the Carescrian added, chuckling, then he turned to the pair of gaunt A'zurnians who would take his field piece back into the hills.

One wore the battered tricornered hat of a highly placed A'zurnian nobleman, the other was totally bald with a huge red welt from his prominent nose to his right ear. Both were filthy and disheveled. Their wings had been cruelly snapped from their backs, ripped away, leaving long, ragged blades that moved slowly, uselessly, while they talked. Except for a few facial differences, they were alike as twins, he thought with a twinge of pity. But then, emaciated people all tended to look alike. He had discovered that long ago in Carescria: Cheeks sunken, joints swollen, dressed in tattered rags that hung in shreds from their bony frames. Yet in these hollow eyes burned sparks of hope and deep, bitter anger. These wrathful men would soon make implacable enemies for the conquerors of A'zurn. No fear of death remained among them. Each long ago relinquished all hope for his life.

Barbousse had just finished reviewing the controls one last time. "Any more questions, gentlemen?" the big rating asked with a grin. "We want to be sure you put these mechanical brutes to the best use possible."

"Thanks to your patient instruction, we have none," said the one with the tricornered hat. "My colleague and I will master the machine with practice."

182

"At one time," the second one croaked, holding up a spindly forefinger, "we were masters of many machines. Fine machines...."

"But few weapons among them," the other said with surprising vehemence. "When we have scourged Triannic's plague from our homeland, we shall never again neglect that part of our responsibilities."

"Nor forget a brave Imperial lieutenant named Wilf Brim—to whom we credit all success of the mission," the scarred one added. "Someday," he said, "when a new generation of A'zurnians have regained our heritage of flight, we shall properly thank both you and Starman Barbousse. Meanwhile, there are ways to appropriately express our appreciation in a more current time frame."

Brim smiled with embarrassment, fighting a lump in his throat. "Just keep on fighting," he interrupted. "Live and win! That's thanks enough for any of us." Then he saluted the two gaunt warriors before they could continue, and followed Barbousse down the ladder. "Good-bye and good hunting," he shouted as his feet hit the grass. An instant after he cleared the hull, the traction engine roared and the field piece lumbered off after the others toward the protection of the low hills that formed the lower boundary of the city. In the control cabin, the man with the tricornered hat was saluting him through the armored glass. Respectfully, he returned the salute, then turned and sprinted desperately after Barbousse for the shuttle, which was half buttoned up and clearly ready to lift. Only the aft hatch was still open, with a gaggle of BATTLE COMMs crowding up the ladder.

"COME ON, you worthless Fleet types," Hagbut yelled from the opening. "Anak's ahead of schedule. Get a move on it!"

Running for all he was worth, Brim glanced over his shoulder—nobody was there. He and Barbousse were the last off A'zurn! Somehow he found strength to run even faster.

The shuttle was already moving forward when he followed Barbousse onto the ladder, shaking with exertion. It was climbing vertically when the big rating dragged him by his arms through the opening, panting desperately.

The next days became a confused mélange of wailing sirens and sprinting crew members—beginning with a full-emergency takeoff when *Prosperous'* powerful Drive crystals shook her massive hull like a storm-driven leaf. Every few metacycles, alarms clattered in the liner's bridge as sensitive detectors picked up long-range BKAEW locator probes from the enemy battlecruisers, but the return signals were evidently too weak to betray the Imperials' location, and after a time the probing came less frequently, finally ceasing altogether on the morning of the third day.

Raid Prosperous was over.

***

During the return to Gimmas-Haefdon, two personal messages from widely separated sources caught Brim's attention immediately. The first, from Effer'wyck@Haefdon, had been sent only metacycles after his release of the A'zurnian hostages. It contained the following lines penned—he assumed—by Margot herself. "Wilf the Helmsman flies faster than Fate: Wilf is he who rides early and late,/Wilf storms at your ivory gates: Pale king of the Dark Leagues, Beware!" Her short message ended with the cryptic sentences: "Today, Wilf, I begin to earn my own way in this awful war. Think of me." This time, it was signed simply "Margot."

Brim wasted little time puzzling over the words during his return flight; he was relishing plans for discovering their real meaning (among other things) in person. Instead, he sent a short note of thanks, signed only "Wilf," then settled back to dream of his next rendezvous at the Mermaid Tavern.

The second message, from Borodov@Sodeskaya/983F6.735, contained another cross-reference to the *Journal of the Imperial Fleet*. This article was much nearer the front of the file and started:

> Gimmas-Haefdon (Eorean Blockading Forces) 228/
> 51995: Sublieutenant Wilf Brim from I.F.S. *Truculent*
> played a decisive role in the recent A'zurn raid. Leading
> 25 men and eight captured mobile cannon under the
> command of Colonel (the Hon.) Gastudgon Z.
> Hagbut, X_{ce}, N.B.C....

The usual debriefing followed *Prosperous'* planetfall at Gimmas-Haefdon, this time conducted by a dried-out commander who may well have been as skilled in his profession as Margot Effer'wyck, but infinitely less pleasant to Brim. It seemed as if the cycles crawled by before he returned to *Truculent*—and the base COMM system.

He called up her code the moment he entered his cabin, but found to his dismay that Margot was "temporarily reassigned and unavailable for personal contact." Emergency messages, he read, could be directed to her usual address, so long as the sender harbored no illusions concerning time of delivery. And no date was set for her return.

With a grim sense of foreboding, he now began to seriously question what she might have meant by earning her own way in the war. But his subsequent efforts to learn anything resulted in dismal failure—everywhere he tried. Personal inquiries were turned away at the Technology Assessment Office by low-level clerks, and his own clearance was insufficient to gain him audience with anyone who might have access to further information. It was as if she had disappeared from the Universe.

So he sent a number of messages to Effer'wyck@Haefdon—all remained unanswered, and he finished the remainder of *Truculent's* refit amid varying shades of gloom to match the weather outside. Not even the obstreperous return of the Bears from Sodeskaya really helped, though a sudden increase in his meem intake considerably dulled the worst pangs of loneliness.

A brief ceremony celebrated Barbousse's promotion to Leading Torpedoman, then a few Standard Days later, *Truculent's* lengthy refit was complete. Two weeks of space trials proved out her new systems, and Haefdon's perpetual storms once again ebbed to insignificance in the aft Hyperscreens. The perceptive Collingswood wisely saw to it that Brim's responsibility—and metacycles at the helm—were greatly increased during this, his second tour on blockade. And with this extra duty, the image of Margot Effer'wyck once more began to fade from his mind's eye. In time, her memory became bearable once more, but only just. Clearly, her "reset" had been much more successful than his.

7

Partway into an endless early morning watch, Brim and Theada attended *Truculent's* helm while most of the crew snatched a few cycles' badly needed rest below. In the nearly deserted bridge, only occasional warning chimes and snatches of disjointed conversation disturbed the muted rumble of the generators. Off to port, a bleak asteroid shoal crawled diagonally astern beneath the bows as though the destroyer were skirting the surface of some infinitely large inclined plane.

"Good morning, friend Wilf," Ursis said cheerfully, materializing in a display globe. "What gradient have we outside?"

"Morning, Nik," Brim said, peering at his readouts. "Looks like it's shifted a bit, now that you ask."

"So," Ursis mumbled, entering data via an overhead console.

"Let her fall off a few points to starboard nadir, Mr. Chairman," Brim ordered. The steering engine sounded for a moment, and the oncoming stars shifted slightly in his forward Hyperscreens.

"Course nine ninety-one, orange," the Chairman reported.

"Very well," he acknowledged, studying *Truculent's* decks by the glow of a smoky dwarf blazing overhead. He swung his recliner aft, scanning the trunk of the KA'PPA mast and twin globes of the directors. Farther back, he cursorily checked the scorched cowling of their torpedo launcher flanked by the hemispheres of W and Z turrets. All appeared in trim, as usual. He had just reached above his head to start a suite of power system checks when a shadow fell across the main console. He looked up to find Gallsworthy leaning over Theada's recliner.

"Take a break, son," the senior Helmsman muttered, indicating the bridge exit with his thumb. "I'll keep the seat warm while you're gone."

"But, Lieutenant," Theada protested, "I just had a..."

"You look tired, Theada," Gallsworthy said sternly. "Tired."

"Oh. I, ah, see, Lieutenant," Theada agreed, fairly jumping out of the recliner.

Gallsworthy nodded. "Give us about ten cycles," he said.

"Aye, Sir," Theada said, squeezing his way into the main bridge corridor.

Gallsworthy thumped into the recliner and frowned, drumming his fingers on the console. "I guess I'm a messenger today," he said, glowering at Brim. "Collingswood's asked me to pass on a bit of information she doesn't really want to talk about."

Brim nodded, trying to appear indifferent—but inside he was all curiosity. Collingswood normally needed no intermediaries. She said what she wanted—when she wanted. "Yes, Sir?" he asked.

"She's got herself dunned with another xaxtdamned Admiralty detail," Gallsworthy explained. "Has to 'volunteer' some of the crew. Only..." He pursed his lips and drummed his fingers again as if he were having trouble with the words. "Only," he repeated, "she got a few extra parameters with this order. Nobody's supposed to know about 'em. But you're a special case, in her eyes." He scratched his head for a moment, then nodded as if reaching some internal accord. "I guess I agree with her," he said with a frown, "for whatever that's worth, Carescrian."

Brim's curiosity was really piqued now. Senior Helmsmen never shared personal opinions with people who reported to them. He waited. Gallsworthy would get it all out in his own good time.

"What it boils down to," the man continued at some length, "is that you, your friend Ursis, Theada, Barbousse, and a couple of ratings are going to form a temporary team—Regula will brief you in a couple of cycles about it. And she's put Amherst in charge of the whole thing."

Brim nodded within. So that bothered her! He calmly scanned the instruments, waiting.

"She wanted you to know," Gallsworthy said presently, "that she didn't make the Amherst assignment by choice. That part came in a personal note from Amherst's father—you've heard of Rear Admiral Amherst, I'm sure."

Brim nodded sourly. He'd heard, all right. According to Borodov, the Admiral had been among the loudest and most vocal opponents to the passage of Lord Wyrood's Admiralty Reform Act. It certainly showed in his son.

"The old boy decided Puvis needed a bit more exposure in the media. Maybe a couple of medals to help the next promotion." He chuckled gruffly—and uncharacteristically. "Probably you had something to do with that, punk, what with those articles you got in the Journal. So whatever happens, figure it's your own fault, one way or another."

"I'll try to remember that, Sir," Brim said, more than a little relieved it wasn't something worse. Life as an everyday Carescrian was still fresh enough in his mind that he could put up with quite a bit of harassment.

"Thank Collingswood sometime. I'm just the messenger," Gallsworthy said. "And, yeah, there's one more thing."

"Sir?"

Gallsworthy nodded his head, indicating the systems console farther back in the bridge. "You have the job of telling Ursis. He's not going to like this at all."

***

Within the metacycle, all four officers sat awkwardly together in Collingswood's cramped cabin, Ursis' bulk crowded in a center position. The Captain (dressed, as usual, in her worn sweater) was explaining what little she knew about the mission. "The Admiralty wouldn't give me much detail. Not even where you are going. Just that it involves a very small starship, some sort of attack ship, I imagine. That and a mercifully—for me—short duration: three Standard Weeks maximum, they say." Her eyes looked at Brim with a twinkle of humor. "These little side trips are getting to be a habit with you, Wilf," she said.

"Aye, Captain," Brim agreed with a grin.

"At any rate," she continued, "the requirement is for four officers: someone in command, two Helmsmen, and an engineer. That ought to tell you where each of you fit. Plus a Torpedoman and a crew of six general-purpose ratings. I'll be sending Barbousse to run that lot for you."

"Barbousse," Amherst gasped with raised eyebrows. "Why, he's only just been promoted to that rank. Besides which, the big lout has absolutely nothing between his oversized ears, er, Captain."

Collingswood's eyes narrowed. "I believe," she said patiently, "Barbousse will serve quite admirably. His records indicate a number of assignments within that duty category."

Amherst sniffed, glancing first at Brim, then at Ursis. "Bloody lowbrow crew, if you ask me," he grumped peevishly.

Brim glanced at Ursis. The Bear scowled.

"That will be sufficient, Lieutenant," Collingswood warned Amherst. "You will carry out the assignment as ordered, whatever your personal feelings. Is that understood?" Her quiet voice had suddenly turned to hullmetal.

"Yes, Captain," Amherst agreed hurriedly. "I, ah, understand."

"Good," Collingswood said. "Because I am also permitting the mission to proceed as organized, while harboring some rather serious reservations of my own."

"Well!" Amherst started, then clearly thought better of it and abruptly shut his mouth.

Collingswood closed her eyes and tapped her toe. "Since I have little more information to impart," she said stiffly, "I declare this meeting at an end. We rendezvous with your pickup ship in approximately two metacycles; it will, I am assured, take you to your mysterious destination. Good luck to all," she said in a clear sign of dismissal. "I am sure I do not have to remind any of you that I expect performance that reflects favorably on the Imperial Fleet and on *Truculent*." Then, abruptly, she busied herself at a console.

"We shall do all in our power, Captain," Amherst muttered stiffly, leading the way from her cabin. Brim followed Ursis and shut the door quietly behind him.

"Try to report to the transport hatch on time, you three," the First Lieutenant said. "I shall leave it to your judgment who should be responsible for notifying Barbousse." Then he hurried self-importantly down the ladder and disappeared into the next level below.

Brim looked at Theada and smiled. "Don't worry," he said. "It won't be all that bad. Besides, Amherst has no objections to your pedigree at

190

all." He patted the younger Helmsman on the back. "Go down and pack for a three-week trip; we'll meet you at the hatch. All right? If we all stick together, everything will come out all right. You'll see."

Theada nodded his head and smiled bravely. "I guess," he said uncertainly. Then with a grimace he followed Amherst down the ladder.

Brim stood and shook his head and looked at Ursis. "Wonderful," he said with a wry grin. "Just thraggling WUN-der-ful."

The Bear frowned. "Perhaps, Wilf Ansor, is not as bad as seems, especially in light of, shall we say, 'special' information Captain Collingswood provides."

"How can that be, Nik?" Wilf asked. "We both know what he's like when he's got the wind up."

"Just so," Ursis growled quietly. "And for selfsame reason, I for one will never unthinkingly follow orders from him again. Nor, I suspect, will you."

Brim nodded. "You're right, Nik," he said. "Never again."

"Therefore," Ursis pronounced, holding his hands at his chest, palms inward, "we may be only team can operate successfully, given circumstances." He narrowed his eyes and looked Brim directly in the face. "Others might well hesitate crossing him—as I once hesitated—with same disastrous results."

"I was as guilty of that as you," Brim interrupted.

"'Guilt' is Imperial word looks only toward past," Ursis observed with a smile. "One of most useful truisms from my homeland. This duty is only in present and future. Yes?"

"It is."

"Then Lady Fate smiles once more on tired old Empire," Ursis said. "Let us notify large compatriot, Barbousse, and prepare for whatever Lady has in store."

***

Shortly after midwatch, the "volunteers" gathered at *Truculent*'s main hatch in time to view their rendezvous. Directly on schedule, a light cruiser swooped up out of the blackness and pulled smartly abreast. "Brand new," Ursis observed. "One of new Nimrons, from her silhouette."

"I.F.S. *Narcastle*," Brim read, squinting through the Hyperscreens.

"That one's just finished fitting out," Theada said. "They must have called her in from her space trials." Outside, brows connected with a muffled series of clangs. Only moments later, air hissed into the passage and a mooring crew unsealed the main hatch.

"Look lively," Amherst whispered impatiently. "I shall brook no slackers while I am in command." Motioning the others to hurry, he shoved Barbousse roughly toward the transparent tube. Brim frowned. Something was definitely bothering the First Lieutenant. He briefly wondered what it was as he followed Barbousse into the hatch.

On his way through the tube, he got a better look at the new starship. She was shaped like an oversized lance and appeared twice the length of *Truculent's* angular hull. Like all Nimrons, she was specially built for high-speed reconnaissance work supporting battle-fleet operations in deep space. Accordingly, she was also lightly armed for her size, carrying only six small turrets on rings about a third of the way from bow and stem. A scant superstructure was topped by a sharply raked control bridge, and six hefty Drive plumes merged from oversized blast tubes exiting just behind her aft turret ring.

Inside, she smelled every bit as new as she was. Ozone, sealant, hot metal: all the familiar detritus of a starship—except the odors of life. Those latter took time to accumulate. And she certainly had been called in from her space trials. Civilian contractors everywhere he looked. Even the tube operators were dressed in the distinctive silver and green spacesuits of the big commercial shipyard at Trax.

The team was met at the opposite air lock by a tight-faced lieutenant commander with a large red mustache and narrow-set eyes, who regarded them as if they were some special brand of nuisance. "This way, gentlemen," he directed unceremoniously, directing the way down a narrow companionway to a large cabin clearly intended to house portions of a permanent crew. "I shall have to ask all of you to stay here for the remainder of the trip," he said. "Someone doesn't want you mingling with any of the trials crew we've got on board—too many civilians and all that sort, you know."

"By whose authority, Commander?" Amherst protested peevishly.

"Mine will do as well as any, Lieutenant," the officer said, pointing to the lieutenant commander's rings on his cuff. "And besides," he added as he slid the door shut in Amherst's face, "I'm not authorized to talk to any of you, either."

Brim shrugged and looked at Barbousse, who was standing politely with his five ratings. "What do you know about this?" he asked out of the side of his mouth. "You always have advance word about what's going on."

Barbousse chuckled quietly. "Aye, Sir," he admitted. "That I usually do—but not this time. It's caught me as much by surprise as you."

Moments later, the steady rumble of the cruiser's Drive increased to a deep thunder, and Brim watched through a small Hyperscreen scuttle as the familiar shape of *Truculent* dwindled rapidly in the distance.

Ursis cocked a furry ear for a moment, then frowned. "The flight crew is certainly in a hurry to go somewhere," he said. "Drive crystals are wide open, from the sound of things." He settled into a recliner, crossed his legs, and folded his hands across his chest.

"Just what do you think you are doing, Lieutenant?" Amherst demanded angrily.

"Relaxing, Lieutenant Amherst," the Bear said as he shut his eyes. "Until someone lets us out of this cabin, it seems to be the most intelligent thing we can accomplish."

Brim and Theada spent a few moments in desultory exploration of what little there was to see in the room, but eventually thumped into recliners beside him. Barbousse and the other ratings followed suit.

Amherst continued to look annoyed, but clearly had no acceptable rejoinder to any of them. "Oh, very well," he said lamely. "I shall, ah, notify you what is expected next."

"I look forward to that," Ursis grunted quietly. In a few moments more, he was snoring.

The team was confined in the cabin for more than two Standard Days, during which time the sound of the Drive never slackened from its original HIGH setting. They transferred to a large, curiously rust-colored shuttle craft only when the Narcastle had driven deep into a very empty-looking portion of the galaxy.

***

Their mysterious destination turned out to be a barren, irregular chunk of red-oxide rock orbiting an isolated gas giant where none of the star formations looked familiar to Brim. A flattened, bubble-shaped structure perhaps one hundred irals in circumference clung to a reasonably "level" section of the rock—colored to blend into the background. As the shuttle dove toward landfall, a worried-looking Amherst nudged the pilot and pointed below. Outside the bubble, three mean-looking attack ships hovered in the stillness at the end of short mooring beams: Examples of an entirely new type of starship with comparatively short range but often capable of speeds in excess of 150 LightSpeed. Many Helmsmen—including Brim—thought starships with such capabilities might well become dominant in many types of future applications. All three of these were of League manufacture, and all appeared to be heavily armed.

"Don't let our STSs bother you," the pilot drawled through a reddish mustache as he turned onto final approach. "All three of those little tubs down there belong to us." Oddly, his name was Blue, though his hair was red, crested to a remarkable degree, and his complexion a chalk-like white. He had a narrow face with a thin nose and long freckled hands. He wore no battle suit (strictly against Imperial regulations in a shuttle), only a rumpled fatigue uniform with soft, casually scuffed boots that looked far more comfortable than military. He also handled the big shuttle as if he had been born at its controls.

Brim chuckled to himself with a strong suspicion that Blue and he would have much in common, as backgrounds went, but elected to keep his silence. The subject of pasts wasn't one of his favorites, either. He peered down at the enemy attack ships—clearly Collingswood's "little starships"—and felt his curiosity piqued again. What now?

***

Inside, the bubble structure was divided into a warren of "rooms" by partitions that did not quite touch the curviform top. Everything about the structure looked ready to be dismantled at a moment's notice. Military gray prevailed nearly everywhere, though occasional areas were finished in more humane colors. The air was uniformly dry and almost unappetizingly without odor, a common attribute of such tiny, self-contained way stations that recycled the same limited set of atoms to sustain life in the midst of the lonely void.

After a squat, gruff-looking woman with Mechanic's blazes on her collar took charge of Barbousse and his ratings, the officers followed Blue into a narrow companionway. This ended in a severe cubicle containing a few display cabinets and a circle of uninviting field chairs, clearly some sort of conference room. Before they could sit, a door opened at the rear. "Gentlemen," Blue announced, "Colonel Dark."

Long-legged, slim, and graceful, Colonel Dark was dressed in the sleek blue coveralls of Lord Wyrood's Imperial Intelligence Service. On her, the tight uniform revealed a great deal more than it concealed. Her complexion was almost chalky white and she wore long jet-black hair in a braid that coiled all the way to her knees. Her eyes were large, almond shaped, intelligent, and hard. As she spoke, she fingered a curiously shaped obsidian fragment that could only be a splinter of hullmetal: Some grim personal reminder, Brim considered, and decided he wanted to know nothing more about it—ever.

"Special-duty crew from I.F.S. *Truculent* reporting, Colonel," Amherst began importantly. "I am Lieutenant..."

"We are aware of everyone's identity, Lieutenant Amherst," Dark interrupted in a soft, husky voice, nearly ignoring his salute. "While you are here on Red Rock 9, we shall have little time for amenities of any kind." She bit her lip as she unconsciously worked the hullmetal fragment between long, well-manicured fingers. "Sit down and listen carefully," she said. "You have approximately two days to qualify for the mission."

As he took his seat, Brim glanced quickly at Amherst. An ill-concealed look of astonishment had taken root on the First Lieutenant's face. He was clearly unprepared for military conduct outside the strict rules of Fleet protocol.

"If you prove to us you can master an STS, the operation's 'go' and you'll have all the details you want. If you can't, we'll simply scrub the whole thing and send you back home with our thanks for making the try. But..." She paused significantly in midsentence to look each officer squarely in the eye.

Brim felt his eyebrows raise.

"But," Dark repeated, "a surprise attack mounted by the Leaguers on another starbase—it doesn't matter which one—deprived us last night of your backup crew. So if you don't make it, the mission won't happen at all, and a very important person will probably die. Additionally, the Empire will lose a lot of information it vitally needs for its survival."

Amherst suddenly looked concerned, almost frightened. He opened his mouth as if he were about to speak.

Dark held up a warning hand. "Don't ask questions, Lieutenant, until after your crew masters operation of the Leaguer STS. Before you have accomplished that, I have nothing more to say."

***

Brim and Theada spent the next half-day buried in a captured STS simulator while the others learned what they could about the attack ship's systems makeup from Imperial databases. Brim had never flown anything like the little starship, but was immediately impressed with its possibilities. Then, following a short rest period, the entire team donned battle suits and pulled themselves along zero-grav lifelines to the ships themselves.

"Apparently, they want us to use the one marked E607," Amherst said on the suit circuit, pointing to the rightmost of the three docked starships. "They say they keep the others here for spare parts."

Closer inspection proved this to be true. Two of the attack ships were clearly missing important components, with hatches opened to the emptiness of space and holes yawning blindly in the control cabins in place of Hyperscreen panels.

E607, however, was ready to fly: A deadly wedge of raw destructive power. Overall, its sharply angular sixty irals described nothing so much as a narrow, single-edged ax head turned on its side with a small control cabin located midway along the length of its upper surface. On either beam, angular outriggers extended forward from the squared-off stem, each virtually filled with a powerful Klaipper-Hiss type—41 antigravity generator. The ship's wide, keen-edged bow was deeply notched on port and starboard extremes to accommodate torpedo-tube doors in the beam ends of the hull. Between these, a squat, dome-shaped turret housed a 60-mmi rapid-fire disruptor. Aft of the rakish control cabin, a spacious well deck extended to the stem, bounded on port and starboard by the breech ends of the torpedo launch tubes and storage for the single reload carried for each. Offset a few irals from the center of the well deck, a row of twelve repulsion rings ran over the stem from a squat autoloader. These marked the little ship's limited capability to strew star mines in its path. Her flat bottom was clear from bow to stem except for an oversized weapons dome housing a powerful 91-mmi disruptor. Within the crowded hull, a single Drive crystal provided thrust for HyperLight dashes and occasional long-distance cruising.

Inside, the cramped control cabin was laid out in a conventional half circle with the two Helmsman's positions facing the forward Hyperscreens. Along the starboard side, a systems console extended to the air lock in the aft bulkhead, and, curiously, included activators for firing the big 91-mmi in the ship's belly turret. Miscellaneous controls, including those for the torpedo tubes and repulsion rings, were built into a neatly organized collection of panels that made up the port control array. The rapid-firing disruptor forward was operated directly from either of the Helmsman's consoles.

Once Ursis stabilized the ship's power, Brim doffed his battle helmet and sniffed the cabin's thin, stale air, taking stock of the uncomfortable seats and drab, strictly functional decor around him. "Grim" was probably a good characterization, he thought. Leaguers built fighting ships with only three real abilities: flying, fighting, and surviving. Everything else was sacrificed to the minimum necessary for operational reliability—including crew facilities. Two small cabins composed the single acquiescence to living occupancy. They were crammed under the forward deck between the torpedo tubes: a two-bunk cabin for officers, a four-bunk cabin for ratings. It wasn't merely uncomfortable, it was xaxtdamned near to being unacceptable. He shrugged. Only tough, dedicated crews survived on these grim little ships. "Fire up the generators, Nik," he said, nodding to the Bear as he perched his bulk atop an undersized recliner. "Let's get this bucket out in space."

Ursis nodded, checked the immediate area outside, then hit the start sequencer. Moments later, the big generators shuddered into life, filling the crowded cabin with a savage, uneven thunder that shook the hull with brutish power. The Bear busied himself with various displays and controls for a few moments until the uneven tumult quieted to a steady rumble and the deck ceased to tremble. "Both generators are standing by, Wilf," he announced with a thumb in the air. The hull rang with vents clanging shut, and the air lock rattled.

Brim checked his own readouts, then looked at Amherst from the left Helmsman's seat. "The ship is ready when you are, Lieutenant," he announced.

"You may proceed," the First Lieutenant sniffed, nodding conspicuously down his nose. But his manner failed to hide the sweat standing out on his forehead—in the coolness of a battle helmet he had yet to remove.

"Aye, Sir," Brim said, squelching one more flash of anger. As the power director came up on forward thrust, he nodded to Barbousse. "Cast off, fore and aft," he ordered.

"Aye, Sir," the big rating said, and spoke into a small personal communicator.

Outside, balanced on the decks, four of *Truculent's* borrowed ratings wearing huge reflective mittens to protect their hands, raced up to extinguish the ship's mooring beams, then dogged down protective hatches over the optical cleats and jogged across the deck to the control cabin. He waited until the men were inside, then watched for his signal from the bubble house aft. Presently, a ruby-colored beacon began to strobe in the darkness at the far end of the asteroid.

"Safe takeoff vector dead ahead," Theada reported.

"Got it," Brim acknowledged. He entered the course manually on the flight director (small starships seldom carried Chairman systems), then called for full military power and stood on the gravity brakes. Again, the cabin filled with the brutish sound of surging generators, and the deck began to vibrate beneath his feet. He glanced at Ursis, who grinned and yanked his thumb in the air.

"Let's go, Wilf Ansor," the Bear growled in a huge voice.

Brim winked and returned his attention to the controls. He'd no sooner released the gravity brakes when the beacon—and all of Red Rock 9—instantly vanished astern in a bellowing surge of power from the generators. Zero-gravity takeoffs all tended to be rapid, but the captured STS was in a class by itself! He grinned; he hadn't had so much fun since he'd flown the little JD-981s at the Academy.

During their next two watches, the team worked tirelessly, exercising each of the ship's flight systems at high speeds, first in free space, then through a crowded asteroid reef orbiting the gas giant at a slightly lower altitude. After two close brushes with disaster (the last of which badly pitted a quadrant of the ship's unprotected Hyperscreens), Brim began to get the hang of things.

"Voof!" Ursis exclaimed admiringly as the Carescrian completed a particularly complex course. "'Wind and cold seek lakes and trees, but Bears claim only wolves,' as they say on the Mother Planets. Wilf Ansor, my friend, you exceed yourself!"

Brim laughed and cranked the skittish little ship into a vertical turn across the reef, huge rock clusters scorching past on the port side in an avalanche of riotous color. "Once you do something like that on a Carescrian ore barge," he yelled over the thundering generators, "it seems pretty easy in something like this."

"You will concentrate on flying, not talking, Lieutenant Brim," Amherst warned through tight lips. "Have you forgotten so quickly what you did to the Hyperscreens?"

Brim glanced up at the pockmarked screens. "I haven't forgotten, Lieutenant," he acknowledged, biting his lip to control his voice. At the same time, he noticed that sweat was now running freely from Amherst's face. The man was afraid!

On his way back to Red Rock 9, he fairly skimmed the surface of a particularly jagged asteroid—and smiled with satisfaction as he watched Amherst squeeze his eyes shut. The Universe kindly provided more than one way of extracting life's little dollops of revenge, he noted with silent satisfaction.

***

The eleven *Truculents* passed a second set of watches exercising the ship's weapons systems (during which, Barbousse accurately torpedoed a ship-sized asteroid), then invested a short period in HyperSpace running on the Drive crystal. When they finally returned to Red Rock 9, an abrupt message recalled them to a meeting with Colonel Dark—immediately.

"Welcome, gentlemen," the almond-eyed woman said as the tired crew clambered into the conference room still dressed in battle suits. "It seems my call for assistance from the Fleet was answered this time with reasonably competent Blue Capes." She smiled for the first time that Brim could recall. "Sometimes we get the best," she continued, "often the worst. It depends on the captains involved, I suppose. Regula Collingswood seems to have done us proud."

"You mean we qualify for the mission?" Amherst asked, a genuine look of concern on his face.

"The team has indeed qualified, Lieutenant," Dark answered, "but only in the merest nick of time. At that, I have been forced to delay your departure until commencement of the second watch tomorrow— my ground crew needs additional time to replace Hyperscreen panels damaged by the initial sloppiness of your Helmsman, Lieutenant Brim," she said pointedly.

The Carescrian felt color rise in his cheeks as he mentally braced for more criticism. Instead, for the second time he watched Dark's face break into a smile as she turned to face him. "Don't take my 'sloppiness' too much to heart, Brim," she laughed suddenly. "No one expected you could do what you've done at all—and you've triumphed." Then her face darkened. "But it also means you now have the actual job to accomplish. And when your crewmates hear all the details, they may wish your Helmsman's talents ran more toward singing or sculpting, perhaps, than piloting a small starship."

At that moment, Brim noticed Theada and Ursis glance uneasily toward Amherst; he followed their gaze. The First Lieutenant had again broken into profuse sweating, though Dark kept temperatures low in her conference room. The Carescrian winced to himself. Somehow, trouble was coming, and he was reasonably sure the least of it would be with the League. But before he could fret about the situation, Dark began her final briefing, and no time remained for anything but concentrating on the mission.

During the remainder of that watch and well into the next, Dark described their task in detail: flying the STS to the very heart of Triannic's League—almost within sight of the great capital planet of Tarrott itself—executing a tricky landfall on Typro, a barren mining planet, retrieving an important Imperial spy, then retracing their steps to a rendezvous with an Imperial warship. "On the surface, it sounds simple," she said. "We've set up three time windows for the pickup. You will determine which one to use after you arrive on the basis of safety: Yours and the operative's." She fingered her hullmetal fragment absently and frowned, staring bleakly across the room. "Unfortunately," she continued, "I have only described the easy part—your mission as originally planned was quite straightforward and relatively free from risk. However, recent developments have made the job somewhat more symmetrical in that it now involves a difficult part, too."

Brim looked at Ursis and grinned in spite of himself. The Bear silently rolled his eyes to the bubble ceiling.

"First, you must travel to Typro and return in a little more than three Standard Days' time," Dark continued. "That's when the Leaguers will discover these STSs of ours are missing from their inventory." She paused a moment, then shrugged. "We acquired them in a rather unusual fashion we'd rather you didn't know about," she added. "Just in case you find yourselves guests of our black-suited friends, the Controllers."

Amherst abruptly excused himself from the room.

"The second unknown is the real reason we have set up this operation in such a hurry," Dark explained, ignoring the First Lieutenant's hurried exit as if he never existed. "We very much suspect our agent has been compromised," she said, "and I am sure you understand what this means to you. If it is true, they'll be waiting around Typro with open arms and give you a very special reception, one with every trick they can muster."

***

Early in the first morning watch, Dark resummoned Amherst, Ursis, Brim and Theada, this time to her office, which was just as cramped as Collingswood's aboard *Truculent*. E607 was moored just outside a transparent wall section behind a console. "You're scheduled out today, gentlemen," she began when the scuffling of chairs ceased. "And I have a few last-moment items you'll need to complete your mission." She smiled, caressing the hullmetal fragment with her fingers. "First," she said, turning to point to the ship, "see if you can find anything different about your Leaguer attack ship since you last saw her. I'll even provide a hint: Concentrate on the control cabin."

Brim peered at the raked-back structure, taking in every detail he could see, naming every appurtenance and protrusion. Nothing looked different or even out of place. He turned to Ursis, who met his eyes, frowned, and shrugged in resignation. From the corner of his eye, he disapprovingly watched Amherst studying Dark herself instead of the ship, then scanned the control cabin one more time before he finally gave up. When he looked, the Colonel's eyes were directly on him.

"Well, Lieutenant?" she queried.

Brim gulped and shook his head. "Whatever it is you've done, Colonel," he said with a resigned smile, "you have certainly hidden it well from me."

Grinning with obvious satisfaction, Dark swiveled her chair to face the room. "Good," she declared, "because if you haven't spotted it when you're sitting right on top of it, then the Leaguers certainly won't notice out in space." She directed their attention to the ship again with a flick of her head. "Look at the KA'PPA tower, gentlemen," she said, "right under the globe. What do you see there?"

Again, Brim peered out at E607. He followed the short KA'PPA tower to its transmitting globe, squinted, then snapped his fingers. "Universe!" he exclaimed. "I missed that completely. You've got two beta feeds on the A input, don't you?"

Dark laughed. "Right you are, Brim," she said. "And only one of them is real."

"Voof!" exclaimed Ursis. "Beautiful job, Colonel Dark."

"Good as Sodeskayan engineering, Lieutenant?" Dark asked with a grin.

"Well," the Bear said with a shrug and a twinkle in his eye, "perhaps not that good—but good enough to fool this Bear!"

"Ha, ha! Excellent answer, Ursis," Dark said. "Now let me tell you what the left beta feed really is, because you are definitely not looking at two of the same device." She smiled almost proudly. "It's what the boffins call a BURST attachment: Operates with your regular COMM gear. I don't have any idea how it works, but it does—sends a whole bloody message in less than a billionth of a click. On anybody else's COMM gear, it's automatically filtered out with all the other static spikes in space. This one can recognize a BURST message and translate it."

"How easy is it to use, Colonel?" Ursis asked.

"Like slipping on a ca'omba peel," Dark quipped. "We've got yours wired in; you'll find a couple of extra goodies on your COMM cabinet. No voice or video. Works just like a KA'PPA, in that sense—symbolic output only."

The Bear nodded. "It sounds fine to me, Colonel," he said.

"Unfortunately," Dark continued, "we haven't had much luck with another important portion of that COMM cabinet: Your authentication key."

Brim mentally winced. Not good at all. Every military starship in the Universe carried some kind of device to return a properly coded "authenticator" signal when "challenged" by similar equipment aboard another vessel. The coded authentications were changed on a random—but regular—basis, and if E607 didn't have an up-to-date authenticator, then the fact that the little attack ship was an authentic Leaguer ship would have little effect at all.

Dark grimaced from her recliner. "Oh, we've got one for you to use right now," she said. "But it's just about expired. We simply don't think it will hold out all the way through your mission—especially if you must use the last of your three time windows." She laughed humorlessly. "The League has selfishly failed to send us the next one in the series for E607, so you'll be on your own if you're in enemy territory when the one you have goes invalid." After a few more words, she wished each of them good fortune, pressed their hands one by one, then sent them on their way.

***

Within the metacycle, Red Rock 9 again vanished in the aft Hyperscreens, and E607 was running HyperSpace, on course for the barren mining planet of Typro, a destination deep within the League. A final message came from Dark about three-quarters through the next watch. It arrived as their first BURST interception: "'Closing this base immediately,'" Barbousse read from the COMM cabinet. "'After Typro pickup, fly course 794 by 819 on 6153E. Imperial warship will: (1) intercept your course, (2) assume care and feeding of spy, (3) complete your orders. Good fortune to all.'"

Through it, Amherst sat in his command recliner in stony silence, his eyes unfocused, as if he had abandoned reality for some safer, more acceptable existence within. To Brim, the man seemed to be deep in some sort of shock. He shook his head uneasily. A critical juncture was imminent, and he sensed he would be deeply involved when it came.

In the metacycles that followed, the First Lieutenant began to find his tongue again, but by now, he had undergone a profound change. Vanished was the arrogant Puvis Amherst Brim had known. He was replaced by the withdrawn, sweat-soaked stranger who had first shown himself on the League starship *Ruggetos* just before its recapture by Praefect Valentin.

At first, Brim attempted to ignore the behavior, as did the others, with inconsequential small talk. But constant interruptions as to "How much farther?" and, "Are you sure the authenticator is in place?" finally broke through their common restraint.

"What's the matter with him, Wilf?" Theada whispered from the side of his mouth. "He's acting crazy."

Brim shook his head and frowned. "I don't know," he admitted as the ship veered suddenly toward a space hole off to port. He carefully eased the helm back on course. "Maybe nothing," he ventured.

"Nothing?" Theada protested. "Don't try to hand me that, Wilf Brim. Universe, it doesn't take a bloody genius to..."

"What is this talk about?" Amherst demanded anxiously. "What's the matter?"

"Change over on the power supply, Lieutenant," Brim lied over his shoulder in a soothing voice. "Perfectly routine."

"Very well," Amherst said uneasily.

Brim turned to watch the man more closely. So did Ursis.

"Perhaps the mission risks too much," Amherst said, silhouetted against the steady glare of the flowing Drive plume aft. "A crew of eleven and a valuable starship for one spy is not a good bargain in my estimate." He turned in his seat. "Is this not so, Barbousse?"

The big Torpedoman jumped as if he were bitten. "I, ah-" he started.

"Not so much of a risk as all that, Lieutenant," Brim interposed. "A simple pickup is all. We've been in much more danger in *Truculent*, you know."

'That is not the point, you...Carescrian," Amherst snapped, biting his lip.

"Then what is the point, Lieutenant?" Brim asked gently.

"It's...it's..." Suddenly, Amherst's eyes narrowed. His face contorted in a paroxysm of hate. "Oh, no!" he hissed. "You'll not do that to me. You and the rest of the low-life scum—Bears and ratings. And that brazen whore Dark. Trash! That's what you are. Trash!" He jerked himself around in the recliner and pointed toward the right-hand Helmsman's seat. "And you'd better watch yourself, Theada; they'll drag you down with them!"

In the shocked silence that followed, Ursis checked his readouts, then rose to his feet and moved slowly to Amherst's side, where he placed a hand on the man's shoulder. "Lieutenant Amherst?" he asked in a gentle growl.

"Take your filthy paw from my uniform, animal!" Amherst grunted, his eyes suddenly clearing. "How dare you touch my person? Remember that I am still your commander!"

Ursis removed his hand, looked at it a moment, then nodded to himself. "You are still in command, Lieutenant Amherst?" he asked gravely.

"Of course I am still in command," Amherst said as he got to his feet and strode toward the tiny sleeping cabins as if nothing unusual had occurred. "What could have made you ask that question?"

"We may yet discuss such a subject, Lieutenant," Ursis growled after him, then returned to his console and the power systems. Save for the steady rumble of their Drive, the remainder of the watch passed in near silence.

***

A few metacycles prior to the first time window, Brim eased the little ship out of HyperSpace and proceeded toward Typro on generators alone. Now deep within League territory, he openly followed a main spaceway as if the STS were part of a normal, everyday mission. The authentication key on the COMM console chimed now and again as passing ships challenged their identity, and the mission appeared to be running a normal course, as planned. During the last metacycle, however, something had begun to gnaw at his peace of mind, though he couldn't quite put his finger on what it was. Something about their approach was ever so slightly out of kilter, and it worried him. Any rock hauler knew it was the little details that do you in, and he scoured his mind for them—to no avail.

Far below and to port, an outbound freighter saluted them. Barbousse returned it promptly—his KA'PPA reply was not even complete before the authenticator chimed.

Brim watched the lights as the key reset, then checked his flight instruments, initiated a long systems self-test sequence, and lined up the navigation follower; it was a hair out of alignment. He was feeding in a series of adjustments from the master console when it finally hit him. The authenticator! Why was a merchant ship challenging him?

"That was a merchant ship a few moments ago?" he asked Theada suddenly.

"Th-That's what the salute said," Theada answered vaguely as he concentrated on a diagnostic logic run.

"A merchantman?" Ursis asked, turning from his console. "What was a merchantman?"

"The starship that just passed us," Theada answered, this time looking up to see what was so suddenly interesting. "Said he was a merchantman."

"I see," Ursis said. "And he used an authentication key?"

"That seems to be the case, Nik," Brim acknowledged.

"Merchantmen don't use authentication keys," Ursis growled.

"You noticed also," Brim said with a chuckle.

"What is all this talk about?" Amherst demanded from the companionway.

"The merchantman we just passed, Lieutenant," Brim answered, peering at a red light blinking suddenly on his overhead panel.

"What about the merchantman?"

"Someone aboard used an authentication key on us, Sir," Brim explained over his shoulder as he switched to a backup cooling system for the steering gear. The red light extinguished.

"So?" Amherst said. "Is there anything wrong with the authentication key?"

"Well, Sir," Brim said, "most merchantmen don't carry an authenticator. It's a piece of specialized military gear, more or less."

"I know that," Amherst snapped. "And this idle talk is the best entertainment you can dredge up to while away your time?"

"Well, actually, Sir," Brim said, "I was pretty serious about the whole..."

Amherst cut him off with an imperious wave of the hand. "Don't bother me with the details, Brim. You are permitted to speak among yourselves. Just be certain you pay very close attention to the job of flying this horrible little starship." He shivered and took his place at the commander's console.

Brim turned to Theada. "Jubal," he said, "you and Barbousse check the other ships we've passed in the last metacycle. See if they saluted as civilian types and then kicked off the authenticator, too."

"Aye, Sir," Theada said, slipping from his seat.

Brim slowed their approach speed to provide extra time to act—just in case.

The younger Helmsman returned with Barbousse in only a few cycles. "We've passed eight of them, Wilf," he replied with a look of concern. "A mixed bag, mostly, but all commercial, and each one challenged our authenticator."

Brim looked over at Ursis. "What do you think, Nik?" he asked.

"Strange," the Bear pronounced. "Eight out of eight, so far, and all civilians. Makes me wonder."

"Right," Brim agreed. "Not to mention the fact that we've encountered no warships of any class."

"None until now," Theada interrupted tensely. "Look what just matched courses with us up ahead." He pointed through the forward Hyperscreens.

Brim peered into the darkness where the stars were occluded by a monstrous shadow. "Military?" he said.

"That's what the Challenge just said," Theada acknowledged. "Gives the ID number as DN-291."

"DN?" Ursis repeated. "That's the League designation for heavy cruisers, but what does '291' stand for? Smallest DN number I can recall is 408."

"Old one," Theada said, snapping his fingers. "Of course. All two-hundred and three-hundred series cruisers were retired a couple of years ago. At least."

"You suppose they kept a few for perimeter defense?" Ursis mused. "Like ultraheavy patrol craft."

Brim grimaced. "For perimeter defense maybe, but surely not as patrol ships. I doubt if two-hundreds are maneuverable enough for that kind of work." He shook his head. "No, Nik, it's my guess that old DN-291 comes out only for special projects."

"Special projects?" Theada asked.

"Of course," Ursis interrupted with a grin. "With a flotilla of so-called civilian patrol craft. Correct?"

"I think so, Nik," Brim said, watching a blue navigational beacon wink far off to port. "It's the way I'd set things up myself, probably."

"I don't follow you," Theada said.

"Nor do I," Amherst complained from the hatchway. "You Carescrians are certainly not very articulate. It probably has something to do with your second-rate educational standards."

Brim gritted his teeth. "Must be, Sir," he said. "I only formed the idea while we were talking."

"Well?"

"Yes, Sir. The way I see things, Colonel Dark's fears that our spy was compromised appear to have been well founded."

"What does that have to do with the cruiser?" Amherst interrupted nervously.

"I think DN-291 is part of a special group, Lieutenant," Brim grunted as the little attack ship abruptly swerved to nadir in a gravity draft. "And the patrol ships supporting her include the supposedly commercial/civilian ships that have been tripping our authentication key for the last watch or so." He thought for a moment while he gentled the ship back on course. "My guess is that they're out to catch both our spy and the ship sent to bring him out."

"It explains why we haven't seen any regular patrol ships," Ursis added.

"Make sense to you?" Brim asked Theada.

"Yeah, Wilf," Theada agreed, looking up from a navigational fix. "It does."

"I suppose it does make some sense," Amherst volunteered. "I never had much hope we would find this 'spy' of theirs. Perhaps we should abort the mission and return home immediately."

Brim raised his eyebrows. "Oh, no, Sir," he ejaculated. "I never suggested anything like aborting the mission. We'll simply have to be a bit more cautious when we go in—maybe skip the first window and just skirt the area."

Suddenly, Amherst's face went pale and sweat began beading on his forehead again. "No?" he cried sharply. "Well, I am in command of this ship, and I say we return home now, before we catch up with that battleship."

"Cruiser, Sir."

"Whatever it is, I order you to turn back now!" Amherst demanded.

"But, Sir," Brim protested, "we can't just turn around and leave without at least trying to pick up that spy. Why, something like that would be murder, plain and simple. We've got to make at least a couple of tries."

"How dare you question my order?" Amherst spluttered, angrily rising to his feet. "Lieutenant Brim, you will immediately place us on a reverse course and, and..."

"Enough!" Ursis rumbled, stepping suddenly to the center of the cabin. "Amherst," he said, "I made solemn promise to myself you would not again destroy mission if I could prevent—and I shall now carry out promise."

"What?"

"Sit down," Ursis said, seizing the First Lieutenant's arm and forcing him back in the command recliner. "Is meaning what I say, you should believe."

A clearly startled Amherst looked first at Theada, then at Brim, eyes widening in dawning fright. "You are not going to permit this to occur, are you, Brim?" he implored. "He's calling for mutiny."

"I support Nik completely," Brim said quietly. "And you now have a choice which you must make immediately: either lead the mission like an officer or relinquish your command. We shall not tolerate another episode like the one on Ruggetos. You understand, I am sure."

Amherst's face turned scarlet. "I shall have both of you arrested and thrown into..."

"Not here you won't," Ursis growled. "Now consider carefully choice Lieutenant Brim gives you—I would not be so generous."

"I...I..."

"Your choice, Amherst. Quickly," Ursis said. "We shall overtake the cruiser in the next few cycles. We cannot be busy immobilizing you during that time."

"Well...I..." Amherst looked imploringly at Theada. "D-Don't you want to go home?" he asked.

"I'd love to, Puvis," Theada said. "But first, we've got to at least try to pick up that spy."

"Barbousse?"

"I've sent one of the men for some rope to tie him up, Lieutenant Brim," Barbousse said, ignoring Amherst completely.

"Your choice, Lieutenant?" Brim asked.

Amherst looked around the room for support. There was none. He took a deep breath, choked back what sounded like a sob. "I-I shall remain in command, then," he whimpered, his eyes overflowing.

"Good decision," Brim said. "Go to your cabin and don't return to this deck until we tell you to. Understand? We'll get you home as soon as we accomplish our mission."

"Heavy cruiser coming up to starboard, Wilf," Theada said as the first warning sounded from the proximity alarm. The little attack ship was already tossing heavily in the big warship's gravity wake.

Brim nodded. "Barbousse, let's ready that salute—the recording they gave us on Red Rock 9."

"Aye, aye, Lieutenant," the big rating said, sliding to the COMM console.

"Bastard's making sure he gets good look at us," Ursis commented. "He's been edging our way since he turned on our course."

"I'll gladly give him the look he wants," Brim chuckled darkly. "We're legal outside, even if he wouldn't particularly like what he'd see in here." Ahead, the big ship continued its drift to port. It was clearly visible through the Hyperscreens now.

"Talk about your weird starships," Theada said. "Look at that, would you." The old cruiser was stubby and humpbacked, with a confusion of wart-like turrets protruding from its ungainly hull as if sown at random like wild seeds. Many of the larger protrusions were connected to others by great flying bridges and walkways. Four huge turrets ringed the hull a quarter of the way from the stern; each mounted two huge disruptors. The stubby weapons reminded Brim of the ugly disruptors in Hagbut's captured field pieces—from the size alone, they promised to be a thousand times more powerful at their lowest setting. A squat, complex deckhouse stumbled forward from the turret ring where it terminated in an awkward, thrust-browed bridge that gave the whole ship a look of primitive stupidity. Formidably armed, though, if taken altogether, Brim thought abstractedly as he flew his little attack ship carefully past. But the insubstantial Drive openings aft made it obvious she would be clumsy and difficult to manage in HyperSpace. He guessed the same would prove true under antigravity generators as well. He watched Barbousse's salute expanding out from the KA'PPA: "ALL HAIL NERGOL TRIANNIC— CONQUEROR OF THE STARS." It was followed immediately by the cruiser's response: "AND RIGHTFUL RULER OF THE COSMOS—ALL HAIL!" Brim chuckled to himself for a moment. Margot would love that! Then, suddenly they were past, running in smooth space again, and the cruiser was receding aft, slipping back to starboard from where she had come.

"Score one for the *Truculent* team," he cheered. "We've passed!"

"Glad to see that one go," Theada swore.

"No more than this Bear," Ursis agreed. "You saw size of disruptors?"

"I noticed," Brim said, grimacing. "I'll definitely avoid that ancient rustbucket, anytime I can."

***

A quarter metacycle before their first possible rendezvous, E607 was rapidly bearing down on the pickup zone with Typro now a recognizable globe hiding the stars ahead. Brim patted the little BURST section on his COMM console. "Nothing more than a symbolic display panel and some controls," he said to Ursis. "But we've got a lot riding on it."

"Spy is having a lot more yet," the Bear growled sardonically. "I would not trade places."

"Lieutenant Brim," Barbousse interrupted unsurely, "would you look at this?"

"What's up now?" the Carescrian asked.

"Reception committee orbiting Typro, from what I can see, Sir," the big rating said. "Switch one of your displays to the long-distance target scanner for the torpedo system."

"Got you," Brim said, switching the spare globe on his own console to the torpedo display. He squinted, then nearly gasped. "Universe!"

he exclaimed. "They really are ready for us," he said. "Looks like they've got at least four ships orbiting there—waiting for somebody."

At that moment, the BURST gear chimed twice. "The time window begins," Ursis observed. "We have a prompt spy."

Brim's display filled immediately: "TIME WINDOW ABORT," it read. "DANGER TO PICKUP CRAFT."

Brim nodded his head. "Guess we now know who those orbiters are," he said as he altered course slightly. "We'll still have a look at things as we pass." He shook his head bleakly. "BURST an 'aborted', Barbousse," he ordered. "Whomever that poor bastard is down there, he's got trouble up to his ears."

As they passed Typro, the resulting confusion of challenges and authentications between E607 and the orbiting ships soon revealed there were five large patrol craft. "They're not making it easy," Brim groused while the planet receded in the distance.

"True," Ursis acknowledged with a frown. "'When rocks and crags tremble before great storm, Nemba cubs run for joy'."

"As they say on the Mother Planets, Nik?"

The Great Bear grinned, diamond-studded fangs reflecting the colored lights of his readouts. "You must be part Sodeskayan," he declared. "Never have I met a human who understands so much."

***

They spent the subsequent watch concealed close by a deserted, mined-out asteroid. Then, as the second time window opened, they once again cautiously approached little Typro with Barbousse's eyes glued to the long-distance target scanner. "Ships are still there, Lieutenant Brim," he reported after a time. "But now I see six of 'em."

The BURST gear chimed again. Barbousse was at it immediately. "Same thing as last time," he reported. " 'Danger to the pickup craft'."

Brim shook his head. "If he doesn't let us get into a little danger pretty soon, we'll never get him home."

"Probably," Ursis commented from his console, "the spy knows that as well as you. He's a brave one, all right. It must be difficult to send that signal—myself, I should want out as soon as possible, and damn the danger to the pickup crew."

"Me, too," Brim added, his mind working furiously. "Unfortunately, it is also getting xaxtdamned close to the limit of our authentication key, after which we don't move around so freely." He shook his head as they moved past the little planet, their authenticator answering challenges from all six patrol craft. "BURST the spy that we'll be back in the next window," he said to Barbousse. "And tell him that we're coming no matter what."

"ACKNOWLEDGE" and "THANKS" soon appeared on Brim's BURST display. He grimaced as he cruised past two of the patrol craft—big and powerfully armed. He listened to the authentication key working in the background and thought of the trapped spy hiding helplessly on the surface below. "I'm glad I don't have that kind of work," he said to no one in particular.

Ursis nodded from across the cabin. "I, too, Wilf Ansor," he said soberly. "Whomever he is, he has paid his dues in this war."

***

Brim got the bad news when the last window was still a quarter of a metacycle in the future.

"I count five patrol craft this time, Lieutenant Brim," Barbousse reported from the target scanner.

Brim nodded. He'd expected the patrol would still be in place—after all, the Leaguers were in home territory. They could afford a waiting game. "Action stations!" he ordered. He was definitely going in to get the spy. He simply didn't know how—yet.

With turrets manned, the attack ship's control cabin lapsed into silence except for the all-dominating rumble of the antigravity units in their outriggers. Brim drummed his fingers on the console and shrugged. At least they'd had no trouble with the little attack ship. Like a lot of League equipment, she wasn't particularly pretty or even sophisticated. But she was fast and reliable with a superb pair of antigravs. He nodded ironically to himself. She was c'lyents ahead of any similar starship the Admiralty had conjured up for the Imperial Fleet.

Ursis looked over sympathetically and smiled. "Could be worse, friend Wilf Ansor," he said. "At least E607's giving no trouble."

Brim grinned, pointing his thumb at this chest, "That's the same thing I've been thinking," he said. "And..." Abruptly, the Carescrian brought himself up short. "Sweet thraggling Universe, Nik," he said. "That's it. What we need is a malfunction to get us in there."

Theada rolled his eyes. "Oh, WON-der-ful," he quipped. "Whose side are you on, Wilf?"

Ursis chuckled. "Perhaps he has not yet defected at all," he said as he turned to Brim. "You are solving problem by looking at it from different angle, I assume, Wilf Ansor."

"That's right, Nik," Brim asserted. "So far, we've planned everything around this tub working flawlessly—and I'll bet the Leaguers have set up their trap expecting pretty much the same from whatever kind of starship comes along to pick up the spy. But I'll bet nobody's looking for something that doesn't work very well."

"Universe—of course," Theada exclaimed. "Any pickup craft would abort its mission if it had trouble. Sure..."

"But how about the malfunction?" Ursis asked with a grin. "How are you going to do that?"

Brim held up a finger, grinned, then turned to Barbousse. "Think you can operate that equipment for launching space mines?" he asked.

The big rating rubbed his chin and frowned, studying a section of the control panel before him. "'Nadzur' is the word for 'mine' in Vertrucht, isn't it, Lieutenant Brim?" he asked.

"Sure is," Brim said.

Barbousse nodded. "And I know 'imbal' means 'load'. I heard someone say that while we were tryin' to start those field pieces back on A'zurn." Passing his hand over part of the controls, he turned a whole sector to flashing green, then rubbed his chin. "Yes, Sir," he said presently, "I can work it. Looks like we've got ten mines on board."

Brim grinned. "That's it, then," he said. "Here's my plan. In the next couple of cycles, you're going to kick one of those out into our wake and immediately detonate it. From any distance at all, it'll look like we've had one great-grandsire of a malfunction."

Theada grimaced. "A space mine," he whispered with awe in his voice.

"The worse we can make it look, the better," Brim continued. "Because right after that, we're going to broadcast on the intergalactic emergency channel that our steering's gone."

"Oh, I get it," Theada exclaimed. "Out of control."

"Right," Brim said with mock melodrama. "Heading for a crash landing on Typro." He laughed grimly. "Bet you didn't expect anything like a crash landing, now, did you?"

"No," Theada agreed. "I suppose I didn't expect anything like that. But the longer I work with you, Wilf, well, it gets easier all the time."

***

"All weapons systems are energized, and I've got a star mine in the first hoop," Barbousse reported, glancing at the warty globe suspended in the forward-most repulsion ring. Twelve identical rings formed a flux tunnel extending over the stern and into the little starship's wake. At a gentle chiming, he nodded to the COMM cabinet. "Incoming BURST message, Lieutenant," he announced.

Brim turned to his own BURST display. "MISSION ABORT," it read. "TOO RISKY FOR YOU. MUCH OBLIGED ANYWAY."

"I expected as much," he said, biting his lip. He narrowed his eyes and turned to Barbousse. "Send, 'No options. On our way. Where do we meet?'"

All eyes were on the COMM now. The display flashed. "DAMN FOOLS," it read, "AND THANK VOOT! CABLE ROUTE 981, ZONE 54G, OPEN LORRY W/YELLOW CANISTERS. NUMBER 8 ON CAB ROOF. GOOD LUCK."

Brim checked his charts of Typro and nodded. "All right," he said. "Everybody set?"

"Let's do it," Ursis said. "Our spy is clearly ready to go, too."

Brim turned in his console to face Barbousse. "Let the mine go," he said tensely. "And blow it up as soon as it's safe!"

"Free..." Barbousse said as the deadly star mine accelerated aft through the repulsion rings and disappeared into the darkness. "Detonating." Immediately, a terrific flash pulsed the Hyperscreens. This was followed by a glowing, burgeoning, mountain-sized cloud that rapidly enveloped them in a paroxysm of flame and concussion.

Eyes slitted against the glare, Brim wrestled desperately with the controls as the little ship tumbled in the fiery blast, generators surging wildly. "Get ready on the KA'PPA, Barbousse," he shouted over the blazing confusion outside. "Standard code sent in the clear!"

When the worst was passed, Brim turned the controls over to Theada and fought his way back to the COMM cabinet. "BEWARE," he KA'PPAed in Vertrucht. "NAVIGATIONAL MENACE. BLOWN STEERING ENGINES. KEEP AWAY. SHIP OUT OF CONTROL. BEWARE." Then he regained his Helmsman's console and began to maneuver the little starship in awkward-looking, wobbling loops, each carefully calculated to bring the ship a little closer to Typro.

Momentarily, the authenticator began to chime with almost constant challenges. "That's got somebody's interest," Brim grunted with satisfaction as he skidded into a wild turn to port nadir, the spaceframe creaking with strain. "They'll want to use short-range COMM in a moment, Barbousse. Switch it up here to my station—voice only—no video!" As a tiny area on his center console glowed green, he swerved again sharply to port. "Beware," he broadcast in Vertrucht. "Internal explosion...Steering failure...Ship out of control...Beware..."

Suddenly, a blank COMM globe sprang to life. "E607, do you receive us?" a voice asked in Vertrucht.

"Audio only," Brim said after a few moments. "Video must have gone in the explosion. Beware! I am out of control!" He pulled through a tight loop to get a better look outside.

"So we observe," the voice said. "You are generally heading toward an area that is temporarily forbidden."

Brim swerved sharply, spotted the ship high to port, then sent the attack ship into a series of flat, wavelike spirals that made the deck shudder between their feet. "What in the name of Triannic do you expect me to do about that, fool?" he exclaimed. "You must have seen the explosion back there. If I could steer, I'd be nowhere near you or your xaxtdamned forbidden area!"

"Well, you will have to do something," the voice said, then stopped in mid-sentence as Brim abruptly turned and headed for him on a collision course.

"Look out!" the Carescrian yelled at the top of his lungs. With his new heading, he was upon them in mere clicks...past in a fraction of another, both ships swerving desperately to avoid disaster. Then the Leaguers were lost again in the starscatter as Brim called up full power and thrashed corkscrewing once again toward Typro. "Beware!" he yelled into the short-range COMM. "Keep away!"

"Universe, yes, do keep away," the other ship broadcast to the others. "They almost collided with us!"

The authentication key chimed again. Moments later, a woman's voice inquired sternly, "What is your intended heading, E607?"

"Presently vectoring toward possible emergency landing on Typro ahead," Brim answered, sensing a far stronger personality here. "There's not much I can do about it."

A long silence ensued, after which the woman's voice said, "Good fortune to you then, fool. None of my ships will approach in your struggles." Brim smiled. He hoped he never had the chance to continue that short conversation.

Other voices questioned him for a considerable time and the authentication key chimed incessantly. But all gradually faded in the distance as Brim wobbled toward his target, which by now almost filled the Hyperscreens ahead. Soon, it was amply clear he'd brought his ragtag ship's crew safely through Typro's blockade! He hoped it wouldn't turn out to be a one-way trip. Dark's authentication key had little time remaining!

In less than a metacycle, features of the arid surface began to define themselves—ragged mountains, dry riverbeds, the dim flicker of occasional cities. As the attack ship staggered deeper into the thin atmosphere, wisps of glowing plasma began to lick at the corners of the Hyperscreens, then spread rapidly to the hundred and one protrusions on the hull until they trailed a long, glowing corkscrew of ions like the meteor they had become. Gradually, Brim reduced his course perturbations, flying more and more in a controlled manner until finally, no more than ten thousand irals from the surface, he leveled off and flew a straight and level heading. "Universe!" he laughed, wiping mock perspiration from his brow, "with all that 'damage' to the steering gear, I didn't think I could bring her in at all."

Aft, Amherst slumped in a recliner, head lolling from side to side. "He's only passed out, Lieutenant," Barbousse reported.

"We're entering Zone 5," Theada said presently, pointing below through the Hyperscreens. "It's sort of delineated by the mountains and that scar somebody once called a river."

"Very well," Brim replied as he cranked the ship in a wide circle. "Do you suppose that's Cable Route 981 running along the edge of the scarp?"

"Only one I can see," Ursis said. "Of course, who could tell in this desert?"

Brim's eyes followed the ground scar where the cable had been laid.

About a third of the way to the mountains, two dust plumes crawled along the endless wastes. The second plume was considerably behind the first, but from its size, it was either a much larger vehicle or it was moving faster—or both. "If that first one's our spy," he said, pointing through the Hyperscreens, "he's going to have company very soon. Anybody see anything else moving?" he asked, easing the attack ship into a wide circle.

"None," Theada said as the ship returned to its original course.

"Just those two," Ursis agreed.

"All right," Brim said, "we'll go down for a closer look." He rolled the attack ship on its back, then nosed over into a steep dive that brought them above the second vehicle in a matter of clicks. "Ugh," he grunted aloud. Below was a typical Leaguer battle crawler with three turrets, the kind that ambushed his little convoy back on A'zurn, only this one looked bigger, even from the air. "Let's check on the other one," he said, opening the power gates slightly. The distance evaporated.

"Open lorry," Ursis observed.

"With yellow canisters," Theada added.

"And an 8 on the roof of the cab," Brim finished. "It's our man, I'll bet. Send: 'Which way is Avalon?'" he called back to Barbousse.

Only a few clicks later, his display flashed, "VOOT'S BEARD! YOUR ATTACK SHIP FOOLED ME. THOUGHT I WAS CAUGHT SURE. ALREADY GOT A BATTLE CRAWLER ON MY TAIL." Only moments later, a huge column of dirt and flame shot up to the lorry's right as the battle crawler began to pull in range. The attack ship bounced when the second blast followed on its heels, aimed this time at them. "CAREFUL," the BURST display spelled out. "POWERFUL BATTLE CRAWLER."

"So much for our cover," Brim muttered, hauling the attack ship around into a vertical bank toward the battle crawler and pulling off the lift vector. They fell like a stone toward the desert floor with both disruptors blasting wildly at the squat, ugly shape in the distance. Only a few irals from the ground, he whipped the little ship level and jammed on the power. All three Leaguer turrets were firing now. The attack ship bucked and bounced through the blasts; debris smashed off the Hyperscreens and rattled along the decks. Suddenly, a huge ball of fire from Barbousse's 91-mmi erupted at the battle crawler's bow, sending a shower of rocks and debris hundreds of irals in the air. The big machine reared and skidded sideways in a cloud of dust, then resumed its progress at a somewhat reduced rate of speed, wobbling violently.

"Got his cable follower!" Barbousse yelled exultantly as they flashed overhead. But the battle crawler's turrets were clearly unaffected and the firing continued almost unabated. Brim snapped the attack ship around and set up another low-level firing run. This time, Barbousse found his target much earlier, and the whole area near the enemy vehicle exploded in a welter of powerful blasts.

Suddenly, a thundering detonation sent the attack ship skidding wildly off course with loose articles whistling about like shrapnel and the cabin acrid in swirling black smoke. A monstrous grinding shrieked through the spaceframe as the left outrigger touched down and skidded across the plain in a cloud of dust and debris. Brim struggled with the controls, helplessly watching the his attack ship slide into a ground loop—then the hull ricocheted from a flat outcropping of desert rock and somehow wobbled level, trailing a long column of dirty black smoke that thinned and disappeared as Ursis calmly manipulated the N-ray mains and extinguished the fires.

"Our ninety-one's gone, Lieutenant," Barbousse yelled above the din. "Battle crawler blew the whole ventral turret away, he did."

Brim continued to fight the controls, achieving first an even keel, then an immediate turn away from the battle crawler with a maximum acceleration dash toward a run of low, rocky hills, the generators bellowing angrily in overload.

"What are we going to do now?" Theada yelled in frustration as they pulled into the lee of the palisades and set up a low holding pattern. "Our little 60-mmi won't even dent that armored cockroach, and the spy's still out there with nothing but a good head start."

Brim bit his lip, concentrated. Quickly. Quickly. "The mines!" he shouted. "Of course! Even a near miss ought to be enough to take a battle crawler out for good. Right, Barbousse?"

Barbousse grinned. "One star mine coming up, Lieutenant," he said.

"Wait a cycle!" Ursis interrupted suddenly. "The spy: Is he far enough from the blast zone? We don't want to take him out, too."

"Easily far enough by now, Nik," Theada answered. "Especially in this thin atmosphere. Remember, he was almost beyond the range of that battle crawler—and those big hummers shoot a long way."

"Very well," Brim said through clenched teeth. "Here we go." Wind roared across the great rent in the bottom of their hull as he banked gently to let the speed build up. Then he cranked the little ship over into a dizzying vertical turn that barely cleared the barren hillside. Jagged rocks whizzed by only irals from their starboard generator. By the time the battle crawler was back in sight, they were accelerating wildly and blending into the background. They took the big machine completely by surprise—in the last clicks, Brim pictured its crew huddled over the traction controls in an attempt to drive with no cable followers.

"Star mine's...free!" Barbousse yelled. Brim heard the hum of the repulsion rings, then the attack ship flashed over the battle crawler, still accelerating. Two more near misses by the Leaguers sent rock and debris over their stern before the whole world turned a blinding white: No shadows, no details, only white. The Hyperscreens dimmed, flashed on again.

And then the shock wave...

Incredible noise. Perhaps no noise—maybe all noise. The impact became an entire existence. One moment, they were speeding across the desert floor, the next, a giant hand smashed the little ship sideways like an insect. Brim struggled with the controls, easing the hull this way and that, instinct alone guiding his hands and feet as he fought to soften the shocks to the spaceframe. Then they were tumbling mindlessly through a gigantic storm of pure flame. Outside on the deck, only hullmetal survived: Covers, attachment points, cables, all their accessories either burned or melted in long runnels along the deck. In the back of the control cabin, someone was screaming over the suit channel in the gagging, fright-choked voice of a wild animal. Brim glanced over his shoulder. It was Amherst, tears streaming from his cheeks, faceplate sprayed with spittle. Nothing could be done for him. He tried to ignore it.

Then, quickly as it came, the firestorm disappeared and they were once again flying in clear air. Amherst's insane screaming died to a series of wracked sobs, then faded to silence. "By Voot's meem-stained beard!" Ursis roared in glee. "It is possible we may yet survive in spite of our fearless Helmsman." The control cabin erupted in laughter— but only for a moment.

"COMM channels are going full tilt," Barbousse reported from aft. "I think the whole Universe is yapping at once. Maybe you'd better listen in, Sir," he suggested.

Brim nodded. "Take the controls," he said to Theada, then brought up a COMM display. It took only moments to discover that every patrol craft in the vicinity was on its way at full speed. He squandered a few clicks to inspect the result of their mine. Most of the blast had gone upward, blowing out the top of the atmosphere. All that remained was a shallow, blackened crater perhaps a few thousand irals in diameter—that, and a still-rising pillar of dust and debris topped by a great roiling cloud with a curious wisp on its top.

"Looks like we stopped him," Theada commented dryly.

Brim nodded solemnly. "Yeah," he said, scanning the terrain. In the distance, he found the little wisp of dust again and smiled grimly to himself. "All right, *Truculents*," he said, "let's go pick up our spy. We're going to have a lot of company in a very short time—and none of them will want to help us."

***

Moments later, they were back over the lorry. "IF YOU'RE THROUGH PLAYING WITH THAT BATTLE CRAWLER, LET'S GO HOME," the spy sent.

Brim laughed. "Tell him we'll do that," he said to Barbousse as he eyed the cable right-of-way. It went straight as a die, all the way to the horizon. He nodded his head. "Send this as I say it," he ordered. "'Put the lorry on automatic. We must pick you up on the fly. Affirmative?'"

"YOU BET," appeared almost instantly in the BURST display.

Brim turned to Amherst, who was now awake and keeping a frightened silence in the recliner. "Will you help, Lieutenant Amherst?" he asked.

"Help you, Carescrian? On this insane mission?"

"You could help," Brim said as he eased the ship over the speeding lorry.

"I shall help none of you!" Amherst hissed. "You are only doing this so you can show me in a poor light to my superiors." In the corner of his eye, Brim watched the First Lieutenant fold his arms and close his eyes.

"Is no longer with us, Wilf Ansor," Ursis growled.

Brim nodded. "Very well," he said. "Nik, do you feel reasonably strong today?"

"Strong enough," came the reply. "What is it I can do?"

"I need somebody out there by the boarding ladder to guide me when I bring this crate alongside the lorry—then lend a hand when our spy climbs on board. Feel up to that?"

"Unless spy is too fat for lifting, Wilf Ansor," the Bear laughed. Brim heard him pull his helmet on.

"Just in case we do get a fat one," Theada interrupted, "I think I'll join Nik out there, if that's all right with you, Wilf."

"I welcome any assistance," Ursis grunted.

"Go to it, Jubal," Brim replied with a grin. Presently, the two appeared on E607's open utility deck, leaning into the wind and clipping their safety cords to eyelets built into the deck. Each had a coil of cushioned life-saving cable over his shoulder.

Then there was time for nothing but concentration. He made a final thrust adjustment, pulling above and to one side of the speeding lorry. His attack ship was nearly sixty irals in length and twenty wide; the spy's lorry little more than a third in any dimension. He made no attempt to delude himself concerning the difficulty of the job—this one would make barge piloting look easy! Starships weren't made for precision work at low speeds and navigational tolerances measured in irals. It would take only one sideswipe by his gravity pods and the whole trip would be wasted. He concentrated on the lorry, flying by instinct alone. "How are we doing out there, Nik?" he asked into the short-range COMM.

The Bear peered over the rail. "A little too far left, Wilf," he said, "but just about right height."

Gingerly, Brim nudged the controls to starboard.

"A couple irals closer yet," the Bear said. "Tell spy to open door now, but still too far for jumping."

"Send, 'Open your door'," Brim ordered Barbousse, then nudged the controls still further starboard.

"Watch!" Ursis said sharply, holding a warning hand aloft. "Is almost enough."

This time, Brim willed the ship's change.

"Perfect," Ursis declared. "Hold right there. Spy has got door open. I'm throwing him the end of this rope. Tell him to tie under shoulders."

"Got it," Brim said through clenched teeth, half afraid to move for fear of bumping the ship into disaster. "Send, 'Tie the cable securely under your arms'," he said to Barbousse. A moment later, Ursis lofted the coil.

"Missed!" the Bear growled in frustration.

"Proximity warning's beginning to flash, Lieutenant," Barbousse called out. "We'll have company any cycle now."

"Very well," Brim acknowledged. But there was nothing he could do as he watched Ursis coil the cable for another try. It was now—or it was never for the spy. If he was going to escape from this planet, he would have to fly the ship out in the next few cycles. He could not sacrifice his crew for one spy.

Again, the Bear lofted his coil. Brim gritted his teeth. "Please don't miss," he whispered to himself.

"Spy got it that time," Ursis said, relief sounding clearly in his voice. "And is tying under his arms. Can you move just a little closer again, Wilf? We have drifted few irals."

"Wilf!" Theada suddenly screeched. "Pull up. An overpass! Dead ahead!"

Brim looked up—even at their low ground speed, the bridge was only a few clicks distant. "Hang on to that rope, Nik!" he yelled, then, "Barbousse, tell him to jump, now!" After that, he had no more options. He waited approximately one more click, then bunted the ship over the bridge, flinging both Ursis and Theada to the limits of their safety cords as he zoomed over the top. He heard Ursis grunt from the shock.

"Don't lose him, Nik," Theada whispered in a strangled voice as he fought to wrap the cable around himself. "I've got it now. You go pull him aboard!"

The spy—dressed in a nondescript Leaguer space suit—was now clinging desperately to the ship's rail with both hands and feet as Ursis arrived at his side. Less than a click later, the Bear hoisted him to safety, and all three struggled out of view toward the air lock.

Brim immediately hauled the little starship around on a low-altitude trajectory perpendicular to the cableway, watching the lorry speed away in the distance. Considerable time would elapse before someone discovered anything wrong with that, he thought—as if it mattered anymore! Every ship in the League seemed to be on its way to investigate the explosion of Barbousse's star mine.

Then his thoughts were abruptly shattered by Ursis' deep bass voice, which—normally placid in all circumstances—was strangely reduced to little more than an awed whisper.

"Princess Effer'wyck, Your Majesty," the Bear stammered over the suit circuit. "W-What in the name of Great Mother Bear are you doing here?"

The name struck Brim like a thunderbolt. "Margot?" he called over his shoulder incredulously.

"Wilf?" a weak but unmistakable voice answered in surprise.

"Margot! Greta Universe!"

"Jubal," Ursis growled, "perhaps you could take the controls while..."

"Oh...ah...yes. Right away, Nik," Theada said as he raced for the right-hand Helmsman's seat.

Heartbeats later, Brim lifted the Leaguer space helmet to reveal a tumble of golden curls. Margot's face was streaked with dust and perspiration. "Universe," he whispered again in amazement. "If I'd had any idea..."

She smiled—and frowned. "If I'd had any idea." She shook her head. "I still can't believe it's you, Wilf." She was silent for a moment as if she were gathering strength. "No sleep...," she said, "...four days. I'm all right. Need to rest though."

"Wilf!" Theada called shakily from the helm. "I think we're going to need you up here right away at the controls. Company's arrived."

"What's the best way out of here?" Brim asked, taking Margot's arms and looking into her tired eyes.

She thought a moment. "Zone 5 here isn't usually patrolled much during daylight." She shrugged. "A few light picket ships. But there's

226

talk about some crazy old cruiser. I tried to get some information about that, but I had to leave."

"We've seen that one," Brim assured her. "It's real." Then he frowned. "Best bet's up, then?"

"Straight up, Wilf," she said. "And keep on going right out into deep space. That's what I'd do, anyway."

"Sounds good to me," he said. "We'll try it."

While Brim made his way forward to the helm, Barbousse swept Margot into a spare recliner beside the unconscious Amherst and helped reseal her helmet at the neck. "Just in case, Lieutenant Effer'wyck," he said grimly as he took his place at the weapons console.

Brim turned in his seat and squinted through the aft Hyperscreens: As Theada warned, two flying objects were in pursuit, but still too distant for him to determine a type.

"What now?" the younger Helmsman asked.

As he took over the controls, Brim shook his head and smiled. "We are going home, Jubal," he said simply. "Right away." With that, he set the generators to EMERGENCY MILITARY and pulled the powerful little attack ship into a vertical climb with Ursis working the power consoles in an orderly frenzy of movement.

The two ships following also pulled into a climb, but whatever their make, the attack ship handily outdistanced them, and they soon disappeared into the ground clutter below.

"Left those two nicely enough," Theada commented.

"Too bad we couldn't outrun their KA'PPAs," Brim said. "We'll have a welcoming committee waiting for us out there ahead."

"I see them in the long-distance BKAEW already, Lieutenant," Barbousse said calmly.

"As I am sure they have us in theirs," Ursis growled.

Just then, the authentication key sounded, but this time with an ominous clanging like an alarm, which it was.

Brim shook his head. "That's it for the authentication system," he warned. "The key's run out."

"The battle crawler was onto us anyway," Theada snorted just as space flashed violently in a rolling ball of pure energy that detonated just off the port beam.

"Authentication is now a very moot point," Ursis rumbled. "Let us see how well that 60-mmi projector forward works against this new enemy."

"Look like four of those little N-81 picket ships Lieutenant Effer'wyck warned us about," Barbousse reported. " A lot thinner skinned than the battle crawler."

Theada concentrated on the firing controls. Brim watched the turret index across the forward deck. Moments later, a stream of energy blazed from the disruptor, accompanied by a rumble that vibrated the deck. A flash in the far distance ahead blossomed into a glowing orange puffball, then subsided.

"Missed!" Theada fumed amid a welter of return fire that smashed at the attack ship's thin hullmetal sides like rolling thunder. The ship bounced sharply as a jagged section of hullmetal railing was carried away with an ear-jarring crash and a cloud of sparkling radiation. "Sure wish Anastasia were here to run this thing."

Brim frantically zigzagged all over the sky trying to avoid the bursts. "Thank Voot they only carry a couple of 70-mmi's on board," he said through gritted teeth. "But eight of 'em can mean real trouble."

A second volley of fire burst from the attack ship's nose, resulting in a brief flare-up ahead. "Make that three N-81s," Theada said proudly—and with a little surprise in his voice as well. He was immediately drowned out as he sent off another volley of discharges. He peered into the target scanner. "Scattered the bastards that time," he said. Outside, the return fire slackened considerably.

"That's the way, Jubal!" Brim exclaimed. He listened to the miraculously steady beat of the two rugged Klaipper-Hiss generators blasting them ever faster through space, then glanced back at Margot in the recliner and felt his heart soar. Dirty and tired beyond all reason, she was anything but the sensuous woman with whom he rather goatishly desired to share a bed. He sensed his feelings toward her had developed a lot farther than that. Glancing at Ursis, he was rewarded by a wink. As usual, the Bear seemed to read his mind.

Soon, Theada began to index his disruptor again. "What do you think?" he asked Brim.

The Carescrian smiled and scanned the heavens. "I think we're going to catch it from all sides pretty soon, Jubal," he said. "So keep an eye peeled. And make every shot count—because it will. If we can break out into open space, we'll be all right. Not much the League builds can catch this class of starship running flat out on its Drive crystal." He felt the ship tremble as Ursis dumped their emergency power cell into the energy supply.

"If we do not need it now," the Bear explained with a grin, "we probably will never need it."

And abruptly the enemy returned, their patrol vessels rushing in this time from all sides. Space came alive with flashing detonations. The attack ship bounced through volley after volley, shouldering aside a succession of hits, but the punishment soon began to tell. A whole section of port Hyperscreens suddenly dissolved into a network of flaming cracks, then went dark. A direct hit carried away the three aft repulsion rings from the open utility deck. Five simultaneous flare-ups smashed their bow off course and blew the cowling from the starboard plasma injectors, though the generator miraculously continued to function normally. Theada had the 60-mmi back in action immediately. Now, however, the attackers were widely separated. Desperately, he fired this way and that, but to little avail, he hardly had time to aim before he was forced to change his target. Outside the remaining Hyperscreens, space was now alive with explosions of dazzling light and radiation. The little ship bounced and bucketed through the concussions as Brim desperately zigzagged in all directions.

Moments later, the Hyperscreens pulsed again, this time remaining dark for a full five clicks while the whole control room shook with a massive series of thunderous tremors. Loose gear clattered to the deck as the bow erupted in a cloud of sparks and debris that smashed back along the deck and grated deafeningly along the walls of the control cabin. Green sparkling radiation cascaded over the control cabin and vomited into the wake; when it cleared, the 60-mmi was completely gone, replaced by a jagged, glowing hole.

"Where did that come from?" Brim exclaimed over the din of the straining generators. "Wasn't even a direct hit!" Two more stupendous explosions erupted off to starboard, smashing the attack ship off course again and pulsing what was left of the Hyperscreens.

"Sweet thraggling Universe," Theada exclaimed. "I see it! Over there, just coming up from the shadow of the planet."

"The old cruiser!" Brim yelled as he suddenly realized he had flown into a classic trap. The little patrol craft were actually herding him like a grazing animal. His mind raced furiously as he crankled wildly through the sky. With no more disruptors to use against the patrol craft, escape was virtually impossible; any way he might choose to go, the huge disruptors of the cruiser could easily destroy him. Yet the only way out now was past the old ship. He made his decision swiftly. "Barbousse," he yelled, "prime those torpedo tubes!"

"They're primed, Lieutenant," Barbousse declared presently.

Brim swung the attack ship's shattered bow toward the cruiser and sighted carefully through his target display. He set his jaw and frowned. A bad deflection, that, low and close to the disk of the planet, but it was the best he was going to get. "Here we go!" he yelled. More explosions battered the racing attack ship in every direction, but each time Brim fought his way back on course. As they approached, space itself seemed to catch fire with shattering detonations and radiation from the big ship's disruptors. "Ready," he yelled.

"Ready," Barbousse answered tensely.

Outside, a torrent of explosions ripped the blackness of space. Brim gritted his teeth and held a steady course while he struggled to acquire the target. He had only a single chance. Every passing click was an eternity.

"Now," he called at last. "Fire both!"

The attack ship jumped as the powerful Leaguer torpedoes blasted from their tubes on either side of the ruined 60-mmi disruptor turret.

"Torpedoes running, Lieutenant," Barbousse confirmed.

"Reload!" Brim ordered, skidding to port just in time to avoid a whole string of monstrous detonations. Powerful machinery whined and labored on either side of the deckhouse as the spare torpedoes were drawn from their storage canisters and inserted into the torpedo tubes. An eternity later, two thumps announced the task accomplished.

"They're primed, Lieutenant," Barbousse announced.

"Fire both!" Brim shouted.

Again the ship jumped.

"Torpedoes running."

By now, every disruptor on the old cruiser that could bear was in rapid fire at them. "Ready the Drive, Nik," Brim warned.

"The Drive is already on standby, Wilf," Ursis assured him.

Brim judged the fast-narrowing distance carefully. Hesitated one more click, then, "Fire it off!" he yelled.

The single Drive crystal came to life at the precise instant the first two torpedoes found their target—they struck dead amidships with an immense explosion that immediately hid the middle third of the old cruiser with a roiling ball of blinding flame and radiation. And now E607 was rushing down at it with the acceleration only a Drive could provide.

"We're going to hit," Amherst shrieked over the suit channel.

A milliclick later, the second two torpedoes slammed into what remained of the Leaguer's midsection, a dull glow boiling out into surrounding space until her hull opened like a rotten fruit. Her KA'PPA mast subsided slowly into the seething mass of energy, then suddenly took off in the opposite direction like a missile. Simultaneously, another glow began forward until the whole ship seemed to collapse inward in a massive explosion of starflame. Slowly, she rolled to starboard, her massive hull breaking raggedly into two parts at a gaping hole in her side.

Brim steered straight for the opening, he was too close and too fast for any other choice. The little attack ship pitched and rolled in the awesome shock waves. Then they were through to open space in less than a click, Brim steering by instinct alone. He remembered an instant of great ruined galleries, flame, and destruction on either side—and debris. Something huge had smashed past the control cabin, ripping a deep gash along the deck and opening the spare torpedo compartment like a ripe ca'omba. The Drive surged for a moment all out of control; a colossal hammer stroke smashed at the hull; then Gandom's V_e effect started and moments later they were in HyperSpace. When Brim turned in his seat, the giant wreck was only a flicker in the aft Hyperscreens, with the Drive growling raggedly beneath their feet and the generators spooling to a stop in their scarred outriggers.

"It probably looked as if we blew up with the cruiser," Theada commented in a voice still weak from excitement. "We were on our way into HyperSpace before we cleared the wreckage."

"No doubt," Ursis grumbled. "Unfortunately, whatever it was we collided with nearly did for Drive, too." He frowned at his readouts and rubbed his jaw. "Hundred and ten LightSpeed is best speed we'll get in HyperSpace, unless, of course, you wish to be out of phase with time."

Brim shuddered. Everyone knew about occasional time castaways. He decided long ago he preferred death—of any kind. "Can we maintain a hundred and ten?" he asked.

"That, fortunately, poses no particular problem," the Bear replied.

Brim shrugged. "Let's go for it, then," he said. "Even a little Hyperspeed is better than none at all."

"As you say, Wilf Ansor," Ursis said. The Drive continued its uneven thunder.

Brim quickly took stock of the rest of the ship. All in all, it appeared to be in reasonably workable form, considering the treatment he'd given it during the last few metacycles. In the corner of his eye, he saw Margot remove her helmet; Barbousse was at her side in a moment. She looked at Brim through tired, bloodshot eyes, her face so drawn she was hardly recognizable.

"I-I watched that, Wilf," she said with awe in her weak voice. "I watched you. No wonder you're building such a name for yourself."

"Desperation, as usual," Brim said as his cheeks burned. "I can't seem to do anything unless I'm in trouble."

"Oh, Wilf," Margot pouted with a tired grin, "you are impossible, aren't you?" She smiled sleepily, then her eyes closed and her head lolled onto her shoulder.

Barbousse opened her space suit at the wrist and gently counted her pulse. "She's asleep, Lieutenant," he asserted with a wink. "I think you've got this mission just about complete."

"Not until we get that lady aboard her pickup ship," Brim said. "But I guess even I'll be surprised if we don't pull that off pretty soon, considering what we've come through so far." Then he turned to Amherst. "All right, Number One," he said without emotion, "now we're on our way home, as you wished. You'd better get yourself cleaned up and back in command."

***

E60T's rendezvous with Margot's pickup ship took place only

metacycles after they limped from the boundaries of the League at 110 LightSpeed. This time, they were not met by a lightly armed reconnaissance craft. Instead, the massive form of I.F.S. *Defiance*, a heavy cruiser, hove into view in what was left of the forward Hyperscreens—signaling imperiously for an immediate linkup.

After Brim matched speeds and came alongside, the ships were quickly connected by mooring beams and a brow extended from the cruiser to the attack ship's scarred and dented well deck. In moments, the Carescrian found himself alone with Margot in the control cabin, the others conveniently hurrying through the air lock after Ursis, who had Amherst firmly by the elbow.

Brim carefully slaved his controls to the larger *Defiance*, then slipped from the helm and made his way aft: where he bent over Margot's sleeping form and gently placed his hand on her shoulder.

She opened her tired eyes slowly, blinked, then opened her arms. In a moment, Brim embraced her. "How I've dreamed of holding you," he whispered, his heart beating out of control.

"I've dreamed of you, too, Wilf," she said breathlessly. "It got me through the bad times back there." She trembled. "I never did that reset we talked about back at *Prosperous*," she said. "I couldn't."

Brim felt a thrill course through his whole body. He looked into her bloodshot eyes. "Nor did I," he said with a passion he had never before experienced. Then their lips touched, hers soft and wet against his. For a dizzy moment, the war ceased to exist—only Margot and her lips and her breath and her arms and her crazy, crazy wet lips...

Abruptly, someone was hammering on the aft Hyperscreens. Brim surfaced just in time to see Barbousse knocking gently from the well deck. Behind him, Amherst was leading a group of officers from *Defiant* through the wreckage toward the air lock. The newcomers were dressed in elegant battle suits that clearly had never seen a battle. "We've got visitors, Margot," he warned.

She continued to hold him for a moment, then released her grip. "I want you to hold me again, Wilf," she whispered, peering intently into his eyes. "I don't know how, but, 'Can e'er I bid these joys farewell?/No greater bliss shines out among the stars'."

"I'll get to where you are somehow," Brim said, Lacerta's poetry glowing like a brand in his memory as the air lock hissed. He got to his feet unsteadily, his heart racing.

"Together," Margot whispered while he helped her from the recliner. Then the others were inside, doffing their helmets and looking around the little control cabin as if its clutter might stain their battle suits. "Princess Effer'wyck?" a bowing commander inquired, ignoring Brim as if he were part of the ship's equipment. The man was short, and inside his helmet he wore a too-neat mustache.

"Lieutenant Effer'wyck, if you please, Commander," Margot corrected. Then, turning to Brim, she said, "I shall remain on Avalon for a time, Wilf. If Fortune wills, we shall meet there. Otherwise, Haefdon." She touched his hand, then reached for her space helmet. "Thank you forever," she whispered. Less than a cycle later, she led three of the officers through the air lock, across the ruined well deck, and out of Brim's sight.

The remaining officer placed a hand on Amherst's shoulder and scanned the burned and splintered deck outside. "Looks as if the rescue wasn't all that easy, Puvis," he said, removing his helmet. He was tall and elegant, even in a battle suit. Like Amherst, he had a long patrician nose, narrow-set, sensitive eyes, and another perfectly groomed wisp of mustache.

Amherst colored. "Ah...no. It w-wasn't, Uncle Shelgar," he stammered, looking at Brim pleadingly.

"We accomplished our mission, Commander," Brim said. "That's the important part."

"Yes, you brought the Princess back," Shelgar said, nodding his head, "thereby avoiding a large and nasty galactic incident." He laughed. "She won't do that again, I'll tell you—they've reassigned her permanently to Avalon this time. Why, when the Emperor found what she was up to, he was furious. Perfectly furious."

"She is next in line for the throne of Effer'wyck, isn't she?" Amherst observed. "Sort of a crown princess, except they don't use the term there." He frowned. "How did she get herself such an assignment in the first place?"

"A strong-willed youngster," Shelgar chuckled. "They say she usually gets what she wants." He smiled. "And from what I hear, she did a perfectly superb job of what she was doing. All very hush-hush, you know." He took a moment to stare at the wreckage-strewn decks, peering intently at the jagged, blackened hole where Theada's 60-mmi used to be. "But," he continued, holding up an index finger, "I did not remain on your, ah, bridge here to discuss the Princess. I have orders for you, Puvis, and also for what is left of this little attack ship of yours."

"Sir?" Amherst asked.

"First," Shelgar said, "you are ordered to return with us in *Defiance*— your father's personal and direct wishes, of course. He will want to bestow your decorations himself."

"I see, yes," Amherst said, his eyes brightening for the first time since the mission began. "I have a few things in the cabin, forward," he said. "If you will be so good as to pass the remainder of the orders to Brim, my Helmsman, I shall be ready to leave momentarily."

Shelgar nodded and watched Amherst disappear into the companionway before he turned to Brim. "So you are the Carescrian Helmsman," he said, folding his arms and smiling.

"Yes, Sir," Brim answered uncertainly.

"Regula Collingswood speaks highly of you, Lieutenant," Shelgar said. "I assume you flew the mission?"

"Some of it," Brim answered.

"I won't ask any embarrassing questions, Brim," Shelgar asserted with an ironic smile. "I've already formed my own guesses about the nature of young Amherst's contribution from what I long ago learned of my brother's son." He winked. "So I also won't bother to read the official version when it appears in the *Journal*." He laughed quietly. "Enough of that," he said. "Politics disgust me, and time grows short. I think you'll like your orders; they get you to Avalon just as soon as you can coax this clapped-out wreck to fly you there."

"Did you say Avalon, Sir?" Brim asked, heart suddenly racing.

"Well, close enough," Shelgar said. "You're to take what's left of this attack ship back to the Technical Intelligence Center on Proteus, Brim. Afterward, you can catch a return ride to *Truculent* from any of the five planets of Avalon. And I shall convey the same information about you to Her Majesty, the Princess Effer'wyck. If I am any judge of quick looks, it will no doubt soften the shock of her reassignment. Especially if you were to, ah, spend some leave time on Avalon herself when you finish with the boffins on Proteus."

Brim felt his face flush. "Th-Thank you, Sir," he gulped. "But...wouldn't it be a lot quicker if she were to ride with us? Even with this damage, we'll be traveling at better than one hundred LightSpeed, while you'll be..."

Shelgar laughed heartily. "Nice try, Lieutenant," he said, "but it's my belief that the Emperor wants Princess Effer'wyck safely under his jurisdiction in as much safety and comfort as possible."

"Aye, Sir," Brim replied. "Probably *Defiance* is a much better idea."

"I doubt if the Princess will agree," Shelgar assured him with a chuckle. "And speaking of orders, Lieutenant—which we weren't— the text of yours ought to be finished downloading by now into your COMM system; read it for the details." He grinned. "Incidentally, Regula asked me to pass this along, too." He took a small metal box from a pocket on his forearm and passed it to Brim. "I just so happened to have one of these lying around in my kit—mine once, now it's yours. You can pass it on yourself someday."

Brim frowned and opened the box. His heart stopped. "Congratulations," Shelgar said. "From what I hear, you've earned it, full Lieutenant Brim." He laughed. "You'll find we've downloaded all the documentation for that, too. If it's high-flown boredom you're after, it'll make good reading." He clapped the speechless Brim on his shoulder as Amherst reentered the control cabin. "Ready, Puvis?" he asked, placing his helmet on his head.

"I certainly am, Uncle," Amherst replied, donning his own helmet. He turned to Brim. "Take care of things as well as you can without me, Brim," he said.

Brim gritted his teeth. "I shall do that, Number One," he said.

"Yes, I'm sure you will," Shelgar said, pushing Amherst into the air lock before him. He winked at Brim as he stepped through himself. "I shall pass along that information we discussed," he said. "And congratulations again." Then he was gone.

Brim grinned while the remainder of the *Truculents* clambered through the air lock, ripping off their battle helmets and congratulating him for his promotion all at once. Scant clicks later, mooring beams to

Defiance winked out and the big starship bore up for Avalon, disappearing in the blackness with an emerald glow that lingered for nearly a quarter of a metacycle before it faded away.

Miraculously, Ursis and Barbousse had procured large bottles of Logish meem—apparently from the emptiness of space itself. Brim laughed, basking in the warmth of their good wishes, happily clicking goblets with each in turn (first full and right side up, then empty and upside down). Inside, however, his glee stemmed from a different source altogether. He was going to Avalon—and Margot. Somehow, a mere promotion in grade paled in comparison!

***

With refueling stops, it took the *Truculents* nearly three Standard Days to nurse the crippled attack ship into native space, but at last E60T's cracked and scarred Hyperscreens began to fill with the glittering star swarms that comprised the heart of the Home Galaxy. In due course, the mighty triad of Asterious blazed forth like a giant beacon suspended above the Universe, drenching all it contained with a glorious golden radiance. Soon, Brim could make out the three individual stars, tumbling within their virtual globe, each trapped within the others' gravity bonds. At last, the five blue-green worlds hove into view: Proteus for science, Melia for commerce, Ariel for communications, Helios for shipping, and the colossal city-planet Avalon herself, throbbing epicenter of an empire that spanned the very galaxy and beyond.

Brim's orders specified signing the attack ship over to the scientific community on Proteus, and accordingly (on the third day of the voyage), he slowed to Hypospace, rounded the Vernal-204 space buoy, and set up his final approach to the gleaming planet of Imperial science. With the attack ship's seemingly indestructible generators rumbling steadily in his ears, he was passed through to the military sector and entered the spaceport traffic pattern when the last flickers of reentry plasma cleared from his Hyperscreens. Below sprawled three circular clusters of buildings and laboratories known through the Empire as the source of nearly half the important military technology developed in the last hundred Standard Years.

He eased E607 into the downrange leg of the traffic pattern while Theada trimmed ship for a dry-land planetfall. As the Klaipper-Hisses

237

began to spool up, a Military Harbor Master appeared in Brim's COMM display and cleared them on to the complex.

"All hands to stations for planetfall. All hands to stations for planetfall," Theada announced on the ship's speakers.

Brim rolled left through an abbreviated base leg for immediate transition to final amid running footsteps and alarm buzzers as Barbousse and Ursis raced to their positions. When the ship righted, he lined up on one of the long Becton-type, gravity-cushion tubes (commonly used in place of water for hard-surface touchdowns), carefully pulled off more lift, and established a gentle glide angle, checking the nose in relation to the near end of the fast-approaching tube. Steady as a rock. He smiled. Couldn't mistake this for Haefdon— no wind!

He made one final power reduction directly over the green-flashing ALPHA beacon, then energized the lift modifiers, held his speed steady, and waited for the approach lights to loom up as he rumbled in over the end of the tube. E607 settled solidly onto the long gravity cushion as its shadow dashed in from alongside and became a blurred spot beside them on the right-of-way. When Brim sensed a definite hover, he dumped the modifiers and completed his roll-out with gravity brakes alone, generators rumbling at idle.

His instrument panel was already a satisfying mass of flowing colors and patterns by the time he taxied from the tube at the second turnoff— and amid wild cheering from his travel-weary crew, he finally parked the little ship at a special gravity pool near the military terminal. E607's first and only military mission was complete.

***

"Text messages for you, Lieutenant Brim," Barbousse announced suddenly from E607's COMM cabinet, his voice nearly lost in the commotion of technicians clambering through the little ship from three separate brows. During the last Standard Week, all four *Truculents* had spent nearly every waking moment wringing out the little Leaguer attack ship for the Imperial Foreign Technology Service.

This latest mission had been the most demanding so far—and Brim, especially, looked forward to the three or four days' of leave that had been promised. One way or another, he was determined to spend some time on Avalon. "What do they say?" he asked, busily shutting down the flight systems.

"Appear to be personal, Sir," Barbousse yelled. "You'll probably want to display them yourself, beggin' the Lieutenant's pardon, of course."

"I see," Brim said as he activated a COMM globe over his control panel. The short text message cascaded instantly across the display:

> Wilf,
> I am required to attend the Godille function as representative of my dominion. Shall I see you there? I believe the Admiralty has deprived you of any excuse to decline. (Regrets Only)
> —Margot

Brim's heart raced as he read the first few words. Then he frowned. "Godille function? Admiralty?" He looked up just as Ursis switched over to external gravity, and almost fell out of his recliner. Swallowing hard, he wrested control of his heaving stomach, then turned to yell hotly at Barbousse. "Are you sure you got all of that?" he demanded. "It doesn't make any sense at all."

"Which one, Sir?" Barbousse asked solicitously. The big generators were spinning down now, and it was a little easier to talk.

"I only got one message," Brim yelled, his voice now far too loud in the little control cabin. Everyone turned to stare at him—he felt his face flush.

"But which message, Lieutenant?" Barbousse asked again.

Brim gritted his teeth. Personal his foot! "The one from Margot," he answered in capitulation.

"Oh," Barbousse said with raised eyebrows. "That's the second one, Lieutenant. The first one must have got lost."

"Thraggling WON-der-ful," Brim fumed.

"I'll send it again," Barbousse said.

Brim thumped back in his recliner, feeling a dozen pairs of eyes at his back. "Thanks," he said, pulling in his neck. Then he swiveled rapidly to face his audience. Eight technicians were expectantly looking over his shoulder at the message globe. "As you were!" he thundered. They scattered to eight tasks elsewhere in the suddenly quiet control cabin. Then the first message cascaded across the globe:

> TO: Wilf A. Brim, Lt., I.F. @ Proteus.991E
> FROM: Lord Avingnon B. Wyrood @ Admiralty/ Avalon
> Lieutenant Brim: Your attendance is hereby commanded at a court divertissement by His Majesty, Crown Prince Onrad in tribute to the Honorable Archduke of Godille.
> - 12 Pentad, 51997:
> - Lordglen House of State: Twilight:0:00
> - Grand Boulevard of the Cosmos, Avalon
>
> BY ORDER OF HIS IMPERIAL MAJESTY GREYFFIN IV, GRAND GALACTIC EMPEROR, PRINCE OF THE REGGIO STAR CLUSTER, AND RIGHTFUL PROTECTOR OF THE HEAVENS.
> (formal attire)
>
> --
>
> Personal to Lt. Brim: Take the Morning:00:00 R-37 Shuttle to Imperial Terminal, Avalon. Transportation will be standing by at the Quentian Portal. A formal uniform awaits your arrival at the Lordglen House.

—A. K. Khios, Secretary to Lord Wyrood

That made some sense of things—at least as much sense as inviting a Carescrian to a court affair in the first place. He laughed. Margot's work for a certainty. Well, if that was the requirement to see her now, then so be it! He'd faced up to some of the best the League could throw at him so far. Avalonian society couldn't be very much worse than that!

Later, on a tram from the landing field, Brim told the others about his invitation.

"The Lordglen House?" Theada exclaimed. "Universe, Wilf, that's one of the fanciest official palaces of all. How'd you get an invitation there when we stay at the Visitors' Quarters?"

"Friends in high places," Brim laughed evasively, feeling color rise in his cheeks. "Besides, it's just until we ship out tomorrow night."

Ursis laughed and clapped Brim on the shoulder. "I think perhaps you do have such friends, Wilf Ansor, but perhaps not whom you think." He smiled. "I shall be most interested to discover who your sponsor really turns out to be."

***

Brim never found himself in Avalon's Grand Imperial Terminal without a total sense of architectural majesty. Taken altogether, the huge structure could only be described as incredible with its immense, cloud-filled ceiling, soaring hundreds of irals over a thousand crowded ramps and concourses that wound among terraced gardens and colored lagoons. It was a fitting metaphor to represent the civilization that conceived and built it. Awesome—like the vast collection of worlds and stars it connected.

Making his way to the bustling Quentian Portal, Brim scanned dozens of curbside lanes for his transportation. A bus? A van? He idly noticed a huge chauffeured limousine skimmer thread its way carefully through the crowd and draw to a halt amid "oohs" and "ahs" from the street throng. He watched with interest as the chauffeur dismounted—somebody important was slated for that vehicle (or, he chuckled, a Bear on leave). He continued to scan the other lanes for his own ride.

"Lieutenant Brim?" a voice asked.

Brim turned in surprise to confront the chauffeur, who was small, dressed entirely in light gray, and appeared to be totally bald (bare scalp gleamed all around his peaked cap). "That's me," he said doubtfully.

The man motioned toward the huge skimmer waiting at the curb, sleek, shining, and important. It looked for all the world like some great water creature poised for attack. "Your transportation to the Lordglen House, Lieutenant," he said, a small blond mustache twitching as he spoke.

Brim felt his eyebrows raise. "That's for me?"

The chauffeur laughed. "All the way to Lordglen," he said.

"You're sure I'm not supposed to drive you?" Brim joked as he strode toward the stately vehicle. "Looks big enough to take a Helmsman."

"Only in traffic, Lieutenant," the chauffeur retorted good-naturedly as he opened the door for Brim. "This time of the day, I can probably handle it myself." Without another word, he climbed into the driver's compartment and the powerful skimmer glided out of the station.

Avalon City proper was laid out in a vast grid of forested parks and urban recumbence at the edge of huge, placid Lake Mersin, actually a sizable inland sea. The Grand Terminal was constructed on an artificial island and connected to the city proper via a wide causeway named for August Thackary Palidan, first starship commander to circumnavigate the galaxy.

Cruising the causeway at high speed, they soon swung onto tree-lined Verecker Boulevard and began to follow the shore. Brim looked out at magenta waves beyond the twisted kilgal trees as they swept past. The chauffeur was maneuvering through the heavy traffic with a light and skillful hand; Brim relaxed in the deep cushions of the seat, enjoying every bit of luxury he could absorb.

They breezed past a cool, mork-shaded park dotted with sparkling fountains full of splashing children. Brim reflected on how long it had been since he'd even seen a child and shook his head. Before he reported to Gimmas-Haefdon, he guessed. War and children didn't mix so very well, as he so sadly knew.

Traffic was heavier as they neared the inner metropolis, and the closer they came, the more the lanes in both directions contained limousine skimmers similar to the one in which he rode, many decorated with embassy crests. One great black machine from the Bright Triad at Ely pulled opposite them in an adjoining lane just as its emergency beacon came on, flashing frantic red, white, and orange in an eye-startling, random sequence. The shining vehicle accelerated quickly, skillfully dodging other traffic and rapidly disappeared in the distance.

To the right, they passed the shimmering Desterro Monument with its colossal spiral of sculpted flame commemorating discovery of the Cold Tetrad of Edrington, center of a gravity drift that collected space debris and invaluable historic artifacts from a million years of space travel. A traditional Mecca for peacetime tourists, the monument was presently overrun by hundreds of gawking cadets and Blue Capes from all over the Empire. Brim smiled. As a cadet, he'd visited more than once himself.

In a matter of cycles, they were gliding over the first great ruby arch crossing the Grand Achtite Canal, each end of the wide, translucid span guarded by immense crystal warriors gazing at the same section of the sky (as indeed their sculptor had determined they would). Brim recalled a tour guide once pointing out that three similar bridges crossed the canal far downstream at regular intervals, each guarded by the same crystal statues that stared eternally at the same section of the sky: the Achtite Cluster. To the left of the bridge apron, Brim's eye caught the great domed tower of Marva thrusting silver and gold above the skyline with its fluted sides and curious winding concourse that spiraled all the way to the dome like a sparkling vine. Old Queen Adrien herself once lived and studied there before she set off in her little Durax III to discover Porth Grassmere on the far side of Elath. It was a place all Imperial Helmsmen knew—and appreciated.

Farther along, they passed Avalon's famous Kimber Castle, where Cago JaHall composed *Solemn Universe* and other classics of the same idiom. In later years, Dalgo Hildi had also lived there, but by the time she finally arrived in Avalon, her active career was nearly over. The graceful old building was presently fronted by crystal scaffolding, and workers appeared to be treating its carved metal facade.

While they continued on into the historic Beardmore sector, Brim noted heavy construction wherever he looked. New buildings were going up on nearly every block. Older structures were being rebuilt, scaffolding and cranes everywhere. A good sign, he considered. Avalon was beginning to recover from the initial shock of the war, looking toward the future again, and perceiving the first glimmerings of possible victory.

He sat back, breathed deeply, and sank deeper into the luxuriously padded seat, feeling the smooth power of the skimmer and the skill of its driver. As they swung through the spacious Courtland Plaza with its famous three-tiered Savoin gravity fountain and onyx reflecting pool, the Imperial Palace momentarily came into view across an expanse of carefully tended gardens and manicured forests. Huntingdon Gate was its usual confused mass of traffic (a reputed challenge even to Avalon's finest chauffeurs). Then the view was obstructed by the squat, glass-walled Estorial Library, where Hobina Kopp first presented her Korsten Manifesto a full two hundred Standard Years prior to Brim's birth. The library had a special poetry section, which he promised he would one day peruse at his leisure—but as usual, not this trip!

At last, Brim's limousine swung onto the long, park-lined Boulevard of the Cosmos and began to slow. Moments later, it stopped gently in a curving driveway before a gracefully understated jade-stone portico: the sprawling Lordglen House of State. It was still early in the day, and the spacious receiving plaza was empty, but Brim could imagine what it would be like later when the guests began to arrive.

A white-gloved footman in a bright red coat and white breeches saluted and opened the door for him. "Lieutenant Brim, Sir? Right this way, please," he said with a smile that instantly dissipated the awesome personality of the building itself. Brim rapped "thanks" on the glass separating the passenger and driver compartments, then followed the footman through an imposing two-story doorway. Inside, they crossed a wide entry hall, boots clicking on the flawless obsidian floor. Above, an enormous gold and crystal chandelier reflected light from thousands of polished facets, and at the far end of the room, twin alabaster staircases curved upward to an ornate balcony jutting gracefully above an elaborately carved archway whose polished ebony doors were presently closed.

The footman led Brim up the left-hand stairway and through a carved-gold arch into a short hallway whose domed ceiling depicted allegorical scenes painted in an old-fashioned and elegant style. Midway along the left-hand wall, they entered a lift to the fifth floor, where Brim was presented a large golden key and shown into an elegant suite furnished with exquisite period furniture and decorated by a collection of artifacts that, even to an untrained eye, were clearly worth the price of a large starship.

"Welcome to Lordglen House, Lieutenant," the footman said as he opened the heavy drapes. "Lord Wyrood has instructed me to attend to all your needs. I have placed a complete formal uniform in the closet to your right, and attempted to provide other, more basic necessities—which you will encounter in the usual places." He bowed. "Should you find I have missed items here and there," he added, "you have only to ring. My name is Keppler; I shall be at your service promptly." With this, he bowed again and exited the room backward, closing the double door quietly behind him.

Brim shook his head as he looked about the tastefully ornate room, a long way from Carescria, this! He peered through the window into a courtyard of perfectly shaped flowering panthon trees whose glowing fruits made the quadrangle look like a miniature Universe of starry galaxies when viewed against the dark paving stones. A stately fountain danced placidly at its center. He squeezed his eyes shut for a moment; this level of wealth transcended his understanding completely. He shrugged. None of it had much importance to him anyway. The only reality here was Margot. Once she arrived, everything else would fade to nothing.

***

Brim fidgeted impatiently as he tested the fit of his borrowed dress uniform before a full-length mirror: white tunic with stiff, gold-embroidered collars, epaulets, and high cuffs, dark blue breeches with gold stripe, knee-high parade boots (like polished hullmetal), white gloves, and peaked hat. A rich, red-lined formal Fleet Cape was carefully draped on the bed, certainly nothing like the cheap copies he had rented at the Academy.

He felt a growing sense of excitement as he counted off the cycles before he would see Margot—it was impossible to sit anymore. He paced back and forth across the thick carpet, its softness wasted beneath his boots. Each cycle seemed longer than its predecessor, even though months had passed since the evening he shared with her on Haefdon. And those now seemed like moments. Outside, a gentle breeze moved the panthon trees; the weather was perfection. An omen, perhaps? He laughed to himself. All moments with Margot were perfection, so far as he could remember; he doubted she would disappoint him tonight.

As he stood staring at the patio, a distant chime sounded importantly. Then, in moments, a soft knock came at his door. "Come in," he said. "It's unlocked."

"About ready, Sir?" Keppler asked as he stepped into the room. "The reception is under way in the ballroom."

Now that it was time to go, Brim suddenly began to fret about the other guests. Wealthy people, of a certainty. Influential. Powerful.

He was no more than a simple Helmsman. What could he have in common with any of them? What could he say worth listening to? Would he make a fool of himself? Suddenly, he felt tired. He wished he could have made other arrangements to see Margot. He never had a chance.

"You look splendid, Lieutenant," Keppler said. "They'll all be jealous, especially with your action record." He helped Brim place his cape properly over one shoulder in the latest fashion. "Now stand back," he ordered imperiously. "Let me make a last-moment check."

Brim suffered further adjustments to his collar, cape, and an offending epaulet before Keppler was finished.

"Perfect, Sir," the footman said finally as he nodded his approval. "A number of important people down there expect to meet you, so you'll want to look your best." With that, he gently propelled Brim from the room and into the lift.

Only a few cycles later, Brim found himself returned to the balcony at the head of the double staircase. Voices and soft music surged from below as elegant couples filed slowly in from the portico and disappeared through the doorway beneath his feet. He paused for a moment, reflecting on his failure to submerge a natural Carescrian irritation with these scions of wealth and privilege. While they enjoyed unbelievable comfort and luxury, men and women of more humble origins were elsewhere locked in mortal combat to protect the very Imperial existence. Why were these people exempted? Then he grimly laughed at the folly he had just concocted. Here he was, himself dressed like the worst sort of professional courtiers—and in the absolute thick of it! He snorted and started down the staircase, contemplating his own double standard.

The huge ebony doors were open now, eight gray-clad footmen with ornate symbolic pikes flanking either side. Beyond, an elegant throng preened and pirouetted: polished officers in the colorful uniforms of every friendly nation in the galaxy, seas of half-revealed bosoms and lavish gowns in every hue and pattern art and science could conjure, humans, Bears, A'zurnians, and the less-numerous races. At the center of the high archway, a majordomo dressed in bright green tunic with dark trousers and green boots bowed as Brim approached. "Your name, please, Lieutenant?" he asked.

"Wilf Brim," Brim declared. "A Carescrian." He looked the man directly in the eye.

"Ah, yes, Lieutenant Brim," the majordomo said. "A thousand pardons. I should have known." He turned on his heel and led Brim into the ballroom. "Lieutenant Helmsman Wilf Ansor Brim, Imperial Fleet," he announced, thumping the butt of his pike loudly on a special square of flooring. "I.F.S. *Truculent*."

A few heads turned indifferently, but the announcement was generally lost in the babble of the crowd. And, from what Brim could see as he stepped into the room, his rank alone would relegate him to the very depths of unimportance among most other guests whose ranks he could identify.

From inside, the room was high and huge, though a soft light level held the overall effect well within the limits of Brim's comprehension— longer than it was wide, with an ornate, domed ceiling covered by gold and silver designs in the form of a sinuous Logis vine. Three monstrous chandeliers like the one in the anteroom hung along its centerline. One wall was a solid bank of mirrors, the others were covered by rich-looking tapestries. The floor was a continuation of the flawless obsidian outside.

While Brim stood orienting himself in the heady atmosphere of hogge'poa, meem, and a hundred fragrances of perfume, a tall commander with a wisp of a mustache and piercing blue eyes appeared from the revelers, smiled, and clapped him on the back. "Brim, my good man," he said, "so glad you could make it. I'm Avlin Khios, secretary to Lord Wyrood." He waved his hand apologetically. "Sorry your invitation arrived with so little notice. We hoped you might be able to make it anyway." He grinned. "Understand you had an exciting mission, what?"

"'Exciting' is probably as good a word as any, Sir," Brim acknowledged with a smile. "The important thing, though, is that we were able to see it all the way through."

"Yes, I understand," Khios said with a knowing grin. "Well, her Effer'wyckian nibs is certainly on tonight's guest list." He took Brim's arm and propelled him into the center of the crowd. "But until the young lady actually does arrive, we have some people who want to talk to you. Not many of them have the opportunity to meet real fighting men."

Brim felt a goblet placed in his hand as he passed a pair of footmen.

The shallow vessel made his passage through the crowd even more difficult than before. As he passed a red-faced Army officer, the man spit, "Carescrian," bitterly at him as if he were repeating an impolite word. Then, within a few more clicks, he was centered in a ring of smiling young officers who wore the badges of the Admiralty Staff—and curious looks on their faces.

Khios named each as Brim greeted one after the other with the handshake he learned in the Academy (Carescrians normally avoided touching anybody, at least during a first meeting); their names were promptly forgotten in the rush of questions that followed.

"You've actually been in one of their starships?"

"What were the cannon like on A'zurn? Were they easy to drive?"

"Were they hard to start?"

"League torpedoes are good, aren't they? How'd the J band stand up after the radiation from those mines?"

To his surprise, Brim quickly began to sense an underlying mood of serious interest—certainly the questions coming his way were founded on well-informed backgrounds. As the group continued to probe, Brim rapidly found he was not talking to the vacuum-headed courtiers he originally thought they might be. Rather, it seemed he was surrounded by a group of dedicated staff people: behind-the-scenes decision makers who, so far as he could ascertain, were probably far more valuable contributing to an office work group than fighting the war somewhere in a battle zone. In the ore barges, one learned quickly to respect anyone who was willing to make a genuine contribution to almost anything.

During the next few cycles, he answered each question as honestly as he could, within his limited knowledge. It was difficult to make noncombatants understand that one often fought more by calm reaction to impressions and reflexes than by detailed study of anything specific. He was patiently giving his third impression of E60T's handling characteristics when the gathering was interrupted by Khios. "I've got to steal Lieutenant Brim for a while, gentlemen," he said, breaking into the circle to re-grasp Brim's arm. "We have a couple of executive types who insist on meeting him now."

Brim nodded politely at the smiling officers and lifted his hands palm upward. "My apologies, gentlemen," he said. Then he turned on his heel and followed in Khios' wake through the festive atmosphere of music, perfume, and beautiful people. The secretary stopped nearly all the way across the big room at a small, unobtrusive archway leading off among the hanging tapestries. He rapped gently on an ornate door before he pushed it open, nodding for Brim to follow.

Inside, soft lighting, walls of elegant display cases, magnificent furniture, and deep carpets identified the room as one of the ultra-private drawing rooms everyone heard of but seldom saw, rooms where the very course of history could be charted quietly, and frequently was. Two tall officers stood talking before a blazing fireplace: One a human, the other a flighted being from A'zurn. Their uniforms were heavy with ponderous badges of rank and decoration.

Khios stopped approximately halfway into the room and bowed from the waist. "Your Majesties," he said. "May I present Lieutenant Helmsman Wilf Brim, Imperial Fleet, on detached duty from I.F.S. *Truculent*." Then he rose to his full height and indicated the two men. "Lieutenant, Crown Prince Onrad, your host, and Crown Prince Leopold of A'zurn." Startled, Brim saluted while Khios clicked his heels and bowed once more, then silently exited the room, closing the door gently behind him.

Nearly panicked and alone in the center of the room, Brim set his chin, collected himself as best he could, and strode purposefully to a position a few respectful paces before the two young dignitaries. He bowed, then stood looking first at one and then the other. "Your Majesties," he said, seizing his emotions with an icy calm, "I am honored."

Onrad spoke first. He looked to be approximately Brim's age and was powerfully built, with the square jaw and thick neck of a natural athlete. Expensively attired, his basic dress was the tailored blue uniform of a vice admiral. "So you are Wilf Brim," he remarked, "the Carescrian who has caused all that trouble for Great Uncle Triannic." His broad smile nearly squeezed his eyes shut. "Ha, ha! Well, your partisan campaign to prove out old Wyrood's Reform Act certainly seems to be working impressively." He nodded to the A'zurnian beside him. "Isn't that right, Leo?"

Crown Prince Leopold exuded an ageless, almost ethereal restraint which, in its own understated manner, stood out like a beacon from all the heavy magnificence of the ornate drawing room. His folded wings reached at least six golden irals from the floor, his eyes were the huge eyes of a hunter hawk, and his look conveyed the very soul of dignity. Here was a man who never acted in haste, nor passion. He was beautifully clothed in the elegant, old-fashioned uniform of a brigadier general, and he stood with one polished boot on the high hearth. He also smiled at Brim, his an analytical and questioning smile that seemed to test its recipient without so much as a touch of challenge. "A 'gentle and daring leader,' as my cousins put it," he said. His eyes narrowed and he seemed to look into the very soul of Brim's existence. "A 'complete' leader."

"There, Leo," Onrad interrupted hotly, "tell that to the anti-Wyrood idiots. They are hard to convince."

Leopold sighed and stared into the fire for a moment. "Even they will learn, Onrad, or surely none of us will survive this tumult." He nodded his head. "But those very factions will eventually learn—because the Wilf Brims of this Universe have the strength to persist, and in the final analysis, they do not." Then he reached to the top of the great carved mantelpiece and took a golden chest in his hands. Stepping to a position opposite Brim, he opened it and extracted a tiny crystal image of a winged being: The same figure Brim instantly remembered from the twin pillars outside the quarry on A'zurn where Hagbut and his troops were held prisoner. It was suspended on a small red ribbon. The Prince smiled again. "I have sent all the meaningless text that goes with this to Gimmas-Haefdon, Lieutenant," he said. "The only importance is that you understand how much your actions were appreciated in Magalla'ana and that we shall never forget your dedication to your mission and my countrymen." He grinned a momentary, lopsided grin. "Lieutenant Wilf Ansor Brim," he said, "in the presence of your liege, the Crown Prince Onrad, I award you the A'zurnian Order of Cloudless Flight." He peered deeply into Brim's eyes. "Wear it proudly," he said. "The decoration has never before been awarded to a groundling." Then he fastened the ribbon to the left breast of Brim's tunic and resumed his original position at the fireplace.

Brim bowed again. "Thank you, Your Majesties," he said. The A'zurnian nodded.

"And see that you take good care of my cousin Margot," Onrad added with a grin and a half-sensed wink. "I have a distinct feeling you constitute the only reason we shall be honored with her blond presence this evening."

Brim felt his face flush. Then he boldly returned the Prince's smile. "I shall certainly attempt to do that, Your Majesty," he said quietly. After this, he stepped back, saluted, and exited the room, closing the door softly behind him. Outside, he stood for a moment gathering his thoughts. Mentally, he felt as if he had just come through a pitched space battle. Then he shrugged to himself. It certainly was a long way from the ore barges—not an inconsiderable accomplishment for a Carescrian!

He made his way back into the growing crowd, accepting another goblet of meem and unsuccessfully scanning the room for Margot's blond curls when a small stir occurred at the entrance doors.

"Her Serene Majesty, Princess Margot of the Effer'wyck Dominions," the majordomo announced in a voice notably louder than before. The babble hushed, and heads turned expectantly.

Brim felt his breath catch as she swept through the door on the arm of First Star Lord Beorn Wyrood. No longer was she merely an attractive military officer, she now radiated that particular beauty exclusively reserved for the wealthy and powerful. She was magnificent.

She was wrapped in a meem-colored, full-length gown that crossed in front and tied at the neck, leaving her creamy shoulders and back stunningly bare. A matching sash nipped her waist, and a daring slit revealed enough of a long, shapely leg to considerably raise Brim's temperature. Around her neck, she wore an enormous, single-drop StarBlaze that flashed with an inner fire as she laughed and chatted with the First Lord.

"...had no idea the party was that important," someone whispered behind Brim. "She hardly ever attends these affairs."

"Voot's beard," another said in a low voice. "She's wearing the Stone of the Empire!"

"And LaKarn isn't anywhere in sight."

"Noticed that."

Brim watched transfixed as a small crowd formed around the couple. In a moment, both crown princes appeared, laughing and talking.

Then, the A'zurnian was bending close to Margot, she whispering in his ear. He grinned his lopsided grin and pulled himself to his full height, scanning the ballroom with his enormous eyes—which lighted on Brim and stopped. Smiling, he spoke rapidly to Margot, then she was peering Brim's way, too.

Their eyes met; she smiled—and frowned. In a moment, she was on her way through the crowd, never taking her eyes from him.

And in that instant, Wilf Brim knew for a certainty he was hopelessly in love.

9 Margot reached Brim amid murmured admiration from the gathered revelers, took his hands, and kissed him lightly on the lips. "Wilf," she whispered with a breathless smile, "I knew you'd manage it tonight—'Fresh evening winds have blown away all fear/From my glad bosom, now from gloominess!/I mount forever'."

Stunned for a moment, he could only stare at her blue eyes, moist lips, and perfect teeth. Never had he seen so much of her shoulders, the swell of her small breasts. He felt his heart rush. "Margot," he said in a whispered croak. "How wonderfully beautiful you are."

She laughed. "I suppose I am a little more presentable than the last time you saw me," she said, her voice mellow and beautiful over the sparkling background of music and conversation. She touched the A'zurnian medal on his tunic and smiled, looking him directly in the eye. "I'm very proud of you, Wilf," she whispered.

Somewhere far away, detached words announced the arrival of someone named Godille, but Brim hardly noticed. He wanted nothing in the Universe more than taking Margot Effer'wyck in his arms and holding her tightly. It was as if they were alone in the room.

Abruptly, she seemed to read his mind. She took his hands in hers and looked into his eyes. "Not yet, Wilf," she breathed almost inaudibly. "I have additional functions I must perform with my new assignment on Avalon—and we shall have to share each other for a while tonight." She gently guided him toward the lights and music,

253

pressing his arm; her perfume was the very soul of seduction.

The dance floor! Brim almost froze. He'd learned exactly enough about social dancing to minimally satisfy his infrequent social commitments at the Academy—nothing more. Helmsmen especially had little time for anything else but flying. "Margot..." he warned, but he was already far too late. Abruptly, he found her in his arms... and they were moving, she flowing with the music, he stiff and suddenly a little frightened.

"Universe, Wilf," she laughed in his ear, "you are a horrible dancer, aren't you?"

"I know," he agreed. "Maybe we ought to..."

"Won't work," she laughed. "You'll have to finish this set with me no matter what." She nearly touched his nose with hers, looking deeply in his eyes and smiling. "Oh, Wilf, relax," she said. "Here, hold me like...this. Yes. That's better."

Brim suddenly found her fitted comfortably against him, her soft cheek pressing his. And it was easier. He felt her body—her breasts. He breathed her perfume, felt his movements become one with hers. He held her tighter.

And the music stopped.

In a rush, the world returned while she slowly released him. He held her hands, desperately trying to stop time's headlong rush. "I don't want to let go, Margot," he heard his voice say; his heart was beating out of control.

She shook her head and placed a gloved finger to his lips. "Our time is later, Wilf," she said. "Trust me. For we shall finish the evening together—pretending it is the Mermaid Tavern again."

Then Brim felt a hand on his shoulder. He turned to confront a beaming Prince Onrad.

"We meet again, Lieutenant," the nobleman said warmly. "May I interrupt your reunion with my blond cousin?"

Brim bowed. "My liege," he said, gritting his teeth in spite of himself.

"Cousin Onrad," Margot said with an abbreviated curtsy. "What a pleasure."

Onrad laughed with a twinkle in his eye as the music began. "I shall interpose myself only temporarily, Brim," he said mischievously. "We princes seldom venture into hopeless contests, especially those that are clearly lost before the play begins." Then he bowed to Margot, took her in his arms, and they were instantly swept into the rush of dancers.

Brim soon found himself with another goblet of meem as he listened to the music and watched couples whirl by on the dance floor. His eyes strayed momentarily to a lovely oval face framed in a halo of soft brown hair. He looked away in embarrassment, but his gaze was drawn back like iron to a magnet.

And her eyes were waiting. She smiled and met his glance. Brim found himself moving through the crowd.

"Lieutenant Brim," she said with a curtsy when he stepped to her side. "I hoped I should meet you tonight."

Brim bowed. "I am honored, Ma'am," he said. "But I didn't catch..."

"Cintha," she said. "Cintha Onleon." She had enormous eyelashes, a tiny nose, and perfectly shaped lips. Her tightly fitting gown was tawny gold and reminded Brim of nothing so much as a large flower bud whose petals were just beginning to open. Like Margot's, her skirt was also slit high along one side, but the overall accent was clearly on bosom—white, stunning bosom.

And while they talked and drank, it became amply clear to Brim that neither he nor she had anything remotely interesting or important to say to each other—only empty, hackneyed words. He was mostly fascinated by her ample sensuousness, she (at least by her conversation) in his battle experience and later a shared bed.

It was not enough. He actually welcomed the Army officer (with large, red-veined ears), who noisily foisted himself upon them and provided opportunity for escape to another part of the room, alone.

In this manner, much of his evening passed: a tall, slim Marsha in revealing black lace followed Cintha—and was herself followed by a petite Beatrice scantily dressed in ruffled pink. Each was fascinating in her own way—and most probably available for much more serious dalliance. But none was Margot Effer'wyck. He discovered to his surprise that good looks and willingness—long his primary standards—were no longer nearly enough to satisfy the person whom he had lately become. Now he also required fascinating conversation, professional accomplishment, even a bit of elitism. He shook his head. Carescria was a long way off, indeed!

Now and again, he caught sight of Margot dancing with (he assumed) important guests—always someone different, always someone of considerable rank. And each partner appeared to be completely enthralled as she laughed and talked and danced. Often, he saw her standing centered in groups of admirers, constantly smiling and drinking with apparent girlish abandon.

Twice, she returned to him for a single—wonderful—dance set when she placed her cheek against his and he never even noticed if he was dancing or not. The second time, her eyes were even more heavily lidded than usual. Her cheeks had a pinkish tinge, and she held him tighter than ever before. "Voot's beard, Wilf," she whispered in his ear, "I've never seen so much good Logish meem; Uncle Wyrood's certainly opened his best cellars for us tonight." She giggled musically, then hugged him closely for a moment as the music ended—and as he was beginning to feel embarrassing sensations in his loins.

Finally, after what seemed like an age of eternities, the crowd began to thin and Margot returned to his arms to stay. "The time of sharing is past, Wilf," she whispered. "Now I shall have you all to myself." They strolled into the coolness of the plaza—almost empty now—and made their way under the panthon trees to the fountain he had watched from his room. She brushed a dusting of tiny glowing blossoms from his hair and stared into his eyes, smiling enigmatically. "'Night sublime, Oh night of love'," she recited in a whisper, "'Oh smile on our caressing;/ Moons and stars keep watch above/Our splendorous night of love'."

Fervently, Brim completed the stanza, written more than a thousand years in the past by the ancient composer Giulietta. "'Cycles fly, and ne'er return,/Our joys, Alas! are fleeting. /Only memory's flame will burn/For spells that ne'er return'."

Avalon seemed to fade completely, the half-heard orchestra now played from at least a galaxy away, and the gentle rush of the fountain wrapped them in a warbling cloak of privacy. Above the dark gables of Lordglen, Avalon's twin moons—both glowing at full disk—flooded the plaza with a golden shadow of magic. They stood silently for a moment before he drew her toward him, eyes closed and arms around his neck. And his whole Universe became two wet, pouted lips.

Brim felt his body trembling as he held her and breathed in the sensuous fragrance of her perfume. He opened his eyes. Hers were open, too; he read in them all he needed to know. "Margot," he whispered while their lips still touched. "I want..." He swallowed and shook his head. "No," he said, "I need to make love to you. And I need to now."

Her eyes continued to look into his, but the heavy lids became heavier still. "Finally," she breathed with a sleepy smile. "For a moment, I was afraid I might have to ask you." Then her eyes closed and she covered his lips with hers, pressing herself against him for a long time before, arm in arm, they made their way back indoors again.

"I have a whole suite upstairs," Brim suggested in the privacy of the music-filled room. "We could be alone there in a matter of cycles."

She laughed quietly as they made their way through the dancers to the great ebony doors. "Nothing would give my dear cousin Onrad more pleasure than to watch me rutting in bed with you," she said in a low voice. "Which he surely would—from all angles—were we to make our tryst here in Lordglen." She shook her head. "No, Wilf, I think we shall take our pleasure elsewhere, where no one will dare invade our privacy."

Brim raised an eyebrow.

"At the Effer'ian Embassy," Margot said firmly. "I live there now. And believe me, Wilf, no recorders invade the privacy of Princess Effer'wyck, at least not in her own bedroom."

***

Aboard Margot's chauffeured limousine skimmer, Brim struggled to maintain his decorum. It was evident she was troubled by problems of the same nature, for she shifted position every few clicks and squeezed his hand nervously a number of times. At last, the great vehicle glided to a halt beneath a small, dimly lighted portico. "The servants' entrance, Wilf," she explained with a wry smile as a huge green-liveried footman with eyes politely averted opened the door of the limousine. "I hope you understand."

Brim laughed quietly. "I know any man at the ball would gladly kill if he could trade places with me at this servants' door right now," he said, kissing her hand. He helped her to the pavement, then followed as she led through the portico doorway, along a narrow corridor (also clearly made for servants—Brim knew that part of the Empire well!), and into a service lift. Less than a cycle later, he stood inside her softly lighted bedroom. Peripherally, he could sense an entire suite of incredible luxury, but none of it held any importance: Only Margot mattered now. With his pulse thundering in his ears, he half heard the door latch shut, and she was in his arms, her breathing as rapid and urgent as his own. She teased his mouth with her lips and tongue.

And suddenly her arms were no longer around him.

He opened his eyes just in time to watch her reach for something behind her neck. She smiled seductively, gently arched her back, then drew the crossed halves of her bodice from the pointed whiteness of her bare breasts. A moment later, the skirt and sash too lay in a heap around her ankles. She wore only lacy briefs underneath. Heart pounding out of control, Brim stared down at the knobby pink aureoles of her swollen nipples, the half-sensed network of delicate veins in the creamy skin beyond. He felt his arms begin to shake uncontrollably, looked deeply into her heavy eyes.

"Hurry," she whispered as he fumbled out of his own clothes. "Oh Voot, Wilf, it's so...you're so...beautiful..."

Naked, he pulled her trembling shoulders close to him again, gently kissed her open lips while his thoughts went whirling to all corners of the Universe. Then they stumbled off toward her huge, canopied bed...

***

Long before dawn, Brim sat on the edge of the bed, breathing her pungent scent on his cheeks and stroking the damp golden thatch beneath her stomach. She sighed and shivered as his fingers moved upward over the firm mound of her abdomen, strayed for a moment at her buried navel.

He thought of his hands. They were soft—Helmsmen didn't dare grow calluses. But nine or ten years earlier, they wouldn't have pleasured her so. Then, those same hands were hard as any other Carescrian miner's. He forced himself to dwell on them for a moment; it never hurt to remember one's origins, especially in the middle of such unbelievable luxury and intense pleasure.

"Wilf," she whispered at length, guiding his face down to her own. "What am I going to do about Rogan?"

258

Brim shrugged and bit his lip. "I suppose I should feel a little guilty about him," he said tonelessly. "I know you two are in love."

She shook her head. "'We seldom are as that we seem', she recited pensively. "'Truth has its little masquerades./Appearance doth protect the dream'."

He moved closer to her on the bed and sat quietly while she sorted her thoughts.

"What the Empire can't know—what you don't know," she continued after a considerable lapse of time, "is that I never have loved him." She looked at him and smiled in resignation. "Oh, he comes here with me. I'm not fool enough to hope you'd believe he doesn't. Not after what you've seen of me tonight. But aside from that, we're little more than close friends, locked into a rather dismal little courtship based on nothing more interesting than political necessity." She smiled ironically at him. "Our child will eventually rule both the whole Effer Cluster and the five industrial centers of the Torond." She laughed. "Shrewd old Greyffin IV saw that quickly enough; soon as my father produced a female. He set the whole thing up on the day of my birth. When Rogan had passed fifteen natal anniversaries."

"Does LaKarn love you?" Wilf asked when she finished, suddenly afraid of her answer.

She smiled and shook her head, staring up at the ceiling. "Sometimes when we are here, he says he does—for a few cycles. But aside from those moments, he appears to be much more interested in his career at the Admiralty."

Brim laughed quietly. "I seem to remember recently bleating earnest protestations of love myself," he said. "Probably at about the same emotional juncture as he."

"Did you mean them?" she asked, suddenly sitting up to face him.

He met her gaze evenly. "I meant every word I said, Margot," he pronounced carefully. "Then and now."

She drew his face to hers, kissed him lightly on the lips. "I believe you, Wilf," she said. "As I believed you then."

"And LaKarn?" he asked.

"I don't know," she said. "Honestly."

Brim snorted. "In any case," he pronounced in mock seriousness, "I now have an everlasting quarrel with my Emperor."

"You needn't," she said with unexpected concern. "I told you Rogan is usually a great deal more concerned about his career than anything I have to offer." She closed her eyes for a moment. "Sometimes, it gets pretty lonely."

Brim shook his head helplessly. "I'm sorry," he said. Surprisingly, he found he actually meant it.

"Don't be sorry," she said. "It's helped bring us together, I suppose."

"Us?"

"Well," she said, her eyes sparkling with impish humor, "you've probably guessed I have little desire to exist as a blushing virgin."

Brim grinned. "After tonight, it would be difficult for you to claim anything like that," he said. "Blushing or otherwise."

She laughed. "We did take care of any lingering doubts, didn't we? But it still proves my point."

"Which is?"

"Well, just about the time you returned from your first mission, he hadn't been by for a couple of months. And..." She shrugged, clearly a little embarrassed by her own words. "You're cute, Wilf. Sexy. Besides that, I was, well, you know...in the mood."

"I think I have the picture," Brim said, feeling himself blush, too, in spite of the present circumstances.

"Anyway," Margot went on quickly, "I didn't think I'd have much problem getting you between the sheets. Girls with legs like these never do. Except..."

"Except?"

"Except you quickly got to mean far too much. I've suspected I love you since we were in the Mermaid Tavern. I'd have gladly shared anywhere with you that night. A broom closet would have been fine. And that's awful."

"I don't understand."

"You're going to have to understand," she said, suddenly serious again. "Because I can't shirk my duty as a princess, Wilf. This thing with Rogan is a lot bigger than anything I am now or ever will be. It won't just go away by itself. In fact," she said seriously, "it may never go away."

"Universe," Brim said, gritting his teeth.

"And how you fit into the scheme of things is something I'm going to have to work out," she said presently. "By myself. I find I can't think very intelligently when you're around like this."

Brim grimaced, guessing what was coming next. "I hope you're not going to ask me to..."

"Yes, I am, Wilf," she interrupted firmly. "Until I come up with some acceptable answers, you've got to stay out of my life. Probably, it'll be harder on me than it is on you. But the politics of this little triangle in which I seem to find myself centered affects too many people—worlds."

"What if you find I don't fit?" Brim asked. "Do I have any rights? After all, this thing is pretty important to me, too."

Margot smiled sadly. "First, I've got to satisfy my obligations as a princess. Then we can start working out some sort of relationship between ourselves—if, indeed, one can really exist."

Brim closed his eyes and shook his head sadly. "All right, Margot," he said, running his fingers through her golden curls. "After today, I'll wait until you work things out—take as long as you wish, I suppose. I may not like it much, but I'll do it. 'I wish what you desire—/Our wishes reconciling./Your whims I still admire,/And wish to keep you smiling'."

She kissed him softly on the lips; he felt the stirring in his loins.

"But today is only today," he reminded her, "and I know I'm going to need you again before I go."

Margot glanced momentarily into his lap—and grinned happily. "Wanton," she chided in mock reproach. Then she kissed his nose playfully and lay back on the rumpled satin bedclothes, smiling happily. "You've already had so much of me you couldn't finish the last time— but, oh how I want you to try at least once more."

***

Considerably later, with early morning sunlight filtering in at the sides of the heavy draperies, Brim quietly left the warmth of Margot's bed and dressed himself in his badly wrinkled formal uniform, most of which still littered the floor where it had dropped. He looked down at her as she slept, face framed in yellow ringlets, then gently pulled a sheet over her shoulder. Brushing her cheeks with his lips, he gathered the meem-colored gown from where it lay, placed it neatly over a chair, then silently exited the room, closing the door gently behind him. He stood for a moment in the early morning silence of the ornate hallway, reflecting that he might well have already spent the most beautiful, exciting night he would ever experience. He wondered when, or indeed if, he would ever sample the same pleasures again, then shrugged. One paid a high price, he observed, when trading the relative simplicity of Carescrian hopelessness for the complex life in which he now found himself embroiled. At one time, he would never have so much as dreamed of a first night with such a woman, much less worry about others that might follow! He shook his head bleakly. Were it possible to undo everything since his entrance to the Academy, he would change nothing. Margot was clearly worth any effort. But the emotional price of hope was high, indeed.

He was met at the bottom of the lift by the same liveried chauffeur who delivered them to the servants' entrance the night before, this time, the man was dressed in a light gray uniform instead of the distinctive green habit peculiar to the House of Effer. He was tall and powerful looking, with a huge, square chin, piercing gray eyes, and a warm smile. "Good morrow, Lieutenant. I am Ambridge Hogget, Margot's chauffer," he said in a rich bass voice.

"Good morrow, Freeman," Brim replied, returning the man's smile. "I recognize you, Sir."

The chauffeur beamed. "What are your wishes this morning, Lieutenant?" he asked. "I am at your service."

"I'll gladly settle for a ride to the Lordglen House," Brim replied.

"No more than that, Lieutenant? Perhaps we could tidy up your uniform while you breakfast?"

"A ride will be more than sufficient," Brim said.

"You shall have it, then," the man replied with an approving nod. "I'll fetch the skimmer."

Within a metacycle, another limousine—this one quite unmarked—deposited Brim under the glowing portico of the Lordglen House, and before midday he found himself again at the Quentian Portal of Avalon's Grand Imperial Terminal. As luck would have it, he arrived too late for the Proteus shuttle, by no more than five cycles. The next was scheduled three metacycles hence. He spent more than two of them on an uncomfortable bench regaining some of his lost sleep, then started on his way through the terminal toward the shuttle's departure gate.

Shortly after he stepped onto blue Concourse 991, his eyes were drawn to a bright red dress and golden curls below as the walkway moved across orange 55. Heart racing, he peered over the glowing azure balustrade. It was Margot—no mistaking her ever again. She was arm in arm with a highly decorated commander. No mistaking him either. Rogan LaKarn. Brim felt his spirits plummet to despair. Gritting his teeth in jealous anger, he stepped back to the center of the moving concourse and continued on without looking back. He bit his lip as his mind's eye peevishly tortured him with imagined scenes in Margot's bedroom, the one he had left no more than a few metacycles before!

Then he snorted in the midst of his hopeless frustration. If nothing else, his recent efforts would certainly serve to benumb the edge of LaKarn's bedtime pleasures. He laughed a little to himself about that. It helped some. But not enough.

***

"'Civilization Lixor,'" Theada read aloud as he stared into a display in *Truculent's* nearly deserted bridge. "'Number of stars: one; number of planets: twelve (one habitable); Total Population (Census of 51995): 8,206,800; Capital: Tandor-Ra; Monetary Unit: Arbera'.'" He slouched in the right-hand Helmsman's station with his feet propped comfortably on the center console perusing *The Galactic Almanac (And Handy Encyclopedia)* for 51997. "Don't ya just love it?" he asked grumpily, waiting for a test routine to terminate.

"Yeah. I love it," Brim snorted while his own diagnostic routine splashed vibrant colors across the left-hand console before him. He idly brought the same information to a more convenient display and continued to read for himself:

> Lixor is the only habitable planet among 12 satellites orbiting Hagath-37 (binary red and green star of eclipsing separation 3.0°) occupying a strategic location in the 91st Province astride three cross-galaxy trade

routes (R-99183, C.48-E-7, and 948.RJT) that skirt massive and treacherous asteroid shoals extending for hundreds of c'lenyts in all directions. Twice the size of Proteus, this planet orbits with an Arias19 type of synchronous rotation that perpetually directs the same hemisphere toward its star. Nearly 100% of the population inhabits this hemisphere, tropical at that portion nearest the light, temperate at the zone of transition ("Lands of Shadows"). The dark hemisphere is little used except for starship landing facilities. Inguer and Vatthan are the largest star ports...

Outside in the perpetual nighttide of a military dockyard near Inguer, the dim, fog-shrouded world almost bashfully revealed itself in the feeble glow of three reddish-blue moons. Now and again, a restless breeze shredded the flowing mist enough that Brim could see a few irals of *Truculent's* frost-caked deck. Occasionally, there were glimpses of the glowing gravity pool below and sometimes the dark outlines of capable-looking patrol vessels berthed nearby, including a compact battleship of unique Lixorian design. He shook his head. For all practical purposes, this end of the crazy world made even Haefdon seem like a tropical paradise in comparison.

Five Standard Months—a lifetime, almost—had passed since Avalon and the luxury of the Lordglen House of State. Even the heady pleasures of Margot's bedroom dimmed in the pitiless, grinding confusion of all-out blockade warfare. The busy, hardworking Princess herself had become a magnificent chimera, especially now that her messages had nearly ceased to arrive again.

Theada completed his suite of checkouts, then, smiling wearily, started aft toward the bridge exit (and wardroom). Brim initiated still another long diagnostic routine on the master console and listlessly returned his gaze to the *Almanac*.

Resources and Industries
Although half of the habitable land mass is forested, Lixor contains much productive land on which

Lixorians have attained high efficiency in agriculture.
Of the total land area, 9.9% is cultivated, 2.5% pasture.
Chief agriculture outputs include grains, vegetable oils,
fibers, and logus products.

Main natural resources are forests, a vast asteroid belt
containing rich deposits of metal, and solar power.
Other forms of energy are imported. Commerce
(including a thriving armaments industry) employs
35% of the work population, agriculture 7%. Lixorian
hullmetal is of special value for reaction-chamber
vessels. Other ores produced are metallic zar'clinium,
lead, copper , metallic zar'clinium, hullmetal, and a
"thriving armaments industry."

Commerce indeed, Brim laughed grimly to himself. Everybody
desperately needed Lixorian goods, Imperials and Leaguers alike
(*Truculent's* own reaction chambers were encased in superb Lixorian
hull metal). He continued to read.

History and Politics

Lixor is a parliamentary democracy with a king as head
of state and a prime minister as principal operating
officer...

The Government holds permanent memberships in
the Trans-galaxian Educational Cooperative, LANN,
EC, and United Independent Trading Council.
During the present hostilities, the nation remains
neutral, maintaining time-limited, renewable trade
agreements with all major powers. Approximately .1
percent of its Gross Product (GP) is distributed in aid
to developing civilizations.

The *Almanac*, as usual, used polite words to describe what Brim
(and disdaining people all over the galaxy) regarded as a distinctly non-
polite situation. The avaricious Lixorians sold everything and anything

they could manufacture to both sides of the great galactic struggle with no compunction whatsoever, even while pontificating vociferously about their abhorrence of war. Brim shook his head. Lixorians had it all their way, it seemed. Playing both sides against the middle, they kept the major combatants constantly reminded of a (very real) need to "protect" irreplaceable Lixorian industries. So long as both sides depended on Lixorian output, neither dared to destroy it. And Lixorian coffers swelled accordingly, in conjunction with their small but expensive military space fleet, which included ten very powerful space forts on "formed" asteroids placed strategically in orbits around their planet.

Defense

Full mobilizable strength exceeds 750,000. Military service is compulsory. A sphere of ten powerful, permanently manned forts constructed from large asteroids and towed into place protects the single inhabited planet. Each fort is armed with enormous disruptors of special Lixorian manufacture. The starfleet is powerful considering the size of the civilization it protects but is mostly limited to numerous small craft (mainly LightSpeed-limited torpedo-and cannon-armed patrol craft) optimized in the direction of high acceleration and maneuverability for synergism with the space forts. Three small area-defense battleships of the Reneken class complete this efficient defense organization.

The right to buy Lixorian goods was negotiated by treaty every two Standard Years, when prices were raised to the threshold of outright economic pain, then a few Arberas more, all of which had to do with *Truculent's* arrival on the strange planet hardly more than a Standard Day earlier.

With the present treaty only Standard Weeks from expiration, the Lixorian Prime Minister had at last "permitted" Greyffin IV's Imperial Government to petition for new terms. *Truculent*, outbound from her patching at Gimmas-Haefdon, was fortuitously available at the time and commandeered by the Admiralty to carry a team of economic negotiators who would hammer out details of the new agreement, but not sign it. The latter was reserved for more impressive diplomats traveling aboard a powerful battlecruiser squadron with a highly classified arrival schedule.

Shortly after planetfall, Gallsworthy and Pym had taken one of the launches to fly Collingswood, Amherst, and the negotiators into a resort area near Tandor-Ra where bargaining sessions were scheduled to begin on the morrow. Now the destroyer and her crew awaited return of their principal members and the launch before returning to the blockade zone.

At last finished with his final set of diagnostic routines, Brim wearily pulled himself from his recliner and started aft toward the chart room and the bridge exit, the end of another seemingly endless watch.

He never made it from the bridge.

"Lieutenant Brim," Applewood called from the COMM console. "A KA'PPA for you marked, 'Most urgent emergency priority'."

Brim raised an eyebrow and turned toward the signal rating; one whole section of his console was flashing the bright blue of a top-priority transmission.

"Overrode the bloody mail and Admiralty messages, it did, Lieutenant," Applewood grumped. "Have to restart the whole sequence now."

"For me?" Brim asked, ignoring the other's complaints.

"From the Captain," Applewood replied, his bald head shining in the strange moonlight. "Funny stuff goin' on, Lieutenant. COMM bands are full of craziness. Noise and strange talk like Leaguer jargon, kind of. All over..."

Thoughts of rest forgotten, Brim hurried to the COMM console. "Let's have the message," he said, frowning.

Applewood generated a text globe. "MOST URGENT EMERGENCY PRIORITY FOR WILF BRIM @ TRUCULENT FROM COLLINGSWOOD @ TANDOR-RA," the message began. "CONFERENCE AREA UNDER HEAVY AIR BOMBARDMENT BY THREE LEAGUE DESTROYERS (BELIEVE ZAGRAIL CLASS). LAUNCH

DESTROYED." The transmission stopped abruptly with the words, "YOU ARE IN COMMAND."

"Is that all?" Brim demanded.

"Don't think so, somehow," Applewood grunted as he busily tried to pick up more transmissions. "But my readouts indicate a time-out on the data stream. I think maybe they lost their KA'PPA, or..." He stopped in midsentence. "Here, Lieutenant," he said abruptly. "Here's somethin' else now. Broadcast in the clear, audio and video. Look." He activated a display globe:

> Citizens of Tandor-Ra: The League is aware your mediators are about to negotiate a new economic treaty with the Universal scum from the Empire. Heed this personal warning from Nergol Triannic delivered by units of His mighty starfleets:
>
>> "We shall tolerate no special terms for the crawling spawn of Greyffin IV. Keep in mind it is only by *Our* goodwill that you continue to do business with this filth from Avalon. Should you grant favorable terms at this or subsequent meetings, *We* shall know and you will mark *Our* anger well."
>
> My ships will return in a few cycles to administer a second warning. Note carefully that we do not attack Lixor or Lixorians. Therefore, we shall consider it an act of war should any Lixorian forces take hostile action against us. (signed) K. L. Valentin, OverPraefect, S.M.S. Grothor.

Valentin! Narrowing his eyes, Brim lost no more than a few clicks as he made up his mind. "Mr. Chairman," he ordered quietly, "pull Collingswood's message up on every ship's console so people don't waste time asking questions, then sound ACTION STATIONS. By authority of the Captain's orders, I am taking immediate command of this ship."

"Acknowledged, Lieutenant," the Chairman intoned. Brim retraced his way forward among the consoles amid alarms sounding from the companionway. Valentin! The same Valentin, possibly? He shrugged, already too busy to give the matter more than passing thought. Less than a cycle later, the first of *Truculent's* flight crew began galloping onto the bridge and into their battle suits.

"Rig ship for immediate lift-off, Jubal," Brim yelled as the younger Helmsman activated the right-hand console. "Nik! I'll need full military power soon as you get the antigravs on stream."

Without a word, Ursis smashed off the main power limiters, then dump-started both generators at the same time. Brim had never been aboard a starship, anywhere, when the power drain was enough to dim the bridge lights. *Truculent's* nearly went out. But the consoles held their function, and with the deck shuddering violently beneath his feet, he listened as the big machines began spinning up.

"Anastasia," he shouted over the rising sound, "I'm going to need every weapons system you've got! Disruptors. Mines. Torpedoes. The whole toot and stumble."

"How about a couple of rocks?" Fourier quipped from a display.

"Great idea," Brim laughed. "If you got some, keep 'em handy. You never know."

"Generators are running and ready at standby," Ursis reported from a display.

Stunned, Brim looked at his own instruments. "Universe," he gulped, "you did that in four cycles."

"I am in a personal hurry to see who this Valentin is," Ursis said with tooth gems flashing.

"Thanks, Nik," Brim said. He meant it. Outside through the swirling fog, he saw the base had suddenly come alive. Everywhere lamps were doused, but moonlight revealed heavy traffic on the access roads as crews raced for their vessels. Soon mooring beams began to wink out, but not a ship moved from its gravity pool.

"Tandor-Ra's broadcast orders that none of the ships outside are to lift, Lieutenant," Applewood reported momentarily. "Sent the best part of the message in the clear, they did. And nobody who's already up is to interfere in any way."

"The bastards," Brim snarled through clenched teeth. "The xaxtdamned, credit-grabbing, Lixorian bastards are going to let those

Leaguers get away with this." He pounded his fist on the arm of his recliner, watching analogs feverishly stowing loose equipment on his own frosty decks below.

"One does not anger customers when one's business is minding a store," Ursis growled without looking up from his console.

Wash from idling generators all over the pool area had cleared the air, and the whole group of ships was now centered at the bottom of a great open-topped cylinder whose walls were made of swirling tendrils of fog. "Special-duty Starmen close up for takeoff, Mr. Chairman," Brim ordered.

"At your command, Lieutenant," the Chairman answered. More alarms went off below and the mooring cupolas lighted.

"Testing alarm systems," Maldive's voice sounded from the chart room, and the bridge jolted as the Chairman verified functioning of *Truculent's* steering engine. "Thrusts in all sectors, Lieutenant."

"Very well," Brim said. He raced through the remaining pretaxi checks, then turned to Theada. "Jubal," he ordered, "you finish the rest of the preflighting with the Chairman while I taxi her out, because if she'll fly at all, we're going up."

Theada nodded silently. He knew...

"Mr. Chairman," Brim ordered next, "have the men in the cupolas single up all moorings; then immediately switch to internal gravity."

"Aye, Lieutenant."

"Stand by for internal gravity!" Maldive warned from her console. The sickening transition passed quickly; Brim was nearly too busy to notice as he watched mooring beams wink out all around the ship.

"I'll speak to the Harbor Master now," he said.

Nearly a full cycle passed before an ashen-faced Lixorian ground controller appeared in one of Brim's displays. "Ground to Imperial DD T.83," she said in a shocked voice. "We...we're u-under attack near Tandor-Ra, and they won't let us..."

"Imperial DD T.83 to Ground," Brim interrupted. "I've already heard. I am about to taxi out for immediate takeoff on Becton tube 195.8."

"Ground to T.83: you are cleared to taxi," the Controller said. "No traffic in the pattern."

"T.83 to Ground," Brim replied evenly. "I intend to shoot any traffic I find in the pattern, so you will clear no one until after I'm gone. Do you understand?"

"Ground to Imperial DD T.83: we understand. You are cleared to Becton tube 195.8 for immediate takeoff; wind five forty-five at thirty-eight."

"Imperial T.83 copies," Brim answered, then peered at Theada. "How's the old rustbucket check out, Jubal?" he asked.

"She'll taxi, Wilf," Theada said, "but I'm not done with the lift-off checks yet."

Brim smiled. "Don't let me keep you, then," he said, and turned back to his COMM display. "Imperial T.83 to Ground," he continued as he peered into the fog. "Proceeding to Becton tube 195.8 for immediate takeoff."

"Helm's at dead center," the Chairman prompted.

"Stand by to move ship," Brim warned on the blower as he checked his readouts and control settings. "Let go all mooring beams, Mr. Chairman. Dead slow ahead both, Nik."

"All mooring beams extinguished," the Chairman reported.

"Dead slow ahead both," Ursis acknowledged. *Truculent* moved smoothly off the gravity pool.

"I'll take the helm now, Mr. Chairman," Brim ordered, steering a course for the Becton tube.

"You have the helm," the Chairman acknowledged.

"Lift-off check's complete, Wilf," Theada reported presently. "Chairman claims she'll fly."

Brim nodded and continued picking his way through the foggy maze of dark taxiways. No border lights guided his path this morning, only hints of direction from the bleakness beyond the Hyperscreens and the glowing instruments before him. When he finally reached the tube, he immediately pivoted the ship into line and locked the brakes. "Full military ahead, Nik," he shouted. All other noise on the bridge was quickly drowned by the sudden rush of the generators.

"Ground to Imperial DD T.83: Becton tube is active—go get the bastards, *Truculent*!"

"Imperial T.83 to Ground: we'll do our best," Brim promised, watching the brake indicators go out on his console; at once, the powerful destroyer began its astonishing acceleration along the tube. Airborne in a matter of clicks, Brim maintained a nearly vertical climb through 960,000 irals before he nosed over and headed straight for the horizon, still under maximum acceleration.

"What're you doing, Wilf?" Theada asked with a concerned frown. "We just got to this altitude; now you're down again?"

"Relax, Jubal," Brim answered without turning around. "It's only a relative altitude. I'm going to skim the horizon. It's an old smuggler's trick I picked up at the mines years ago. We're now heading straight for the opposite hemisphere, the one closest to Hogath-37, where the Leaguers are trying to tear up our Tandor-Ra conference. What I'm doing is getting a good running start while I keep as much of the planet between them and us as I can."

"A smuggler!" Theada exclaimed, pointing across the center console in mock horror. "I knew it!"

Brim laughed. "Too true, Jubal, my friend," he said. "We Carescrians just naturally get mixed up in all sorts of evil deeds!"

"Incoming coded KA'PPA, Lieutenant," Applewood interrupted from a display. "From Cap'm Collingswood."

"I'll have the KA'PPAs as they come," Brim answered, "Just read 'em."

"Aye, Sir," Applewood said. "'Collingswood to Brim: Lost KA'PPA COMM temporarily,'" he read. "'Hear you have taken off without my orders: good man. Good hunting! Imperial battlecruisers due to arrive in one to one point five metacycles should you require assist. Of interest to you and a few others: that OverPraefect Valentin probably has a familiar face. Message ends'."

Brim turned to nod at Ursis.

The Bear grinned back. "Possible..." He kissed his fingertips. "Even with poor odds, I personally welcome the opportunity to find out."

An image of Barbousse suddenly materialized in a nearby display. The big rating silently grinned for a moment, then kissed his fingertips, too.

Brim smiled grimly, watching *Truculent's* apparent altitude diminish with perceptible speed. "We'll make a bit of trouble for the bastard, no matter who he is," he growled into the displays as the destroyer surged forward through increasingly dense atmospheric layers. Livid orange tongues of plasma streamed from every protuberance on the hull. Aft, the whole ship trailed a fiery wake of disturbed atoms.

"Stand by all weapons systems," Fourier warned on the interCOMM.

"Standing by," a chorus of voices answered.

"How much ground clearance are we going to have?" Theada asked nervously from the side of his mouth as he stared in fascination through the forward Hyperscreens.

Brim chuckled. "Not much, Jubal," he replied. "How close, Mr. Chairman?"

"On this heading," the Chairman replied presently, "*Truculent* will clear the ground by a minimum seventeen hundred fifty irals."

"Oh, plenty of room," Theada said a little breathlessly.

Their actual perihelion occurred so quickly that Brim only sensed an instantaneous transition from apparent descent to ascent, although *Truculent's* control settings remained unchanged. Off to port, he'd glimpsed a small city for a moment—they'd have no glass in their windows anymore. Probably have a few caved-in roofs, too. Time to worry about paying for that damage later.

"I see 'em!" somebody exclaimed. "Six points to port and low to the horizon."

"We're tracking," another voice said quietly. "*Zagrail* class ships all right. Long-range destroyers."

"You've never seen one of those, have you, Wilf?" Fourier asked.

"Only read about 'em," Brim admitted.

"Xaxtdamned fine ships. They can outmaneuver a scalded skarsatt."

"I'll keep that in mind," Brim said, lowering *Truculent's* bow until he could see three irregular shapes against the starry background. They were arranged along a staggered line formation and returning for their second attack on an arrogantly steady heading: Clearly expecting no more opposition than their first pass received from fort or starship. The Carescrian smiled with grim satisfaction. This time, OverPraefect Valentin was in for a nasty surprise—whomever he might turn out to be. In his display, he watched the firing crews at their Director consoles, listened to their familiar litany of deflection and ranges. "We'll take them in order, Anastasia," he said quietly as he adjusted course toward the leading enemy ship. "Closest first."

"All disruptors prepare to engage forward," Fourier said. "Target bearing red for five."

"Range ninety-one hundred and closing rapidly."

"Steady…"

The enemy ship was long and cylindrical, built as a single hull instead of independent modules on a K tube. She had a high, thin bridge and nine turrets distributed evenly forward, 'midships, and aft in triads circling the hull. Brim wondered if he might be looking at his special adversary as he scanned the distant vessel. There was quite a score to settle.

"Shoot!"

Truculent's deck bucked violently as all seven disruptors went off in a blinding eruption that lit space around the enemy destroyer like a tiny nova. A flame glowed for a moment abaft her bridge, then abruptly winked out.

"Got 'im, first shot!" somebody yelled gleefully as Fourier poured salvo after salvo at the enemy ship, starting a number of fires and blasting a large piece of debris into the wake.

None of the three attackers was fighting back yet, Brim noted. His tactics of surprise had served him well. He imagined the chaos Fourier's seven big 144s must be causing in the lead ship and wondered what the reaction would be in the two nearby asteroid forts whose big disruptors—quiet so far—nonetheless bore directly on his present position.

Finally, ragged return fire began to flash outside from the enemy ships. "It's mainly from the second one," Brim yelled to Fourier. "We'll give them a bit of trouble next." He put the helm over and hauled the ship onto a collision course with the next enemy destroyer.

Fourier nodded. "I see him," she said.

"Bearing orange nine forty-six."

"Up a hundred."

Brim watched the forward turret index a few degrees to port, rise slightly, then lower. Unseen, he knew the others were retracking to the same target.

"Steady…"

"Shoot!" *Truculent* was closer to this one, and the targeting was accurate. Great pieces of flaming wreckage began to fly off the enemy ship.

The first and third destroyers were now recovering from their initial surprise; to starboard, space erupted in a ragged welter of return fire. *Truculent's* deck kicked with the first long-range hits from the third enemy ship, but the effort was far too late for Brim's intended victim. A shattering explosion suddenly sent the second raider skidding off course to nadir, all but one of its turrets paralyzed or blasted to silence.

"Looks like he's had it," somebody observed.

"I'll have a spread of torpedoes into him, Anastasia," Brim ordered. In a matter of clicks, a salvo of five big Mark-19 torpedoes flashed past the bridge from the launcher, leaving a trail of blinding ruby fire in the starry darkness.

"Torpedoes running," Barbousse's deep voice intoned on the voice circuit.

Brim immediately canted *Truculent* round toward the third attacker. "Give him everything we've got!" he yelled to Anastasia over the bellowing generators.

"New target bearing blue four forty-one at eleven ninety-two."

"Shoot!"

Again, *Truculent's* powerful battery turned space into a concussive inferno, this time around the third enemy ship. Then the whole Universe lit from aft. Startled, Brim swung in his recliner, gritting his teeth. Were the Lixorian forts finally joining the fray? On whose side? He was immediately relieved to see what remained of the second League destroyer melt completely into a roiling cloud of livid energy from his torpedoes. Every port gleamed like a fiery eye along the hull before the ship burst again into a stupendous flowerlike pattern of flame and debris. He watched an entire turret assembly fly off into space like a runaway holiday rocket.

"That got the Leaguer bastards!" somebody yelled jubilantly.

"Universe," another whispered aloud, "look at that burn."

Suddenly, Brim was nearly knocked senseless against his seat restraints as a stunning explosion went off just abaft *Truculent's* bridge and caved in a corner of the chart room. The cabin atmosphere blew out in a single, tremendous draft that took two navigation consoles with it and filled the bridge with whirling shards of jagged hullmetal and Hyperscreen crystal. Chaos ruled momentarily as agonized screams filled the voice circuits and half a dozen consoles disappeared in great sparking eruptions of energy. The Carescrian felt a heavy weight bounce off the back of his recliner—his faceplate was suddenly covered with a spray of redness, that smeared as he tried to wipe it away. He turned in time to see a headless corpse crumple in a greasy red puddle beside him, belly ripped from crotch to the shredded stump of a neck. Still in its helmet, the severed head bounced like a child's toy at Theada's feet as the gravity pulsed in the shock waves.

Truculent's hull jolted and vibrated as more hits came aboard from the third enemy destroyer. One particularly powerful blast burst amidships, took the port launch with it, and opened the hull at the officers' quarters with a fiery plume. Brim knew instinctively he had just lost all he owned: His sister's picture in its little charred frame passed his mind's eye for an instant, then he snapped himself back to reality and hauled the destroyer around in a hard turn to port amid a howl of strikes from small weapons that shattered what remained of the aft Hyperscreens and filled the bridge with more jagged pieces of flying crystal.

In the corner of his eye, he saw someone crawling along the main corridor bubbling blood from a dozen holes in a barely recognizable battle suit. Suddenly, one of the larger rents unsealed in a red mist that sprayed nearby consoles a dark, sticky-looking crimson. Whoever it was stopped crawling and spasmodically reared upward before crumpling onto a tattered, blackened shred of star chart. Brim read the word MALDIVE on the nametag.

He bit his lip. At least he wasn't worried about the forts anymore. The Lixorians were clearly following orders and staying out of the action. He turned to watch the first destroyer they had encountered. Fourier had just redirected two of *Truculent's* ventral turrets at her. Burning in three or four locations along her hull, the *Zagrail* was returning the fire, but only intermittently; clearly, hits had been scored on critical control centers, though the ship's propulsion systems appeared to be undamaged. At least, Brim noted with satisfaction, the Leaguers were making no attempt to continue their attack on Tandor-Ra below.

Off to starboard, the third destroyer was turning with them. Two of her turrets were out of commission, with disruptors pointed at useless angles. The other seven, however, were firing rapidly and accurately, matching *Truculent* shot for shot. Brim wondered if she might be the ship carrying Valentin, then decided at the moment he had no time to care.

Soon the two ships were racing parallel courses across the bright disk of Lixor, *Truculent* silhouetted against the light, her opponent in the much-more-enviable position of blending with the darkness of space, at least so she appeared from Brim's console. Below, his own decks were a ruin, littered with debris and punctured in at least a hundred locations. Fires were reported in three damage-control zones. A nearby display presented the heavily armored sick bay crowded with more than twenty bloody bodies waiting for healing machines that were already full. Flynn could be seen feverishly rushing to this one and that, trying to handle the sudden overload. He was a fine doctor, Brim knew that from experience. But a lot of *Truculents* were going to die before this day was over, despite all the man could do.

He didn't opt for a closer look in the sick bay since the bridge itself was beginning to fill with acrid black smoke from fires raging in what was left of Collingswood's cabin. Metal fires, for certain, he noted. Nothing burned like metal once it caught.

Another explosion jarred the deck: This one in the Communications cabin joining A turret to the lower part of the bridge. Miraculously, the voice circuits held, but the deck buckled dangerously beneath his boots. And soon the smoke was worse than ever.

"I'll have a square pattern of five torpedoes," Fourier ordered. Moments later, five torpedoes flashed from the launcher: two high, two low, one in the center.

"Torpedoes running," Barbousse intoned.

"That ought to show them!" somebody yelled in the ruby glow.

"And how!" another started.

"Oh, no!" a third voice exclaimed in dismay as the enemy destroyer reacted with unbelievable speed, executing a series of tight maneuvers that cleanly evaded four of the speeding missiles. The fifth torpedo— evidently unexpected in a square salvo—excised a small deckhouse from the hull just aft of her small superstructure in a cloud of flying debris. It did not, however, encounter anything sufficiently solid in the framework to set off its charge, and continued on into space without inflicting any important damage.

"Afraid of that," Fourier snapped angrily. "Still, it didn't hurt to try."

Another welter of shots erupted close to the starboard bow, smashing the forward docking cupola and sending jagged hullmetal splinters whizzing through the Hyperscreens in a dozen places.

"Voof!" Ursis roared through clenched teeth as he grabbed his left forearm. Brim could see his battle suit sealing off a ragged wound in a spray of blood. The Bear pounded his console in high dudgeon. "Now," he pronounced solemnly, "that bastard Triannic is really in trouble!"

"Look out!" somebody else yelled. "Jubal's caught it..."

Brim glanced to his right in time to see Theada slump facedown onto shards of crystal littering his console, the Hyperscreens shattered in front of his station. Blood flowed freely from somewhere beneath his head and dripped in a puddle at his feet. "Somebody get a pressure patch up here!" the Carescrian yelled, then cranked *Truculent* around in a climbing turn as the first ship desperately took evasive action to escape his attack. The Leaguers acted only just in time. The space they would have occupied erupted in a deadly salvo of closely spaced blasts as Fourier growled in displeasure.

On the bridge aft, Brim glimpsed a crew with laser axes and power pries fighting three smoky radiation fires in what was left of the chart room and trying to free somebody pinned to the deck by a fallen support. Deep in the hull, he scanned a generator room turned to near chaos. Huge, charred holes had been opened by hits on either side of the keel, but miraculously, Borodov kept the oversized Admiralty N-types churning out their enormous output of raw antigravity waves. *Truculent's* speed was a major reason she was still in one piece now that the enemy ships had at last joined forces. Near one shattered power console, part of a rating still sat in the recliner, burned completely away from the waist up. Beside one of the blast holes, a leaking body hung limply impaled by three long needles of hullmetal, melted then thrust inward at the time of impact.

While two blood-covered medical ratings gently eased Theada from his console, Brim watched the second enemy ship turning toward him again. Fourier's disruptor crews wasted no time in blanketing it with a barrage of shock and radiation. The Leaguer's KA'PPA tower went in a blinding flash of light and a shattered launch sailed straight down from its mountings, only irals from a direct hit beneath the bridge. Brim smiled grimly. They'd felt those salvos, all right.

Then, with a blinding flash, *Truculent's* spaceframe again heaved convulsively, gravity pulsed, and loose debris bounced around the interior of the wrecked bridge like a swarm of heavy insects. A second explosion followed on its heels, this one all the way forward in the hull. It spun the destroyer like a toy. Brim fought the controls with all the skill he could muster. Flames and angry sparking radiation obscured the bow and boiled into their wake. When it cleared, *Truculent's* A turret was replaced by a jagged, blackened hole from which clouds of radiation swirled along the top decks. No hope for that crew, Brim thought as he followed the deadly billowing mist aft where it passed the wreckage of W turret, still apparently intact except for an innocuous-looking hole near the slot for the disruptor, which pointed uselessly off to port.

Then a third tremendous hit battered the ship. Brim grabbed his console as the gravity pulsed again and more loose debris cascaded across the wrinkling deck plates. This time, the steady thunder of the generators began to fade into hoarse, staccato rasping. He glanced around the decks through the Hyperscreens: No new damage topside, at least none he could recognize. The hit was on *Truculent's* bottom. And it didn't require much imagination to understand she'd taken serious damage. Fresh radiation was already curling into the wake from below, and their speed was beginning to fall!

Everybody seemed to be shouting on the voice circuits. All over the smoldering bridge, damage-control teams were desperately clearing debris. Smashed figures desiccating in torn battle suits were stacked like cordwood in the shredded remains of the chart room.

Instinctively, Brim ducked as more violent explosions went off close overhead, lighting the shattered wreckage on the decks below with a dazzling glare. He scanned Borodov's power exchange in a nearby display. Heavy clouds of radiation billowed overhead, and in the background, actual flames fed on some source of combustion from another wrecked systems console. Borodov's soot-covered helmet appeared in the display.

"How bad is it, Chief?" the Carescrian asked.

The old Bear shrugged and considered a moment. "*Truculent* has seen better days," he pronounced slowly. "Last hit destroyed important control logic for starboard generator; it runs pretty much out of control now. But it runs."

"And...?" Brim asked.

"And," Borodov went on, "we can still steer and run full speed. But doing the latter will quickly destroy the damaged generator."

Brim felt the speed drop noticeably. He watched the third enemy ship again turning toward him. Moments later, the first ship also turned. Both Leaguers could see he was in trouble. "Full speed, if you please, Lieutenant Borodov," he said quietly.

Borodov shrugged. "Full speed it is, Wilf Ansor," he said, busying himself at his console.

Fourier urged her disruptor crews to even more exertion, and somehow the rate of firing did increase, with telling effect. Bright flashes winked all over the enemy hulls. Additional metal fires began to belch clouds of sparks on the third enemy ship, but she continued to employ her disruptors with the same deadly accuracy. Return fire sprayed *Truculent* everywhere; her hull jumped and pounded as they burst aboard.

Somebody started screaming over the voice circuits again, but a long time passed before the bloodcurdling sound registered in Brim's mind above the general pandemonium. He turned in his seat to confront a medical team pulling Fourier from her console. Her suit was horribly burned at the neck, and her hands desperately tore at the shredded hole in her shoulder. One of the medical ratings placed a pressure patch over the opening while two others held her arms. The screaming abruptly turned to a liquid gargle, then stopped altogether. Brim turned back to his controls, gritting his teeth as the team dragged her limp figure aft toward the chart room.

"Starboard generator will fail within three cycles, Wilf Ansor," Borodov reported from below. Brim glanced at Ursis.

The Bear nodded confirmation.

"I suppose it will have to fail then, Chief," Brim said. "Keep it going as long as you can."

Borodov smiled broadly. "Give 'em great grief, Wilf Ansor!" he yelled over the din as he returned to his readouts.

In the corner of his eye, Brim caught Ursis grinning, too. His thumb was raised in the Universal human sign of approval.

Then there was little time to notice anything except the battle. "Stand by to concentrate all fire on the number-three ship!" Brim yelled at Fourier's replacement. He noticed the man's gloves were almost instantly soaked in blood from the console. "Let's go, then!" he yelled. "One last try!" He skidded *Truculent* into a tight descending spiral, then suddenly hauled back on the helm until he was flying on a collision course—with all remaining turrets firing as fast as their crews could recharge the 144s.

This unexpected attack once again took the enemy ship by surprise. The Leaguer captain instinctively put up his helm and attempted to climb out of *Truculent's* way; it was the worst thing he could do. Brim's remaining 144s all concentrated their fire on the enemy's steering gear just forward of the Drive openings. Pieces of hull metal blasted loose as the big disruptors tore at her hull. Suddenly, a terrific explosion ripped the enemy's midsection, followed immediately by a second and a third. A deckhouse blew off in a shower of sparks and glowing clouds of radiation. Then, slowly but inexorably, the ship began to shear off course.

"Get another spread of torpedoes in there!" Brim yelled, skidding *Truculent* to open a clear line of fire for the torpedo launcher—which fired as soon as it bore on the target. Five ruby sparks flashed past the bridge from aft; Brim watched them on their way, noting that this time, his scalded skarsatt had done the outmaneuvering. Then the target was obliterated in a stunning ball of flame that pulsed rapidly four times before it defined itself into a roiling cloud of livid energy that consumed what remained of the enemy ship like a minute star.

Brim put his helm over only just in time to avoid the cloud of debris, then aimed the ship once again toward the first enemy vessel. "Give 'em everything we've got left!" he yelled—just as the damaged port generator gave out with a thunderous rumble that shook *Truculent's* spaceframe to its very keel.

In spite of his struggles with the controls, the destroyer slewed around out of control, stars sliding across the Hyperscreens like a billion speeding comets on parallel tracks. Brim almost had to bring the ship to a halt before the steering gear would accept its new offset parameters.

"B turret seems to be jammed," someone reported.

"And we've no power to the torpedo flat," Barbousse added. "That last salvo did it for my part of the power exchange."

Brim nodded to himself as he carefully eased *Truculent* around to face his final opponent, now warily closing in for the kill. Seriously afire in a number of places, the *Zagrail* was not in much better shape than her Imperial adversary, but with propulsion systems evidently intact, she now had an insurmountable advantage. Brim shrugged grimly and continued to fly as best he could; if nothing else, he'd stopped the raid on Tandor-Ra. Perhaps that might make up for what was in store for the destroyer under his very temporary command.

He suddenly remembered Collingswood's mention of Imperial battlecruisers and glanced at his timepiece. He'd been fighting for more than a metacycle and certainly needed the "assist" she mentioned. The big ships were due any cycle now. He gritted his teeth. If he could just buy himself a little more time...Then he laughed ironically. Last-moment rescues only happened in fables to princes and kings. In all probability, Carescrians simply didn't qualify.

Outside, the enemy destroyer approached on an asymptotic curve, always toward the port side where *Truculent* had no operational disruptors to bear. Brim tried to turn with it for a forward shot, but to no avail. When he tightened up on the port helm, the steering engine created intense interference patterns with the operational generator and actually opened the effective radius. Helplessly, he stood by as the enemy ship positioned itself, watched the turrets index around to point directly at his bridge.

"Message from the enemy ship," somebody yelled above the confusion. "Full video an' all, if you please!"

Brim cleared a display. "I'll take it at this station," he growled, guessing who was on the other end. The globe flashed, glowed, then manifested the image of a handsome masculine face: Blue eyes, blond hair, dimpled chin. The Carescrian grimly nodded to himself. The Valentin.

"Ah, Brim," the elegant visage hissed, peering out of the display with a look of amused surprise. "I thought it might be you from the first transmission."

"Well, Hab'thall?" Brim snarled as he kicked the steering engine. It was just sufficient to surprise the opposite Helmsmen and get in a brief volley from C turret. Three shots landed with bright explosions; Valentin's port-side launch arched away in a series of tight loops trailing flame like a small comet. The OverPraefect's image jumped wildly in the display.

"That foul trick, Brim," Valentin snarled, "was the last—lucky—gasp of your contemptible existence." He glowered from the display in high dudgeon. "Today, I shall finish what I started more than two years ago. For Dame Fortune has finally deserted you, Carescrian—and your thrice-damned ship!"

Brim kicked the steering engine once more, but the Leaguer Helmsman was wary this time. Now there were no more tricks left from the Carescrian mines. With Valentin's execrable laughter ringing in his ears, he desperately scoured his mind for a way to prolong things until the battlecruisers might arrive. "Well, Hab'thall," he commented derisively, "I see they demoted you after your last blunder."

Valentin's eyebrows shot upward. "Demoted?" he protested. "You would have done well to study League Fleet ranks, fool." He pointed proudly to the ornate device embroidered in metallic thread on his perfectly tailored cuff. "I," he pronounced, "have been made an OverPraefect—promoted, Brim. Not demoted! The same rank as your full Commanders, Lieutenant. "

"Is that right?" Brim said derisively. "Old Triannic must xaxtdamned well be scraping the bottom of his bedchamber slops bucket if he's forced to promote the likes of you. Voot's beard, Valentin, you've never been able to complete a mission yet, when I'm around." He peered into the display with mock concentration, wrinkling his nose. "Something about me sets you on edge, doesn't it, Hab'thall?"

"Capcloth! Carescrian scum!" Valentin raged in a high, choked voice. "I shall show you what it means to be on edge." He turned to someone outside the display and nodded. "Carefully, though," he panted. "I want this to be slow. Make certain our Imperial friends have plenty of time to savor their agony." He laughed nervously. "Yes," he hissed in clear anticipation, "so they enjoy every shot!" Then he raised his hand and Brim's display went blank.

"Apparent end of transmission, Lieutenant," a rating reported.

Brim nodded. "Very well," he said to himself. He turned to face the enemy ship and waited grimly, wishing he had even some of Fourier's rocks to throw. They would have been every bit as effective as his disruptors now, and a thousand times more satisfying!

He glanced around *Truculent's* battered bridge, littered with bodies and Hyperscreen shards. Not many of the old crew alive now; only Ursis and a few scattered ratings waited defiantly at their consoles, staring into the enemy disruptors. Clearly Valentin was keeping his promise to draw things out, enjoying his moment of triumph. Brim nodded again. Let him! The battlecruisers were on their way, and even if he were not around to see it, the OverPraefect's predilection for torture might cost him dearly.

As he sat watching the enemy ship, he thought about the Lixorian forts. In *Truculent's* present position, at least three of them could bring their big disruptors to bear, save the ship doing a job they were built to accomplish. But all were silent, watching as the Leaguers prepared to cut his now-helpless destroyer to pieces. He took a deep breath. Though he would soon be blasted all over the Universe, he would die with disdain for every preening Lixorian businessman on the surface who sucked sustenance from the troubles of others. Much as he hated the black-suited Leaguer Controllers, he could easily generate more respect for them than for the rapacious bastards who lived on the planet below. At least Controllers had moral fortitude to cleave to some cause other than pure avarice.

Across the emptiness, a single disruptor flashed. *Truculent's* deck jumped as the bolt of energy crashed home just forward of the bridge in a shower of sparks. A second flash, and the 'midships deckhouse erupted in a cloud of radiation. Through a display, Brim scanned the glowing wreckage of the wardroom. Most of it was now open to space; great starry holes yawned where Greyffin IV's picture used to hang. He wondered momentarily about the fate of old Grimsby, but couldn't see the pantry—and the damage-control sensors there seemed to have lost any ability to function. In the long, shocked silence that followed, he thought of Margot; his mind's eye saw her as she was the night they met in that same wardroom. Then the softness of that memory was blown away by a stunning jar as a bolt landed in the petty officers' mess directly below his feet. More Hyperscreens shattered beside him; splinters tweaked his battle suit in a dozen places. A sharp pain burned his arm. He looked down to watch a charred hole sealing itself on his right forearm. The deck bucked again as three direct hits destroyed the torpedo launcher behind him.

"Sorry, Nik," he yelled to the Bear. "I did the best I could."

Ursis shrugged and smiled fatalistically. "I am not troubled by impending death, Wilf Ansor," he growled. "I only regret I did not tear that Hab'thall from limb to limb when I had chance."

"Universe!" somebody exclaimed in a trembling voice, "why doesn't he get it over with?"

"Do not attempt to speed Lady Fate," Ursis laughed over the voice circuits. "She often requires time for her miracles—which we badly need, as Universe knows."

"I can't stand any more of this!" somebody else shrieked, but her voice stopped abruptly, interrupted by a blinding light that erupted just aft of Valentin's ship. The spreading burst of raw energy sent the enemy destroyer tumbling out of control like a child's toy and laid *Truculent* on her beam ends. Terrorized screams filled the voice circuits; many of the Imperials no longer had visual access to the outside. Stunned, Brim automatically eased the destroyer back on to her original orientation, just in time to watch the Zagrail hesitate in its flight for a moment, then angle off into space at top acceleration amid a whole barrage of the huge flare-ups—the battlecruisers had finally arrived.

It was about xaxtdamned time!

10

Brim ultimately missed destruction of the third enemy ship (except to note a great pulsing light coming from somewhere off to starboard). Instead, he had been searching the darkness for a large object that appeared to separate from the doomed starship in its moment of hesitation before the attempted escape. Debris or possibly a cutter? Or had he imagined the whole thing? Whatever it was, it failed to register on any of his displays. Shaking his head, he reluctantly abandoned his search to watch the great Imperial battlecruisers *Benwell* and *Oddeon* heave majestically into view, their glowing disruptors returning smoothly to parked positions on their foredecks as they approached.

"Incoming messages, Lieutenant," a rating yelled.

"I'll take 'em here," Brim ordered, reluctantly abandoning his search. Whatever escaped Valentin's doomed flagship had long since disappeared among the stars. Momentarily, a globe materialized a familiar head and shoulders on his console.

"Your Highness," Brim stammered.

"Wilf Brim, as I live and breathe," Prince Onrad drawled from the display while he stroked his chin thoughtfully. "Certainly glad you take better care of my blond cousin than you do of His Majesty's ships." He raised his eyebrows in mock disapprobation. "Poor *Truculent's* a proper mess."

Brim felt a rush of emotion. A choked laugh of relief escaped his throat. "Couldn't help it, Your Majesty," he sputtered. "They just showed me how to fly 'em at the Academy; didn't say anything about taking care of 'em."

"Ha, ha! Good point, Brim," Onrad laughed. "We ought to send you to teach the class, then, for I meant what I said about the proper mess you've made. It's totally proper. You've saved much more than just a conference, you know, and I am told you faced three enemy ships. I saw only one badly damaged survivor fall victim to our disruptors. So if my count is accurate, you must have destroyed two others while you were at it. Correct?"

"Correct, Your Highness," Brim answered, "but two were one too few. That third ship you destroyed nearly got us."

Onrad grinned. "Just like you xaxtdamned Carescrians. Always biting off more than you can chew." Then his face became serious. "I thank the Universe we arrived in time," he said slowly. "You and your crew have accomplished much important work today—more than I suspect most of you know. It will be good to see you suitably rewarded." He smiled again. "Right now, I'm going to turn you over to Admiral Penda here, but I shall expect to see you in person back on Avalon as soon as it can be arranged. Good work, Brim—and share those words with your crew. Today, each of you is a hero, in the fullest sense of the word."

Brim's display faded, then returned with the gray visage of Star Admiral Sir Gregor Penda, Imperial Fleet; no mistaking that round face and medium beard. The man had been part of almost every important news summary for the past five years, good and bad. His piercing eyes looked as if they had never admitted to a moment's doubt about anything, nor had they remained long shadowed by unanswered questions. Bold, decisive, and brave beyond all question, he was generally acknowledged to be the greatest tactician in the known Universe, as much feared by his enemies in the League as admired by Imperial colleagues. "Congratulations, Brim," he said with a pleased smile on his face. "You seem to have saved much of the Empire's face as well as the conference. However, from the looks of *Truculent*, your medical officer would probably welcome a hand with the wounded. Am I right?"

Brim thought of the crowded nightmare in Flynn's sick bay. "I'm sure he would, Admiral," he said.

Penda nodded. "We'll make the diplomats wait while we do

something about that," he said. "The Empire needs all the crews like yours it can get—preferably alive." He passed instructions quietly to someone out of view, nodded a few times, then turned back to Brim. "I shall have Benwell alongside in a moment, Brim. We'll stow the protocol this time and do the maneuvering on this bridge. If I'm not mistaken, your own steering gear is shot to pieces."

Brim looked outside and felt the color rise in his face. *Truculent* was weaving all over the sky. He pulled back on the power until his course steadied.

"You look surprised, Lieutenant," Penda laughed.

"Universe," Brim groaned, his eyes raised to the shattered overhead Hyperscreens.

"That's all right, Brim," the Admiral chuckled. "Judging from the hole in *Truculent's* bottom, I doubt if the Fleet can come up with many Helmsmen who could have done as well; old Borodov's already notified our engineers you have performed a navigational miracle."

In moments, the colossal battlecruiser was carefully pulling alongside, towering over *Truculent's* tiny frame like a great mountain range. Brim shook his head in wonder; one brush with that immense bulk would reduce his little destroyer to a wrinkled piece of hullmetal foil. Momentarily, he succumbed to a flash of galloping claustrophobia; it passed rapidly when he considered that even assistant Helmsmen aboard *Benwell* were among the finest in a whole galaxy. He grinned at himself while a brow extended from the giant hull. Far overhead, he could make out tiny figures looking down from the bridge. He stood and saluted. They all returned his gesture. It was one of the proudest moments of his life.

***

The TRANSpool skimmer drew to a halt in a cloud of swirling ice particles, which quickly dispersed in Haefdon's everlasting wind. "Thanks," Brim said, stepping into ankle-deep snow despite recent efforts by one of the base's ubiquitous (and largely unsuccessful) pavement scrubbers. Early evening chill was raw on his face as he scanned the bleak inland repair yard. He'd got only a fleeting impression of it in the darkness the previous night after a frightful landing between the two deep-space tugs that towed *Truculent* home. Now, after a desperately needed rest, he had returned to sign Collingswood's destroyer over to the ship salvagers.

Salvage berth 189-E, itself, was a typical clutter of weather-beaten buildings in faded gray, heavy machinery, rusting wave guides, wheels of snow-covered cable—all surrounded by the requisite forest of ever-moving shipyard cranes. And what remained of *Truculent* hovered inertly on an oversized gravity pool, swaying uncertainly in the veering wind, centered on a tangle of mooring beams rigged by indifferent salvage-yard laborers. A rusty, oversized brow squeaked and rasped on unkempt bearings as she moved.

"Want me to wait, Lieutenant?" the driver probed gently from behind.

Brim guessed the woman had a lot of experience with people like himself. Ships could work their way into a person's soul. And when they were hurt... "Thanks, but this may take awhile," he lied, turning back to the skimmer. "I'll call for another ride when I'm finished." In truth, little more remained for him to accomplish at all so far as *Truculent* was concerned. A cycle or two at most, then the doughy little warship was no longer a part of his life—except for the memories.

The driver nodded. She understood. "There's COMM gear in the shack with the metal roof over there," she said, pointing off across the pool. Then she saluted (almost as if she meant it) and drove off into the snowy evening silence, her navigation lights persisting like ruby wraiths in the darkening grayness.

Brim pulled the Fleet Cloak closer around his neck and shivered as he turned once more toward the ship. When he'd viewed her from one of the tugs on the way home, she hadn't seemed quite so damaged. Not out in space where she was meant to be. But here in the waning moments of a dreary Haefdon day, she was dreadfully transformed. Power chambers extinguished, her whole structure had cooled. Ice and snow dulled even the Hyperscreens over her buckled and warped bridge (or, rather, what remained of those Hyperscreens). Her decks were everywhere mottled by the bright blue of temporary pressure patches, and unsightly braids of thick multicolored cables ran through temporary holes punched in her hull from ugly machines blinking evilly on the periphery of the pool. She'd been despoiled of most everything that could be removed before the long tow home even began, including the workable disruptors. Now, during his absence, they'd taken even her one remaining launch. Except for a great throng of remembrance, the stout little ship had become a lifeless, stripped hulk.

With a deep breath (one he would never admit was a sigh), Brim started grimly for the brow, his boots squeaking in the powdery snow. Around him, the first lights began to sparkle on the cranes like bright stars in rapidly moving constellations. Others winked on here and there in windows of the sheds and control shelters. But he could sense no warmth in any of them. The whole salvage complex—all of it—reeked somehow with the stench of death.

Out on *Truculent's* empty decks, the wind seemed harsher and colder. Brim's ears caught the distant, crackling thunder of a lifting starship, and he suddenly found it difficult to face the ruin around him. He shivered again as he carefully picked his way across the icy, buckled hullmetal toward a temporary shelter they'd rigged as a main boarding hatchway. The cover itself was unsealed; he fought it open against the wind and stepped into the empty darkness beyond, stomping snow from his boots on the grating. Maldive's station was long gone, as was poor Maldive herself. With so many of the others, they'd given her remains a Blue Cape's traditional sendoff into Universal emptiness. Her entry desk, along with *Truculent's* ornate sign-in register, had been reduced to subatomics in Valentin's final orgy of destruction.

The ship's interior even smelled empty; a damp staleness assaulted his nostrils, redolent of a faint but pervading scent of—he wrinkled his nose—death. No amount of scrubbing could ever rid this hull of the blood that had dried in so many cracks and seams.

Switching on his torch, he closed the hatch and started forward along the companionway, boots echoing hollowly in the empty stillness. He had gone only a few steps before the beam reflected from a spot of brightness on a blackened, wrinkled bulkhead. Frowning, he stopped, aimed the torch: "I.F.S. TRUCULENT. JOB 21358 ELEANDOR BESTIENNE YARD 228/51988." The metal plate still shone as if it had been polished within the last day, which on closer inspection he knew it had. By force of habit, he brushed a few strokes with his own sleeve. Someone in the skeleton crew had been polishing regularly all the way home.

Brim smiled thoughtfully. Who? It could have been any of them; they all loved the ship in one way or another: Nik, Borodov, Barbousse, the handful of Starmen left alive. Except himself. He'd been too heartsick to wander far from the bridge.

Farther along, he paused by the entrance to the wardroom; it was now only a rough blue patch in the bulkhead, shaped like a hatch. Not enough of the riddled walls beyond remained to permit shoring-up operations, so they'd sealed the whole area off instead. Everyone took the easiest way out of solving problems in space; starship repairs were a whole lot easier in the controlled environment of a gravity pool. And in spite of his gloom, Brim found himself chuckling about Grimsby. The ancient steward had been sealed inside his pantry by an early hit; they'd found him there calm and rested the morning after the fight. Grimsby was a survivor.

Up the ladders past the ruin that was once Collingswood's cabin, he ended his climb in the twisted wreckage they still (almost jokingly) called a bridge. Now even the last of the consoles were dark—those that remained on the wrinkled deck plates. Most of the duty stations had been removed previously, either by Valentin's disruptors or parts—desperate scavengers from nearby Imperial blockade ships who swarmed to the battle site even before it was judged DD T. 83 should be towed home for salvage. Brim walked slowly to the right-hand Helmsman's station: A most valuable console, it remained only because it was necessary for landfall operations. He turned his torch on full power to melt frost covering the cracked Hyperscreens before him. Outside, it was quite dark now, but the snow had stopped and the air was clear. Round patches of light gleamed dully under the repair yard's ubiquitous Karlsson lamps.

As he stared out into the night, he could just see the blackened circle where A turret was once mounted. It reminded him of Fourier, herself blasted from existence like most of her beloved guns. In death, she traveled near Maldive somewhere, forever headed out into the Universe toward peace—if, indeed, such existed anywhere. Beside him, Theada's console had been removed and was certainly serving even now in another needy ship, salvaged like the young Helmsman himself. It would be a long time before Theada was sufficiently healed for a permanent return to duty. But he had survived, thanks largely to Admiral Penda's quick action moving wounded crew members from the overcrowded charnel house in Flynn's sick bay to the giant and superbly equipped hospital aboard *Benwell*.

Brim sat in the recliner to wait for the manager of the salvage team, remembering that only metacycles previously, he had used every bit of his skill—and a little more—fighting these same controls to a standoff as the two space tugs eased *Truculent's* almost helpless hulk down from a temporary parking orbit. He shook his head in wonder. The transition from roaring, flaming reentry chaos to the stony silence that now enfolded the bridge was nearly unbelievable.

As he sat, he wondered what Lady Fate had in store for himself. Clearly, *Truculent* would never need a Helmsman again. His own message queue at the base officers' quarters mentioned only that orders would be forthcoming, not when. He would hear something after the ceremonies tomorrow, he assumed, then shook his head. Somehow, he had been dreading that honor ever since Prince Onrad's message, informing him *Truculent's* heroes would be decorated at home on Gimmas-Haefdon rather than on Avalon. It made sense, the way the Prince put it: Avalon did appear to have quite enough in the way of ceremonies. The celebration would do a lot more good at this bleak outpost, where it would not be lost among the glitter of a hundred important functions.

He smiled to himself in the darkness. He found he didn't really care what happened at the moment, only that something new was in the wind. That was enough. For the present, he was glad enough to have the almost unbelievable luxury of a few metacycles to waste on himself.

It would have been nice, he considered, had Margot been... Then he squeezed his eyes shut, forcing all thoughts about her from his mind. With her permanent reassignment to Avalon, it was clear she had already made a decision denying him any more of her life. And he'd accepted that pragmatically. There was, after all, a yawning gulf between the future queen of a large star cluster and a Helmsman lieutenant not seven years from the Carescrian ore mines. He nodded to himself as he had so often done in the past few months. An unbridgeable gulf.

293

Outside, the lights of a skimmer caught his eye as it churned along the main highway, then slowed and swung through the gate, drawing to a stop before *Truculent's* salvage berth. Brim watched its single passenger disembark and make his way toward the brow. A nearby Karlsson lamp revealed him to be none other than Bosporus P. Gallsworthy himself. Gallsworthy? He'd already been promoted to Lieutenant Commander and reassigned to important Admiralty duty on Avalon. And the man certainly couldn't plan a long visit to this burned-out hulk; he was scheduled to depart on the *Robur Enterprise*, which left for the capital in no more than two metacycles.

Presently, footfalls sounded on the ladder to the chart room, then the senior Helmsman strode into the bridge. "Thought I'd find you here, Brim," he said with a chuckle. "Sentimental dunces like you always fall in love with the xaxtdamned-fool ships they fly."

Brim got to his feet and shrugged good-naturedly. "Guess I can't help what I am, Commander," he said.

Gallsworthy almost smiled. "I guess you're doing all right, Brim," he allowed. "But I lie a lot, too. So you'll never be sure."

"I see, Sir," Brim mumbled as he fought his own smile to a standstill. Coming from Gallsworthy, those words were high praise indeed.

The man shrugged. "I didn't come here to pass compliments, smart alec," he growled. "Seems I'm doomed to be Collingswood's messenger boy until I actually board the xaxtdamned ship for Avalon." He laughed a little and looked Brim in the eye. "Somehow, for the Captain, I never seem to mind." He frowned. "Don't exactly know why."

Brim kept what he hoped was an impassive face. He could make a good guess why.

"At any rate, Regula's all tied up today with important business, which, by the way, involves you, punk, so she sent me to find you and tell you what she's done before you get the news as an official surprise." He actually did grin at this juncture. "I doubt if you'll have many objections."

By this time, Brim's curiosity was just about to go nonlinear. He nodded and steeled himself. One couldn't hurry Gallsworthy. The man simply had a hard time with words.

"Tomorrow," he continued at length, "after the ceremonies, you'll receive orders for your next ship. She's I.F.S. *Defiant*, a brand-new light cruiser in final design right now at Eleandor-Bestienne." He stopped for a moment and frowned. "It's where old *Truculent* was launched," he said in an almost choked voice. "Xaxtdamned rustbucket anyway. Always needed trim on the starboard helm."

Brim laughed to himself. Perhaps he wasn't the only one who ever loved a starship.

"*Defiant's* first in a new subclass of very light, high-speed cruisers," Gallsworthy continued after a moment. "Something else indeed. More'n half again the length of old *Truculent* here, nearly triple the crew—with the same top speed. Serious xaxtdamned warships. Built on the same principle as battlecruisers, only a lot smaller; they'll use 'em for leading convoy defenses. Typical combat group has three of 'em with four or five destroyers. Damned near maneuverable as those Leaguer *Zagrails* you went up against, but armed with nine big 152s and a whole raft of smaller stuff. And they've got propulsion that'll knock Ursis' eyes out."

"Nik, Sir?" Brim interrupted in spite of himself. "He's assigned, too?"

"Yeah," Gallsworthy said. "Collingswood's asked for him, too. Old Borodov's heading for the Admiralty like me. He's an Archduke back in Sodeskaya, ya' know—serving in our Fleet only because he feels he should. He'll be assigned to the General Staff next go-around."

"Borodov an Archduke?"

"Brother of the Sodeskayan Knez," Gallsworthy assured him.

"Voot's beard," Brim said. "Who would have thought something like that?"

"And Captain Collingswood? She's commanding *Defiant*?"

"Of course, Collingswood's commanding. Who else would bid for the likes of you and Ursis on her crew? Especially in senior positions."

Brim shook his head. "In what positions, Commander?" he asked dizzily.

"Senior," Gallsworthy reiterated. "I don't know why, either. She must see something in you two young pups I've never seen. Xaxt, she's busy right now pulling the right strings to set that up. It's why she's not here telling you this herself."

"Universe..."

"Yeah. My words exactly."

"Who else is coming over to the new ship from *Truculent?*" Brim asked.

"Not many," Gallsworthy answered. "Course, there aren't a lot of you alive after that last action, either. Aside from ol' Grimsby, Flynn and Barbousse are the only others I know of." He frowned. "Actually, I think Regula said she was bringing Barbousse along to keep you and that damned fancy Bear friend of yours out of trouble." He chuckled. "Barbousse. Now there's a real Blue Cape, by Voot."

"Yes, Sir," Brim said. He had no arguments about that...

***

Only cycles following Gallsworthy's departure, Brim met the salvage crew on *Truculent's* starboard deck just inboard of the brow (as required by some ancient and obscure Fleet protocol), then placed his mark with a logic scriber in the prescribed half dozen places on a tabulator board. "For the Captain." Then he was through. After that, he picked his way quickly over the brow and around the gravity pool to the shed with the metal roof.

Waiting for the TRANSpool skimmer to arrive, Brim found he could not bring himself to look back at the ship. It was as if he had just deserted a longtime friend in the middle of adversity—something Carescrians simply did not do. Mutual assistance was fundamental to survival itself in the grinding poverty of that far-off mining district, and Brim's sense of guilt in breaking this basic life tenet was almost overwhelming. He stood with his back to the littered gravity pool and stared out into the darkness, trying to concentrate on the future, not the past. Somehow, he wasn't very successful.

He traveled all the way back to the officers' quarters in near silence, then made his way directly to the Great Central Wardroom in the main building. He determined he would need an awful lot of meem to wipe the last few metacycles from his memory. An early start was not only advisable, it appeared to be a necessity.

He quickly found his need for drowning memories was not in the slightest unique. Ursis and Borodov had preceded him to the darkened, music-filled Great Wardroom by at least a metacycle. They were already well into a workable cure, each puffing his inevitable Zempa pipe and helping fill the room with the rich odor of hogge'poa.

"Aha, fryind Wilf Ausorevich," Borodov slurred in a melancholy voice, raising his empty glass upside down. "At least you have finished vith thankless task." As always, two young and (Brim assumed) attractive females fawned at either side of the elderly Bear. Somewhat less than soberly, they also raised their empty glasses to the Carescrian.

"Come, tonight we will drink manyeh, manyeh toasts to old *Truculent*, eh?" Ursis said, stumbling to his feet, "Devil take damned Valentin! Voof!" He handed Brim a large, ornate goblet and indicated an enormous collection of Logish and Sodeskayan meem bottles on an adjacent table, most of which were still relatively full.

As evening progressed into night, these vessels were duly emptied—and just as duly replaced by the quiet, efficient staff of the Great Wardroom. Brim's melancholy eventually gave way to fuzziness during endless Sodeskayan aphorisms and declamations on the memory of DD T.83. Each was punctuated by a toast in the Sodeskayan manner by first draining a freshly filled goblet, then reverently reciting the age-old Sodeskayan litany, "To ice, to snow, to Sodeskaya we go!"

"Bears can always dance with lyittle storm maidens, but who can escape volf's golden fangs?" Borodov growled. "Voot take it!"

"To ice, to snow, to Sodeskaya we go!"

"Is no great triumph watchink mountain winds freeze lakes," one of the females said as she rose unsteadily to her feet and smoothed her skirt. "Except those havink much to do wyith zest of life." The Bears nodded their heads wisely as she sat.

"Yes. Is fact!"

"She speaks truth in that."

"Yes...To zest of life, and to *Truculent*! Mayeh her atoms continue aboard other heroic ships, in tradyition set byeh original crew!"

"To *Truculent*. Mayeh this salvage brink disaster to Nergol Triannic!"

"To *Truculent*. Long mayeh her atoms sail stars!"

"To ice, to snow, to Sodeskaya we go!"

"Conflict loves great warmink breasts of Mother Planets," Ursis slurred emotionally.

"True," Brim said absently from his chair as he mopped spilled meem from the leg of his trousers.

"Yes...yes...conflict," the Bears shouted.

"To ice, to snow, to Sodeskaya we go!"

"To atoms of old *Truculent*! Mayeh theyeh sail stars forever!"

Shortly after the change of the last watch, the Great Wardroom began to empty, but *Truculent's* wake continued unabated. Brim was by now feeling little residual mental pain, but something still bothered him, and it had everything to do with the ship. He tried to concentrate more on the toasts.

"To ice, to snow, to Sodeskaya we go!"

"Frozen logs, like Holyeh Grayeh Rocks of Nodd, are truelyeh not stuff of scyience!" This latter nearly brought the Bears from their seats as they doubled up laughing.

"To *Truculent*! Never forget!"

"To ice, to snow, to Sodeskaya we go!"

Brim's mind had begun to drift by now on a pleasant, muzzy lake of meem. Were the Bearish aphorisms actually beginning to make sense? Was that Captain Collingswood entering the Great Wardroom on the arm of a rather ordinary-looking Blue Cape?

Collingswood!

Brim struggled to put himself together as the couple approached. The Captain was now in the lead as they threaded their way among the tables. Her escort wore a triple insignia on his collar. Brim counted its parts carefully. One thick and two thin rhomboids. He counted them again as the two reached their table. A vice admiral. Somehow, he was not surprised.

"Ah, Captain Collingswood!" Borodov remarked jovially, his speech suddenly more precise. "Our evening will be complete only if you and Sir Plutron join us for early morning libation." He bowed. "May I present two of most beautiful Sodeskayan intelligence officers, just arrived from Mother Planets: Spa'rzha Cherdak and Ptitsa Pro'tif."

The two young Bears giggled and curtsied. "You won't have to remember our names if you'll stay," they laughed.

"Please," Ursis said as he rose, his voice also without accent. "We shall consider ourselves doubly honored."

Brim smiled. "Yes, please," he echoed from atop two wobbly legs. He knew he was in no shape to utter anything more complex.

Collingswood turned to the Vice Admiral, who now stood by her side. "I should love to join these people, Erat," she said, looking into his eyes.

"And so should I," the Admiral said. "Spa'rzha, Ptitsa, I am most honored to make your acquaintance." He chuckled. "We Imperials can use all the intelligence we can locate." He was short and thin with bushy brows, gray hair, and a fleshy nose. He was also clearly involved with Collingswood in a relationship that had little to do with the Fleet. His deep-set eyes fairly shouted how he felt about her.

"My friends," Borodov said, "we are, this morning, in company of Vice Admiral Sir Erat Plutron, Commander of Fourth Battle Squadron." He began to introduce the other members of the party.

"I'm going over here for a moment," Collingswood called to the Admiral. "I should like a few words with Lieutenant Brim while I have the opportunity."

Plutron smiled. "I don't think I shall be jealous," he said to Brim with a wink.

Brim nodded and held up his hands. "N-No contest, Admiral," he said, then moved a chair from a nearby table beside his, holding it for Collingswood while she sat. "Good m-morning, Captain," he said, returning clumsily to his own chair. He was very much aware his words weren't coming out as well as they should. Bears, he concluded with no little envy, had an unbelievable tolerance for meem.

Collingswood smiled. "Relax, Wilf," she said quietly—the others had suddenly been drawn into vigorous conversation with Admiral Plutron. "I have been far more intoxicated than you on occasion, for the very same reasons."

Brim felt his brow knit, but he kept his silence.

"I shan't preach long," she said, pouring herself an admirable dollop of the best Logish meem (a woman with clearly patrician tastes). "I have other matters to occupy my mind tonight besides *Truculent*. But then, old DD T.83 was not my first ship, as she was yours." She fastened her eyes on his. "It may not help much at the present, but you should know that you did a superb job in that last battle.

Remember that. You may have had your first ship blown out from under you, but you accomplished your objective admirably—against astronomical odds." She smiled and raised her eyebrows. "The three-to-one ship ratio you faced was an impossibility in the first place. Add to this the fact that you were also up against one of the League's most promising, most highly decorated, and probably most clever young Fleet commanders. The whole episode says much for your ability—as well as your accomplishments. You did win, you know."

"Except," Brim interrupted, "I t-think Valentin got away in one of the xaxtdamned launches, beggin' the Captain's pardon."

Collingswood laughed. "I thought you'd notice that," she laughed. "I did, too. *Truculent's* Chairman was broadcasting the whole thing to me real time in Tandor-Ra. The Admiralty would love to believe they're rid of the likes of that Hab'thall. But I think not. I talked to Erat about it—he feels the bloody criminal got away, too. Evidently, the League trains its officers to desert if a ship appears doomed. They do it a lot, you know. And I don't think it would have been a good bargain risking all those lives in Flynn's sick bay against the capture of a few worthless Leaguers. Do you?"

Brim bit his lip. "Thanks, Captain," he said. "But a lot of them died anyway. As you well know."

Collingswood reached and took his hand. "Lots of people die in wars," she said quietly. "It seems that's mostly what they're all about." She smiled. "You almost died yourself—on your first mission. A matter of pure chance, I think. You did the best you could; that's all any of us can ask. Living or dead."

Brim could only stare into her brown eyes as she spoke. "And so far as *Truculent* herself is concerned...certainly I loved her. I've loved all my ships." She looked him in the eye. "But never forget, Wilf Brim, she was only a ship. Hullmetal, rivets, crystals, and a couple of oversized antigravs. No life there. No personality. Only what we lent to her while we were aboard. And we took it with us over the brow when we left; never forget that." She narrowed her eyes. "Yes," she ruminated in an uncharacteristically hard tone of voice, "we all feel bad old *Truculent's* gone to the breakers. But we'll take her personality along with us to *Defiant*—you, me, Ursis, Flynn, Barbousse, even crazy old Grimsby. And *Truculent* will never die. Just as they'll salvage her parts, we'll salvage her soul."

Brim shook his head. The talk had finally uncovered his sore spot. "Except I was the one making decisions when they all died, Captain," he said with renewed gloom. He could hear the others at the table discussing comparative Drive systems with great animation. Admiral Plutron was also a person of far-flung knowledge.

"Finally," Collingswood said triumphantly. "I believe we're finally at the heart of the matter."

Brim raised an eyebrow. "The heart, Captain?"

Collingswood smiled. "The heart, Wilf," she repeated. "If you accept command responsibility, you also accept costs. It goes with the territory. In the most crass terms, it has to do with resources and the fact that nothing is free—simple thermodynamics. As a commander, your resources are ships and lives, including your own. You put what you are willing to gamble on the line, then play toward some goal as best you can. At the end, you have either won that goal or lost, always at some cost of your resources. It's as simple as that. If you win, you measure relative success by comparing your actual cost against the value gained."

Brim's mind was beginning to function again a little. "I guess my goal was..."

"Your goal—which you instinctively knew without any orders from me—was to prevent further attack on Tandor-Ra. At least until Penda and the battlecruisers arrived." She looked him in the eye. "Did you do that, Wilf Brim?" she asked.

Brim pursed his lips. "I did that, Captain," he said—a little proudly, in spite of himself.

"You're absolutely right you did," Collingswood said. "And don't you ever forget it."

"But the price," Brim said, wincing at the thought. "Universe..."

"That part belongs to me this time," Collingswood answered. "Because, in effect, I ordered you out there on an impossible mission. I set the price I was willing to pay, not you, Wilf Brim." She smiled. "Of course," she said, "I didn't expect to pay the whole wager when I put you in charge. And...I didn't."

Brim could only shake his head.

"Oh, don't try to talk, Wilf," Collingswood said. "Simply think about what I have said. Objective and price, those are the touchstones. When you work them out for *Truculent's* last mission, you'll find you accomplished my objective at a bargain. You not only saved a city— with all the lives that involves—but a treaty, as well. And there's no telling how many lives that treaty will eventually save." She laughed and sipped her meem. "Then," she said, "there's the matter of the enemy ships. Your score stands at one ship for two—actually one for three, since the last one would probably have gotten away had you not disabled him before *Benwell* arrived at the scene. Not a bad score in anybody's book, I should think. How do you really feel about that battle, Wilf Brim?"

"Well..."

Collingswood laughed. "Wilf," she said, "I think I have made my point. If you continue to let this *Truculent* thing bother you, then it is clearly your own doing." She turned her head toward Admiral Plutron. "I, on the other hand, have urgent matters on my mind, so if you will excuse me, Lieutenant, we shall see each other next at your decoration ceremonies tomorrow."

"Aye, Captain," Brim said. "And I th-thank you for including me in *Defiant's* crew."

Collingswood smiled warmly and shrugged. "If you still want to sign on with me, after what I have put you through," she said, "then I am quite gratified to have you aboard."

Shortly after that, Collingswood and her admiral took leave of the Sodeskayan table amid wishes for safety, prosperity, and long life from each to all. Not much later, Borodov also rose, stretching his arms sleepily. "Is an early metacycle for elderly Bears," he said, glancing at his timepiece. "I think I shall turn in now. Tomorrow promises long metacycles of wakefulness, for I accompany the Prince back to Avalon." He looked at Brim and grimaced in mock anticipation. "Even Bears are sometimes afflicted with hangovers, Lieutenant," he said. Then he disappeared with Pro'tif on his arm.

After a final goblet of meem, Ursis accompanied Brim to his room. "Since you started on Sodeskayan meem," the Bear explained, "this

Sodeskayan has the responsibility to insure you find the way to your room, eh?"

Brim shrugged. Were the truth known, he felt a little woozy on his feet, besides, the Bear's room was nearby, and he felt his own responsibility toward his friend. In the end, they assisted each other, with added help from Cherdak, who also professed responsibility for making sure Ursis arrived at his room safely. The Carescrian decided he wouldn't ask any questions about that. The threesome decided (after much serious discussion in committee) to take a shortcut through a spacious courtyard. The night was still clear, miraculously so for Haefdon. Brim scanned the stars as they walked. Suddenly, Ursis and Cherdak picked up their ears.

"Big one comink, Nik," Cherdak said, turning her gaze toward the ocean.

"Indeed," Ursis said presently. "Listen, Wilf Ansor—you should be able to hear it any moment. Sounds like battleship."

Brim listened, peering sightlessly at the sky and concentrating on sounds from the night. There. A low rumble—more felt as a vibration than heard—growing stronger by the click. Soon it was shaking the pavement beneath their feet. All three looked up at the same time to watch a whole flotilla of destroyers blaze through the cold air. This was followed immediately by a monstrous collection of lights and flashing beacons that glided rapidly overhead with the cascading thunder of a thousand lesser starships. And even in the relative darkness, there was no mistaking those majestic lines: *Queen Elidean* herself, first of the five greatest battleships ever constructed (she alone had tear-shaped shelters at the tips of her bridge wings). Then the great vessel passed behind the roofline of the officers' quarters.

Ursis laughed as the tumult began to ease and they continued across the courtyard. "Your Crown Prince Onrad travels in style, if I may say so."

Brim saluted his friend. "If it turns out that you may not say so," he pronounced in mock seriousness, "then I shall take it upon myself to say it for you." He rubbed his chin and shrugged as if he had suddenly reached a difficult decision. "In point of fact, I have recently divined that such mode of travel is probably even more comfortable than the average Carescrian ore barge. Now what do you think of that, Sodeskayan?"

"Deep thinking, Brim," the Bear replied, nearly tripping on a raised paving tile. "Deep thinking indeed."

Cherdak smiled and got a better grip on her countryman.

The two Sodeskayans delivered Brim to his door only cycles after they stumbled out of the sixth-floor lift. The Carescrian never was able to remember getting himself into bed, nor neatly hanging his uniform in the wardrobe.

***

Brim came muzzily awake before his alarm chimed him out of bed. He didn't bother to open his eyes—clearly he was not finished sleeping, and his thoughts were still muddled from the night before.

Besides, he was still glowing from an erotic dream to end all erotic dreams. About Margot, of course, and oddly enough (now that he thought about it) set right here in the room he occupied. He sighed; the xaxtdamned thing was so real, it might really have happened. His mind's eye could still see her mounted astride him, eyes glazed, red-flushed face twisted into a ravishing mask of effort and delight while her pelvis moved urgently backward and forward, scraping his groin with her coarse, wet gold until they both erupted, howling like maniacs in great, throbbing explosions of delight. Their coupling was even better than he remembered from Avalon, as if the Universe were atoning for time they'd spent apart. If that made any sense at all. If anything in that sort of dream had to make sense.

As he recalled, she'd arrived in the dream out of nowhere—awakening him as she climbed into bed, her clothes folded neatly on a chair by the door.

He smiled as he lay in the lonely darkness. Even dreaming, he'd been too affected by the powerful Sodeskayan meem to take much advantage of the situation. Except, of course...But that had been totally automatic.

She'd giggled happily when she discovered his condition, and placed her lips beside his ear while blond curls tickled his nose. "That's wonderful, Wilf," she'd whispered. "You've come through splendidly. I shall now take care of all the rest." It was the most beautiful dream of his entire life.

He sighed again and shifted to a more comfortable position—where he suddenly encountered a warm, smooth curve that had absolutely nothing to do with an empty bed. Neither did the perfume he'd been breathing, come to think of it.

He felt himself go rigid. Heart suddenly thundering in his ears, he moved his hand along the softness. And he was awake this time, all right. The curve was very, very real. He carefully opened his eyes to a mass of golden curls on the pillow beside him.

"M-m-mm, Wilf," she said sleepily. "Ready for more?"

"S-Sweet, thraggling Universe," he mumbled. It was all he could manage before she rolled toward him, threw her leg over his hip, and smothered his mouth with her wet-crazy wet lips.

A long time passed before either of them said anything sensible at all.

***

"How in the name of Voot himself," Brim demanded as dim morning light glowed through the window, "can you sit here naked in bed with me and say you are going to marry him? I mean, how?"

Margot smiled impishly, resting her back against a pillow. "Watch my lips," she said. "I...am...going...to..."

"Universe!"

"Oh, Wilf, for crying out loud—which you are going to make me do before long—I don't love him. You certainly must know that, by now. I'm just going to marry him. That's all."

"That's all? Universe, Margot. I mean..."

"I know what you mean, Wilf," she said. "And even if my life isn't my own to live as I choose, I don't intend to give you up. My wedding to Rogan LaKarn won't produce a marriage: A partnership is more like it. He doesn't want me. He's got somebody else, too, you know. A couple of somebody elses, in fact."

"Well, that's not my case, Margot," Brim replied. "You know I want you—I've just never wanted to own you. Or anybody else, for that matter." He looked her in the eye. "But I xaxtdamned well want to make sure nobody else gets to make that claim, either."

"I understand," she said, nodding her head. "Universe knows I feel the same way about you."

"That's good," he answered, "because there is something else." He was talking very seriously now. He'd given the matter months of thought on blockade duty and was quite ready to discuss it in a Universe of detail. "What I need—all I need," he went on emphatically, "is to know that I'm the one special person in your life, permanently. I need that relationship because I need you."

She looked him in the eye. "You have that already, Wilf," she said. "It's one of the few parts of my life they can't control with the excuse that royal duty calls for it." Then she took a great breath and put her hands on her stomach, staring down into her lap. "But will you still believe in that relationship when this belly of mine is swollen with his child?" She looked up and pursed her lips. "That, Mister Brim, will be the true test for us both. And it will happen. They'll expect heirs immediately after the war."

Brim closed his eyes and winced. "Heirs," he repeated, emphasizing the plural form of the word. "Ouch."

"You didn't think it was going to be easy for either of us, did you?" Margot asked. "Listen, Wilf, in the not too distant future, I'm going to have to encourage you to find yourself some...ah...temporary sleeping companions. Either that or you'll end up like a celibate lots of the time. And it's my bet that if I ask for something like that, I'll eventually lose what little I have of you."

Brim started to protest, but she continued before he could speak.

"This love we think we share will have to be so terribly strong it can last through quite a bit of adversity, especially now that I'm permanently reassigned to Avalon. Just trying to see each other is going to be xaxtdamned difficult. It was no easy matter getting a berth aboard *Queen Elidean* so I could be here for your ceremony today. And I am required to return with her when she casts off early this evening." She laughed resentfully. "After my little spying sojourn to Typro, Uncle Greyffin IV is doing everything in his power to keep me safely within the Imperial sphere on Avalon. At least until I produce that heir."

Brim nodded and smiled gently. "I guess we'll spend a lot of our lives skulking, then," he said.

She sighed and took his hand. "I should dearly like to find some nicer words, Wilf," she said, looking down at her manicured nails. "But I suppose it is precisely what everything boils down to. Turns out it's commonly accepted practice among us of the so-called *ancienne noblesse*, if that's any help. Otherwise, we'd have royal marriages falling apart all over the Empire. Can you live with something like that?"

"Can you, Margot?"

"I asked you first, Wilf Brim," she laughed quietly. "But, yes. I can live with it." She looked him full in the face. "I've spent a lot of time weighing the question of 'us'; now I'm ready to commit." She grimaced. "I can't find a nice way of putting this, but it's got to be said. Rogan and I have, well, played the beast with two backs a number of times since you and I first made love on Avalon. And never once has it changed the way I feel about you. Not even when it was especially good, as it honestly has been on occasion. Like you, I have certain nerves down there; tickle them properly and it...feels good." She pursed her lips and squeezed his fingers. "Life is going to be damned difficult over the long stretches we'll be apart. But the most difficult times of all will come when we do see each other and cannot touch."

Brim nodded. That made abundant sense. "How long before the wedding?" he asked.

She took a deep breath and frowned. "Sometime during the summer season in Avalon next year," she said. "I shall have to set the actual date soon after I return."

"And until the wedding?" Brim asked.

"Until the wedding—and *after* the wedding—we'll skulk, Wilf Brim, just as we're skulking now. Whenever we can be together." She smiled (and frowned). "The more we practice, the better we'll be: At skulking as well as other, more interesting activities. Starting right now." Her eyebrows raised and she smiled salaciously. "It's still more than two metacycles before Cousin Onrad presents your decorations, and I need you. 'Like a king fulfill then my life/Fill my unsatiated soul/With all the bliss of paradise!'"

***

Miraculously, the morning continued to hold fair, though telltale cloud formations promised an expeditious return to Haefdon's more conventional meteorological fulsomeness not too many metacycles hence. The frozen world had almost become placid by the time Brim stood at attention in dim midday light. Behind Headquarters Plaza, flags rustled crisply in the chill breeze. From the corners of his eyes, he could see ranks of Blue Capes lined on either side as far as they'd cleared the melting snow; representatives from hundreds of organizations comprising Gimmas-Haefdon. He smiled to himself. Margot was among them somewhere, watching, sharing the moment with him, as were Borodov and Ursis. The two Sodeskayans stood to his right, with Borodov in a center position as befit his great seniority. Nearby, a single rank of ratings, including Barbousse, waited for their own decorations.

Distant thunder from a lifting warship momentarily drummed his ears, then faded into the yellow-gray sky. Someone in the formation sneezed. Another coughed. Brim smelled the nearby sea as it tossed itself to vapor on the jetties and boulder-protected causeways. At last, the main doorways to headquarters were thrown wide by white-gloved Imperial Marines. They moved in perfect unison, a professional honor guard if Brim had ever spotted one. He wondered idly how the beautifully attired escorts would face up to a day's terror on blockade duty. Presently, a military band yerked out one of the brassy war marches from nearby Glamnos-Grathen, then Crown Prince Onrad emerged from the building. He was followed by a number of high-ranking naval officers, including Gimmas-Haefdon's commander, (the Hon.) Rear Admiral Dianna C' J' Herrish, Vice Admiral Eug'enie Drei'ffen, commander of the Sixth Battle Squadron; Star Admiral Sir Gregor Penda, Admiral of the Imperial Fleet; and First Star Lord Beorn Wyrood!

Brim was stunned. He had trouble even imagining such an assemblage, much less seeing one—especially walking toward him. For a moment, his knees felt more than a little weak. Then the feeling passed in a wave of relief. These sage visitors from the Admiralty had little interest in any of the *Truculents* as persons. Rather, they were using the little ceremony to personally address the commoners of the Fleet. He took a deep breath, then smiled inwardly. If admirals really had that sort of need, then Wilf Brim was glad for an opportunity to assist—after all, they'd brought him a long way from the Carescrian ore mines.

***

Mercifully, none of the senior Fleet officials had many thoughts to inflict on the gathered *hoi polloi*. Brim listened to their words echoing hollowly from military voice amplifiers. He even concentrated, and appreciated the praise he heard for men and Bears. He was especially gratified to hear Lord Wyrood state that, "the Carescrian Wilf Brim" had done much to prove his Admiralty Reform Act (and that a number of new Helmsman Academy slots would be opened in honor of his accomplishments). But when he attempted to probe below the glossy surface of their flawlessly delivered words, he encountered the same lack of basic understanding that characterized the absentee owners and controllers of the mine operations in which he'd once toiled.

No matter who you were, it seemed, once you reached—or surpassed—a certain level of command, you eventually lost contact with the reality of the work being done—mining, fighting, either one. Herrish, Drei'ffen, Penda, even Wyrood spoke in vainglorious terms of "glory," "bravery," "heroism," and the like. Brim wondered if any had ever lived on a blockade line, where the most common terms were more like "terror," "desperation," and "death." He wasn't sure if anybody aboard old *Truculent* ever did have time for heroism. He was xaxtdamned well sure he hadn't himself.

Then he relented...a little. Unlike the mine controllers, it actually seemed as if these officers wanted to say something worthwhile. In their own manner, they cared, partly to save their own skins, of course. But nevertheless, he felt they did care. And at least for now, it was enough.

Laurels were awarded after the speeches (Were they afraid to lose their audience otherwise?). The admirals stood in a line facing the Blue Capes, Prince Onrad in the center. On one side, Admiral Penda dispensed medals; on the other, Lord Wyrood called out names from a tabulator board. "Utrillo Barbousse, Torpedoman," Wyrood boomed.

Brim watched the big rating stride impassively to a point directly in front of the Prince and salute as if such an encounter had been a daily

309

occurrence for years. Gallsworthy's words suddenly echoed from *Truculent's* ruined bridge. "Now there's a real Blue Cape."

Each medal accompanied a short, personal conversation with the Prince that invariably sent the recipients back to their positions on the plaza with outright smiles breaking through their carefully nurtured military *sangfroid*. Brim was so thoroughly mesmerized by the proceedings that when the next name called was "Ursis," he found himself almost unprepared to follow!

He watched with a heightened sense of concentration while Onrad spent an even longer time in conversation with the younger Sodeskayan, until the Bear's words suddenly broke everyone within earshot into gales of very genuine-looking laughter. Wiping his eyes, the Prince clapped Ursis' shoulder and said something with a great smile beaming on his face. Then he turned to Penda, took the proffered decoration, and pinned it to Ursis' collar. They saluted. A smiling Nikolai Yanuarievich Ursis returned to his position on the other side of Borodov, and the name "Wilf Ansor Brim" boomed hollowly from the loudspeakers.

Ears roaring suddenly in a nonsensical attack of pure stage fright, Brim felt himself moving across the pavement. Mentally, he jerked himself around as he walked. There was nothing different between this and his first meeting with the Prince back on Avalon. He snorted quietly as his mind came back under control, and he stopped the prescribed three paces from the line of nobles, saluting energetically.

"Well, Lieutenant Brim," Onrad remarked with a distinctly pleased countenance. "You seem to be turning up in my life with some regularity these days." His eyes strayed past Brim's shoulder to wink at someone in the formation of Blue Capes. He laughed. "That pile of blond curls atop my cousin yonder seems to turn up often in the same places." He shook his head. "Coincidence, of course," he said.

"Of course, Your Highness," Brim assured him.

Onrad stood in silence for long moments, considering. Finally, he shook his head. "You know, Wilf," he said in an underbreath, "aside from my own considerable masculine jealousy, I think she's made a damned fine choice." He chuckled quietly. "As if what I think means anything to the independent likes of her!" Then he became serious. "Unless I miss my guess—which I don't all that often—you have just accepted a hard road with her." He took Brim's elbow. "It's a damned important road, and it requires one very strong man to follow it." He pursed his lips. "Of course, it's none of my business; I simply have a habit of butting in where I shouldn't. Take good care of her, Wilf. Someday, she'll probably be the most powerful woman in the galaxy, and then she'll need love—real love—from someone who doesn't have an ax to grind." He winked. "But then, I couldn't know anything about you two." He smiled. "Coincidence she's come all this way, of course."

Brim bowed. "Coincidence, of course, Your Majesty," Brim said with a straight face.

"Good for you, Wilf," the Prince said with a smile. "You will do well." Then, once again, he became serious. "And I did come here to present you with a reasonably significant decoration. Although it is probably only the first (and the least) of a whole series of medals I shall pin to your cape over the next period of years—if we survive, of course." He turned to Penda. "The Imperial Comet, please, Admiral," he ordered.

Brim felt his heart skip a beat; he actually questioned his ears. That medal was only given...

Onrad laughed. "I caught the look in your eye just then, Wilf," he said. "And though it was Regula Collingswood who put you in for it, I was damned proud to sign my name beside hers. You deserve the medal." He grimaced. "You should have been decorated for the part you played in the A'zurnian mission, too," he continued. "Old Hagbut killed that one, though. I found that out through my Army sources, but I couldn't do anything about it. I've got to back up my senior officers, even when they're wrong."

Speechless, Brim could only shake his head for a few moments. "I am terribly honored, Your Majesty," he finally stammered.

"Actually, I think I am, too," Onrad said with a grin. "I shall look forward to our next encounter, my Carescrian friend. They always seem the result of some interesting excitement."

The Prince's words were a clear sign of dismissal. Brim stood at rigid attention while Onrad fastened the device to his collar just below his badge of rank. That finished, he stepped back to salute. "I shall indeed look forward to our next meeting, Your Highness," he said.

Then, turning about-face immediately, he marched back to his place in the line.

From this opposite vantage point, he had no trouble locating Margot in the assembled sea of Blue Capes. She had been standing in the front row, directly behind him throughout the whole ceremony. And her wink, this time, was all for him.

***

Borodov closed the ceremony by receiving two medals: one Imperial and one Sodeskayan, before his reassignment to the Admiralty in Avalon. Afterward, the nobles followed Onrad back to the headquarters building in (approximate) step to additional marches from Glamnos Grathen, at which time the formation of Blue Capes disintegrated into a sea of happy cheers. Brim dodged to Margot's side in a matter of clicks. She shook her head happily amid the noisy throng and smiled as she took his hand.

He thrilled at the soft warmth before she abruptly released him. "The first of those look-but-don't-touch encounters, I suppose?" he said ruefully over the hubbub.

"Neither of us can complain about the touching we got to do this trip," Margot laughed quietly, looking at him from the corner of her eyes. She touched her back and laughed ruefully. "I shall be stiff for weeks—and a bit sensitive you know where." Then, capriciously, she took his hand again. "Parting is one of the more painful ways we shall perpetually pay for the pleasure of being together," she sighed. "And *Queen Elidean* departs for Avalon in less than two metacycles. I shall have to be aboard almost immediately. Will you walk with me to the brow, Wilf? It may be a long time before we talk alone again."

***

The vast battleship looked much like a great humpbacked island as it hovered beside the quay. Rumbling at idle with the muted thunder of sixteen antigravity generators, *Queen Elidean* was indeed ready for immediate departure; a chill layer of air hung over the whole pierhead, and the water round about her massive footprint rippled and stirred in swirling patterns of alabaster froth. High overhead on the topmost bridge, Helmsmen performed last-moment systems checkouts, jabbing here and there at unseen controls.

Brim and Margot arrived at the 'midships brow after successfully avoiding every shortcut from headquarters either of them could think of. "Onrad's not here," he observed hopefully. "His royal pennant isn't flying from the *Queen's* KA'PPA yet. You've probably got the best part of a metacycle before they even single up her mooring beams."

Margot laughed quietly. "There's no putting it off any longer, Wilf," she said firmly. "I must board now. Otherwise, I won't be able to make myself go at all. I don't want to leave you any more than you want to leave me, you know." She bit her lip. "Our early morning kisses must suffice us for a while. Too many people are watching." She held out her hand.

Brim took it in his. "I wish I had any idea when I shall see you again," he said. "Whenever that turns out to be, it will seem as if I have waited a lifetime."

"But at least not forever, Wilf," she said. "And I shall write this time, enough to make up for the months of silence I put you through. We have years of 'skulking' ahead of us. I know that sounds pretty awful, but for me at least, it's a whole lot better than giving up completely. And who knows, some day..."

"I shall gladly skulk until my dying moment, Margot," Brim said, barely holding back emotions that threatened to make a fool of him on the crowded quay. He swallowed hard, then raised her hand to his lips. "'Alas, how soon the cycles are over,/Counted us out to play the lover'," he quoted, the words rushing to his mind from nowhere.

"Oh, Universe, Wilf," she choked, her eyes brimming, "I can't say good-bye." She fumbled an ornate signet ring from her finger and passed it into his hand. Then without another word, she abruptly thrust herself into the throng filing into the brow.

Brim stood for a long time staring dumbly after her until he realized a number of the Imperial Marine guards were regarding him with ill-concealed suspicion. He shook his head as he turned to leave the boarding area. Onrad had been very right. His choice would be a hard road, indeed.

***

Toward the end of the afternoon, Haefdon was rapidly settling back to its normal mien. Raw, wintry wind gusted remorselessly from the polar regions, blustering along the drab beach and bringing with it sure promise of snow—joined by occasional whiffs of overheated logics from the Theo-21 repair yard across the bay. Outbound along a narrow finger of tumbled rocks that jutted into the tossing gray water, Brim pulled his Fleet Cloak tighter around his neck, turned up the heat, and continued toward a dark, abandoned beacon clinging in rusty desperation to the last vestiges of stained, weather-smoothed rock. Its base was nearly lost in the lashing surf. It could be a wet perch to watch from, he knew, his face breaking into a smile. But he also knew it would be well worth any discomfort.

Behind him, in the waning light, *Queen Elidean* had been singled up for some time now. Her escort of ten powerful R-class destroyers was already aloft and thundering through the leaden skies as each took up position for the battleship's lift-off. Only cycles earlier, he'd watched them rumble out toward the horizon, turn, and hold for a moment while glittering clouds of ice particles rose like summer storm clouds a thousand irals beyond their stems. Then, moments later, the reverberating blast of antigravity generators reached his ears as the sleek escorts raced in pairs over the surface of the water and soared effortlessly into a darkening sky.

The Carescrian lowered his head as he picked his way over man-sized boulders that formed the last few irals of the ruined pier, eyes squinting from the blowing saltwater that now ran in rivulets from his cloak. His arrival at the beacon coincided with the first snow squall, which passed quickly enough and actually seemed to clear the air as he ascended corroded rungs toward the long-dark beacon. In a few cycles, he was well above the spray and settled onto a wide, rusting girder with a surprisingly dry view of both the quay and the ocean.

He was not a moment too soon. In a matter of clicks, great optical hawsers flashed to the battleship from four waiting deep-space tugs, a final network of mooring beams extinguished, and the great starship began to shrug aside the long gray rollers as she slid majestically toward open ocean—and space. She passed Brim's vantage point only cycles later, her port tugs rumbling by a few hundred irals out on the sound.

With a smile, Brim observed the orderly confusion on their bridges, then looked up at the great battleship ghosting through the wintry air like some monstrous sea creature unaffected by wind or wave. Even at idle, the beat of her incredible generators shook the old pylon where he sat in a shower of rust flakes. He squinted up at her great casemates—individual disruptors in the main battery were longer and far heavier than the attack ship he'd ridden deep into League territory. Many of the deckhouses were nearly as large as old *Truculent* herself. Sweeping beacons flashed everywhere; a thousand lighted scuttles gleamed in sweeping parallel rows along her graceful hull. Countless analog machines scurried everywhere along her decks, stowing landside gear before it was forever lost in the takeoff. And somewhere aboard was Margot. He squeezed her ring in his pocket and lifted his head toward the bridge as it moved grandly past. It was too far away to make out more than moving silhouettes, but he could swear one of them waved. He'd shown her where he would be.

Snow began again before the big ship was out into the takeoff zone, but Brim could still see her when she turned parallel to the shore and the hawsers winked out from the space tugs.

Like her escorts, she paused while great clouds of backwash became a whole miniature storm system (complete with flashes of lightning!). Then, unbelievable thunder filled the air—became part of the very Universe—while the great ship gathered herself and began to move over the water once more, her footprint throwing great curving waves to either side until, just abreast Brim's beacon, she lifted. Simultaneously, four of her escorts swooped through the cloud cover to take up station on each side, and the five powerful warships climbed like a single existence to vanish slowly into the rolling storm. Mighty sounds from the squadron's passing echoed for a long time before they eventually faded into the booming of the ocean's everlasting surf.

***

Before Gimmas' feeble radiance departed completely, Lieutenant Wilf Ansor Brim, I.F., climbed from his perch and began picking his way back among the rocks toward the shore. Around him, little remained in view except the empty wharf, the pounding water—and the snow, which by now had grown into a hissing blizzard. He shrugged as he walked; none of the dirty weather mattered. He was nicely warmed from within. He had part of Margot now. And somewhere halfway across the galaxy, Collingswood's new ship was becoming reality, with a whole different kind of "pick and shovel" warfare for him to master.

He touched the comet on his collar; he'd come a long way to get that. Not much more an ex-miner could ask for, now, was there?

As he neared the shore, he spied two figures making their way toward him through the snow: A large man and an even larger Bear waving what could only be a colossal bottle of...meem! The three met in the last moments of daylight, passing the bottle among themselves and clapping one another on the back in great apparent hilarity. Then arm in arm, they started landward and disappeared into the driving snowstorm singing, "To ice, to snow, to Sodeskaya we go!" over and over again until their voices merged with the howling wind and pounding surf. Not long afterward, the quiet flakes covered their tracks in a soft, uniform mantle of white.

END

COMING SOON!
"Director's Cut" Books & Full-Cast,
Unabridged Audiobook Special Editions:

GALACTIC CONVOY
THE TROPHY
THE MERCENARIES
THE DEFENDERS
THE SIEGE

And the All New continutation of the best selling Wilf Brim Saga:

THE TURNING TIDE

8 1/05